Heir of Blood

LOST FAE QUEEN TRILOGY

E. R. JENSEN

TRIGGER WARNINGS

Miscarriage
Forced marriage
Graphic fight scenes
Controlling family members
Suicidal thoughts
Prejudice

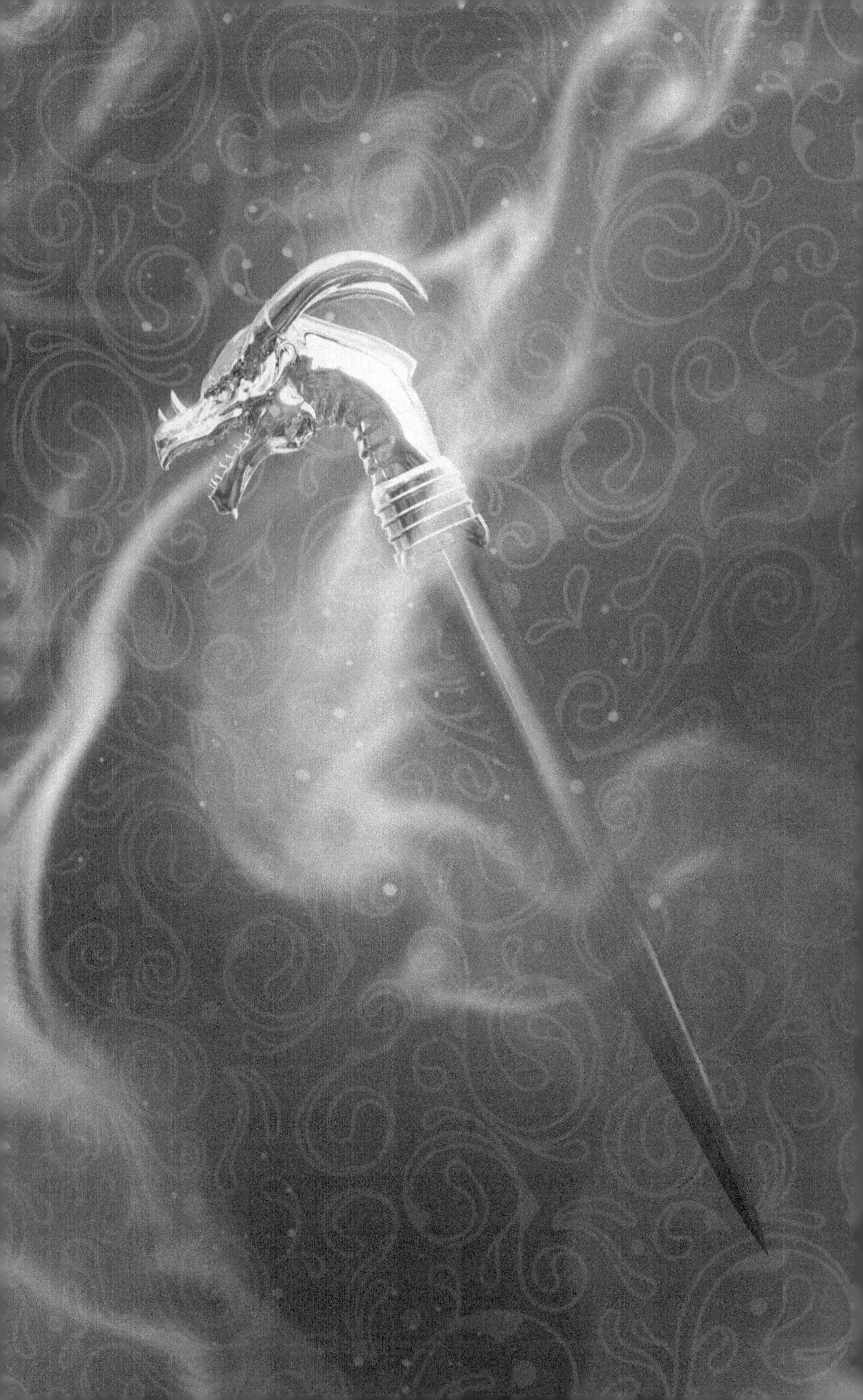

OTHER BOOKS

The Lost Fae Queen Trilogy
Throne of Dusk
Heir of Blood
Crown of Emeralds (*coming 2026*)

Twisted Talent Series
Hoodwinked in Hotlanta
Spellbound in Spud City

JADE WILDS
COURT
LOCHAN SGÀILE
WHISP
EMBERGATE
WEST IRON
EMBER MOUNTAIN
COURT OF DUSK
COURT
GLASS OASIS

MOON
ICKET
EMERALD
MINES
EMERALD VALLEY
EAST
SILVER
COURT OF DAWN
E SUN
T
N
W
E
S

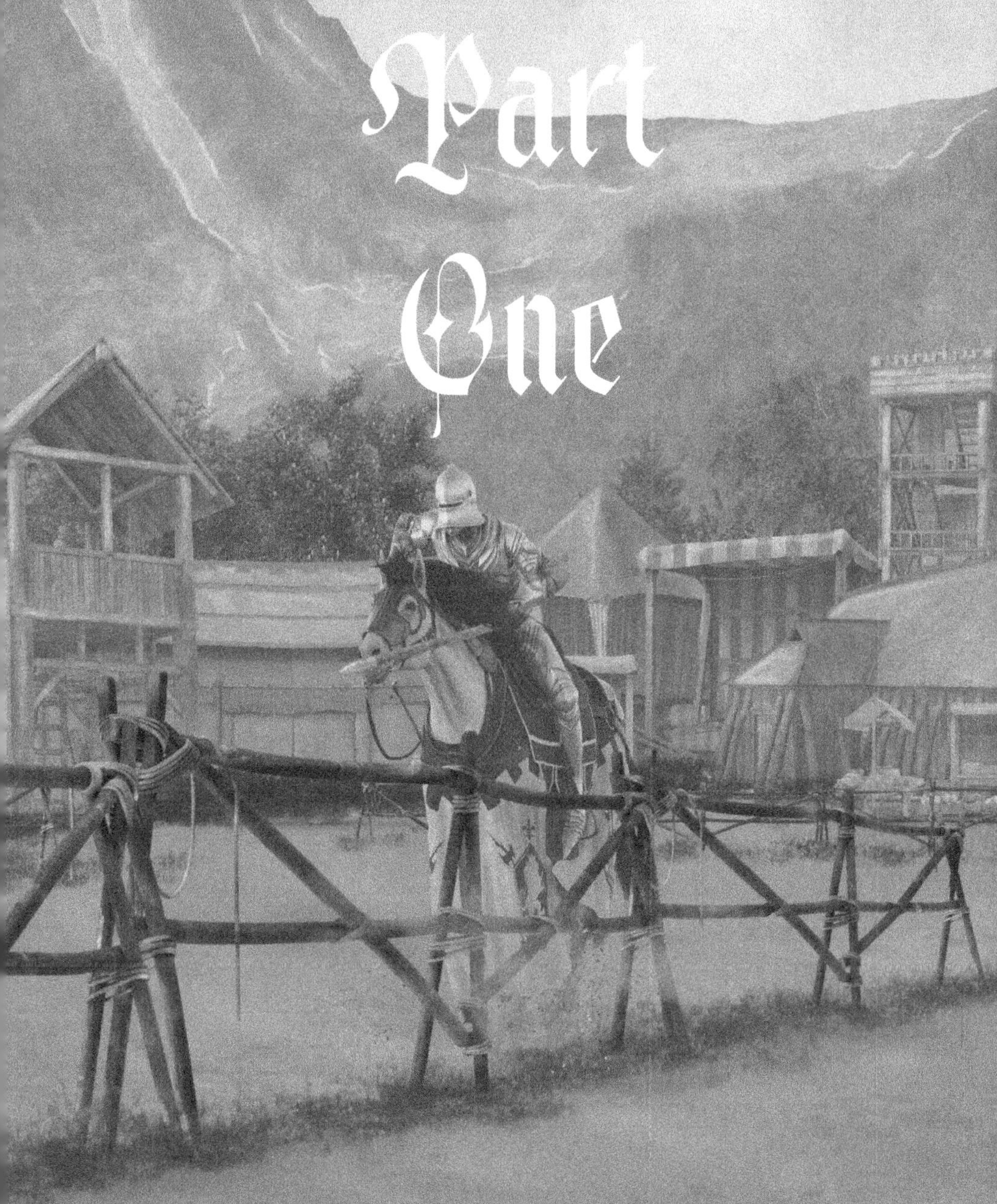
Part
One

One

SERAFINA

The gold-encrusted carriage pulled by four white horses rolled through the massive gray stone city gates topped with large gold spheres. I peered out at the vaguely familiar, white-painted storefronts with shiny gold awnings lining Helias Way, the main thoroughfare to the palace. Twelve years ago, I was fleeing for my life. Now, because of my uncle's unexpected death, I was returning to take my place as heir of the South.

Returning alone. King Leonard had denied my request to bring my best friend, citing Fae were not welcome in his palace.

Except I'm half-Fae, and he's welcoming me. Anger swelled within my chest that my grandfather would demand I return but deny my simple request of bringing a companion. *I will discuss the matter with him when I arrive*, I thought, adding it to my growing list.

I brushed a strand of hair behind my ear, frowning as I realized if I was going to be the heir to a human kingdom, I had no choice but to cancel my engagement to Prince Tanyth, the Fae ruler of the Court of Dusk. Sadness filled me. Tanyth had shown me nothing but kindness, and now I was turning my back on him. *A ruler of a Fae court should understand the need to fulfill a responsibility to a court or kingdom*, I reminded myself, but it didn't make me feel much better. I disliked breaking agreements, no matter how big or trivial they were.

While I had anticipated needing to negotiate with my Fae grandfather, King Pharaan, ruler of the Court of Dawn, to get approval to marry Prince Tanyth, I knew it was futile to ask King Leonard. Even if he were to agree to it, which was impossible, the three other human kings were unlikely to acknowledge the authority of a Fae, regardless of his being my husband and rightfully a co-ruler of the South.

A hard bump jolted me out of my thoughts as the carriage climbed the last hill to the palace. I caught a glimpse of my reflection in the windows when the sunlight hit just right. My russet hair was coiled on top of my head with a heavy crown of gold and what felt like hundreds of pearl and gold pins stabbing my skull. I was wearing a heavy ivory dress with an overlayer of gold lace and short, pointy shoes that I was certain had been created by a man who had no idea how it felt to wear them for hours on end. *I look like a princess. The test will be if I can behave like one.* I'd spent only a few hours in the carriage, and I was desperately wishing for the comfort of a tunic and pants with my sword strapped to my side.

The closer we got to the palace, the slower the carriage moved. Within the last hundred feet of our approach, it dawned on me why King Leonard needed me and couldn't just name a long-lost family member as heir. *The mines.* Each of the human kingdoms—North, South, East, and West—possessed sole control over a metal mine. The ability of the mines to produce metal ore was tied to the royal family of each kingdom. Not having an heir meant a kingdom risked collapse if its ruler died without a surviving family member.

Deep down, I understood why it needed to be me and not someone else. No matter how difficult it was to believe, no one else was left. When I departed Gaskal twelve years ago there had been five heirs standing between me and the throne, and all had perished. I was no stranger to accidents and illnesses that claimed lives.

The carriage brakes squeaked as we rolled to a halt. I took a deep breath and winced. The headache that had plagued me since my departure from the Court of Dusk was still determined to drive me mad. *I can do this*, I told myself and threw my shoulders back, willing myself to at the very least appear confident and ready to face my grandfather and his court.

A guard wearing the gold-and-white livery of King Leonard's palace opened the carriage door and offered me his hand. I took it and stepped out of the carriage, careful to get my dress all the way out. I recognized my grandfather immediately, though he had aged over the past twelve years. His thick white beard and thinning white hair topped with a large gold crown were still the same. A heavy white fur-lined cape was drawn around his shoulders against the chilly wind.

Surprisingly, aside from the guards, no one else was in the welcoming committee. Growing up, I spent very little time at the palace, and honestly, I had no idea who my grandfather was close to or who would have attended my arrival. I knew he had advisors, of course, but there was much I needed to learn while I was here. About my grandfather, his court, and his expectations of me as heir.

I prayed that once the stress of settling in passed, so would the headaches. Without Commander Meriel's healing knowledge or magic available to me among the humans, I could expect little help from the human medics.

"How was your journey?" my grandfather asked in a clipped voice as he met me halfway down the steps. He took my hands in his and gave them a hard squeeze. I stifled the urge to yank my hands back. In many ways the opposite of my father, King Leonard had never had a warm personality; that was likely, I mused, one of the things that drove the wedge between them.

"Uneventful," I replied carefully. I had napped through most of it and assumed mentioning the fleeting glimpse of what might have been a snow leopard was only going to stir up trouble.

"Glad to hear it. Given the circumstances of your departure twelve years ago, I will admit I was concerned that you would come under attack," King Leonard explained.

My throat felt dry at my grandfather's admission. It also explained why there had been such a large escort. *Clearly he doesn't feel I am capable of defending myself. What does he think I did among the Fae? Knit?*

My work would be cut out for me to prove to my grandfather—*and* my future subjects—that I was qualified to rule them.

Am I? a dark part of myself asked.

I dug my nails into my palm. It would do me no good to doubt my abilities. *Would the king have demanded I take my place as his heir if he truly thought I was incapable of leading the South?* Unfortunately, I did not know him well enough to have the answer, though I couldn't tell what he would gain by naming me heir if he thought I was only going to destroy his kingdom.

"There are refreshments just inside while they finish preparing lunch," my grandfather announced, then offered his arm stiffly to me. I gave him a hesitant smile, which he did not return, placed my hand on his arm, and let him escort me inside.

Two

TRISTAN

For thirty years, I had been bound by a blood contract to Prince Tanyth and the Court of Dusk as lord commander. Many times had I wished he would release me, yet now that the contract had been destroyed, I almost missed it. Not because I wanted to be treated like I was nothing more than a slave, but because I had set responsibilities and expectations to meet. These past two weeks marked the first time in my entire life I was free to make my own choices. *It's going to take time to get used to.*

I frowned. I shared a soulmate bond with Serafina, which meant I technically wasn't free. I was bound by magic to the love of my life. Except ever since Prince Tanyth had caught us together—an act he had forbidden—the prince had taken Serafina out of my reach, deep within Dorcha Palace, and the bond had been muted between us. No matter what I tried, so far I had not been able to resolve the issue.

I rolled onto my side, staring at the canvas of the tent. Sleep eluded me. Outside the tent, I could hear the hoot of an owl and croak of bullfrogs in the nearby pond. I chose a campsite far enough from the city wall to reduce the chance of being noticed and to avoid hearing the loud noises that human cities seemed privy to at odd hours throughout the night. I took a deep breath, held it, and then released it. Forcing myself to shut my eyes, I counted backward from ten.

I gently pushed Serafina onto the couch in the library. I could tell from the longing in her eyes that she was ready for me. I kissed her, then slid my cock inside of her. Her body was perfect, as though we were made for each other. I started with a slow in-and-out rhythm, making sure she was okay with our position, then increased my speed. I was surprised when she started lifting her hips in time with my strokes. The effect was electrifying as she sent me deeper and deeper. I felt her folds tightening, and her heartbeat sped up. Her fingers lightly gripped my hips in encouragement, digging into me as I quickened my strokes, relishing how well our bodies fit together. One more thrust sent her over the edge, and I followed almost immediately after. I kissed her as our bodies spasmed together, and then I felt it—the magic uncoiling between us.

I brushed her mind with mine, and I could feel hers right at the surface. "Serafina, I love you," I said into her mind.

"I love you too," Serafina replied.

I lifted my eyes from Serafina's and was staring into a teal face with blue-black hair in a single braid. Travaran growled, "Betrayer."

Thrashing in the covers, I woke up to find myself alone in my tent. Neither Serafina nor Travaran was with me. *Travaran is dead, and Serafina is certainly secure within the palace by now.* I knew it was not going to be simple to see her. Fear clung to me. *What else did Tanyth do to her?* I had spent too long obeying Prince Tanyth's orders to believe that all he had done was tamper with the mating bond. Not when the prince favored cruel punishments for those he disliked.

A sharp ache in my lower back was a painful reminder of how terrible the prince could be.

Prince Tanyth came up right behind me. His legs brushed mine, and I could feel his hips against my butt.

I ran my hand over my face, trying to drag myself out of the memory.

A sharp blade pierced my lower back. It pulsed with magic as Tanyth twisted it, casting an eerie green glow across the stone. If the wall had not been in front of me, I would have collapsed from the fierce pain. Dragonfang.

A chant rose in the stands. "Tristan! Tristan!"

I massaged my lower back with my hand, hoping it would alleviate the ache. I didn't know enough about Dragonfang to have any idea what being stabbed by it meant, other than it couldn't be good. *Not as long as Prince Tanyth has it in his possession.* I knew that Fae magic objects were not inherently good or evil. It was the wielder who determined how they were used.

As the tiger leaped, I did a two-handed thrust straight up with my sword, impaling it. Lifeless, the tiger fell like dead weight on top of me. No matter how hard I tried, I could not get the tiger's body to move. I was thoroughly trapped.

Rubbing my hands on my pants to get rid of the clammy feeling, I took a deep breath, forcing myself to focus on the present.

I cannot change the past. But I can control my future and hopefully influence Serafina's.

One of the last things Tanyth had said to me about Serafina was that she was "safe." I realized now that there were different interpretations of "safe" and that it was possible Tanyth had merely meant that he knew exactly where she was. I'm sure he considered most of the Fae creatures in the dungeon cells "safe." I had spent too long in the Court of Dusk to believe that she was truly safe if I was meant to take Tanyth's word for it. The idea that he had somehow orchestrated this gnawed at me. *How would Tanyth benefit from Serafina becoming the heir of the South? Or even the queen?*

A sliver of fear tried to take hold in my mind. *Can I win Serafina back? Or did Prince Tanyth corrupt our love for each other in a way I can never overcome?* Unexpected circumstances—Serafina a prisoner, me the lord commander of the Court of Dusk—had led to us meeting, but did we really know each other? If this was truly a chance to do things all over again, would I be her choice?

I had done many horrifying things in Prince Tanyth's name. *Am I worthy of her love and forgiveness?* I had to believe I was, or I might as well return to the Court of Dusk. There was only one path for me now, the one that would bring me back to Serafina's side. *Whatever it takes.*

My mind, body, and soul wanted to get Serafina back, but I was going to have to be patient. I could not rush into the palace and steal her away. Maybe I would have been able to do that twelve years ago, when she had lived with her parents in the city among the other humans, but now, as heir, she would be under close watch and reside within the palace. Besides, she might not appreciate it if I stole her away in an attempt to win her back. *I'm assuming she doesn't want to be in Gaskal. What if I'm wrong?*

Studying the sliver of forest through the gap in the tent flaps, barely visible in the dark, I debated my next move. I desperately wanted to save Serafina, but now that I knew where she was, perhaps I could get help. It would be a long shot, but at this point very few options were available to me. I would not be doing Serafina justice if I wasn't willing to pursue all options.

I packed up my gear and vanished it, using my magic to store it along with other important belongings such as my weapon, ready to be called upon when needed. Serafina's human grandfather had called her back to Gaskal. Maybe her Fae grandfather, King Pharaan of the Court of Dawn, could help me get her out again—or at least get in contact with her.

Three

King Leonard led me into a room that I assumed was used for guests waiting for meetings with him. At one end of the room were built-in white shelves full of knickknacks—rocks, miniature statues, and a toy-sized horn, to name a few. The long wall had windows with heavy gold drapes pushed back to reveal a view of the statue garden. Upon closer inspection, I noticed the windows were actually doors that opened onto a small balcony.

A long black dining table was set at one end with a gold tea service, biscuits, and plates for four. *This must be where lunch is happening too.* I wondered who the other two people would be. I racked my mind for memories of who had been close to my grandfather but drew a blank. I hadn't spent much time at court growing up, but when I had, paying attention to my grandfather and his nobles was the last thing on my mind. Not that I could blame myself. The last time I'd set foot in the palace prior to today was when I was ten.

"Lunch will be here soon. While we wait, please relax and have some tea," my grandfather said and poured us both cups. Though the words sounded welcoming, his tone was cold. *As though he's merely going through the motions of polite host.*

Not wanting to stir up trouble within the first hour of my arrival, I took the cup and sipped, nose wrinkling at how strong the tea was. *This must be how he likes it.* I set the cup down. "When are we going to discuss what I'm doing here?" I asked, unable to hold the question in any longer.

Eyes narrowing—either in annoyance or anger, I couldn't tell—King Leonard took a sip of his tea. Long moments ticked by as I waited for his response. "We will do that tonight. Your arrival was later than expected, and I didn't want to keep my guests from their lunch any longer."

Pressing my lips together, I kept my response to myself. *He's blaming me for delaying their lunch? What a ridiculous notion.* I shifted on my feet, immediately regretting it as the pointy shoes squeezed tighter. Glancing at the bottom of the dress, I debated if I could ditch the shoes without him noticing. The hem was above the floor, and as I shifted, I caught glimpses of the shoes. *I guess not.*

There was a light tap on the door. A servant walked in and announced, "Lord McCormack and his daughter, Lady McCormack."

Lord Theo McCormack was a short, reed-thin man with medium-brown skin, sharp gray eyes, and close-cropped pewter-gray hair. He wore a navy-blue jacket with gold buttons, a white satin shirt, and matching navy pants with gold piping down the side of the legs.

Lord McCormack walked toward us, and I sucked in a breath as a young woman close to my age stepped out from behind him. Raven-black hair cascaded around her shoulders in ringlets, framing her delicate face. Her skin reminded me of caramel, and her eyes were a shade darker. I knew immediately that she was his daughter—the shape of their chins and noses was identical.

Lord McCormack bowed deeply to both of us, and his daughter dipped into a curtsey. "May I present my daughter, Violet."

Violet's selection of a dusky purple dress was fitting given her name. *Was it her choice to wear purple or her father's?*

Keeping my question to myself, I replied, "Nice to meet you."

"Lord McCormack's lands are near our eastern border. He is my trade supervisor, as well as ambassador for negotiations with the Lord of the East," King Leonard explained.

Nostrils fluttering, I inhaled a breath. *I fought the Lord of the East and his knights in the battle at Emerald Valley. A battle that happened because the Lord of the East's greed led him to breach the trade treaty with King Pharaan and the Court of Dawn—silver in exchange for emeralds.*

"Are you quite well?" asked my grandfather coldly.

"Fine. I was just recalling the battle at Emerald Valley," I replied. If I closed my eyes, I knew I'd be able to see the ranks of the Lord of the East's knights as they came down the hill toward the Fae.

My response earned me a sharp warning look. *Not a suitable topic*, I mused, wondering if it was not suitable at lunch or for a princess to speak of at all.

"Pardon me, Your Highness. You were at the battle at Emerald Valley?" Violet asked.

Amusement flooded me, and I met Violet's gaze. "Yes. I fought side by side with the Fae warriors and defeated the Lord of the East."

Violet's gaze slid to my ears, then back to my face. "You're not Fae. Why would you fight with them?"

"I'm half-Fae and spent the past just over eleven years at Jade Wilds, a Fae training camp," I replied smoothly. I could hear my grandfather's feet shifting in agitation. I didn't care. *He's not my master.* He had refused to tell me anything prior to introducing me to our guests. I was merely stating facts.

Violet opened her mouth to ask me another question when her father cut her off. "Look, lunch has arrived."

Servants strode into the room and set a covered plate at each of the four set chairs. *How convenient.* Not wasting any time, I sat down on the side that had the two place settings. I anticipated my grandfather would sit at the head of the table. Thankfully, Violet slid into the seat next to me. I guessed the purpose of this lunch was for me to meet Violet; otherwise, there would be no logical reason to have postponed it. Discussing logistics of trade with Lord McCormack sounded like a task for King Leonard, not a princess. *Unless he intends to thrust me into the middle of learning the inner workings of the kingdom.*

The covers on the plates were removed, revealing a chicken breast, candied brussels sprouts, and red fingerling potatoes. As I ate, I half listened to my grandfather's conversation about a negotiation over the price of wood and grain. Halfway through the meal, when it became clear that my grandfather and Lord McCormack weren't going to include us in their discussion, I shifted in my seat so I could more readily talk to Violet.

"What does a typical day look like for you, Violet?" With no knowledge of Violet beyond what duties belonged to her father, I decided this was the best question to open our discussion with.

Violet gave me a slight smile. "My mother has taught me how to run the household. My day starts with tackling the correspondence that has arrived overnight. Then, I talk to the cook regarding her menu for dinner. If my father is home, we will eat in the dining hall. If he is away, then we typically eat in the kitchen. Once my indoor tasks are complete, I go into the stable and help the grooms with our horses."

"Do you ride?" I asked.

Violet's smile widened. "Of course. When my brother was still home, he taught me how to train horses. Now that he is gone, I have taken over. Or as much as I can. I keep them exercised, at least."

I was intrigued that Violet knew how to train horses and that her father allowed her to do so. I was tempted to ask if she knew any weapon skills, but I was afraid to broach the subject in present company. The last thing I wanted was to get Violet in trouble in front of the king, who I had a feeling didn't believe women should use weapons.

Searching for a safe topic, I finally settled on, "Do you come to the palace often?"

Violet shook her head. "No. Usually Father only brings me once a year or so. Though he comes quarterly to give the king updates, my father does not permit me to be involved in the trade agreements, so there isn't much for me to do at the palace."

"Would like to visit more often? I would enjoy the company," I said. Excitement coursed through me. Violet was comfortable with horses. I could go riding with another woman.

"I would love to," Violet said eagerly.

Four

TRISTAN

With the dissolution of my contract with the Court of Dusk, I no longer had any restrictions on when or how I used my magic. Star portals had long been the fastest method of traveling for Fae, though not all Fae could make one given the immense amount of magic they required. Standing in the forest next to where I had camped the night before, I closed my eyes and gathered my shadow magic to me. When I had enough, I raised my hand and created a shimmering gray oval of pure magic. Nostrils flaring as I exhaled, I took a quick glance around to make sure no one was going to try to follow me through and then stepped into the portal. The next step took me out of the portal and onto the road that would lead me to Uaine Palace and the Court of Dawn.

Born and raised in Glass Oasis on the border between the Court of Dusk and the Court of the Sun, until I was exiled to Embergate for training, I had never had the opportunity to visit Uaine Palace, though like most Fae, I had heard stories.

Nothing could have properly prepared me for what I saw when I reached the top. The hill sloped gently downward toward Uaine Palace and its city. A short stone wall marked the perimeter.

Even from here, I could see how carefully it had been planned out, with streets in precise lines intersecting at ninety-degree angles. The palace was surrounded by a high wall of green granite with light-gray stone spires soaring toward the sky. Several of the towers had green windows. I wondered if they were colored glass or merely an illusion crafted with magic.

I shoved a tremor of fear away. The Court of Dusk and the Court of Dawn were not exactly on good terms with each other. I focused on my task—asking King Pharaan to help free Serafina of her obligation to the human king. Walking briskly, I followed the road, hugging the edge in case there were any other visitors moving at a faster pace than I was. The design of the city—no gate barring entry as I crossed under the delicate archway and wide, smooth streets—was a stark contrast to the darkness at the Court of Dusk. *Dorcha Palace doesn't even have a city. Besides, if it did, who would be brave enough to live there?*

As I worked my way toward the palace, my presence did not go unnoticed. I felt eyes watching me, though if I tried to identify who they belonged to, the feeling went away. I suspected it was only a matter of time before word of my arrival reached the king's ears. I just had no idea what he would do about it, if anything, or if the news had reached him that I had "died" and was no longer the lord commander of the Court of Dusk and under Prince Tanyth's thumb. In all the years I had spent serving Tanyth, the only time he'd directly interacted with the Court of Dawn was at the battle of Emerald Valley, when Tanyth heeded the call to arms. *A battle I was not permitted to participate in.* Instead, Tanyth had taken his heir with him. *And look where that got us. Travaran dead and Serafina captured.* I shuddered and pushed away the memories of Travaran trying to cloud my thoughts, focusing on what was important to me right now: that to my knowledge, Tanyth had never openly challenged King Pharaan, but his dislike of the king was common knowledge.

The gates to the palace were shut. Beyond them, I could see a courtyard with lush green plants and a fountain that I thought might be constructed entirely of emeralds.

A brown-haired female Fae in plate mail with the court's emblem of an emerald and two crossed pickaxes stepped forward, barring my advance. "State your business."

Drawing myself up to my full height, I replied, "I seek an audience with King Pharaan regarding his granddaughter Serafina Wyantha."

At Serafina's name, a flicker of recognition flashed across the guard's face. She studied me. My dark-brown cloak was clasped at my shoulders with a plain silver circle; my dark-green tunic and brown leather pants were deliberately nondescript. As far as I was concerned, I did not have allegiance to any court and would not mislead anyone into thinking I did by openly wearing a court emblem.

"I will send your request. You will wait here until orders come stating otherwise." The guard strode into the gatehouse. Ears straining, I could not make out any words spoken between the guards in the house. I was relieved when another Fae, a blond female guard, departed the gatehouse and went across the courtyard before disappearing into the palace itself. My message would be delivered.

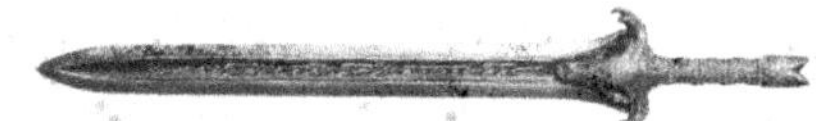

Arms loose at my side and weight distributed between both legs, I took up a comfortable stance and settled in to wait. I hoped my audience would be approved quickly, but I knew it likely wouldn't be. Fae were wary of strangers as a rule. I had time to wait. Serafina was in Gaskal and for the foreseeable future would remain there. Of that much I was certain.

I recalled the first time I saw Serafina at Dorcha Palace. I had returned from hunting a leon.

When I saw the number of guests, I immediately regretted my decision to report without cleaning up first. My black leather vest was clean, but that was it. Smudges of dirt were on my cheeks and bare chest, and I could feel bits of tree bark digging into my scalp.

A russet-haired female stood next to Tanyth, and I realized she was a human as I approached the throne. My lip curled in distaste. The last thing I needed was to deal with Prince Tanyth's latest human prisoner.

A flicker of movement drew my eyes to Bane, the blond-haired, gray-eyed Fae I had trained with at Embergate. Tanyth had denied his request to join me on this hunt. Bane thought it was because he was second-in-command, but I knew better. Tanyth was afraid we would plot against him, and the two of us together would be a credible threat.

Bane smirked at me, then pounded his metal-tipped staff on the stone by the throne. The human jumped, startled, and I shot him a glance.

"Lord Commander Tristan Gilvrye presents to Prince Tanyth a leon shapeshifter!" announced Bane.

It was impossible to ignore the human shaking like a leaf. Is she going to fall over? I wondered. Any show of compassion toward a human would be punished. If she falls, I will have to ignore her. I plastered a bored expression on my face, praying I could sell my indifference to this whole spectacle. If I couldn't, I risked far more than the human's life, because I was not just a Fae. I was a shapeshifter.

The prince's eyes flickered between me and the human, a cold smile on his lips. "Lord Commander, if Serafina passes her arena trial, then you will oversee her training."

My blood boiled with anger. I was used to him assigning me odd tasks, but ordering me to train a human was a first. Especially one who looked like she hadn't been fed in a few days. "Your Highness, her capture alone proves the human has minimal skills. I cannot make a warrior out of nothing."

I smiled as I remembered Serafina's bold response, even then unwilling to be intimidated by any of us. I regretted my reaction, but I couldn't undo the past—only strive to be better for the future. Years of honing my *lord commander* persona to fit what Tanyth expected of me, combined with fear that Tanyth would somehow learn my shapeshifting secret, had caused me to treat her terribly.

We had both gotten lucky when Tanyth found our exchange amusing. Now, thinking back on the confrontation, I wondered if the whole thing had been a test from the moment he captured her. *Would he have killed his own son simply for a chance to interfere with a prophecy?* It was a hard idea for me to swallow.

Tanyth might be evil, but he had still loved his son. I refused to believe he had sent Travaran to capture Serafina just to set certain events in motion. That was too extreme even for Tanyth. *Isn't it?*

The gate rattled and drew me out of the memory. Alas, it was just the pair of guards on patrol relieving the ones at the gate. I ran my hand over my face, wondering if the entire debacle with Serafina at Dorcha Palace had been part of Prince Tanyth's plan—or at least a twisted experiment to find out what would happen if you put a warrior who had spent decades killing humans in charge of training a half-human prisoner. *Or he had lied when he said he didn't believe in the Lost Fae Queen prophecy.*

I couldn't figure out what connection the Lost Fae Queen prophecy had to the one about the three magic objects. If there *was* a connection between the two, then it would explain Prince Tanyth's motives. *Perhaps I can ask King Pharaan if the visit goes well, or at least get permission to peruse his library.* Though the book *Bedtime Tails* held many Fae stories that were also considered by some to be prophecies, it was not the only written record of them. *Bedtime Tails* just happened to be the one that was the most widely distributed.

Hours trickled by. Periodically, I would test the bond, to see if by chance there was a flicker of response from Serafina. I was not surprised that it remained dull.

I straightened as I heard the sound of booted feet. Sure enough, a double column of the king's elite guard approached the gate, their bright-green capes fluttering behind them in the mild breeze. The male at the head of the group, with pale blue hair just visible under his helmet, raised his hand and they halted in unison.

The gates opened just enough for the commander to walk through. "Lord Commander Tristan Gilvrye, I am Lord Commander Onvyr Naero. What is the purpose of your visit?"

Onvyr's golden eyes glittered as he stared at me longer than was polite. I refused to react to his scrutiny or to his apparent knowledge of who I was even though I had not given a name when I made my request to see the king. Very little intimidated me—certainly not Onvyr. "The short version is that I would like to request the king's aid to remove his granddaughter, Serafina Wyantha, from the possession of the Lord of the South."

I opted to omit the use of the human surname, knowing that Onvyr would dismiss the matter as not a Fae concern when he drew the familial connection between Serafina and the Lord of the South. But I was also gambling that King Pharaan had told others in his court of Serafina's existence.

"I see. What is your interest in Serafina?" Onvyr inquired.

"She is my soulmate," I said softly. Onvyr's eyes widened at my revelation. I hoped disclosing that information would help gain the audience I desired.

"My orders are to bring you to the study so you can be more comfortable as you wait. I cannot promise the king will meet with you in person," Onvyr warned.

I nodded. *At least they are allowing me inside Uaine.* "Very well." An idea flickered. "Would it be possible to browse your library while I wait?"

Onvyr gave me an appraising look, then replied, "No. If King Pharaan decides you may stay at Uaine longer than your meeting, then I can escort you to the library. Until then, you must remain in the study."

At Onvyr's signal, the gate was pushed open farther, and the column of the elite guard split, allowing us to walk through the middle. He guided me up the three steps and into the palace. The walls were white marble with green veins here and there. I was surprised by how open and airy it was, though it was far more in line with Fae traditions to build a palace this way than the darkness of Dorcha Palace, which was mostly under Ember Mountain. There were no huge doors barring the way inside, just a large, open archway with smaller arches dotting the wall allowing for air to flow freely into the building. The ceiling was a vibrant green dome high above us. A delicate staircase made of jade spiraled up the dome, though I doubted a Fae would climb it. *More than likely, you'd need to be capable of flying to reach the door at the top.*

Onvyr did not allow me long to inspect the dome. He ushered me down a hallway and into the room I presumed was the study, though I wondered whose study it actually was. The room had a white desk with the Court of Dawn emblem stenciled into the middle. There was one chair behind it with a green cushion and two in front that were plain medium-colored wood. The sideboard matched the desk and was white with the court emblem on the front. It held a pitcher of water and three glasses.

Not that it has room for anything else. The space felt like it would be more suited to a broom closet than a location to conduct meetings.

"There is water and a chair. Either I or someone else will return shortly with an update. Or, if you're lucky, the king will come and speak to you," Onvyr said, though his tone made me think that he doubted King Pharaan wanted an audience with me. Nibbling on my lip, I nodded.

When Onvyr departed, I sat in one of the chairs. *What am I thinking? The whole palace is on edge at my presence. Likely assuming I'm here to carry out Prince Tanyth's dark deeds.* I realized that it had been a mistake to come here. I would have to earn King Pharaan's trust before he would ever directly offer to help me, no matter what the request was.

Five

SERAFINA

S tifling a yawn, I wondered again why my grandfather had decided to have dinner so late. We hadn't yet discussed why I was here, or his expectations of me as heir. There was also the matter that I hadn't been to my rooms since I arrived, though they had been mentioned several times. Writing the letter to Prince Tanyth and calling off our engagement was at the top of my list, even before sleeping. *Though I don't know who would be willing to deliver the message.* I doubted my grandfather would allow me to send one of his messengers to the Court of Dusk.

We were in the massive formal dining room, sitting at the head of a table that was long enough to seat at least fifty. Crystal chandeliers overhead were evenly spaced the length of the table, providing only enough light to guess at what was on our plates.

Lunch this afternoon with the McCormacks had confirmed that my grandfather had an assortment of rooms to choose from, and I couldn't help questioning his motives for eating dinner in here and not a room better suited for two people. *Maybe he is trying to intimidate me.*

I drank water out of a silver goblet, waiting for him to explain whatever we were supposed to be discussing. So far, he had spoken only about the weather and flowers. I was tired and had little appetite. Annoyance simmering, I set my glass down when it became clear that he was not going to get to the point anytime soon.

"Excuse me, Grandfather," I said, trying to keep my voice light and airy. The last thing I needed was to let my emotions get the better of me and start an argument.

His blue-green eyes were focused intently on me. "What?"

"I was under the impression we were going to have a discussion. I do not think the weather or the palace gardens fall under that category," I said sweetly, my fingers crumpling the edge of my dress the only indication of my true feelings.

He huffed out a breath. "You are right. There are several things we need to discuss. First, it is of utmost importance that as my heir, you represent me and the South to the best of your ability. Which means you will wear clothes and partake in activities that are appropriate for a princess. You shall also refrain from having conversations about your time with the Fae and are not to be openly armed."

I pressed my lips together in a thin line. *What else am I supposed to talk about? Flowers?*

He continued, "You will be required to have at least one guard—preferably two—with you always, unless you are sleeping. In addition to guards, you will also be assigned a maid and one or more ladies-in-waiting."

There goes my privacy. I didn't like the idea of constantly having someone glued to my side. Unable to stop myself with anger simmering, I said sharply, "Is that *all*?"

King Leonard stared at me. "No."

Of course not. I sighed, waiting for him to finish explaining what other unwanted restrictions would be placed on me.

"It is also critical that we find you a husband," he said. His expression dared me to object.

I was too shocked to do more than gasp. "Husband?"

"You didn't think I had summoned you to become my heir and would allow you to not have a husband, did you? The line must continue. You must produce a child," he replied matter-of-factly, then added, "Your engagement to Prince Tanyth has been terminated. I would advise you to send correspondence to him."

I dug my fingernails into my thigh under the table. The news that he had terminated my engagement sent me reeling. *How did he find out?* I swallowed, my throat suddenly dry. It had been foolish of me not to anticipate my grandfather's plan. To marry and bear a child. The timing of this conversation caught me off guard more than anything. It was one thing to explain expected behavior, but quite another to tell a clearly exhausted young woman that she would need to marry and produce children as soon as possible.

"I see," I said, my voice shaking slightly.

"I have created a list of qualified suitors, and tomorrow afternoon you will begin meeting with them," my grandfather said.

Tomorrow? I swallowed the word and instead replied with a more suitable response. "I get to choose?" I asked, holding my breath for the answer.

His nostrils flared. "No, the choice is mine. You can provide feedback, but ultimately, it is *my* choice, not yours."

Gasping, I covered my mouth with my napkin, biting hard on my tongue. Coppery blood flooded my mouth, preventing me from responding. *This must be why my parents refused to live in the palace. He wants to control too much of my life.*

Jaw tight, I listened to the rest of his words. "My intention is that by the end of the week we will have a marriage contract, and in two weeks' time, you will be married and busy making an heir."

Heart racing, I struggled to prevent an outburst. I couldn't afford to anger him more. I ground my teeth together. I didn't like how he was dictating my life to me. Even when I was at Jade Wilds, I had had some amount of say in what I was doing. Yet

King Leonard, with his casual tone, acted as though my marriage and creation of an heir was nothing more than a business contract, like the ones he did for trade agreements between territories with Lord McCormack. *Maybe instead of cutting off the engagement, I should write to Tanyth begging him to rescue me from this new hell.* As soon as I thought the words, I dismissed them. Asking Tanyth for help was not a good solution. It would likely end in war between the Court of Dusk and the South, an event I wanted to prevent, not be the cause of.

Grandfather must have noticed my reaction because his next words were biting. "You. Will. Marry. Your mother knew quite well that this could happen should misfortune befall my other heirs."

Anger and sadness washed over me. My mother had known this was possible, yet had never shared the information with me. *Just like she never told me about being the king of Fae's granddaughter.* Fists clenched, unwilling to let him place the blame on my dead mother, I met the king's gaze. "You could have contacted me at any point to ensure I knew it was possible, either when I lived here or once I was at Jade Wilds. It was your choice to leave me in the dark all these years. Perhaps if you cared about the South as much as you claim, you would have done a better job to ensure all potential South heirs were aware of their *duty* before they were called upon to perform it."

Not waiting for his response, I stood up and ran out, back to my rooms. I didn't care if I had broken the protocol; my emotions were too strong. If I hadn't left, I wasn't sure what I would have done. *Something I would've regretted.*

I slammed the suite doors shut behind me. The doors shuddered on their hinges, and I momentarily worried they were going to fall off. Yanking up the hem of my dress, I slid one of my hidden daggers out of its sheath on my thigh. Desperate to get out of the dress, an ill-fitting reminder of what was to come with my new role as heir of Gaskal, I gripped the dagger, and with sharp slices I cut myself out of the dress. I threw it in a heap in the corner, then collapsed to the floor. Sobbing, I wrapped my arms around my knees, rocking back and forth. "I can't do this."

I closed my eyes.

A fragment of a memory came to me: being curled in a ball on a massive bed, hopeless. The desire to end it. Then warm arms encircling me and a voice saying, "I'm here, always." A feeling of safety and love.

I groaned; suddenly it felt like someone was stabbing a knife through my head. I clutched my face with my hands and writhed in pain. Just as quickly as it had come, the pain dissipated, and I sat up and let out a relieved breath. That was the first time the headaches had gotten extreme, and I dearly hoped it would be the only time.

Cautiously, I stood up. When the pain didn't return, a quick glance confirmed I had indeed shredded the dress and was only wearing undergarments. My hands were shaking from a blend of exhaustion, pain, and anger. I knew I was unlikely to fall asleep if I got into bed, not without giving my mind a chance to at least try settling.

Training usually helps. Pushing furniture out of the way, I created a space that would allow me to practice simple hand-to-hand combat maneuvers.

When I awoke the next morning, I momentarily forgot where I was, until I recognized the bed and the room as the set of suites assigned to me at King Leonard's palace. I felt marginally better now that I had a night's rest behind me. *Today is a new day.* Even though yesterday had proven challenging, there had been one bright spot—meeting Violet. I knew Violet and Lord McCormack were visiting for a few days and wanted to make sure I was able to find her today.

I slid out of bed and stretched, then made a beeline for the small desk. There was a stack of paper and a quill conveniently on top.

Tanyth,

I regret to inform you that my grandfather, King Leonard, has called upon me to take my place as heir of Gaskal.
Please forgive me. I never intended for our engagement to end, let alone through a letter.

Yours sincerely,
Serafina

Rereading the letter, it sounded too short, but since I wasn't confident it would not be read by my grandfather, I was afraid to include anything that could be interpreted the wrong way. I folded the letter and stuffed it in an envelope. I found a seal with wax in the drawer; thankfully it was just a plain circle with no emblem. I wasn't sure the letter would make it to Prince Tanyth if I were to use King Leonard's seal.

Task complete, hunger still eluding me, I decided to do sword drills, confident they would boost my appetite. I pulled my sword out of the trunk and went through the warmup drills, followed by the real ones. The sword was a comforting weight in my hand as I worked my way through each of the ten maneuvers and then the combinations.

I was completing the seventh set of combinations when the doors to my suites swung open. I whirled, sword in my hand, to face the intruder.

The intruder was not a real intruder—or much of a threat. I lowered my sword and studied the maid. A round face, a pointy nose, and pale blond hair in a severe-looking chignon made the maid's expression harsh. She wore a plain cream-colored dress with gold satin cuffs and a gold satin apron tied around her waist, and she had a dress draped over one of her arms.

"Princess, we must get you ready. No time to waste!" the maid said, her voice high-pitched from nerves.

Eyebrows shooting up, I placed my left hand on my hip with the right gripping the sword, the tip digging into the oak floors. I stood rooted to the spot. "Why?"

"Your first suitor is here!" she said, wringing her hands, then she turned to the bed and laid out the dress that had been chosen for me.

Inwardly cringing, I kept my face schooled into annoyance at the interruption. "I thought it wasn't until this afternoon?" I said, but based on her actions, I knew it was my information that was wrong, not hers.

"Sorry, Princess, but the Duke of Piore is here," she replied.

"Shit," I muttered, and the maid gasped. I rolled my eyes. In my own chambers, I refused to curb my tongue and only use "words appropriate for a princess."

"What is your name?" I asked so I could address her properly.

"I'm Mary," she said quickly. "Tomorrow you will get a lady-in-waiting."

A lady-in-waiting? I wondered if that was an appointment I got to make myself or another one that my grandfather would do for me.

Quicker than I had imagined possible for one person, she had me dressed and fed a light breakfast, then was ushering me into one of the palace's many galleries. This one had large windows and a balcony that overlooked the rose garden, with a large black piano sitting at one end.

Mary practically shoved me through the door before vanishing. Chin high, shoulders back, I refused to allow my abrupt entrance to set the tone for the encounter with my first *suitor*.

A tremor ran through me, and I clenched my jaw. *This can't be any worse than my first day at the battle camp facing hundreds of unfamiliar Fae.* I strode forward and laid my eyes on the Duke of Piore. He was the same height as me, with short ash-blond hair and dark-brown eyes. His brown coat reminded me of one of the many tree trunks in the Jade Wilds forest.

Disappointment coursed through me, though I had no idea why. I wouldn't have been expecting someone else in the duke's place.

"Your Grace," I said and curtsied.

"Your Highness," he replied, bowing deeply.

"Please just call me Serafina," I said, taking a few steps closer to him. I stayed out of arm's reach, guessing that was an appropriate distance for an unwed woman interacting with a strange man.

"Then you must call me Taylor," the duke replied. "Now, Serafina, tell me about yourself. What is it that you enjoy doing?"

Inhaling softly, I gave him the prettiest smile I could manage. "I spent eleven years being trained by the Fae, and I enjoy fighting with a sword."

Taylor's jaw dropped open in shock at my bold answer, and his cheeks colored. "You fight with a sword?"

My lips twitched in amusement. *What if he had been the one who walked in on me this morning when I was practicing with a sword instead of Mary?* "Yes, Taylor. I can fight with a sword, axe, even my bare fists if I must," I clarified. It was a struggle to keep my composure with his obvious discomfort. *He must like weak women*, I surmised.

Taylor backed up a few steps, putting one of the sofas between us. "If you'll excuse me," he said and then turned and briskly left.

When the duke was gone, I couldn't help myself; I laughed. *What did he expect me to say?* I belatedly realized that the king had asked that I omit talking about Fae, though in my defense I had answered the duke's questions honestly, which I felt was more important than sticking to the king's approved topic choices. I shrugged. *There will be more suitors.*

When my laughter subsided, I realized I was alone in the gallery. Since the king or his advisors had forgotten to tell me the first suitor was arriving early this morning, I had no idea if anyone other than the Duke of Piore was expected or if I was free to do as I wished for the remainder of the day. I hoped it was the latter. A ride with Violet sounded divine right now. Given she had not reacted negatively yesterday when I spoke of training with the Fae, I expected that Violet didn't care if I could use weapons. *A noblewoman training horses is just as uncommon as one trained in weapons.*

I strolled around the room, peering at the large paintings hanging on the walls. Most of them were hunting scenes of some sort with men on horseback and hounds capering around. I was surprised at the lack of images of any females in this room. *Does my grandfather's court still believe in keeping the two genders isolated from each other?* As I considered my question, I realized that I had no idea. Aside from lunch with Violet and meeting the maid, I had not yet encountered any other women.

I don't want to be the center of attention, though. Maybe it is better that I haven't seen many people. I am sure if my grandfather hates the Fae, many of his courtiers share the same sentiment. The fact that I lived among the Fae for over eleven years is not going to help me win them over.

The door creaked behind me. I turned, reminding myself I wasn't in danger and forcing my hands to stay relaxed at my sides instead of in fists.

King Leonard stepped through the door. Eyebrows arched, I took in his riding outfit. He had tight-fitting breeches, knee-high black boots, a short red coat, gloves, and a velvet hunting cap on his head. "I was informed that the Duke of Piore has departed. Since you are now free for the rest of the morning, I thought you might want to join me for my morning ride."

His offer caught me off guard. After I stormed out of dinner last night, I had not expected any sort of casual interaction. *I was hoping to ride with Violet. I suppose this would be a compromise.* The king was holding himself stiffly, and his eyes were hooded and difficult to read. I had no way of knowing if this was a peace offering or another way of him asserting his authority over me. I prayed it was the former and that our shared interest in horses might give us common ground.

Not wanting to overshadow what could be an enjoyable ride with negative thoughts, I allowed a small smile to curve on my lips. "I'd love to." He held out his arm and I slipped mine through his and lightly set my hand near his elbow. *A fresh start?*

"I do need to change first," I pointed out when I realized we were not heading back toward my rooms.

A slight course alteration had us at my suite in a few minutes. "I'll wait," King Leonard said.

"I'll be fast," I responded. He gave me a look of disbelief.

Not wanting to waste any time discussing it, I slipped into my room and shut the door.

The corset laces came undone with less effort than I expected. Letting the dress fall in a heap, I stepped out of it and rummaged in my trunk for a pair of pants, a tunic, and tall boots. Sliding the clothes on, I sighed in relief. The dresses I had worn so far had been extremely uncomfortable. *I need to talk to the seamstress.*

I stepped out of the room and caught the king's shocked expression. "Why are you wearing pants?" he demanded.

I rocked back on my heels and banged the door with my shoulder. "This is what I ride in," I replied.

The king's jaw visibly tightened. I wondered if he was going to retract his offer to allow me to ride. "I don't have time for you to change again," he finally managed to say, then turned abruptly on his heel and strode down the hallway. I followed a step behind, taking the hint that whatever comradery might have been growing between us just minutes before was now most definitely not.

Guards trailed us, and as we approached the stable, more appeared. Some were already on horseback. I should have anticipated that going on a ride with the Lord of the South would never be *just* the two of us. Unlike the Fae, humans did not have magic. The only defense my grandfather had from an attack would be any training he had received and that of his guards.

We strode through the stable doors.

A small black horse with a sidesaddle stood quietly next to a bright red one with a regular saddle. The red horse alternated pawing the ground and tossing its head impatiently. Not knowing what kind of rider my grandfather was, I kept any thoughts of whether or not he should be riding a young, energetic horse at his age to myself.

My grandfather took the reins of the red horse and led it outside before I could say anything. The groom offered me the reins of the black one. I took them and then moved to its side and unbuckled the saddle, sliding it off the horse's back and setting it on an open stall door.

"Princess, you cannot take the saddle off," protested the groom, shooting a worried glance in my grandfather's direction.

I rolled my eyes. I doubted the groom was going to physically prevent me from doing what I wanted. Not with guards and the king nearby. "I most certainly can. I'm the one riding the horse, and I would prefer to ride bareback than in a sidesaddle!" I retorted.

The groom cleared his throat and in a firmer voice replied, "Your clothing will be ruined!"

I raised my eyebrows. I was wearing pants and a tunic, same as him, nothing that would get ruined. I yanked the saddle blanket off the horse's back and tossed it on top of the saddle. Then, wrapping a handful of mane in my hand to help me balance, I jumped up and swung my leg over.

When I was comfortable, I gathered the reins in my hands, gave the groom a wave, and clucked lightly to the horse.

When he saw me astride the horse, my grandfather flushed in anger. "What's the meaning of this?"

"The sidesaddle was unnecessary. Now, are we going to ride?" I demanded, hoping he wouldn't order me to put the saddle back on the horse.

Clenching his teeth, eyes blazing, he said, "The pants were one thing. Riding bareback is another entirely. Get off the horse."

"No," I replied firmly.

"Guards, remove the princess from the horse and escort her into the palace," the king ordered.

One guard placed a tight grip on my horse's reins; another moved toward me and looked as though he was going to grab me by the waist. My whole body was strung tight in indecision. I wanted to kick the horse into a gallop and take off. But I hesitated, because I knew that disobeying the king in a matter like this was not important. It was just a battle of wills. Even if I won, I would not gain much.

I started to swing my leg over to dismount when a motion at the corner of my eye caught my attention. Leg frozen mid-swing over the horse's back, I watched in horror as my grandfather's body convulsed and he toppled off his horse. Suddenly lacking a rider, the chestnut stallion began bucking.

Forgetting me, the guards rushed to my grandfather, but the stallion was wild, with his hooves flying and no regard for the humans around him. There was a distinct possibility someone was going to get hurt, maybe fatally. I leaped off my black horse and launched myself at the stallion, dodging the hooves until I was able to snag the dangling reins. I tugged and half dragged, half led the stallion far away from the fallen king. Eventually, the stallion stopped moving. His heaving sides were lathered in thick, foamy sweat. My tunic was sweat-soaked too, and I noticed my hands were shaking slightly.

Worried for my grandfather but afraid to take my attention off the stallion, I murmured soft nonsense words to him, waiting for a groom to relieve me.

It took a considerable amount of time before a groom noticed I was holding the horse. The guards were still clustered around my grandfather, so I had no way of knowing how he fared, and I was afraid to bring the stallion too close lest he decide to misbehave. *Not that I can blame him. I would have been surprised too if my rider had suddenly toppled off.*

"Forgive me, Your Highness," the groom said, rushing over.

I handed him the reins and jogged over to the kneeling guards. "How is he?" I asked. They were blocking my view. I could tell he was still lying on the ground, but I could not get a clear look at his face. *Please be okay.* I knew he had officially acknowledged me as heir, and if anything did happen and he was incapacitated, I would take his place without issue. The idea of that moment being now, when I had spent barely a day in Gaskal, was terrifying. *I'm not ready.*

"Let me sit up," growled King Leonard.

I sighed in relief at his voice. Regardless of the tension between us, I did not want my grandfather to die. *Is this the illness Commander Meriel spoke of?*

The guards stood and backed away, giving their king space. I held my position and observed him as he sat up. I was surprised that my grandfather would be able to stand up and walk away after having what I suspected was a seizure and falling off a horse. Sure enough, that was exactly what he did. His movements were slow but precise as he sat up and then rose all the way to stand.

"I ordered you to your room," he snapped at me.

I raised my hands as though surrendering. "I was dismounting when you had your episode," I explained.

For a brief moment, I thought maybe his expression softened, and then it was gone.

"I'm fine. Tired, but uninjured." The king turned away from me and his guards closed in, tighter than they had escorted us earlier. As a tight bunch, they escorted the king into the palace.

I took a shaky breath and waited until I could no longer see the king and his guards before I retreated to my rooms as well.

Six

TRISTAN

My eyes snapped open when I felt pressure against my throat. To my chagrin, I had fallen into a light sleep. Threads of dark green magic laced in gold wrapped around me. King Pharaan was standing on the other side of the desk, green eyes bright against his tanned skin. The king's black hair was tied severely at the nape of his neck, making it easy to see his wide gold necklace with its fist-sized emerald. The rumors were true of how imposing the king was. Refusing to let King Pharaan's tactics get under my skin, I reminded myself how aggressive Prince Tanyth was when he wanted to intimidate. Wrapping magic around my throat was minor compared to stabbing me in the back with Dragonfang.

Eventually the magic disappeared, though the king's eyes stayed locked on mine. "Why are you here, Lord Commander of the Court of Dusk?"

Nostrils flared, I chose my words carefully. "I am no longer bound by a blood contract to Prince Tanyth." I paused, watching King Pharaan as his eyes widened in surprise, then continued. "Your granddaughter, Serafina, is my soulmate, and—"

"Not possible," whispered King Pharaan, rocking back on his heels as though I had slapped him.

My eyes blazed with anger at King Pharaan's doubt, and the words were out before I could stop myself. "I love her, and by her own free will, we are mated. You cannot change that."

The king's green eyes snapped with barely suppressed fury and the air around him shimmered with magic, a telltale sign that I had hit a nerve. "Then tell me, Tristan Gilvrye, why is it not possible to feel your mating bond? Why are you lying to me?" King Pharaan demanded.

"I'm not lying. We are mated, but Prince Tanyth did something to her," I snarled, and to my dismay, I felt fur beginning to break out along my hands and arms. Sucking in a sharp breath, I clamped down on my anger and shoved my will against my shifting magic.

King Pharaan caught sight of my hand before the fur completely disappeared and grabbed it, jerking me forward and almost toppling over the chair in the process. "You're a shifter?"

I tugged on my hand, trying to get it back to no avail. He had seen proof; there was nothing left to do other than confirm. "Yes, I am a shifter."

"Show me," the king said.

Deep down, I knew it was not a request; it was an order. *What would happen if I refused?* A shudder rippled through me. The snow leopard wanted out. My secret was no longer a secret. There was even a chance that King Pharaan could have sensed the snow leopard within me if he had not been angry. Prince Tanyth knew I was a shapeshifter. It would spread among the Fae soon enough. I had no logical reason to refuse.

"Yes, my king," I said and bowed my head in deference, though anger still simmered in my veins. He released my hand immediately. I stood up and scooted the chairs out of the way. Then, I focused on the snow leopard.

The change was instantaneous. One moment I was in my Fae form, the next I was a massive snow leopard, making the small room feel even more cramped. I peered at King Pharaan, trying to gauge his reaction. My fur stood on edge, a clear indicator of the tension I felt between us.

The king's mouth moved, though his voice was almost inaudible, even to my snow leopard ears. It only took me a moment to realize that he was reciting the Lost Fae Queen prophecy.

"When tension rises and war with the humans has come, the
Lost Fae Queen will return.
First, she will prove her battle prowess.
Look closely or you might be blinded, for when the Fae Queen
returns, not all will know her, yet everyone will follow her.
Be warned, the Fae Queen must stay pure until the Great Cat
finds her and their souls unite.
With their souls bound, the heir will be found.
The Fae Queen's magic will return, and together they will
defend the Fae from the end of time.
Time is of the essence, or the Fae will fall to the darkness."

Tears glistened on King Pharaan's cheeks. "Serafina is safe with her human grandfather."

In frustration, I shifted immediately back to my Fae form. "She's not safe!" I growled under my breath. Though I was now Fae, I could still feel the elongated canines in my mouth. *Is King Pharaan not aware of everything that has transpired?*

Dark green magic swirls formed around the king, his magic responsive to strong emotions just like mine. "When King Leonard made the request for Serafina to fulfill her duty as heir to the human kingdom, I agreed. His reasoning was logical. I cannot afford to have the gold mines fall into disarray should King Leonard die without an heir. The title is hers by birthright. The Lord of the South's blood runs through her veins in equal amounts to her Fae bloodline." He paused and moistened his lips with his tongue. "You claim to love Serafina. Would you deny her her birthright to one day be the Lady of the South?"

I clenched my fist, nails digging deeply into my palms. *He is my king.* "When it means that we cannot be together because she is bound by human law, yes, I would do everything in my power to free her from that obligation. You of all Fae should understand, since you are bonded." I refused to beg. I loved Serafina with everything I had, but I did not want her family to agree to help because I had begged. I wanted their help because they believed in her.

"Yes, I do understand your feelings, but you must be able to stand in my shoes. Here you are, one of my subjects, who has served the Court of Dusk for decades and murdered many shapeshifters in Prince Tanyth's name. Now you are claiming to be mated to my granddaughter, yet I cannot find a single trace of such a bond on you. Without the magical evidence of the bond, your words and claim are empty. I cannot break a treaty with a human kingdom without hard proof, and from where I'm standing, there is none," King Pharaan explained firmly.

"What about the prophecy?" I demanded, scrambling for some way to make the king understand.

"You are a snow leopard, and it would be reasonable to draw the conclusion that you are the Great Cat. However, it goes back to the lack of proof of your mate bond. The prophecy explicitly states, 'With their souls bound, the heir will be found.' It is unlikely that the prophecy is talking about you and Serafina without that requirement being met. If the order of events is necessary, she cannot be *the* heir it refers to if the bond does not exist."

I choked back an incredulous laugh. "Since when do we take prophecies entirely at face value?" *Besides, we were bonded before she became the heir of the South.* I kept that tidbit to myself, knowing bringing it up would be pointless without evidence of the bond.

"Enough!" bellowed King Pharaan, and the door burst open. A light blue unicorn—Onvyr, I presumed—and three guards filled the doorway, waves of magic rolling off them.

"Your request has been denied based on the lack of proof. Begone, before I punish you for your impertinence," King Pharaan ordered.

I clamped my lips shut as the two guards shoved me out of the room.

Onvyr shifted back to Fae form as we walked. "You are no longer welcome here. Do not linger in the city."

So much for my request to see the library. I sighed. *Maybe I can send word to Commander Meriel, and she will know the answer.* It was a solid plan. Commander Meriel was a seer and had knowledge of many prophecies.

My escort of three ensured that I was safely on the other side of the palace gate before returning to the depths of Uaine Palace. Frustration bubbled up that King Pharaan would give me an audience and then tell me there was no proof of the soulmate bond. *But the king* did *give me an audience.* I had to take that as a positive sign. Clearly the king of Fae cared for his granddaughter. I hoped that if circumstances changed and I had to call on King Pharaan in the future, he would not require proof to take action. Exhaustion weighed me down, and I trudged back through the city, head hanging low. *I'll camp for the night, then return to Gaskal in the morning.*

The next morning, using a star portal, I departed Uaine and its city. Sleep had not eased my disappointment in King Pharaan. *Maybe this was Prince Tanyth's intention. To crush King Pharaan's hope that the Lost Fae Queen would be found in his lifetime, throwing the Court of Dawn into chaos upon his death with no living male heir.*

I shook my head, trying to cast King Pharaan's opinion away. *I must believe in Serafina and our bond. It is real. I just need to figure out how to fix it.* Closing my eyes, I summoned a dark, almost black cloak with a deep hood that I pulled up around my face, then walked down the path toward the gates of Gaskal.

I arrived at Wayside Inn hoping to find Callyn. The inn's close proximity to the gate made it an ideal location for us if we needed a rapid escape. We had split up once I was healed so that I could track Serafina with the plan that Callyn would find me. *Not that it was too difficult to guess where Serafina had been sent. There were only two places she had strong ties to—Jade Wilds and the South.* After the way things had gone at Uaine Palace, worry gnawed at me—worry that the bond was unfixable, and that I was not strong or smart enough to devise a solid plan to get Serafina back without King Pharaan's help.

After waiting in our room for more than an hour, it was clear Callyn was out for the day and I should find something else to occupy myself until she arrived.

My original plan was to lie low and rest. However, tension rolled through me, and I knew resting was the last thing I was capable of. Deciding that a run would help, I discarded the cloak and headed down the stairs.

The innkeeper grabbed my arm as I hit the last step. I bristled at the touch. "What?" I growled, hand dropping to my sword.

"I know you're Fae. That mean's it'll cost ya double to stay here," the innkeeper said in a no-nonsense voice.

I glared at him and he released my arm, taking an involuntary step back. "No."

The innkeeper's lip curled. "It's double, or pack your bags right now."

Grinding my teeth together, I debated what to do. I wanted to leave. *Double?* What a ridiculous notion. But Callyn had chosen the inn, and without her being here, I was loathe to get us thrown out without knowing a suitable alternative existed.

"Fine. We'll pay double," I said in a low voice.

The innkeeper nodded in satisfaction and disappeared around the corner, presumably into the kitchen. I ran my hand over my face and left briskly before the innkeeper could make any more demands. Not wanting to draw attention to myself, I headed out of the city and into the forest. I ran along narrow game trails. A few were hardly trails at all.

The ground, a mix of grass, clover, and dead leaves, gently sloped downward, and I thought I could hear a gurgling creek. Deciding I was unlikely to run across a human if I hadn't already, I took a deep breath and shifted. Falling forward onto my front paws, I stretched. I relished the feel of leaves and leaped toward the creek, bouncing down the slope, over rocks and a few fallen trees.

I drank icy water from the creek, taking in my surroundings and enjoying the freedom and the lack of fear. For far too long, I had lived knowing that if I shifted, it would be a death sentence. It had been that way ever since I had entered training at Embergate. I was no longer within reach of Prince Tanyth, and the blood contract had dissolved. The only Fae I knew of who harbored ill will toward shapeshifters and acted upon it was Tanyth. The presence of Onvyr, a unicorn shifter, in Uaine Palace supported that. Here in the South, I was safe. *Safe from being killed for shapeshifting or the other transgressions I'd committed while lord commander, at least,* I amended. I had no idea how much Fae outside of the Court of Dusk knew about what went on within its borders. I doubted anyone from the Court of Dawn would come after me, but the other two courts were a different matter.

Then there was the matter of a Fae in a human kingdom. The battle between the Court of Dusk and the Lord of the South had happened before Serafina was born, but there were other, more recent conflicts, fresher in human memories, such as Emerald Valley. Would the humans who lived here attack first and ask questions later? Or would they proceed with more caution and acknowledge that likely they didn't possess the knowledge—or the skills—to successfully kill a Fae?

Thirst quenched, I bounded up the far side of the bank and wandered through the forest, letting the instincts of the snow leopard take control.

Seven

SERAFINA

I learned my lesson the first morning; suitors could arrive early. To ensure I would have the time I needed to mentally prepare for meeting with the next suitor, I woke at dawn.

I got dressed in a plain green tunic and brown pants accompanied by soft leather boots. Working my way through a set of stretches, I debated what to do first. *A run.* At Jade Wilds, I would often start my day with a run to help clear my mind. It was also a great way to warm up before starting a training session.

I peered out of the room and into the hallway. A guard stood facing the door, wearing the usual chain mail with the palace livery in cream and gold as a tunic over the top. This guard seemed close to me in age, though his face was clean-shaven, so perhaps that contributed to how young he looked. His light-brown hair was swept back from his face, with an aquiline nose and hazel eyes that widened in surprise as I studied him.

"May I help you, Princess Serafina?"

I smiled. "What is your name?"

"Thomas," he replied, blushing.

Do guests normally not ask guards for their names? It seemed silly to not find out Thomas's name since he had been assigned to me since my arrival.

"Well, Thomas. I want to go on a run, preferably outside," I responded.

Eyes wide, Thomas glanced up and down the hallway as though someone would appear to tell us both that we were misbehaving. "I can show you a good route," he finally replied.

"Wonderful." I motioned with my hand. "Please lead the way."

Thomas did not walk ahead of me, but he did walk at my side, pointing at landmarks and explaining our path. The door we emerged through placed us near the stables. I briefly considered changing plans and riding, but riding would make me less accessible, and I was reluctant to further complicate things between myself and my grandfather.

"We can follow the edge of the wall. There is space to run at least two abreast the full perimeter of the palace," Thomas explained. He then waited for me to set the pace.

I started slowly, wanting to get a feel for Thomas's ability and to check out the surroundings. After two laps, I sped up into a ground-covering run—not my fastest, but judging by Thomas's breathing, the fastest the guard could manage without tiring quickly.

Should I run five more laps or stop and practice sword work back in my room? I mused. Leaning toward running longer, I pulled up short as we got closer to the stables when I saw Violet. Adjusting our course, I jogged over to the entrance to the stable, where Violet was having a lively discussion with one of the grooms.

"Good morning, Violet!" I called.

Violet turned toward me. "Princess Serafina! Good morning. Would you like to join me for a ride?"

Happiness filled me. "I would love to."

I took half a step forward when Thomas's hand touched my arm. "Princess, your maid, Mary, just sent a messenger saying that you need to prepare for your first visitor this morning."

I sighed and gave Violet an apologetic smile. "Looks like we'll have to ride another time."

"Of course, Your Highness," Violet replied with a curtsey.

I stepped closer to her. "Please, Violet, you can call me Serafina. I don't want us to be formal with each other."

Violet looked uncertain. "I will honor your request when in present company, but I do not want to risk the king's wrath by addressing you like that when we are with him or other nobles."

It was an agreeable compromise. I nodded. "Very well. I'll catch up with you later, Violet. Bye!"

Thomas's hand was on my elbow, steering me away. It was tempting to dig my heels in, but it wasn't the guard's fault. He had willingly accompanied me on my run, which meant in the future he was likely to help me with my requests, even if they were not typical for a noble or a princess.

Hours later, I left Thomas in the hallway to my room, intending to change for the second time today, except this time it was escaping the dress in favor of more comfortable attire. I was surprised when Violet and Mary were sitting at the dining table in my room. Both glanced up as I entered.

"Your Highness, Lady Violet McCormack has been chosen by King Leonard to be your lady-in-waiting," Mary explained.

I swallowed my dismay at yet another thing my grandfather had done for me without consulting with me first. "It's good to see you again, Violet."

"Can we help you with anything, Your Highness?" asked Mary.

I gave them both a smile. "Why yes, in fact. I want to change out of this dress and into pants and a tunic."

"Why?" asked Mary in surprise.

"It's more comfortable," Violet and I responded in unison. I smiled at Violet. Mary gave both of us a confused look.

"It's a personal preference," I explained. "However, I will change out of the dress with or without your help."

Mary and Violet both stood up and came close enough to me to help with the dress. I had to admit, having two extra sets of hands did make the task of unlacing a corseted gown much faster than when I had only myself.

Dress successfully removed, pants and tunic settled in place, I snagged an apple out of the basket on the dining table and made for the door. I wasn't sure if I should tell them I was leaving or just leave. *What is proper protocol in a situation like this?* When I was in Jade Wilds, I never had to worry about protocol unless we were training or around Fae royalty. I could just come and go as I pleased on our days off. Here, I felt like I was never off duty.

I stepped out of the suite and Thomas fell into place slightly behind me, a faithful shadow as I strolled through the palace. The idea of taking out a horse for a ride was still appealing. Mind made up, I adjusted my course and headed for the stables.

The stable was quiet, save for the munching of horses eating hay. Wanting to keep things simple, I made my way over to the small black mare's stall. I knew my grandfather had chosen her for me yesterday, and I decided that if all the horses were unfamiliar to me, I'd rather try one that was highly likely to be easy. A box of brushes and the bridle were sitting forgotten on a bale of hay in front of the stall door.

I lightly groomed the mare and then slipped the bridle onto her head. Not wanting to bother with figuring out which was the right saddle, I intended to ride bareback.

I was leading the mare out of the stable when the king appeared, dressed similarly to how he had been yesterday in his riding attire. I kept my surprise to myself. *If I were his doctor, I would not allow him to ride so soon.* Given how much we had been butting heads since my arrival, I kept my thoughts to myself.

"If you are willing to wait for my horse to be prepared, I could accompany you on your ride," King Leonard said.

"I am going to ride bareback," I informed him, making sure we weren't going to have another battle of wills. He was intruding on my personal time. I was not going to give in to his demands to wear a riding habit or to ride in a particular type of saddle.

The king studied me for a long time before sighing. "Fine, but if you fall off, then I will lock you in your rooms and only let you out to eat or meet with a suitor."

I bowed my head in acceptance, confident in my ability to ride. *He may not be aware, but Mother allowed me to start riding when I turned three.*

Our wait was short. Word must have been sent ahead of the king's arrival to prepare his horse. Once mounted, Grandfather clucked to the red stallion, and we began our ride at a steady walk. Though our progress was slow, the rhythm of my mare's stride was smooth, and I found myself relaxing for the first time since my arrival at the palace.

Our entourage grew to twelve guards as we crossed through the gate and out into the meadow on the east side of the palace. With a sharp glance at me—almost a challenge, I surmised—my grandfather urged his stallion into a gallop.

True to her nature as a lady's mount, my mare waited patiently until I urged her forward into a gallop. The breeze tugged at my pants and strands of my hair curled at my checks as excitement bubbled up within me. *Freedom.* The guards strung out around us in a loose circle, watchful of our surroundings and easily keeping pace.

Our horses were almost neck and neck. I tilted my head and gazed at my grandfather. He seemed to be enjoying his ride as much as I was. Unfortunately, the end of the meadow was rapidly approaching. Both horses eased back into a canter, and we rode along the edge of the meadow, then circled back to face the palace.

My heart thumped in my chest, and I couldn't help but smile. *This was just what I needed.* Keeping my eyes on the palace, I ran a hand along my horse's neck, appreciating her velvety fur and the coarse strands of black mane. Out of the corner of my eye, I saw my grandfather tug on his reins, and his stallion dropped from a canter to a walk. I followed suit, but instead of tugging on the reins, I slowed my seat, and my horse immediately eased into a walk.

"You should not tell any of the suitors you ride astride," my grandfather said conversationally.

His comment caught me off guard. I gave him a quizzical look and he elaborated. "Many men find it distasteful for a woman to ride at all. Knowing you ride astride might be enough to send them packing."

I frowned. "I've been riding since I was three. My parents encouraged it. Do you expect me to behave only as a proper *human* woman? I think it's important that my future husband knows what kind of woman he's marrying." *Another topic to remove from my list.*

My grandfather tugged on his beard before answering. "The only thing that your future husband needs to know is that you are a virgin and the future Lady of the South."

Eyes wide in shock, I replied, "You want me to *lie* about who I am?" Thankfully my horse wasn't concerned about my hands vibrating on the reins.

He gave me a sharp look. "Omitting information is not lying. Your duty in these meetings is to present yourself as a princess of the South. Dazzle them with your beauty."

I snorted, causing my mare to shift uncertainly. "I'm not beautiful."

"Perhaps you do not see it because you were among the Fae too long, but to a human man you are beautiful, Serafina," he said firmly.

I still wasn't sure I believed him, but if that was the tale the king needed to be able to justify what he was telling me, then I wasn't going to complain. I was more concerned about his instructions to steer conversations with my suitors away from topics defining who I am as a woman, as their future wife, and as heir of the South. Opting for a safe response, I bowed my head and replied, "I will do my best, Grandfather."

Satisfied, he waved his hand at several of the guards and split away from me. I sighed and watched the king ride away. *I suppose this is what those frequent etiquette lessons were for at Jade Wilds. To prepare me for unlikely situations such as the one I now find myself in.*

Glancing at my guards and wondering what their instructions had been, I decided to put them to the test. With a light touch of my leg and the reins, my horse whirled around and launched into a ground-covering gallop. Leaning forward with the reins loose, I urged her onward. *Let's fly!* Muscles bunching, the mare dug her hooves deeper into the soft grass, and we rocketed forward. The guards shouted behind me, but I didn't care. All too soon the edge of the meadow was just ahead. Breathing heavily, I reluctantly slowed to a canter and circled back toward the palace. I could stay out here for hours, but I was certain that my guards would not permit me to do so. It was a miracle they had not called an immediate halt to my solo gallop. *Unless they couldn't catch me.*

Either way, I knew I needed to go back to the palace. The last thing I wanted was for my grandfather to regret allowing me to ride and forbid me from taking a horse out in the future. Just as working on training helped me settle, so did riding, but in a different way. Galloping on a horse, at least for a short while, felt as though there was nothing else in the world but me and the horse. A chance to let go of the pent-up emotions and be free.

"Princess, we must get back. You need to prepare for dinner," the guard closest to me announced.

"Yes, I am ready to return so I will not be late."

I *did* need to change back into a dress, which was a time-consuming endeavor, even with help from Violet and Mary.

Thrilled by the decision to run yesterday and its positive influence on my mood, I opted to run again at dawn on my fourth day in Gaskal. I knew I needed to create some amount of normalcy for myself, and I intended to use running to create a daily rhythm that would allow me to take care of my own personal needs before being subjected to the nonsense required as the heir of Gaskal.

I stepped outside of my room and Thomas was ready for me with a different route recommendation. I was impressed by his willingness to settle into a routine I was sure was new for him too. Unfortunately, I did not see Violet this time. Not that I expected her to be out at dawn every morning, especially with her new duties as my lady-in-waiting. I opted to cut the number of laps in half, wanting to get in sword practice, which I had been unable to do yesterday due to meeting with two suitors.

The first meeting had started well, but when he began asking detailed questions about what I had been doing the week prior to my arrival, my head began to throb, and he left citing not wanting to wed a woman who had a horrible illness. The second suitor sat in silence; eventually I had to start the conversation, and it was clear I made him nervous. When I mentioned using a sword, he bolted out of the room without even saying a proper farewell.

Brow barely damp with sweat, I entered my suites and went to the chest that had my sword. Thomas had offered to show me a spot in one of the gardens that he thought would be suited for practice. I opened the lid on the trunk, expecting the sword to be on top, but it wasn't. Wondering if Violet or Mary had rearranged my things, I dug through the trunk, resorting to making a pile of the contents. The sword was nowhere to be found.

Frowning, I walked over to Thomas, who was waiting for me by the door. "Can I borrow your sword? I don't know where mine went."

Thomas raised his eyebrows. "It's missing?"

I nodded confirmation. Thomas's hand settled on the hilt of his sword; he looked uncomfortable with my request. "I can send one of the guards to retrieve a sword for you out of the armory. They will meet us at our destination. Will that work?"

I didn't have an alternative option. I understood Thomas's reluctance to hand over his sword; it would be difficult for him to protect me without a weapon. "Yes, thank you."

Problem solved, Thomas led the way to the practice area. We walked around several corners, and then Thomas opened a door and led me outside, into the statue garden.

"Here," he said, indicating the area directly in front of us. There was a statue of a rearing horse on one side with a stone bench; otherwise, it was clear in the middle. "None of the guests come this way, and the servants won't disturb you."

Just as Thomas had promised, a guard with salt-and-pepper brown hair and a bushy mustache entered the garden, a sword in his hands. The guard stopped next to Thomas. "You asked for a replacement sword."

"Yes, I did. Thank you." Thomas took the offered sword and handed it to me.

Instead of departing, the other guard bristled. "I thought *you* needed it."

The muscles around Thomas's jaw tightened. "I did need the sword, for Princess Serafina. An order is an order. You're dismissed."

I watched with amusement as the guard's face reddened. He stared openly at Thomas before looking away and giving him a salute. "Yes, sir."

When the guard was gone, I headed into the center. Unsheathing the sword, I gave it a few experimental swings before entering my starting stance: legs properly spaced, shoulders level, and back straight.

High. Middle. Low, I told myself, starting with the simplest of strikes and blocks. Then, I shifted into the ten training movements. I half expected Thomas to offer to spar with me, but every time I glanced his way, he had a blank expression on his face. *Maybe when we get to know each other better, he will be open to practicing with me.* I knew he must not be too far off; otherwise, he'd never have allowed me to practice. Mishandling a sword could be far more dangerous than two well-trained individuals sparring.

Settling into my task, each movement was fluid, each step calculated. I lost track of time as I practiced, the hour passing much faster than I expected. The scuffing sound of a boot brought my awareness back to my surroundings. Sweat trickled down my back and forehead; I swiped a strand of hair out of my eyes and my hand came back wet. "We should go back. I need to bathe before I see any suitors or the king."

"Sounds good. I will send a message ahead," Thomas said. He stood and walked over to the door back into the palace. When he opened it, he stepped halfway through the door, and I could hear the murmur of voices. A few moments later, he turned toward me. "They will prepare a bath and ensure your breakfast is ready as well."

"Thank you," I replied graciously.

I had to rush through my bath and breakfast. King Leonard sent a message an hour ago requesting me, and no one had successfully delivered it. *Or tried.* I couldn't help thinking that perhaps one of the maids or guards wanted me to fail so that I would leave disgraced. I didn't think it was too far-fetched given how angry the guard was earlier when he learned Thomas was giving me a sword.

Perhaps if I let them get to know me and try to get to know them, they will not judge me on my grandfather's prejudices toward Fae.

Mary stood behind me, tightly lacing the spring-green corset. I braced my feet wide to keep her from yanking me around as she tugged on the laces. My fingers spread over the top of the dress. It had delicate flowers and butterflies embroidered all over. A far cry from anything I would have chosen for myself. *Likely an attempt by my grandfather to enhance my "maidenly" appeal.* I quieted my thoughts, calling forth an image of a glassy lake in a meadow.

"Today, you will have tea with the Lord of Mirae," Mary informed me as she came around to inspect her handiwork. I tried to recall where Mirae was but couldn't. *Likely not in the South at all.* He would be the fourth suitor since my arrival, causing me to wonder how long my grandfather had been planning to call on me as his heir. I doubted this many men were ready at the drop of a hat to wed a long-lost princess. *Unless they all have been greedily eyeing the throne as King Leonard's health has declined.*

"Try your best today, Princess," Mary suggested.

I gave her a withering look. *He must have offered her a reward if she could get me to marry quickly.* This was my life. While I was willing to do as my grandfather had requested and omit mentioning "undesirable" activities I enjoyed, I refused to lie if I was asked about them directly. I was going to spend the rest of my life with one of these men at my side as I ruled the South. At the very least, I wanted my husband to accept me and my interests, even if he was unwilling to participate in them with me.

I mumbled something incoherent to her and opened the door before she could offer any additional advice. To my surprise, the steward, Lord John, was waiting for me. "Your Highness," he said, offering his arm. I set my hand lightly on his forearm and allowed him to lead me to wherever I was meeting the Lord of Mirae.

Our destination was the patio overlooking one of the rose gardens. Beautiful I was certain when the roses were in full bloom, but now, with the plants dormant, it was an odd choice for a location to have tea. *Not my problem.*

The Lord of Mirae leaned against the stone railing, watching as we approached. He had a face that reminded me of a rat, with a long, pointy nose and dark, beady eyes. I let go of the steward's arm and, tipping my chin up, marched over to the Lord of Mirae.

"Good morning, sir," I greeted him, offering my hand, secretly hoping he would not kiss it.

The Lord of Mirae bowed over my hand with precise movements and then took it. I couldn't hide my cringe as his moist fingers wrapped around mine and he placed a very wet kiss on my knuckles. Grinding my teeth together, I waited for him to release my fingers so I could wipe his touch away on the folds of my dress.

"Please just call me Enrico. You are a stunning specimen, Princess," Enrico said, still trapping my hand in his.

Inwardly cringing at the word *specimen*, my patience withered. I pulled my fingers out from his grasp and waved my hand to indicate the table with the tea service that was awaiting us. "Let's sit and get to know one another," I suggested, selecting the seat where I could see my guards and escape route.

I took the liberty to pour us each a cup of tea, then wrapped my fingers around my delicate teacup and brought it to my lips.

Enrico gave me a smile that didn't reach his eyes and folded his hands in his lap. "I know you lived with the Fae for twelve years," he revealed.

I gulped my tea and immediately regretted it as it scorched its way down my throat. *Too hot.* I said nothing, hoping Enrico would prevent me from needing to respond to his statement. Though not widely known, my grandfather had not tried to hide the fact that I had lived among the Fae.

"Hopefully their intolerance for humans taught you how you are expected to behave," Enrico said.

I pressed my lips together before I could blurt something obscene at him. I shot a glance at the guards to see if they had overheard Enrico's words, but they weren't paying attention to us—even Thomas, who usually had my back.

"What do you do for a living, sir?" I asked, keeping my tone light and airy, an attempt to cover my dismay.

"My family operates two of the major trade routes through the four human kingdoms. I primarily conduct inspections of merchandise and ensure we have strong relationships with all our business partners," Enrico said. "I heard you met Lord McCormack. He is one of my close contacts for negotiations with the South."

It was tempting to cut to the chase and tell him that I fought with weapons and rode horses astride and most definitely had not learned proper ways of behaving from the Fae. But my behavior would be reported to my grandfather. I had to at least pretend to be interested, no matter how much I disliked the Lord of Mirae. Hunting for a topic that would eventually lead us to an opening for me to make him leave, I settled for a simple question. "Do you read?"

"For enjoyment, most definitely not. But I am capable of reading if that is what you're asking. Otherwise, I wouldn't be able to manage our trade routes. Correspondence and accounting require one to be educated in reading and arithmetic." He paused. "I'm assuming that you read for your own enjoyment. What types of books do you fancy?"

Taking a small sip of tea to soothe my suddenly dry throat, I replied. "History, warfare, battle strategy, blacksmithing, to name a few."

Enrico chuckled. "Interesting subjects. Quite unusual for a woman who would have no use for such knowledge."

My nose twitched as he presented me with the opening I needed. "That is where you are wrong. I have tried my hand at blacksmithing, fought in a battle, and learned about battle strategy over the years I lived with the Fae."

Enrico's smile twisted into anger and something else I couldn't name. "You are a disgrace. No wonder King Helias requested I come to meet you. He hoped I would be willing to overlook your background with the Fae. Except he failed to tell me that they treated you as one of *them*." Throwing his hands in the air, Enrico shoved back from the table, toppling his chair over. "As much as I want the Southern throne, I do *not* want you for a wife. Good day," he said harshly and stalked past the guards and out the door.

My heart pounded in my chest, and it took a few moments to regain my composure. I knew Enrico wouldn't be happy about what I said, but I wasn't expecting his outburst and admission that he hadn't planned on using me as anything other than a pawn.

A while after the Lord of Mirae departed, I heard the snick of a door. A panel in the wall swung open, and King Leonard stepped out and approached me. "You are supposed to be convincing them to marry you, not making them flee."

I shrugged. "I am being honest. Just as my parents taught me when I was a girl—that I must always be honest."

His lip curled. "I am sure you have other interests besides fighting with a sword, ones that are appropriate for a princess. You are deliberately revealing your interest in weapons to discourage them from continuing to pursue you. I forbid you to continue in this vein."

I frowned. "Perhaps if you were choosing future husbands who were willing to stand by my side while I *rule* the South, there would not be as much of a problem. The Lord of Mirae admitted to my face that he was intending to take the throne and leave me in the shadows as nothing more than a broodmare."

The king's face filled with surprise. *What else doesn't he know about the suitors he keeps sending my way?* As he opened his mouth to speak, a messenger ran toward us and bowed, shoving a scroll at the king. My grandfather turned his back on me and opened the scroll as he walked away.

I sighed and debated what I should do. After tea with the Lord of Mirae and the confrontation with my grandfather, I needed a distraction. My thoughts drifted to Violet, but I rejected the idea. Though I was getting along well with Violet, I had a feeling she was reporting to him, and I wasn't entirely sure she would be sympathetic to my problem. *An outing.* None of the instructions my grandfather had given mentioned entering the city of Gaskal. I certainly wasn't going to ask permission. All I needed to do was change clothes into something a little less ... I glanced down at my clothes, bright spring-green with pink and purple butterflies. *Flashy.*

Mind made up, I headed into my chambers.

Violet met me at the door. "How was the Lord of Mirae?"

I frowned, not sure if I knew Violet well enough to discuss the details. "Not the right fit," I replied, settling on a safe explanation.

"Do you need help with anything?" Violet asked.

"Yes, as a matter of fact. I would like to change into a plain dress. I have an errand I want to run in the city, and if I look like this, I will draw too much attention to myself," I said.

Violet shifted on her feet as though she wanted to respond but wasn't sure if she should.

I blew out my breath. "Speak your mind."

Violet swallowed hard. I watched her throat bob and waited for her to speak. "Why would you want to hide the fact that you're a princess?"

"Because if I go into the city as a princess, people will act differently. I would rather be accepted as one of them than treated like a delicate flower that might break," I said, a tinge of annoyance creeping into my voice. I had been hoping Violet would be my friend, but the relationship was not going to work if she was going to critique all of my decisions.

"I see," Violet replied, then walked over to the wardrobe. A few moments later, she returned with a dark russet dress, similar in shade to my hair. She held it up. "Would this work?"

"Yes, that is perfect," I said, offering her a smile.

Violet proceeded to help me change into the russet dress. I almost asked her to join me on my walk but then thought better of it. I really wanted time to myself.

Going into the shadowed area by my nightstand, I bent over and strapped a dagger around my calf. Tugging the dress down, I moved over to the door.

"Would it be possible to get an appointment with a seamstress? I'm finding the dresses do not fit very well. Since I live here now, I would like to have the existing ones altered and new ones made so I can be comfortable," I queried.

"Yes, I will set up an appointment for you," Violet agreed.

"Thank you." I inclined my head to her and departed, heading down the hallway, toward the kitchen, and out the servants' entrance.

Eight

TRISTAN

Rested and in complete control of myself, I decided to explore the city. After my run-in with the innkeeper the night before, the idea of walking around Gaskal as visibly Fae was less than appealing. Even bundled in a cloak, my height and gray skin were dead giveaways that I wasn't quite human, so I decided to test out a magic glamour. I slid a pendant around my neck—a small, circular piece of obsidian on a thin black cord, imbued with a spell to prevent the humans from knowing I was Fae.

As the magic activated, it sent small tingles over my skin, then settled into place. To begin with, I kept my hood up, but eventually I pulled it down, revealing my dark-gray hair that was tucked behind my pointed Fae ears. I was pleased when no one noticed my ears or could sense that I was actively doing magic.

Even though I was now free to shapeshift whenever I felt like it without worrying about being killed by Prince Tanyth, one of the disadvantages of being in a well-populated city was that I was constrained by what the humans of Gaskal considered normal—and a snow leopard prowling their streets was certainly not normal. The glamour definitely wasn't strong enough to keep the humans from noticing my snow leopard form, and even if

I drew on my shadow magic to hide, I was concerned someone would see me. The last thing I needed were rumors of a large cat wandering the city. Which meant if I wanted to shapeshift again, I'd have to return to the depths of the forest.

I meandered through the streets, browsing the shops. A crew was hastily repainting a wall that had red letters on it. Only one of the words remained: "half-blood." I winced, knowing exactly who the words had been directed at. *The innkeeper is clearly not the only one willing to voice his opinions.*

I was stepping out of a spice shop when I saw her. Russet hair in a loose braid down her back, with wisps framing her blue-green eyes, and a modest brown dress that was a shade darker than her hair. *Serafina.* Longing filled me. I took several steps toward her, but she was focused on someone she was speaking to in the doorway of the shop.

Maybe if I take off the glamour, she'll recognize me. Pivoting, I moved into the shadows, drawing the hood over my head to hide my ears. Taking a deep breath, I removed the pendant and stuck it in my pocket, then walked into the street. The effect was immediate; people who moments before had ignored me now shot looks of distrust my way. It was likely only a matter of time before someone noticed I was Fae—the height difference alone was like a beacon.

Serafina turned toward me. Her eyes briefly met mine and then slid to something beyond my shoulder. Holding my breath, I prayed and waited. Moments ticked by. Just as I opened my mouth to say her name, she stepped off the curb toward me. At the last moment, she adjusted her stride, and our arms brushed for a second, but she continued as though I were merely a stranger standing in the middle of the road. I had to cover my mouth to stifle the moan that escaped my lips as my cock hardened to the point it was painful.

Sadness and hot desire warred within me. *Our arms brushed. I should go after her.* I made it two steps toward the blacksmith shop she had entered when caution got the better of me. A quick glance showed more humans were paying attention; a few were even talking and pointing. One of Serafina's guards was dressed to blend in, but the collar of his tunic was the unmistakable gold and cream of the palace guard. Eyeing me, he started to pull his sword out of its scabbard. I knew I was running out of time before someone called for a city guard. A tall, lanky youth ran into my shoulder hard, and I snarled under my breath.

Get a grip, I warned myself.

Tugging the hood down even further around my face, I drifted into the alleyway and slipped the pendant back over my neck. *She doesn't recognize me.* It was difficult to wrap my mind around that, especially when I had vivid memories of when the mating bond had fallen into place. How it had felt to touch her mind.

As much as I wanted to sweep Serafina into my arms, I knew the risk was too great. If she remembered who I was, the only thing I could predict about her reaction was it was likely to be violent, and whether or not she was aware, she had at least four guards trailing her. The last thing I needed was a very public confrontation with the heir of the South.

Serafina was not in imminent danger from her grandfather, but she was still in a cage. If I were to whisk her away, questions would be raised, and there was a good chance it would send the Lord of the South into a war against the Fae.

There must be a way to get to her, to fix our bond, without start-ing a war. But how? Swallowing hard, I forced myself to evaluate everything. I knew very little. My first step must be to gather more information. Follow Serafina and learn her movements, see where she entered and exited the palace from, and maybe I could come up with a plan.

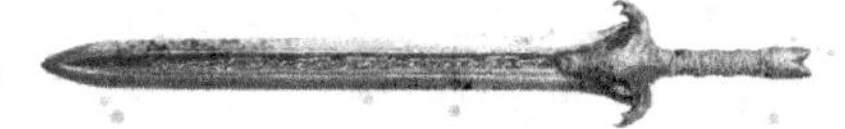

Disappointment filled me. Serafina had lingered in the black-smith's shop, forcing me to leave so as not to draw attention to myself. Frustrated and without a solid plan, I returned to Wayside Inn to eat and prevent myself from causing a ruckus at the blacksmith's.

The wood chairs in the dining area at Wayside Inn had not been built for large humans or Fae. The rungs of the chair dug into my back and hips. I knew I could fix it with my magic, but I was loathe to draw attention to myself. Even though humans could not do magic, there were some who were more sensitive than others and noticed when it was being used.

Pulling my hood up tighter around my face, I resigned myself to the uncomfortable chair. I took a small sip of the ale the server had brought and cringed at the bitter taste. *I can't believe humans enjoy this swill.* Holding the cup to my lips, I pretended to drink more while peering at the customers at other tables.

Taking a deep breath, I let my eyes flutter shut. Serafina failing to recognize me earlier was eating away at my confidence in my ability to get her back. *No path is without bumps*, I reminded myself. I had spent years trying to devise a plan to escape the blood contract I had made with Prince Tanyth. *A few days is nothing. Serafina is alive. We're in the same city. It must be enough for now.*

I heard a thump and my eyes snapped open. I had a dagger at the newcomer's throat before I recognized her. Pale, almost-translucent skin, purple eyes, white hair braided tightly at her temples to keep most of it swept out of her face and the rest loose, draping over her shoulders and back. To top it off she wore tight leather pants and a matching vest with iron buckles. Her scabbard was accompanied by a dagger, and small knives were strapped to her thighs and calves. It was my best friend, Callyn, the only Fae who had never turned their back on me.

Her gaze fierce, Callyn announced, "I have a plan to get to Serafina."

I opened my mouth and then clamped it shut again, looking away. I found it hard to believe Callyn would come up with a viable plan when I had failed in the same amount of time. *Maybe she learned something while I was off seeking aid at the Court of Dawn.*

"The king is trying to marry her off as soon as possible so that he can secure the line of succession with Serafina's child," Callyn explained.

I frowned, not sure how this knowledge would help us. "The king is not going to permit me to be a suitor. I am not a human lord ... or even a Fae lord, for that matter."

Callyn rolled her eyes. "Are you going to let me tell you my idea, or are you just going to complain about everything?"

"Sorry," I said, raising my hands in apology.

"As I was saying ..." Callyn gave me a pointed look, as though daring me to interrupt again. "I did some research to determine what provisions the human laws have if no appropriate suitors are available. If my source is correct, when no suitable husband is available, the king is required to host a competition allowing eligible males to vie for the right to marry the heir."

"Surely Fae cannot compete," I said, letting her words sink in. *A competition.* As a trainee at Embergate and lord commander of the Court of Dusk, I had had numerous opportunities to compete against others to demonstrate my skills. *At the Court of Dusk, it was often win-or-die circumstances*, I reminded myself. I assumed that a human competition for a marriage contract would not require the losers to die.

"I am still investigating, but from what I have determined so far, the laws of the South do not specify that the males in the competition are required to be human. It simply says 'adult males' and then goes on to list some criteria," Callyn replied.

"What are the criteria?" I asked, interest piqued.

"Nothing overly complicated. You must be able to use a sword, run, swim, and possibly ride a horse. There is also a provision for an extra test should there be a tie, but the details on that are unclear," Callyn said.

"That sounds doable," I replied, unable to keep excitement from creeping into my voice. *A chance to win Serafina back without stealing her away.*

"My thinking precisely," said Callyn with a smile.

What about the other suitors? I knew there had to be more. I glanced at Callyn, debating if I should ask. I decided that I didn't want to know. Callyn was as invested as I was in helping me get Serafina back. I was confident that she would ensure I had a legitimate shot. There was no reason to know the exact details of how she accomplished it.

Nine

SERAFINA

One of the guards did a brief inspection of the blacksmith shop, then nodded, giving me the all clear. They quickly agreed to wait outside, presumably not wanting to be stuck in the hot shop. As I wandered toward the back of the building, I could see the waves of heat rolling out of the forge. The steady rhythm of the smith hammering on the metal of his current project was a welcome sound. The temptation to order a custom silver-iron sword was creeping in, especially since my sword was still missing and I wasn't allowed to keep the borrowed swords.

I was the only customer in the shop, which suited me just fine.

"Miss, may I help you?" came a gravelly voice. I could barely make out the smith. He was mostly obscured by the red-orange glow emitting from the forge.

"Not today. I'm enjoying browsing the selection of weapons and watching you work," I replied.

"Shopping for your husband?" he asked, examining me from head to toe.

I guess he thinks I can't handle a sword, I mused. *Or that doing so is unladylike.*

"Something like that," I replied. I didn't have enough knowledge of whether women in the city used weapons to know if I would stir up trouble by correcting the smith and telling him I was shopping for myself. "Do not let me interfere with your work. I will just keep browsing. Thank you for your time." I inclined my head politely and turned my back on him to discourage our conversation from progressing any further.

On one wall was an assortment of axes, shortswords, and daggers. They were all plain, with leather-wrapped hilts and no adornments. I noticed a glass case with a massive lock on it behind a large worktable. Glancing toward the forge to confirm the smith was not watching me, I quietly approached the glass case.

The case was its own work of art: intricately carved mahogany with decorative flowers and vines. I ran my fingers over the wood and was surprised that it was warm. I yanked my hand back and placed it on the worktable, which felt cool to the touch. Hesitantly, I brushed one finger over the mahogany again. *Why is it warm?*

As I studied the wood intently, I noticed the other images hidden in the vines and flowers. Unicorns, dragons, and griffins. Eyes wide, I continued to trace the images with my finger. *Why are Fae animals, which humans don't believe are real, hidden on this case?* Unable to come up with a good answer, I removed my finger from the wood and examined the contents.

The first weapon that caught my attention was a longsword. It had dark-brown leather wrapping the grip and a plain pommel, but the crossguard had a row of emeralds across it. *Expensive.* My eyes drifted over to the next weapon—a greatsword that looked extremely heavy. The blade had a pearlescent sheen to it that almost seemed to move of its own accord.

I rolled my eyes. *It's just the light tricking me.*

On a small shelf was a very delicate dagger encrusted in gems. I shook my head; it seemed as though these were just showpieces. A quick glance out of the storefront window and I realized the sunlight was fading. If I didn't return for dinner, I would be missed. The last thing I needed was for my grandfather to forbid me from going into Gaskal.

Taking a deep breath, I squared my shoulders and walked toward the door. I set my hand on the cool black metal and tugged. But the door wouldn't budge. I pulled it again, and it still wouldn't move.

"What is going on?" I mumbled.

I heard a low cough behind me, and I whirled, fists raised. A Fae female with dark-brown skin stood in the shadows; it was so dark I could barely make out her face. Then she took a step forward, into the light.

I gasped, throwing myself at her. "Ghilanna!"

My best friend's comforting arms wrapped around me. I don't know how long we stood there hugging. Tears dripped freely down my face, but I didn't care.

I leaned back to peer into her face. "How are you here?"

Ghilanna chuckled. "Just because your grandfather would not allow me to travel with you does not mean he can claim owner-ship over me. I am a Fae warrior. I can come and go as I please."

"Promise me you won't let him know you're here. You might not be afraid of him, but he is a powerful human king with many resources. I don't want you to feel his wrath," I replied seriously.

Ghilanna shrugged. "I'll be careful. Speaking of which, don't you need to get back for dinner?"

"How did you know that?" I asked, surprised.

Ghilanna tweaked my nose with her fingers. "I've been here for a few days, hoping you would venture into the city. You've always been fascinated when Fiera did blacksmithing, so it wasn't difficult to guess you'd likely head here first."

I sighed. She was right. I was predictable, and I also needed to go. "Will I see you again?"

"Of course. I promise," Ghilanna replied. I hugged her again and then reluctantly let go. This time, when I tried to open the door, it worked. As I walked back up the street toward the palace, I realized I should have told her about the headaches. Ghilanna might at least have some suggestions.

Next time, I promised myself.

I was surprised when I walked into my suites to find Violet sitting on the couch working on embroidery.

"How was your walk?" Violet asked conversationally.

I opened my mouth to speak, then started coughing. Violet rushed to my side, cup of water in hand. I gulped it gratefully, and the coughing fit finally subsided, but it still felt like there was a dust ball in the back of my throat. "Thanks," I croaked.

"You're welcome," Violet said and returned to her seat on the couch. She picked up her embroidery, and the needle flashed in the lamplight as it moved across the fabric.

I crept closer, curious. Embroidery was not a Fae pastime, and I had had very little exposure to it. "Do you enjoy embroidery?" I asked.

Violet shrugged. "It can be soothing at times. My mother taught me. She felt it was important I mastered it, along with sewing and cooking."

Practical household skills, I thought, but kept the words to myself. "I can cook a few things, but I never had the opportunity to learn how to embroider."

"Do you wish to learn?" Violet replied.

I considered her question. "Maybe someday. Right now, I barely have time to practice the skills I already have. I can't imagine trying to fit in learning a new one. At least not if I want to learn it properly."

"I understand. I imagine you have far more important things to tackle," Violet said.

I felt bad. She was trying to be nice and offering to teach me a new skill, and I had told her I was too busy. "How about this? Starting next week, you can give me an embroidery lesson, and in exchange I'll teach you some hand-to-hand combat and self-defense techniques."

Violet giggled. "I don't think my father would like that."

I shrugged. "If you're going to be my lady-in-waiting, then I feel it is important that you can at least defend yourself. I'm not saying you have to kill anyone. Only buy yourself time until help can arrive. You'd be surprised at how just knowing a few maneuvers can have a significant impact."

"Very well, I accept," Violet replied. "I suppose he can't object if I tell him I'm only following your orders."

I nodded. She had a valid point. One I had a feeling we might be using frequently if my wishes conflicted with Lord McCormack's.

Lying in bed debating whether I could go back to sleep or should get up, I heard a light scraping sound at the door. Rolling onto my side, I stared at the door, half expecting it to open, when I noticed a piece of paper had been shoved under it. Curiosity piqued, I flung the covers off and rushed over to the door. After snagging the note from the floor, I unfolded it.

Go home half-blood filth.

My anger rose, and I crumpled the note in my hand before realizing the guards must have seen something. I yanked open the door, startling Thomas and the other guard on duty.

"Did you see who put this under my door?" I demanded.

Thomas looked at me in surprise. "No one was in the hallway but us, Your Highness."

I waved the note in his face. "Then how did this get under my door?"

Thomas took the note and read it, his face blanching. "I swear to you, there was no one here but us."

Which meant either he was lying or one of them put the note under my door. I had spent enough time around Thomas to feel as though I had a measure of him. The other guard I didn't know. I shook my head and retreated into my room, shutting the door firmly behind me.

The note was a harsh reminder that King Leonard was not the only person in the palace who was not comfortable with my mixed bloodline. I couldn't change who my parents were. *I just have to prove to everyone I am worthy, no matter what blood runs through my veins.*

There was a soft knock on the door as Mary and Violet arrived to help me prepare for the day. Mary carried a tray of food, and Violet had a dress over her arm. I ate and got dressed in silence, allowing me plenty of time to think.

The king was running out of patience with me, and the number of eligible husbands was dwindling. Rumors were flying around the palace that I had used magic on the lords to force them to decline the opportunity to marry me. My grandfather was not doing anything to discourage the rumors, even though he knew very well that I had no magic.

While I might have scared away suitors with my honesty, I was not the only reason the number was dwindling. Violet brought news that the second son of the Lord of the West had arrived yesterday, but the inn he was staying at caught fire in the early hours of the morning and he had burned to death in his room. A few times while I was walking in the palace, I had heard whispers that I might be trying to sabotage my suitors, I made a point of ignoring them. *It's not worth my time.* Besides, the night of the fire, guards had been posted at all exits and entrances to my rooms, so the king knew with one hundred percent certainty that I was not responsible. I was tempted to point out that accidents, such as the fire, were commonplace in a city like Gaskal with thousands of residents in a small area.

The most pressing matter for me was discovering what would happen if we reached the end of his list and I still did not have a marriage contract in hand. *There must be provisions. I can't be the only female heir who isn't already married in the history of the South.*

My thoughts were interrupted by a knock on the door. I stood, expecting my grandfather to come in. Instead, it was his steward, Lord John. He bowed and then sat in the open chair across from me. There were two teacups and a steaming pot of tea waiting for us to drink it.

"Lord John, where is the king?" I asked. I did not like skirting around the topic as many of the courtiers of the Gaskal court seemed to do.

Lord John's lip curled in distaste before he remembered himself. "The king is unwell this morning and has sent me to explain to you what will happen if the last suitor, whom you are meeting this afternoon, does not end up agreeing to a marriage contract."

I took a sip of my tea. No one had ever given me an explanation for the seizure the king had had three days ago. I had no idea if they were common for him or a new development. *Is that what ailed him this morning?* The steward did not seem as though he would appreciate questions from me. I almost wondered if the steward had placed the note under my door. *Though I'm not sure he would gain anything by trying to drive me away.* Letting the tea slide slowly down my throat, I waited for him to explain.

Lord John coughed, then spoke. "Southern law allows for a competition to take place in a situation like this where there are no eligible suitors. The winner of the competition will become your husband."

I sat up straighter in my seat, and Lord John must have noticed. He continued gravely, "You must understand, Princess. If the competition is invoked, then you will be required by law to accept the winner as your husband. No matter who he is. I am aware that you are skilled in weapons, but you are not allowed to compete or to aid any of the competitors."

"I understand," I said, unable to hide my smile. *A competition based on skill, not bloodlines.* For the first time in days, I was excited. *It would not be easy for anyone to protest the outcome of a competition that is written into Gaskal law.*

"Since the competition has a predetermined amount of time and activities, the date and preparations for your wedding will also begin," Lord John said.

Wedding plans. My excitement faded. Distracted by the meetings with the suitors over the past few days, I had conveniently forgotten that when a marriage contract was agreed upon, the wedding would be imminent. *Or it was easier to become absorbed in the distraction than to face reality.*

I knew once a wedding date was set my fate would be sealed. By scaring off the other dukes and lords, I had hoped maybe I could put off the inevitable and could convince my grandfather it was unnecessary for me to marry this quickly. Now the only consolation I had was that if by some terrible misfortune my grandfather died before I was wed, I would no longer need to marry as quickly. I was all too aware that one of my responsibilities as heir was to ensure the Helias bloodline would continue, but I preferred not to rush into a marriage or childbearing.

It felt like ever since the battle at Emerald Valley, I had been rushing somewhere. The betrothal to Prince Tanyth, my return to Jade Wilds, and now here in the South. *Why does everyone have a sense of urgency? Is there some deadline that everyone but me is aware of?*

I tugged on my lip as I considered my grandfather. His urgency was the easiest to understand, given his advancing age and illness. It was hard to fault him for wanting to die knowing that his kingdom would continue without him and not be plunged into war.

Lord John cleared his throat. "There will be a three-day recruitment period for males to come forward and announce their intent to participate and for me to validate their claim to have the minimum required skills. There will be a banquet to welcome the competitors, and then the first task will start the following morning. The tasks will be an obstacle course, a foot race, and a joust."

I had been half expecting him to outline the details of each task, but he did not. The foot race and joust were straightforward, even if jousting was seldom used in human tournaments these days. However, the obstacle course had me baffled. *What kind of obstacles?*

Memories surged through me of training exercises with Fiera and Ghilanna in the forest in pouring rain, followed by one of a leon charging toward me with a chain on its leg.

My head began to throb.

"Princess, are you well?" Lord John asked in concern.

I shook my head and immediately regretted it. "Not really." I pressed my hands against my forehead, willing the pain to go away. The past few days had been blissfully headache-free, making me wonder what had triggered it at that moment. It was clear that stress was not the cause; otherwise, I would be subjected to relentless migraines.

Lord John patted me awkwardly on the shoulder. "I don't have any more information that I am required to give you. Why don't you go to your chambers and rest for a while? I know it is a lot of information to process."

I slowly exhaled and then stood up, wobbling slightly before fully getting my balance. I departed and went back to my chambers to lie down.

Ten

TRISTAN

Guards raced around the city, posting flyers announcing the competition and encouraging gentlemen to sign up. I assumed the other cities in the South were getting the same treatment, ensuring an equal opportunity for males in the entire kingdom to participate. I wasn't sure if King Leonard would send notice beyond his borders. Without much personal knowledge of human kingdoms or culture, I had no idea if an heir marrying someone outside the kingdom would be welcome or frowned upon.

Callyn and I were in our shared room at Wayside Inn, finishing the final preparations for my formal presentation to the king as a competitor. I was sharpening my sword and decided to tell her what had been nagging me. "What if another Fae shows up?"

Callyn chuckled. "I am confident you're the only Fae male who has a strong enough interest in Serafina to not care about the problems that will arise if you do win and marry her. Unless you've forgotten that if you do marry her, after King Leonard dies, you would become king of a human kingdom?"

Doubt filled me. "I would not put it past Tanyth to show up and also enter the contest," I muttered.

Callyn curled her lip. "He won't."

"How can you be so sure?" I demanded. Fae were not well regarded by humans, and though the human competition was likely to be easier than the training Fae went through before becoming warriors, it was not just a matter of winning a human competition. What happened afterward was just as important.

"That's not his style. He would rather sweep in when tensions are high because you're not a human and expect the humans to follow your orders," Callyn said.

I wasn't sure I believed her. Though our relationships with Tanyth had been quite different, Callyn would often share information with me that Tanyth had given her in confidence. I never knew what she had done to acquire that information; there were some secrets that needed to stay secret.

"Don't forget the king still has to approve you as a participant. No one can just waltz in on the first task day and be allowed to join. Even though the rules do not specify that it must be a human male, I am concerned if you show up as you are, it will not go well," Callyn said.

I set down my whetstone and ran a hand over my face. "I know. It doesn't help that I have a history with him. King Leonard is likely not the only one who was present the day I brought him King Lionel's head."

"I have a solution," Callyn said.

I stared at her, waiting for her to divulge it. *I am already using a glamour pendant.* I wasn't sure what other options existed for me.

"I can turn you into a human," Callyn said. My jaw dropped. I didn't know that was even possible. Before I could muster a response, Callyn continued. "Yes. I ran into Marek, and it was among the things we discussed."

I licked my dry lips. "Marek?" My eyes widened when I realized she meant Marek the griffin rider. "He's here in Gaskal?"

Callyn nodded. "Yes. I can tell you about that later. Right now, we need to stay focused." I sighed and motioned for her to continue. "Marek said he can help me cast a spell that would allow whoever is wearing the pendant to become human. In some ways, it is a binding spell, much like what is going on with your mating bond. Your ability to do magic will be nonexistent while you wear it, including being able to shapeshift. But it will be nearly impossible for even a Fae to detect that you are not a human."

Marek and I had a dark history. I was surprised he would have agreed to do anything that would help me. "What kind of bargain did you make with Marek for his help?"

Callyn shook her head. "None. He thinks the pendant is for me, not for you. I did not correct his assumption."

Even though Callyn's reasoning was logical, I did not like this plan. Lying to Marek was one thing, but to turn me into a human, to *lie* about who I am to compete for Serafina's hand, was different. But I couldn't see a way to avoid it. Gambling that King Leonard would not recognize me was a high-risk option. If it failed, I would be executed for murdering a king.

"If I agree to this, when would we do it?" I asked.

"If you give me the obsidian pendant, I'll meet with Marek tonight to do the spell. He said it requires a full moon, so we got lucky that there is one tonight," Callyn replied.

They can cast a spell on the pendant, and I can still back out. It was only that knowledge that had me accepting her offer.

I removed the pendant from around my neck and handed it to her. "Please make the arrangements with Marek."

Callyn stuffed it in her pocket. "I'll head there now."

I nodded and watched her depart, thoughts churning. Even though I desperately wanted to win and officially have Serafina's hand in marriage, the idea of hiding my true self felt a lot like what life was like in Prince Tanyth's court. *I promise to only be honest with Serafina.*

Eleven

SERAFINA

The shift of events, from me needing to convince a suitor that I would be a good wife to the decision hinging solely on the outcome of a competition, meant I had a day of reprieve before I would be required to attend the formal introductions to each man wanting to compete for my hand in marriage. King Leonard needed time for the message to be delivered. If he rushed the timeline too much, he ran the risk of no one entering.

I was desperate to get out of the palace and find Ghilanna—someone I could confide in who wouldn't report to my grandfather. I dug through my wardrobe for another "boring" outfit. The russet dress appeared to have been a onetime find, and my appointment with the seamstress had not been scheduled yet. I chose a pair of black pants and a dark-brown, almost black tunic, part of the clothing I had insisted on being allowed to have that didn't require a seamstress.

As I pulled on my boots, I heard a soft knock at the door. I sighed and prayed this wasn't someone intent on preventing me from having a "day off."

"Come in," I called.

Violet hesitantly entered the room. "Thomas said you were awake. I thought I should see if you needed anything."

"I'm good," I replied.

Violet came over to where I was sitting on the couch. "Can we talk?"

"Sure," I replied, wondering what she wanted to talk about *right now*. I stuffed my impatience down. I had the whole day ahead of me. A few minutes were not going to ruin things.

"There have been rumors around the palace about you, including that Fae drink the blood of humans to live as long as they do. I even heard one person say they thought you wandered the corridors at night in search of victims," Violet said, her face serious.

I covered my mouth with my hands to hide my smile. *Fae drink human blood?* When I was confident I wasn't going to burst out laughing, I responded, "Fae do have a much longer lifespan than humans, but I can assure you they don't drink human blood to live longer. As you would expect from a long-lived species, they also mature slower than humans do. I promise I am not wandering the corridors at night to drink blood or for any dark intention," I explained patiently.

Violet sighed in relief. "Glad to hear it, Your Highness. I will be sure to correct those who think otherwise."

"Thank you. Now, is there anything else you wanted to discuss?" I asked.

"That was it," Violet replied.

"Good, then I will see you later." I stood up and walked to the door.

Not wanting to be waylaid by anyone else, I stuck to the servants' passageways and headed into the city with two guards shadowing me: Thomas and George, a burly guard with gray eyes and wavy shoulder-length salt-and-pepper hair.

Within a few blocks of exiting the palace, I was able to blend in with the city folk. Catching snippets of conversation, I found that the upcoming competition for my hand in marriage was a common topic. Running a hand over my hair, ensuring the scarf was still secure, I meandered toward the blacksmith, hoping the fact that she found me there previously meant Ghilanna would be nearby. *I don't have time to hunt the entire city for one Fae.*

As I made my way, I noticed a cluster of people around a wall. Curious, I pushed my way through until I could see what they were looking at. Someone had scrawled "Kill the half-Fae slut!" across most of the wall in bright-red paint. I covered my mouth with both hands, cutting off a shriek of anger before it could get out. If humans living in the city were painting those words on the wall, then it was highly likely it wasn't safe for me to reveal myself here. Thomas patted me on the shoulder reassuringly. I wasn't alone, but all I had was a dagger. My two attempts at searching my chambers for my sword had only confirmed it was not in my rooms and someone must have taken it. Not that my grandfather would allow me to wear a sword into the city. Without it, I felt exposed. A mob could be vicious, and a dagger with only two guards might not be enough. Cautiously backing out of the group, I continued on my way to the blacksmith.

I was a block away when my guards closed the gap between us. Both were clenching their sword hilts so hard the whites of their knuckles were showing. A moment later, I caught sight of the reason for their reaction. Ghilanna was staring at us from the shadows of an alley. I could see the faint glow of her magic and presumed the guards could too.

I took a step toward her, and a cold hand wrapped around my bicep. "Let go," I ordered, prying the fingers away.

"Our orders are to protect you. Fae are dangerous," the guard protested.

I ground my teeth in frustration. "Yes, Fae are dangerous. So am I. Now let me go. Ghilanna is my friend. I trust her with my life."

The guard hesitated a moment longer and then reluctantly withdrew to his previous position a few feet away. I was surprised

Thomas hadn't stepped in. *Maybe he's worried about how it would look for two guards to be at odds in public.* I briskly entered the alley and embraced Ghilanna, inhaling her familiar scent of jasmine and rose. "I have so much to tell you."

Ghilanna patted my back. "I know. Come, there's a place we can talk nearby without being as visible."

I nodded, intrigued by Ghilanna's choice of location—though after the red paint on my way here, maybe the desire to be less visible had to do more with my safety. *What would people say if they witnessed me collaborating with a Fae in plain sight?* I slid my hand into hers and let her guide me on a winding path through the city. When we halted, a quick glance behind me showed we had lost my guards. *I'm sure it was intentional.*

"We don't have much time," Ghilanna said, yanking a door open and pushing me through before closing it behind us. Her hands glowed as white magic flowed out of them and engulfed the door before disappearing altogether. "That will keep them out if they track us here."

We went deeper inside the building, and I realized it was a small apartment. A bed was tucked against the wall with a simple kitchen on one side and a well-used dining table with four chairs. "Are you going to tell me what's going on? The conversation I was hoping to have shouldn't require this level of secrecy."

Ghilanna blew out her breath. "How much do you know about your mother?"

"Solana!" I gasped, shocked by the topic. "What does she have to do with anything?"

"Just tell me what you know, Serafina," Ghilanna said, her tone more of an order than a request.

I sighed. "We lived here in the city. Just my father, mother, and myself. She would help the healer who lived on the same street as us, and my father did carpentry and mason work. We never went up to the palace unless the summons was urgent. Our neighbors didn't seem to care that Mother was different.

Though I don't recall if they knew she was Fae or not. It wasn't something we discussed."

Ghilanna pressed her lips together into a thin line while I spoke. When I finished my monologue, she gave me a sad smile. "They really didn't tell you anything, did they?"

"Tell me what?" I asked, frowning. *We didn't have secrets in our house.*

"That contrary to your grandfather's hate for Fae and the few other people who are of the same mind, overall his feelings are not shared throughout Gaskal—at least not among its long-term residents. The nobles seem inclined to share his views that Fae are an abomination. My point is that even though you were not aware of it, Solana was well accepted as a Fae, and many hoped she and Gareth would be able to alter the king's view on the matter, enabling the city to be more readily accessible by Fae," Ghilanna explained.

My jaw dropped at the news. *My mother was accepted* here *as a Fae? Then why is there red paint on the walls telling me to leave?*

Ghilanna continued when it was clear I couldn't formulate my thoughts well enough to speak. "Your mother, along with Commander Meriel and some other Fae from the Court of Dawn, believed if humans were given the opportunity to live and work side by side with Fae, the animosity that has existed between our two cultures and species might decrease. Especially when both sides realized how similar we are and the benefits of a friendly relationship."

"We have trade agreements ..." I said.

Ghilanna shook her head. "The trade agreements have been around for hundreds of years. Born of necessity, not because humans or Fae are willing to admit they have anything beyond raw materials to share with one another. What I'm talking about is developing genuine relationships and trust. Not just scratching the surface as has been done in the past."

"I still don't understand why this is important now," I said softly.

Ghilanna gave my hand a squeeze. "Because your mother was laying the groundwork for the day you would take the throne of the South."

I shot upward so fast my chair went flying across the room. "Impossible!"

Ghilanna cast a wary glance toward the door and held her finger to her lips. Exhaling, I carried the chair back over to the table and sat in it.

"The Fae have many prophecies," Ghilanna said. "Your mother, though she tried to hide it, was a seer as well as a healer. No matter what she told you when you were growing up, she knew that there was a strong possibility that you, not a male of the Helias line, would one day sit upon the Gaskal throne. That you would become the Lady of the South. She also knew that if everyone in Gaskal felt the same way as your grandfather did about Fae, you would not survive more than a year as ruler."

A strangled sob escaped my lips. *My mother knew I might be queen.* I wished with all my heart she was still alive and able to explain why she had done what she had done.

"I'm sorry, Serafina. I can't imagine how difficult it is to learn this from me and not from your mother." Ghilanna's voice was soft.

I swiped at the tears, though they kept trickling down my face anyhow. "What about my grandfather's insistence that I marry? Is there any way I can get around that?"

"No," Ghilanna said firmly. "That is one of the laws Solana was worried about but could not find a way to control. The only thing I can tell you is to have faith that the winner of the competition will be an individual who is truly worthy of your hand in marriage. Who will value you for your entire self and not just the crown you will one day wear."

I heard a sharp pounding on the door. "Open up!"

I recognized Thomas's voice. The door rattled on its hinges.

"We're out of time. I'll find you soon. There is so much more to share," Ghilanna informed me. With a wave of her hand, she released the magic on the door. By the time the guards reached me, she had vanished.

"Your Highness! Are you okay?" Thomas inspected me from head to toe while the other guard rushed around the room hunting for Ghilanna.

"I'm fine, and you won't find her," I told him.

George stepped forward, his words biting. "The king will be furious that you were out of our sight."

I sighed. "Why do you even need to tell him? This can just be between us. I swear to you, Ghilanna and I only had a private conversation. Nothing else transpired here."

George exchanged a look with Thomas. If it were only Thomas, I was confident he would not alert my grandfather. But I knew nothing about George. I wished I could manipulate his thoughts to ensure he would do as I asked instead of having to rely on his loyalty to me versus my grandfather.

Ghilanna said there are Fae sympathizers in the city. Do I even know how my guards were chosen or where they came from? Maybe they know about my mother too. But now is not the time to find out. My grandfather did not like Solana. If he got wind that I was asking questions about her, it could cause problems. I would have to tread lightly.

"Fine. We will do as you request, but do not disappear like that again, or we will be obligated to report both occurrences to the king," George informed me.

Nodding in acknowledgment, I departed the apartment with the guards close on my heels. Thoughts churning at everything Ghilanna had told me, I narrowly missed being run over by a wagon. Only Thomas's quick reflexes yanked me out of the way in time.

"Your Highness, you need to pay attention to where you're going. The busy streets of the city are no place to daydream," Thomas said harshly.

"Sorry. Why don't you lead the way to the palace?" I knew I could probably find my way, but Thomas was right, I was very distracted. It would be safer if I had a back to follow.

Twelve

TRISTAN

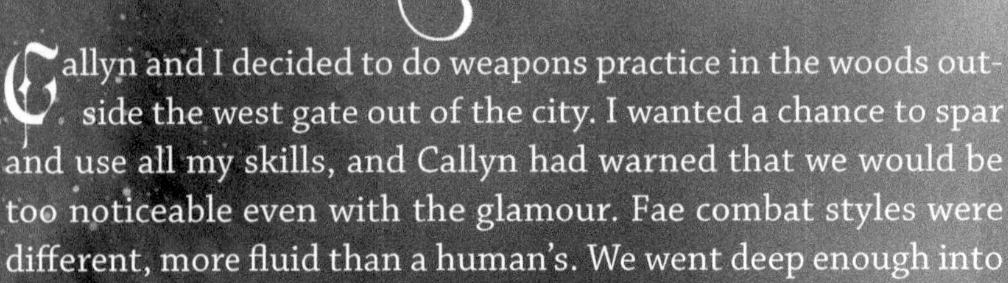

Callyn and I decided to do weapons practice in the woods out-side the west gate out of the city. I wanted a chance to spar and use all my skills, and Callyn had warned that we would be too noticeable even with the glamour. Fae combat styles were different, more fluid than a human's. We went deep enough into the woods to minimize the chance of being noticed.

There was a small clearing and a pile of rocks that looked as though at one point it had been an animal den. *Perhaps a fox,* I thought, based on the size.

I shrugged my pack off my shoulders and unclasped my cloak, folding it neatly on top of the pack. I then called in my broadsword.

Callyn eyed the broadsword. Even with my Fae height, it was quite large. "You're planning on using that in the competition?"

"That would be my preference," I replied. Which particular weapon I used had not been my chief concern.

Callyn shook her head. "You can't use your broadsword. Remember, you're going to look human *and* likely only have human strength. People are going to question how you're man-aging a sword that large. If the spell does sap your Fae strength, you will look ridiculous too. The last thing you need is to draw attention to yourself. Even an axe would be less noticeable."

"For the moment, we're sparring. I don't look like a human, nor do I have a reason to act like one yet. We can worry about my final weapon selection when that critical decision needs to be made," I responded, adjusting my grip on my broadsword and giving it a few experimental swings. Since our arrival in Gaskal, I had limited my training sessions to working on maneuvers without a weapon or hand-to-hand combat—a stark contrast to my daily use of a sword for over four decades. Callyn's words unnerved me. I hadn't considered that disguising myself would also change my strength and stamina as well.

Callyn nodded and her longsword appeared in her hand. Like mine, it was unadorned—a service, not ceremonial, weapon.

We crossed swords, the metal hissing slightly as the blades lightly touched. "One, two, three!"

Exhaling, I stepped to the right and struck low. She blocked. We did a series of strikes and parries with very minimal movement, giving our bodies a chance to warm up.

I watched Callyn closely, and when she rocked back slightly, I took a step forward and began a high strike, aiming for her collarbone. Hoping to catch her off guard, halfway through the strike, I changed angles—a challenge when holding the broadsword in a two-hand grip—and went low. Clearly prepared for such a move, Callyn shifted her stance and blocked easily.

I'll have to try harder. I pivoted to my left, trying to get behind her, but she anticipated the move and turned precisely in time to meet my middle strike with a parry. Wrapping her left hand around the hilt to put all her weight behind the sword, she forced me three steps backward before the pressure let up and she skipped to the side.

My lips twitched, and I switched to a single-handed grip on the broadsword. Callyn's eyes widened at the change. *It's not like I've never used this sword one-handed.* My personal preference was to practice with all types of weapons and methods of handling them, so that as a fight changed, I could readily adapt. Should an opponent injure my right hand, I wanted to be fully capable of fighting left-handed with any weapon, even those that were traditionally considered two-handed.

We gazed at each other, catching our breath. Sweat beaded on my forehead, and droplets trickled from Callyn's hairline down to her chin. Instead of waiting to officially restart our match, Callyn lunged forward, trying to stab me in the stomach, much like the move I had made that had resulted in my first kill at Embergate so many years ago. Gritting my teeth and pushing away the memory, I hastily blocked and retreated a few steps. I was almost into the trees.

I need to get the advantage back. Muscles bunched in my legs, and I leaped forward with a snarl, sweeping the broadsword in an arc that turned into a blur. High strike, reverse into a backhanded low strike, and spin. I maneuvered myself so I was almost behind her. Callyn scrambled to keep up with me. Neither one of us was wearing armor, which meant we had to be careful not to fatally injure one another.

We moved around the clearing, a deadly dance of strikes and parries. In the distance, a glimmer of movement caught my eye. I froze, sword forgotten, as a memory crashed into me.

The clash of swords as King Lionel Helias charged. Sparks flying. Blood dripping down my face. King Lionel on his back. "Negotiate with me." His head rolling away from his body.

"Tristan!" snapped Callyn. I blinked, and the jagged pieces of memory faded, leaving me staring into Callyn's bright-purple eyes. Her white hair was disheveled, with strands escaping her usually immaculate braid and framing her pale face. "Are you okay?"

I closed my eyes and took a deep breath, slowly letting it out. When I opened them, I gave her what I hoped was a reassuring smile. "A memory. I'm sorry to have interrupted our practice."

"Usually you don't get distracted like that. I was worried that the wound in your back was doing something horrible to you," Callyn said, brushing her hand lightly across my cheek.

"No, it wasn't the wound. This is not my first time here in the South. That's all it was. I promise I am fine. Now, did you want to practice more or return to the inn?" I asked, glancing up at the sky to determine how long we'd been out here. My best guess was a few hours, but I had no idea how long the memory had held me.

"We should go back. I'd rather not draw attention by returning after dark," Callyn said.

"We could scale the wall. Or use a star portal. There is no rule that says we must enter and depart through one of the city gates," I reminded her.

Callyn's jaw tightened. "Aside from the fact that you want to maintain a low profile. Rumors will spread if they note that we depart through the gate, don't return, and are somehow walking the streets the next day. Magic is rare here. It would do you good to remember that."

I grimaced. Old habits were difficult to shake. Living with the Fae my whole life, magic had been commonplace.

Callyn picked up my bag and cloak and tossed them at me. I caught them just in time to prevent the bag from hitting me in the face.

As we walked back, I was able to shake off the last of the memory of killing Serafina's great-grandfather under Prince Tanyth's orders and focus on what I would be facing over the next couple of days. "Our plan is that I will be one of the last to present myself. The last, if we get lucky. If I wear the pendant, no one will know I am Fae."

"As long as you remember your human name," Callyn chimed in.

I rolled my eyes. "I am capable of playing the role of a human and sticking to a new name."

"Good. I imagine there are strict rules for the competition, but whether or not provisions are in place to prevent cheating, I have no idea. Unlike Fae, humans do not have magic. Unless the king is in possession of a magic object that will allow him to ensure rules are not broken, we can only hope that the individuals assigned to supervising the competition will be fair."

"It is also possible the other competitors could try to use magic objects to enhance their chances of winning," I pointed out.

Callyn gave me a sideways look. "It's possible. But just like cheating, it depends on how the competition is managed. My assumption is it won't be as simple as being the best."

As we passed through the city gates, Callyn announced, "I have an appointment I need to get to."

I raised my eyebrows in surprise. "An appointment?"

"Yes. Instead of moping around, I've been doing everything I can to try to figure out how to get you some one-on-one time with Serafina," Callyn retorted.

I rolled my eyes. "I have not been moping."

"If you say so ..." Callyn replied.

"Fine, you go off and do your thing. I'm going to see if I get lucky and Serafina goes back to the blacksmith."

After practicing in the forest, I found I was far more focused than before. Eager to try the pendant and attempt to find Serafina, I gathered the items I'd need from my room at Wayside Inn.

Standing in front of a mirror, I studied the obsidian pendant. There were Fae letters around the edge that had not been there before. I ran my finger over them and they shimmered briefly with gold magic. Taking a deep breath, I pulled the black cord over my head, settling the pendant on my skin as Callyn had instructed. An aura of my gray magic appeared around me and then was sucked into the pendant as I watched.

It felt as though my magic was draining away. Clenching my fists, I prevented myself from removing it. *I must do this if I want a shot at the competition.* The Fae letters flashed and then disappeared.

Callyn had not elaborated on what kind of changes the magic would make to me, only that I would become human. My skin, normally light-to-medium gray, altered until it was a shade of tan, as though I was a human who spent many hours out in the sun. Black stubble rapidly thickened into a beard. My distinct pointy ears became small and rounded. Tall even for the Fae, I was not surprised when I shrank. My long slate-gray hair darkened until it was coal-black like my beard, and the length shortened till it brushed the top of my shoulders. My blue eyes stayed the same, as did my clothing, now baggy on my smaller frame.

Blinking, I stared at the human who gazed back at me. *This is creepy.* While I had utilized disguises in a few tasks for Tanyth, I had never needed to physically alter my appearance in such an extreme way. It was going to take some time—time that I didn't have much of—to get used to seeing my new face in the mirror. *It's good I am doing this now and not tomorrow morning.*

Glancing at the table, I caught sight of the sack of clothes Callyn had purchased for me—*human* clothes. She had guessed at sizing. I examined the pants and realized she had guessed quite accurately how much my height would change. They were just a hair too long.

Yanking off my too-big clothing, I replaced it with a pair of thick black wool pants, a burgundy long-sleeve tunic, and a stiff leather belt. There were loops for a longsword and a dagger but no leather sheath. I was grateful my boots still fit. They were plain brown and had no identifying markers that would make someone believe they were Fae versus human crafted.

Satisfied with the new me, I tested out my new name. *Rhys Mongan.* Callyn had not told me how she came up with the name, only that it was the one I had to use.

"I am Rhys Mongan," I said to my reflection. Not wanting to waste any more time, I departed the inn and took a meandering path through the streets of the city to the blacksmith. I picked up tidbits of conversations among the humans. A cluster of women were discussing if each man who had shown up to compete so far was handsome enough for a princess.

Farther down the road, a group of men were debating the merits of brawn versus brains and if the scrawny kid who had been approved yesterday was capable of succeeding against the entry who had a battle record.

What rumors will they spread about me after I present myself tomorrow? To me, it was a waste of time to judge my opponents on one meeting—or no meeting. I realized most of the humans gossiping had not likely seen the entrants in person. They were relying on the words of someone else who had been a witness.

I reached the blacksmith and strolled inside. As soon as I set foot in the door, I could feel a hum coming from the left side of the room. My feet carried me over to a large case with several weapons. My eyes widened as I took in the intricate carvings on the edge of the wood. *What is a Fae cabinet doing here?* I peered into the case and gasped as I recognized the sword with emeralds on the guard. When I was at Uaine Palace, I had seen a painting of a male I had thought was King Pharaan holding the sword.

I puzzled over the matter, unable to figure out why a sword that had been property of the King of Fae would have ended up in a human blacksmith shop.

A cough had me whirling, hand on my sword hilt. "Can I help you?"

I was certain the man was the blacksmith. He wore a well-used leather apron with scorch marks peppering it. Sweat dampened his brow, and his curious hazel eyes gazed at me. The blacksmith's dark-brown hair was pulled back into a knot at the base of his skull. I was mildly surprised a blacksmith would have long hair given the risk of it catching fire.

"I saw your shop and wanted to see what you had available that was ready-made," I said smoothly.

The blacksmith glanced at the case, then back at me. "Are you sure that's all you are doing?"

The words were not accusing, just a simple question. Deciding I could try the truth and see what happened, I responded, "The sword with the emeralds caught my eye."

The blacksmith gave me a half-smile. "It does that. Unfortunately, it's not for sale."

"May I ask why it's here if it's not for sale?" I asked, brimming with curiosity.

The blacksmith shrugged. "A friend asked me to keep it safe." He hesitated, and I wondered if there was more that had been said, but he did not divulge anything else. I let the subject drop, not wanting to pry. We gazed at each other a few moments more before the blacksmith wandered back to his forge. I examined the weapons on the wall for a few minutes. When it was clear that neither Serafina nor any other customers were going to appear, I departed.

I made it fifty feet down the road before I was certain I was being watched. Casting a subtle glance to the side, I could not identify who it was, though I would've sworn I saw eyes staring back at me from the alley. I headed toward a row of shops that had glass storefronts, intending to use the windows to study the Fae following me by their reflection. There was no one behind me, but the feeling of being watched had not disappeared.

Thirteen

SERAFINA

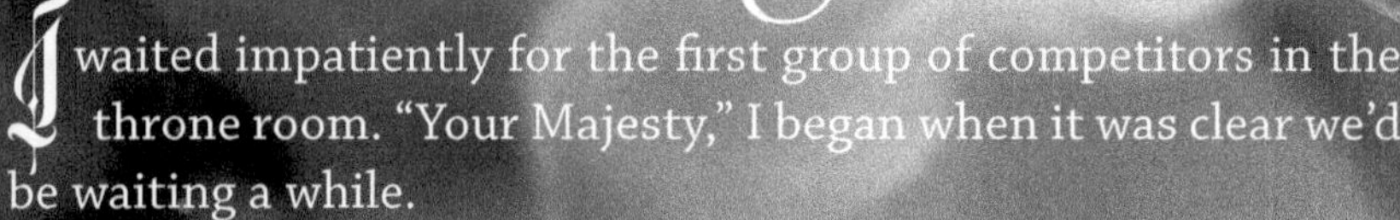

I waited impatiently for the first group of competitors in the throne room. "Your Majesty," I began when it was clear we'd be waiting a while.

King Leonard glared at me. "Yes?"

I swallowed, not wanting to lose my nerve. "I am concerned that there are not enough safety precautions in place. Someone was able to put a vicious note under my door, and my sword has gone missing."

King Leonard's eyes narrowed and his cheeks flushed. "The note was a bad joke by one of the guards, and you are not allowed to carry a sword. I see no reason for you to have one in your rooms."

I pressed my lips together to prevent the angry words from escaping my lips. Inhaling deeply, I took a moment to collect myself. "A sword would allow me to protect myself, and currently I have to borrow one for my practice sessions."

"The only thing you need to practice is how to be a princess. Leave the sword work to men. We shall not discuss this further," King Leonard said and turned his face away to stare at the doors at the end of the throne room.

I tried, I consoled myself. Based on grandfather's comment, I thought he might have ordered my sword removed; clearly he was not concerned it was missing. Nor did he view the note as a real threat. *Hopefully he's right.*

This afternoon marked the first of two set aside for potential competitors to introduce themselves and formally request to participate. Since they were competing for my hand in marriage, I was required to attend every session so they could inspect me and determine if I was worthy of their time.

To hide my boredom, I studied the details of the throne room. Gold fabric was elegantly draped between the white marble columns that marched from one end of the hall to the other. I was standing as directed next to my grandfather's throne. King Leonard perched in an ornate high-backed chair covered in gold overlay that looked rather uncomfortable.

Thankfully, the seamstress had met with me early that morning and, to my surprise, was able to modify one of the gowns my grandfather had already ordered. I was wearing a dark-blue gown with embroidered gold flowers and a thin gold crown. My hair had been curled and draped over my left shoulder. The rest of my wardrobe would be created or modified over the next couple of days, with at least two dresses completed per day. Though my argument to abandon the corset had been denied, I had asserted my opinions on the fabrics and fit: petticoat underneath with a full skirt and a high neckline. Although the corset hinted at my full breasts, my skin was not visible.

Whispers of a memory, banquets where I had been ordered to wear a gown that was almost sheer gold fabric, teased my thoughts. Yet whenever I tried to focus on them, my head would throb. Here in the South, as a princess, the rules were clear: Only after my wedding would a male—my husband—be awarded the privilege of seeing me naked, or even partially naked.

It was one of the things that I found a stark contrast to Fae culture, that humans did not openly talk of sex. Which suited me just fine. I was content to wait for my wedding night to discover the secrets of the male body.

Time passed achingly slowly. After two hours of no guests showing up, I was tempted to ask to be dismissed, but I knew the request would be poorly received. Instead I sat attentively with my hands folded in my lap. The only reprieve I had gotten was when servants brought me a chair after it was clear candidates were not flooding our gates. *Maybe no one will come.*

There was a commotion just beyond the doors, a flurry of movement as the guards snapped to attention, and then Lord John tapped his cane. "May I present Frederick Hunter of Hunter's Hollow, Your Majesty."

I twisted my fingers on the edge of my dress as nerves hit me. Frederick Hunter strode toward us, oozing confidence. He was short with broad shoulders, and his muscular arms were clearly defined underneath his too-tight burgundy tunic. A mop of curly black hair and a mustache that reminded me of a horseshoe added mystery. When he reached the end of the aisle, he bowed to my grandfather and then to me before focusing solely on my grandfather.

"Your Majesty, I am here to request permission to enter your competition," Frederick announced.

Outwardly, there did not seem to be any issues with Frederick, not that a person's appearance could tell you everything. I wasn't entirely sure how my grandfather intended to conduct this preliminary screening, especially when the first task—the obstacle course—was designed essentially to do just that: weed out candidates who were not worthy.

"Frederick, your request is granted. I look forward to getting to know you at the banquet in two days," Grandfather said. *Apparently it's just a visual inspection.*

Frederick bowed again. When my grandfather waved to dismiss him, he departed.

Once Frederick Hunter broke the ice, candidates started to arrive at a steadier pace. Raising my arms above my head, I stretched to relieve a tight spot in my lower back. From the edge of the room where a few guests were observing the introductions, Violet caught my eye. I smiled. *Maybe we can go for a sunset ride when this ends.* Anything would be better than standing or sitting in the chair that had been provided for me.

To my relief, when the last suitor departed, Lord John announced the conclusion of today's approval window and had the guards ensure the last suitor made his way out of the room.

A quick glance at my grandfather showed that he was deep in conversation with the master of the guard. I made a beeline for Violet.

"Would you like to go for a quick ride?" I asked hopefully.

Violet's smile fell slightly. "I would love to, but my father has asked that I refrain from riding due to the influx of men in the city for the competition. He is concerned for my safety."

"I have guards. We'll be safe," I reassured her.

Violet shook her head. "I will not publicly go against his wishes."

I ground my teeth in frustration, searching for an alternative option that would be "safe." "Dinner?"

Violet nodded. "Yes, a meal in the palace would be acceptable."

I noted how specific Violet was, as though she expected me to suggest we eat in the city. "I will make arrangements and then let you know where it will be."

"I look forward to it," Violet replied, then curtsied and walked over to where her father was waiting.

My grandfather was still talking to the master of the guard. Not sure who to talk to, I noticed Thomas standing near the throne. I headed over to him, hoping that he would have an idea of how to arrange a private dinner with Violet.

"Thomas, Violet and I intend to have dinner together, and I am not sure who to discuss this with. So far my meals have been arranged for me," I said. I felt silly asking how to make this request, but the truth was my grandfather had not given me any direction for matters such as this.

Instead of making fun of me, Thomas gave me an understanding smile. "A good question. A dinner request would start with talking to the head cook, Francis Cookie, sending her either a written message or someone to discuss with her directly. It is up to you if you want to specify the meal or let Cookie choose. How much advance notice you give would determine if special requests can be accommodated. Then, there is the matter of the location. Servants can prepare the room of your choice."

"Would it be strange for me to talk to Cookie in person?" I asked, wondering how I was going to decide what room I wanted to prepare if I had not had a tour allowing me to become familiar with my options.

"A little unusual. However, you have not been in residence long. I am sure she would appreciate the chance to talk to you in person," Thomas replied.

"Can we go talk to her now?" I asked.

Thomas glanced around the room, but no one seemed to be paying attention to us. "Yes, we can go now."

The timing of my request was perfect as far as Cookie was concerned. She had been debating what to do with the remnants of a beef tenderloin. Not aware that the palace had access to beef as a source of meat, I was excited to try it. With the number of forests in the South, there was not much dedicated grazing land for cattle; what land there was had been set aside for dairy cows to produce milk and other milk byproducts such as cheese and butter.

Deciding to stick with simplicity, I chose to eat in the small dining room off the kitchen. Our meal was after the king's, which meant Cookie had sent most of her staff away. The smell of fresh bread drifted to our table as we waited for Cookie to bring us the first part of our meal.

"If you don't mind me being blunt, I was not expecting us to eat down here," Violet said.

Not sure how to take her comment, I spoke knowing my tone would bely my defensiveness. "I figured you'd prefer not to be disturbed."

Violet frowned. "I wasn't saying this is a bad location. My mother told me that I should expect a princess to want to be flashy all the time. Showing off jewels, gold, well-appointed rooms. This"—she swept her hand around—"is none of those things."

My lips twitched in amusement. "I'm sure you've figured out by now I am not that type of princess."

Violet gave me a slight smile. "You're right. Which I am fine with. I'm only saying it has been an adjustment, matching my expectations with the reality."

"Have you ever had beef before?" I asked, unable to wait longer.

"Yes. Haven't you?" Violet asked curiously.

I shook my head. "No. The Fae are not fond of it. They prefer the gaminess of freshly hunted meat from wild animals. Though as a whole, Fae eat far less meat than humans do."

"You're in for a treat," Violet said.

I was skeptical that beef would be much better than venison or wild boar. But I would find out shortly. Cookie walked in with a basket of fresh bread and two small bowls of broth. "This will hold you over while the tenderloins finish."

Following Violet's lead, I took a roll and broke it in half, then dunked it in my broth. When the bread was dripping, I took a bite. My eyes widened in surprised at how good the roll was this way. I had never considered dunking it in broth before.

"Great idea," I said.

She shrugged. "That's just how we eat rolls with stew or broth at home."

"Do you have a special way of eating beef?" I asked seriously.

Violet smirked. "With a fork."

I threw a piece of bread at her. She grabbed a roll out of the basket and tossed it at my face. It hit me in the forehead and landed in the bowl of broth, splattering the table and napkin in my lap. I burst out laughing, and Violet did too.

When Cookie came back in, we were both clutching our sides, trying not to fall out of the chairs.

"Something funny?" Cookie teased.

I sobered up and saw her eyeing our mess. "We'll clean it up when we're done."

Cookie set down the plates with the beef tenderloin and an assortment of baked vegetables. "Your Highness will do no such thing. Now eat your beef while it's hot!"

Since the interviews started after lunch yesterday, I made the mistake of assuming I would have time to myself in the morning. Unfortunately, when I set foot outside my door to go for a run this morning, Violet dragged me right back in, citing that the seamstress needed me *again*. I was chomping at the bit to get even just an hour of fresh air and time to myself before getting sucked into my duties as a princess; alas, that was not going to be possible.

Three hours of standing still with the seamstress poking and prodding me with sharp pins and I was desperate for an escape I wasn't allowed to take. Instead I was given five minutes to eat lunch and then was escorted to the throne room for day two of contestant interviews.

My feet were aching and I was desperate for a chance to do anything other than stand still. We had thirty minutes before the opportunity for interviews would be concluded; the window ended precisely an hour before sunset. So far we had interviewed eighteen contestants over two days. My grandfather was hoping we would get two more, which would give us a nice even number of twenty. Preparations for the banquet tomorrow were well underway. In addition to the competitors, there were also guests from the three other human kingdoms. The king intended for the banquet to be a formal presentation of me to all guests and did not want to spoil the event by allowing me to converse with the newcomers until then. I thought it was ridiculous and would have preferred if the competition were a quieter affair.

If I were in his shoes, would I do anything differently? As king, he needs to ensure that his neighbors continue to view us as capable of holding on to our seat of power—and that they know we are abiding by the rules for this competition—so they accept me as Lady of the South. I grimaced. I knew very well that they would never truly accept a woman in that position. They would likely try to give my title to my new husband. I wondered how it was that only men were able to have that title. I doubted that every one of the four kingdoms had been blessed over the years with exclusively male heirs.

Perhaps they just gave the man who married the princess the title, deciding that a woman could be a figurehead and nothing more. Regardless of whether or not that was what my grandfather was intending to do as well, I was not going to become a queen and Lady of the South in name alone. I was going to rule my people. *Just as my mother had foreseen.*

I now knew that all the training I received at Jade Wilds had been designed with the assumption that I would eventually take my place as Lady of the South. The annoying monthly etiquette lessons with an emphasis on both human and Fae cultures had

had a *real* purpose. I was not simply Gaskal's future queen, I was also the bridge between Fae and humans.

I need to talk to Ghilanna. I was confident my best friend had far more information to share than what we had covered in two brief meetings. But we were both afraid of what my grandfather would do if Ghilanna showed up at the palace. *Maybe the competition is the best time.* With the number of guests in residence at the palace and overflowing the inns in the city, would they really notice if she was in the audience?

I was certain there were several things my grandfather had not yet told me about either. Things I need to understand to one day rule—including how the gold mines operated.

Lord John banged his staff on the floor, jarring me out of my thoughts. "Rhys Mongan of Eagle Rock."

My hands were lightly gripping the arms of my chair as a ripple of excitement went through me at the prospect of a competitor who was not from the South. *How far away is Eagle Rock that I've never heard of it?*

Rhys strode down the red carpet with measured footfalls. His back was straight and his shoulders down, and confidence oozed from him. As he approached, I noted his wavy, shoulder-length black hair; long, thick black beard; and tanned skin. He had no weapons but carried himself as though he was highly trained. *Is Eagle Rock where the human kings train their knights?*

Rhys halted at the appropriate spot, several strides away from the thrones, then addressed us. "Greetings, King Leonard and Princess Serafina," he said with a formal bow. "I am here today to request that I be allowed to participate in your competition."

When Rhys finished speaking, his deep blue eyes met mine boldly. I was taken aback that he would do something so reckless in front of my grandfather. My lips parted as we stared at each other, then my vision faded to black. I slumped sideways and caught myself awkwardly on the chair arm. The blackness disappeared, but the whole throne room was spinning. I slid out of the chair and onto my knees, clutching my head, praying the vertigo would disappear.

A tan, calloused hand reached toward me, then was violently pulled away. The guards were shouting, but I was too occupied with nausea and overwhelming pain to pay them any heed.

My grandfather knelt beside me. "Serafina, let us help you."

I cautiously tipped my head up to meet his worried eyes. "I just need water and rest. It should pass." *I hope.* Curled in a ball, I prayed that water and rest were the answer. I wished Ghilanna were here, because she would know what to do.

I could only assume my grandfather gave orders. The next thing I knew, Violet was tucking me into my bed.

Fourteen

TRISTAN

Watching Serafina collapse, with such pain written on her face, I had nearly lost control of myself. With an iron will, I made the smart choice—to depart. Shrugging off the restraining hands of the guards, I gave the king a curt bow and turned on my heel. Whispers spread through the few guests in the audience. I wasn't even sure King Leonard had noticed I was departing.

Tremors of fear mixed with anger ran through my body as I walked briskly away, even as my mind yelled at me to run back to her side. My steps wavered as I headed down the wide cobble-stone road toward the open palace gate. *What the hell has Tanyth done to her?* In the weeks we spent together at Dorcha Palace, I had never once seen Serafina collapse like that, even in the direst of circumstances.

I was just about to pass through the palace gate and re-enter the city when a guard shouted, "Rhys Mongan!"

I turned around with a hand on my sword hilt. I recognized the guard as one of the humans who had been in the throne room. "Yes?" I replied, trying to keep my voice neutral. *It's not the guard's fault Serafina is sick.*

"His Majesty wanted me to relay a message to you. Your request has been accepted if there is no evidence that *you* caused the princess to collapse," the guard said.

I grimaced. Of course King Leonard would be quick to blame the visitor who hadn't even touched the princess for the illness. "I assure you that I did nothing to harm her."

The guard nodded and motioned that I could continue on my way. Heart pounding in my chest, I took the long route back to the inn. A few blocks away, I paused in an alleyway. Callyn emerged from the shadows, her pale braid draped over her shoulder. Her clothing was the same style as mine, but she was not making an effort to hide the fact that she was Fae, which surprised me. *She is in the shadows, though.*

"How'd it go?" Callyn asked.

"Not well. Serafina collapsed in pain. I only know I was approved because the king sent a guard with the message," I said, voice flat.

Callyn frowned. "It almost sounds like magic, but the only Fae I know of who might do that is not here."

"There could be another Fae in Gaskal. Serafina's new position as heir is bound to have attracted attention within the Fae courts," I replied. *Or a human poisoned her.* Either was a viable option. Not all Fae were fond of Serafina's mixed heritage, and I was aware that some had even called for her death when she was training at Jade Wilds.

"How did she seem as you walked in?" Callyn inquired.

I shrugged. "She was fine … until our eyes met."

"Then it must be tied to you. You ran into her the other day and she didn't recognize you but never became sick. Right?" Callyn asked.

I nodded. What she said made sense. If it was tied to me, then it was highly unlikely it was poison.

Callyn continued, "That leads me to believe that her memory has been erased."

"Or bound ..." I whispered, fists curling tight.

Callyn gave me a sharp look. "Can he do that?"

I blew out a breath, anger and sadness flooding me. "Yes. I've witnessed him binding a Fae's magic before. Not merely putting one of those magic-nullifying collars on, but a true binding spell. Since a mating bond is magical, it is possible he was able to bind it and erase her memory, or at least lock it away."

"Do you remember any crucial details?" Callyn pressed.

I tried to remember what exactly Tanyth had been doing when I witnessed the binding. "Coralyn threw magic at Tanyth. Then he used Fleshrender and said, 'Your magic no longer exists.'" I shuddered as a perfect image of Fleshrender entered my thoughts. The blade was black metal, and when the light caught the metal correctly, you could see blood coating it.

I blinked, and Callyn's face was right in mine. "You okay?" she demanded.

"Yes." I shuddered in revulsion. Fleshrender was one of the three magical objects in a Fae prophecy that Prince Tanyth strongly believed was real and was desperate to fulfill.

Become one with flesh
Summon the dragon with his fang
Bloodsong sang with glee
The one who can tame the three
Can maim all foes against thee.

Thanks to me, I thought bitterly. The prince had acquired Dragonfang; now all he needed was the *Bloodsong Grimoire.*

Callyn hissed, "If Fleshrender is the key to undoing whatever binding he put on Serafina, then we are doomed. He keeps it under lock and key within Dorcha Palace, and as much as I love you, I am not willing to go back into Dorcha Palace and gamble that I could get out again."

"There must be another way," I replied. "What if it is as simple as redoing what we did to bond originally?"

"Fucking her, or falling in love again?" Callyn asked, her voice tight.

"One or both, perhaps. The only way into her bed is by winning the competition," I said.

Callyn gave me a withering look. "You are so dense at times. You didn't wait for Tanyth to order you to take her to bed. Both of you made your own choice. Why would this time be any different?"

Anger flared, and I tried to keep it in check. "If the king were to find out—" I began.

Callyn slapped my face. I snarled at her.

"You act as though you are no longer capable of thinking or planning for yourself. Maybe Tanyth tampered with you as well," Callyn said harshly. I bared my teeth. "Both you and Serafina are adults, whether by Fae or human law. There is no reason why you cannot partake in consensual sex. Though I would recommend doing so in secret. Your greatest challenge would be seducing her."

I turned my back to Callyn and moved deeper into the alley. She did have a point. In theory, I could obtain Serafina's consent without having to win the competition. It would require secrecy though, and after what happened at Dorcha Palace, I was reluctant to have a relationship with her that required us to stay hidden. *I don't want to seduce her.* What I wanted was for her to fall in love with me again. *Except she won't be falling in love with me—it would be Rhys Mongan.* I had made my choice to become Rhys to win her hand. Yet now I fully understood what it meant. Serafina would marry Rhys. *How am I going to break the news to her that I'm me?* It was a matter for another day, but one that would have to be accomplished carefully, or I risked losing Serafina for good.

The other thing nagging me about my introduction to the Lord of the South and Serafina was how she had been in obvious pain, though she had seemed unaffected until moments after our eyes met. I shook my head. I would have to decipher that tidbit another day. I couldn't imagine how I would handle life among the Fae, being accepted as a warrior, held as a prisoner for weeks, and then suddenly tossed back into human society as future queen. It was enough for even the strongest to break.

Callyn gave my cheek a kiss. "At least King Leonard agreed to allow you to participate."

I nodded. It was a small consolation that the first step in our plan had been successful. *I must focus on the events I have control over and let the rest play out.*

After a hot but bland dinner from one of the vendor carts on our way back, Callyn and I retreated to our shared room on the third level of Wayside Inn. I removed my tunic as Callyn organized our belongings behind me. I heard her gasp.

"What?" I demanded, peering over my shoulder at her. I dropped my tunic in a heap. She stepped toward me, staring intently at a spot on my lower back. "Do I have a wart on my back?"

Callyn stuck her tongue out at me and created a ball of Fae light, illuminating the spot she was staring at. Her breath hissed out of her mouth. "When he stabbed you in the back ... before ... before you and Serafina mated ... that was with Dragonfang, right?"

Growling under my breath, I walked over to the mirror and angled myself so I could see the reflection of my back. Where the wound had been was an intricate tattoo of a dragon. *I guess the spell on the pendant wasn't strong enough to erase that.*

"You've been marked," Callyn said breathlessly.

Rage flowed through me, and I clenched my fists tight. "The prophecy doesn't say anything about what happens if you're marked." I began the recitation. "'Become one with flesh—'"

Callyn interrupted me. "You are correct that *that* prophecy does not talk about being marked by one of those magic objects. However, it is common knowledge among the Fae that a magical object is capable of marking someone. I'm surprised you didn't learn that as a youngling. Though it is more complicated to get Fae to agree on what that allows the wielder to do to the person who is marked. My biggest concern is if Tanyth knows you are marked, he could be using it to track you. We're not able to ask him, but we need to take into consideration that he knows you're not dead and are in Gaskal," Callyn said.

Growling under my breath, I stalked away from the mirror and finished undressing. *What is Tanyth's end game if he wanted to rip Serafina and me apart only to permit us to be back together? Or maybe he has no idea about the mark.* I was tired, and having more hurdles to overcome was not helping matters. I needed to stay focused on what was in my control. *Attend the banquet. Compete in the three tasks.*

I lay down on my bed. The lumpy wool mattress and coarse sheet were a far cry from the comfortable bed I had had at Dorcha Palace. Not that I cared. I would take my freedom from Tanyth over a comfortable suite of rooms any day.

Fifteen

SERAFINA

The pain in my head after meeting Rhys would not dissipate; even sleep eluded me. The only solution available was to accept the doctor's offering of a sleep draught. After drinking the entire glass of amber-colored liquid, I lay down and shut my eyes, praying that when I woke up, I would feel normal again.

I was walking in a lush forest with soft emerald-green grass beneath my toes. As I walked through the trees, I thought I caught glimpses of a large grayish cat. But no matter how hard I tried, I could not find it—or anything else, for that matter.

I woke up feeling refreshed. I remembered the dream of being in the forest and had a nagging feeling I had been there before, though it wasn't anything like the forest surrounding Jade Wilds. *It's not like I am a Fae seer and able to interpret the nuances of a dream.*

Excitement filled me at the prospect of having the opportunity to get to know each of the competitors vying for my hand in marriage. Several of them had piqued my curiosity during the interviews, including Rhys, the last one to be accepted. I knew I did not have any control over the outcome of the tasks, but I was permitted to offer my favor or encouragement to any of them.

I walked outside into the private yard and took a deep breath. On the other side of the wall was one of the kitchen gardens. I could smell the hints of basil, thyme, and jasmine growing in the herb garden that I knew was the pride of the palace cook staff. Violet had declined my offer to give her a lesson in self-defense, claiming she had mending to catch up on. I let it slide since I didn't want to force Violet to train.

Once again, I had to borrow a sword; my request to obtain a new one had been denied. *Maybe Grandfather thinks if I don't have my own, I will stop practicing.* I began my warmup, slowly and steadily working my way through the ten sword maneuvers several times before adding the combinations in. My grandfather was still cold and distant, and I had had limited encounters with the nobles in the palace. It was becoming clear that if I wanted to get to know the people of my grandfather's court, I was going to have to try without help. It was a challenge to find the motivation when everything was moving at such a rapid pace. Eliminating my morning training would resolve the time issue, but I was concerned not having a small amount of each day to myself would increase my stress and ultimately make matters worse.

Living among the Fae had changed me, as had fighting in a battle against humans. I was not a docile human woman content to embroider or manage a household for the rest of my life.

A memory flickered through my mind from when I was at the battle camp before the Fae faced the Lord of the East. King Pharaan had told me I would have a choice to live with the Fae or with the humans, and yet here I was, *without a choice.* I would do my duty to my kingdom, marry, produce an heir, and then find some way to live my best life here. Forget about the freedom I had had among the Fae. I swallowed hard, wishing there was another way, but I could not see any that would allow me to appease King Leonard's need for an heir without it being me.

A slight scrape on the stone had me whirling, sword raised. Ghilanna dropped down from the top of the wall and landed silently in front of me. "I told you I would find you again."

Casting my gaze around, I could not hide my surprise that Ghilanna had chosen to meet with me in the palace of all places. *Not that I have had a chance to return to the city.* "There are twenty contestants," I informed her, studying her face for a reaction.

Ghilanna didn't even blink. "I am aware. Is there anyone you favor?"

"Not in particular. Though there are a few I am not sure I would like being married to. They seem too self-absorbed," I responded.

"Word has traveled about your collapse after meeting Rhys Mongan. To make matters worse, very few of the humans seem to know where Eagle Rock is. They're suspicious. I highly doubt a human who didn't touch you could make you sick, but I am here to make sure he *didn't* use magic on you," Ghilanna explained.

Relief coursed through me. "There was no magic. I have been plagued by terrible headaches since I returned from the Court of Dusk. Commander Meriel was able to help some, but they seem to arise unpredictably. The one yesterday is the worst I've experienced."

"May I?" Ghilanna stepped forward, her hand raised.

"Of course," I replied, not entirely sure what my friend intended to do. Ghilanna placed her hand on my forehead. Her touch was cool to begin with, then warmed. I could feel her magic spreading through me.

After a few moments, she yanked her hand back with a hiss. "There's magic at work. *Dark* magic. Far beyond my abilities. I'm sorry."

Fear threaded through me that a Fae wanted me to suffer, but I couldn't recall ever having confrontations with anyone that would explain the use of *dark magic*. I snapped my fingers as an idea came to me. "Can dark magic interfere with memories?"

Ghilanna's lips formed an O as she considered my question. "Fae magic can do many things. Seers can see events of the past, present, and future. It would be logical to assume that a Fae could warp a seer's magic to manipulate an individual's memories. I am not sure what there would be to gain from doing that to you. Most Fae who dislike you would be far more likely to execute you than waste their time with something as volatile as dark magic."

"After the battle at Emerald Valley, I spent time as a guest at the Court of Dusk. Then, when my marriage to Prince Tanyth was unexpectedly postponed, I returned to Jade Wilds, which is when I learned of my new status as heir of Gaskal. Other than sending Tanyth a note calling off the engagement, I have not conflicted with any Fae," I told her. None of this made sense. There was no reason that any Fae I'd ever had interactions with would have done such an awful thing.

Then, I had another idea. "What if it's not directed at me, but at King Pharaan?" I wasn't convinced this made much sense. I *was* King Pharaan's granddaughter, but a female Fae could not rule a court.

"A personal vendetta?" Ghilanna asked.

"Yes," I replied.

"Your Highness!" Thomas's voice came from the open doors.

I glanced over my shoulder at him, then returned my attention to Ghilanna. "We're out of time for now. I must prepare for the banquet."

Ghilanna sighed. "I can do some research about headaches and dark magic. When I find the answers, I will tell you."

"Thank you," I said softly and watched as Ghilanna sprinted toward the wall and leaped, landing on top, then disappeared over the other side. Thomas had observed the exchange without comment. I paused in front of him.

"Thank you," I said.

Thomas, usually quiet, surprised me by responding. "I hope your friend can find a solution for your illness. No one I've consulted has had any solid recommendations."

My eyes widened. *Thomas is consulting people about my illness?* I was taken aback by the idea of a palace guard telling others that I was sometimes severely ill. Then, I studied his face and realized he likely didn't intend it to be malicious and that he honestly wanted to help me. "Do the people you consulted know much about Fae?"

"Let's keep this between you and me," he replied, stepping closer and dropping his voice into a whisper. "My mother is a healer, and many years ago she received training from a Fae. She knows more than most human healers."

His revelation caught me completely off guard, though it provided some insight into why he was comfortable around me and had no qualms with Ghilanna's appearance. Unsure what else to say, I settled on returning to my rooms.

Attendants filed into my rooms, bearing a large assortment of items. As they unveiled what they carried, I found myself cringing.

A case full of jewels, several crowns—each more outrageous than the next—and then, of course, my dress. I studied it: a deep hunter-green velvet overskirt with a triangle opening down the middle where gold satin was visible. The gold satin also lined the inside of the flared bell sleeves, and the waist and neck of the bodice had an intricate gold beaded design. I ran a finger over the velvet, smiling at how soft it was. A memory surfaced.

The dress was made of deep emerald velvet. The top was gathered at each shoulder and adorned with large diamond brooches. There were delicate gold chains draping over the arms, but no sleeves. The neckline plunged into a deep V from the neck to the navel and the rest of gown was cascading folds of emerald velvet in a luxurious skirt.

I blinked in confusion, then stared at the dress in front of me. *It must be a dream I had. I've never worn anything but modest clothing my entire life.*

"Are you okay, Princess?" asked Mary.

I nodded. "Yes, I'm fine. The dress is lovely."

"Wonderful. Now we need to get you into it. Then, you can choose which crown you fancy and the jewelry. The king was very specific. You must wear at least two pieces of jewelry in addition to the crown," the maid explained.

I rolled my eyes. *Of course. The banquet was yet another opportunity to put the prize on display. If it wasn't obvious enough how wealthy Gaskal was, since it possessed the coveted gold mines, then jewelry would certainly do the trick.*

Although everyone had been referring to tonight's entertainment as a "banquet," I was mistaken in the assumption that we would be sitting down for a formal meal. Servants moved throughout the ballroom with trays of food and drink, but no formal dining tables were set up. Along the walls, chairs and some benches were available for guests who wished to sit instead of standing or dancing.

The last two days had been dedicated to introductions. Thankfully, tonight I was not required to sit or stand in a particular location and could mingle with the guests. Representatives from the North, East, and West kingdoms were present to witness the competition for my hand in marriage, and, I presumed, to get a measure of me and what role they anticipated I would play in the future of my kingdom.

None of the competitors had claimed to be backed by any of the kings, but I suspected each king had at least one participant they were supporting. *Would it affect me to know which kingdom?* I knew very well that the skills required depended far more on each man's ability and not what political ties he had.

After completing an initial circuit of the room, I claimed a corner of the ballroom near a group of three chairs that would allow me to sit and talk to someone if I chose but kept me away from the throng of people in the center. I couldn't shake the feeling that I had been at a similar event before, but I could not remember when. Parties like this didn't exist while I was at Jade Wilds, and even the graduation party at Emerald Valley was quite informal compared to what I was participating in tonight.

My conversation with Ghilanna had me wondering to what extent dark magic could alter a person who had no magic to call their own.

As I subtly peered around the room, I thought I caught a glimpse of Rhys. I wasn't sure if I should be excited or apprehensive since when we met yesterday, I had almost immediately collapsed from the horrible headache.

I took a half step away from my corner when a cough stopped me. Just to my right was Pierre, the tenth suitor to request to compete. He had short black hair and a thick black mustache. Tonight, he was wearing a teal jacket over a dark-blue, almost purple button-up shirt, and his pants were dark charcoal. My lips twitched in amusement as I realized he looked much like one of my grandfather's prized peacocks.

Pierre bowed with a flourish. "Princess Serafina, how are you this evening?"

I smiled. "Very well, thank you, Pierre. Is the food to your satisfaction?" Small talk was one of my least favorite things to do, but I knew I would have to get used to it.

Pierre flashed a bright smile. "Divine. Would you like to dance?"

The words I'd been dreading. I knew I could refuse, but I didn't want to hurt his feelings. One of my primary tasks tonight was to ensure each exhibitor felt as though he had a fighting chance to win—and that I was worthy of the required effort.

"Of course," I said and placed my hand on his offered arm.

Pierre escorted me to the dance floor, which was surprisingly empty of dancers. *Did they all flock to the drink table at the same time?* I placed my right hand in his left and my left hand lightly on his right shoulder, keeping our bodies a respectable distance apart. The quartet shifted into an elegant waltz, one that thankfully Pierre and I both knew. We moved smoothly across the dance floor, and to my surprise I found that I was having fun.

At the conclusion of the third song, Frederick Hunter approached us while we caught our breath.

Frederick bowed deeply. "Your Highness, may I have the next dance?"

I let my hands fall from Pierre's embrace. "Of course. Pierre, thank you."

Frederick offered his hand, and I set mine lightly in his and allowed him to guide me a few paces away from Pierre before we eased into a contredanse with another couple. We were about the same height. Frederick's expression was serious as we swirled around the room. Such a contrast to Pierre's smile and eager conversation. The music faded, and murmurs of thanks carried across the dance floor as partners changed. I was debating how to politely withdraw from the dance floor when a tall figure approached.

I had to peer around Frederick's head so that I could see who it was. *Rhys.* His black hair was almost blue in the low light of the ballroom. My head began pounding as our gazes met. I let go of Frederick's hand and took a few steps backward, bumping into someone else. "Sorry," I mumbled, trying to weave my way through everyone. Cool fingers wrapped around mine, and I stopped my frantic retreat to see who was bold enough to grab my hand.

Rhys's blue eyes were full of concern. "Serafina," he whispered.

I gasped at his casual use of my name and briskly yanked my hand out of his. "How dare you!" As soon as my fingers left his, the room began to tilt. I swayed on my feet. Rhys cupped my hand in his and gently stroked the back of my knuckles.

The room stilled. Eyes wide, I gazed at him warily. "What magic are you using on me?" I demanded, keeping my voice low. The last thing I needed was someone to hear me accusing a competitor of using magic on me. *Treason.*

"I swear, I am not using magic on you. I am merely holding your hand," Rhys replied, his voice rough.

"Promise?" I queried, then immediately regretted my word choice. Extracting a promise in a room full of witnesses was unwise. Especially when our words could be misheard.

"Yes. On my life, I am not using magic on you. Are you sure you're okay? I can escort you back to your rooms if you're unwell," he offered.

I knew he meant well, but a competitor escorting me to my rooms would be taken the wrong way by the king. "You approached initially to ask for a dance, did you not?"

Rhys nodded. His hair swung over his shoulders, and I had the odd desire to run my fingers through it.

"Very well, then let us dance. Whatever illness was threatening me seems to have resolved itself. I assure you I am fine," I said. Honestly, I wasn't entirely sure dancing *was* a good idea, but I had the sense we were being watched and felt that accepting his offer to dance would be the simplest way to encourage our observers to forget whatever else had just happened.

Rhys held my hand to his lips and kissed it lightly, then bowed. "May I have this dance, Your Highness?"

I was relieved that he had agreed and that he was mimicking the behavior of the others I had danced with. *A safe choice.*

"Of course." As we stepped onto the dance floor, the orchestra music changed and became quite energetic. I suppressed a groan. A volte was not the best experiment to see if I truly was feeling better. Rhys gave me a quizzical look, which I ignored. *A volte it is.*

As we twirled our way across the dance floor, through waltzes, another volte, and even a minuet, I became aware that of the fact that if we were in physical contact with one another, the headaches and illness were gone. However, if I spun away and I looked at Rhys with the physical touch broken, it would return even more intense than before.

The music stopped, and I became aware of how few people were left in the ballroom. Even the king, it seemed, had retired for the night. I stood staring at Rhys, our fingers intertwined. My lips parted, and I took a half step forward before I realized what I was doing and released his hand as though it was burning me. As the room started to spin, I sank to the floor, eyes clenched shut, gasping.

A cool hand brushed my forehead. "You're fine, Serafina," Rhys's voice coaxed me.

I opened one eye, then the other. Tremors ran through me. *Why does his touch send away the illness?* Warnings rang in my head. I could not trust every man I came across. Just because we had had a nice dance did not mean he meant me no harm. He was here to win the competition. This was nothing more than an opportunity for the biggest prize in the South. Giving Rhys too much information about the illness that plagued me and Ghilanna's suspicions could put me in extreme danger.

"You can escort me to my room," I said softly.

Rhys's eyes widened, and I was pleased to have caught him off guard with my words. Using Rhys to leverage myself back to standing, I led him to the side door where Thomas was waiting.

"Rhys is going to escort me to my room. You will follow," I said in a firm voice. I didn't want Thomas to question me in front of Rhys, but I did want him there to guarantee my safety and make sure Rhys would not do anything untoward to me.

Sixteen

TRISTAN

The guard—Thomas, Serafina had called him—watched me closely, his hand resting on his sword hilt. Little did Thomas know that I could kill him far quicker than he could draw the blade. But killing a human for no reason was not on my agenda, nor did I anticipate it would ever be if I had control of my own actions. It would severely jeopardize my ability to get Serafina back. I swallowed hard, ordering myself to focus on the present.

Dancing with Serafina for as long as I had far surpassed any of my expectations for the night. Yet our bond remained dull and unresponsive, despite our prolonged time together. Now, as we walked back to her rooms, my intense need was challenging my control. Her hand in mine sent small sparks through me.

Her immunity to them was disconcerting. Even before we had bonded weeks ago at Dorcha Palace, I had known on some level that she could feel the sparks whenever we touched, her body's reaction and scent a giveaway. The sparks had been the beginning of the soulmate bond forming. Tonight, though, all I sensed from her was relief that the illness plaguing her was diminished by physical contact with me.

When Serafina called Thomas over to us, my initial reaction was hot anger. Until the wisdom of her decision hit me. As the "prize" of the competition, her reputation was also on the line. Being caught unchaperoned with one of the competitors at night would be catastrophic for both of us. I also had not considered how difficult it would be for me to be this close to her without being intimate. Thomas's solid presence kept me grounded.

We halted in front of a large ornate door inlaid with gold fleurs-de-lis. Our eyes met, and my breathing hitched as I dipped my head down, lips parting for a good night kiss.

Thomas shouldered his way between us, breaking the hold I had on Serafina's hand. "You forget yourself," the guard rasped, shoving me with his hands.

Serafina peered around Thomas's shoulder. "I'm sorry," she said before slipping inside her room. When the door was shut and I heard the click of a key in the lock, Thomas stepped back out of my space.

"I will escort you to the door. It would be wise to remember you are not welcome here unless you have an express invitation by the princess *and* an escort," Thomas warned.

We walked in silence for a while, our boots clicking on the polished marble floor. When I estimated we were just around the corner from the main entrance to the palace, we halted. Thomas stood on his tiptoes and whispered in my ear. "Be careful. There are eyes everywhere."

Biting the inside of my cheek, I nodded in understanding. The warning was noted, though odd that Serafina's guard, who didn't know me, would be comfortable enough to give me one. We resumed our trek to the entrance, and Thomas stopped at the door while I continued down to the road and out the large palace gate. *Or perhaps my plan was not as secretive as I thought.* Callyn and I had both been in the city several days before the competition, and she was not actively hiding her presence. *Is Serafina's guard the person who has been following me?* The idea that Serafina's personal guard was taking time away from his duties to follow me sounded unrealistic. A king's spy was far more likely.

I passed the tannery where Callyn and I had agreed to meet, but she was nowhere in the vicinity. *Maybe she decided to go to bed. It is far later than I thought.* I glanced at the horizon, where the dark night was slowly being overtaken by the gray fingers of dawn.

Wayside Inn was empty, save for the cook who was baking the morning bread. Climbing the stairs two at a time, I opened our door quietly, not sure what to expect. The kiss of a dagger met my throat as I shut the door.

I pushed it away with the tip of my finger. "I thought you were sleeping."

"I was, but you weren't exactly being quiet on your way up. What took so long? I thought I'd have to search for you in the palace dungeons," Callyn grumbled, shoving her dagger back under her pillow and taking a seat on the bed.

"Dancing with Serafina," I replied.

Callyn's eyes lit with hope. "Truly?"

I nodded. "Yes, though there is no change in the bond. I was able to gather some information, but I'm not entirely sure how helpful it will be."

"Are you going to share the information or make me guess?" Callyn demanded testily, confirming that she had indeed been asleep.

"An illness plagues her. It is unlike anything I have seen before. When we are looking at each other, she becomes disoriented and experiences intense pain. However, if I touch her, all symptoms go away," I explained.

"Is that why you danced for so long? Because you were touching, and it made the sickness go away?" Callyn asked, standing up and pacing.

"I assume so. I didn't ask Serafina about the illness. I was concerned about being overheard," I responded.

Callyn rifled through one of the bags, looking for something, though I had no idea what. She finally gave up after examining several books. "I have a hunch, but I was hoping one of the books would confirm it before I tell you." She blew out her breath. "I don't seem to have the correct book with me. The problem with binding spells is they can often cause severe symptoms to the person who has been bound. It's possible that because it's your mating bond that has been bound by Tanyth, seeing you triggers the severe reaction, but physical touch is able, on some level, to pierce the binding and allow your bond to behave as it should."

"So, you're telling me that unless I am touching her, anytime Serafina sees me, I am going to make her sick?" The whole idea seemed strange to me. "Why would Tanyth not have accounted for this happening in his spell?"

Callyn shook her head. "I have no idea. The only possibility is that he made the spell for a Fae and did not account for the fact that as a half-blood, Serafina's body is different, and spells potentially would need to be altered to accommodate that."

"Could that mean the spell will weaken over time?" I asked hopefully.

Callyn sighed. "Anything is possible. We just don't know enough. For now, you need to rest. You're supposed to report for a demonstration with the other competitors at lunchtime."

Callyn was right. I had spent far longer than I should have at the palace and only had a few hours to rest. The king had not shared any details about the three phases of the competition other than the first would be an obstacle course, the second a foot race, and the third a joust. I shuddered at the challenge that would await me in the joust. As a rule, horses did not appreciate me, a snow leopard shifter. They could sense the predator, and their natural instincts were to run.

"Good night," I said, and with a flick of Callyn's fingers, the Fae light went out.

Seventeen

SERAFINA

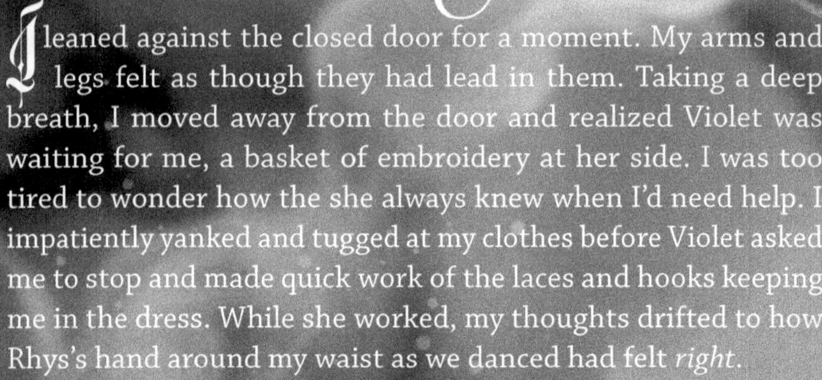

I leaned against the closed door for a moment. My arms and legs felt as though they had lead in them. Taking a deep breath, I moved away from the door and realized Violet was waiting for me, a basket of embroidery at her side. I was too tired to wonder how the she always knew when I'd need help. I impatiently yanked and tugged at my clothes before Violet asked me to stop and made quick work of the laces and hooks keeping me in the dress. While she worked, my thoughts drifted to how Rhys's hand around my waist as we danced had felt *right*.

Unfortunately, with the competition, there were no guarantees that anyone—even a human as clearly meant for the assignment as Rhys—would be successful. No one knew what awaited them in the obstacle course or even where it was located. *By design.* I was certain the king was keeping the information close to his chest. The foot race could be as simple as a short sprint or a marathon lasting days. And the final task, jousting. A loud snort erupted from my nose at the thought of Pierre even holding a lance, let alone taking a hit from another competitor.

In addition to not knowing any more details than the competitors, I also was balking at King Leonard's plan to keep me in the dark about other important matters regarding my role as heir. Indeed, he had been avoiding being alone with me. His reasoning was once I was married, he could finish teaching me everything that I needed to know, along with my husband. *Is this his way of telling me that his intention all along has been to only use me as a broodmare for an heir, and to keep the power of the kingdom exclusively in a man's hands?*

The dress fell around me in a heap, and I stepped out of it, then quickly removed the pins holding my hair up. They plinked to the floor one by one. Violet gave me a disapproving glance but didn't comment; instead, she bent over and started picking up the pins.

"You don't need to do that. Just leave it," I said, surprised that Violet was picking up after me.

Violet lifted her head and peered at me. "May I speak freely?"

I nodded, and Violet continued. "This *is* my job as your lady-in-waiting, to keep your room and things tidy, as well as be your companion." I pressed my lips together, staying silent. The last thing I wanted was for Violet to get in trouble with the king because of something I told her to ignore.

Violet gathered the hairpins into a basket and stood up. "You may not like what it means to be a princess, but that doesn't change the fact that you are a princess."

I opened my mouth to respond, but she held up her hand and kept talking. "I understand this situation is new to you, but if I may offer some advice: Pick your battles with the king. Choose what is worth fighting over and what is better to go along with. For me, that is following my father's rules about not riding in the city where strange men can see me, but because I obey that rule, I am allowed to ride in the meadow here and train horses at home."

I was tired, but Violet did have a point; I was only here because my grandfather wished me to be. *Maybe I push him because I hope that he'll send me away. That I can go back to living in peace at Jade*

Wilds, where I was a warrior and respected. A small part of my mind laughed, because there had been Fae, like Edrym, who had hated me and wished me dead. Scrubbing my hands over my face, I tugged the nightshirt on that Violet had laid on the bed.

"Thank you," I said softly.

Violet offered me a half smile. "I'm not telling you to change, Your Highness, only to consider your actions more carefully. Thomas told me about your bareback ride with the king. A perfect example of when you're pushing against expectations for a worthy reason. When you stood up to the king in that moment, you reminded him who he is dealing with: a highly skilled half-Fae warrior."

I blushed and immediately felt guilty for how I had treated my dress and hair pins. "I'm sorry, Violet. I appreciate your candid feedback and promise I will try to act more like a proper princess going forward. Now if you don't mind, I am exhausted and would like to bid you good night."

"Of course. I'll see you in the morning," Violet curtsied and carried the dress and basket of hairpins through the door into her adjoining chambers.

I climbed into bed. Exhaustion washed over me, and before I could contemplate how Rhys's touch had sent away the sickness, I fell asleep.

Rhys and I danced across the worn wood floor. Pale columns of stone, like sentries, formed a square on the edge of the room. The blood in my veins thrummed in time to the music. A delicate waltz. The headache that had begun earlier was mercifully staying away.

The tempo of the next song was different—stronger and aggressive. Rhys's steps changed, and he pulled me sharply toward him. Our bodies collided and sparks erupted along my skin. Then, he twirled me away from him. As I spun across the floor, my skirt flaring out around me, I caught sight of Rhys's expression—intense desire. My face heated. How can someone I barely know look at me like that? Unwilling to break the magic of our dance, I returned to his arms.

Rhys twirled me away and then brought me back, his steps confident, arrogant, wholly male, and possessive. Every time I spun away, I found myself praying he would pull me back, needing his touch to keep the sickness at bay and to add fuel to the other feelings that I wasn't willing to name yet. Distracted, I stepped on his toe, earning me a warning snarl.

"Sorry," I whispered, cautiously meeting his bright-blue eyes as we whirled around the dance floor, our bodies pressed tightly together. His gaze was fiery and full of desire. All I could think of was Rhys. At a slow moment in the music, he swept me into his arms, and his kiss scorched my lips, demanding. A throbbing at my core began, and when he tipped his head back for a breath, I wrapped my hands around his neck, pulling his face back down to mine.

"Serafina, you have overslept." Violet's voice broke through my dream as she tutted in disapproval and threw the drapes open. Sunlight streamed through the window, and I rolled over, burying my head under the pillows.

The feeling of dampness between my thighs brought me fully awake. Horror washed through me. Afraid at what I would find, I ran my hand between my thighs and nervously inspected it. My fingers were smeared with blood. Muttering a string of curses, I tossed away the sheets and scooted off the bed.

"I need to bathe," I announced.

"You don't have time. You slept too long," Violet said, her voice tight, as though I was going to blame her for allowing me extra sleep.

I raised my eyebrows and waved my arm at the bed. "I started my cycle. I need a bath and some cloth pads if you have those available as well."

Violet couldn't hide her surprise as she approached me. "I apologize, Your Highness. I had no idea that being only half-Fae meant you're still subjected to a human woman's cycle."

I was not entirely awake and didn't feel like explaining that Fae females had cycles that were only slightly longer than a human's. Taking a deep breath to keep from snapping at Violet, I replied in what I hoped was a calm but firm voice, "It doesn't matter. Just call for the bath so I can get cleaned up."

I walked over to peer out the window, wrapping my arms around my abdomen as my stomach clenched and a cramp rolled through me. The last thing I needed was another health problem to deal with. I could not recall how long ago my prior cycle was. I knew I should have had at least one since the battle at Emerald Valley, but the when was eluding me.

Thankfully there was plenty of hot water in the palace. The tub filled quickly, and I settled into it, relishing how the hot water temporarily relieved the tightness from the cramps. I was lathering my hair with soap when I noticed the water was beginning to take on a pinkish hue. *Not a surprise*, I told myself, given I was on my period.

I sank under the water to rinse my hair out, and my whole body contracted. I surged to the surface, gasping. What I thought was a large blood clot floated to the surface of the water. Unnerved, I peered at it and was surprised to see it was more of a sac than a blood clot. *What the hell?* Scooping my hand under it to bring whatever it was closer, I realized that it most definitely wasn't a blood clot. It was a fetus.

Uncertainty washed over me. "That's not possible," I whispered. Glancing at the door, it dawned on me how much this changed. King Leonard thought I was a virgin. Hell, *I* thought I was a virgin. *Did Tanyth and I ... ?* I shoved the thought away, feeling sick to my stomach. *If the king finds out, I have no idea what he'll do, other than blame me for misleading him.*

I ran my hand through my hair, confirming the soap was out. Then, I stood up and scooped the sac into my hands. I took it to the toilet, placed it inside, then flushed. I waited painstaking moments for the water to go down and the bowl to refill, making sure the evidence was gone.

There was a light tap on the door. I was out of time for anything else. I had to hope disposing of it was enough to keep my secret safe. For it must remain a secret, even from Ghilanna. I picked up a thick towel from the small table at the side of the tub and wrapped it around myself, shutting away any thoughts on the miscarriage.

"Your Highness, it's time to dress," announced Mary before pushing the door open to check on me.

When I was dry, Violet brought over my dress. "Where's the corset?" I asked. It was a staple piece of almost every dress in my wardrobe.

"We thought you would be more comfortable without it. If you wear the overcoat, the king is less likely to notice," Violet explained sympathetically.

Relief coursed through me. The snug corset would have been almost unbearable today. As much as I detested having Mary and Violet hovering, I found that they did for the most part have my best interests at heart.

The heavy dark-gold brocade dress felt as though I was wearing two entire suits of plate armor. *What did they make this out of?* I didn't recall this being one of the selections I had made. Wearing something this cumbersome was ridiculous, almost as uncomfortable as wearing a corset would be.

The luncheon was set up so that we ate at long narrow tables. Chairs were placed on one side, and the demonstration would happen in front of the table. This way the guests could eat and be entertained.

I entered and sat near the middle of the table, with my grandfather in a raised chair at the far end. The competitors appeared to be warming up. Lord John was leading them through stretches, then a basic sword drill.

Someone filled my plate with food. I picked at it lightly and was barely aware of my neighbors; they were talking to me, but I had no clue about what. My attention was held by the competitors and assessing their skills. I wanted to know who would be competing for my hand and if there was anyone who lacked sword skills or was exceptionally skilled.

When the warmups were complete, Lord John walked around the men and spoke to them too softly for me to make out his words. Based on the intention of this luncheon, it was not difficult to guess he was giving them their next instructions. To my knowledge, the competition did not specifically require combat, even though having sword skills was one of the eligibility requirements.

Perhaps the suspense of not knowing exactly what each phase of the competition would require was also a test of sorts, meant to judge each man's ability to adapt to circumstances as they arose. Battles frequently required the ability to adapt, and I imagined ruling a kingdom did also.

The competitors organized themselves into groups of five, with the first group including Pierre. A rope fence was placed in a circle around the five men and quiet fell across the room, all eyes drawn to the imminent combat.

Two versus three, contained within a defined space. An intriguing setup, and one I was familiar with, although Commander Meriel's preference had been one versus two if the teams were going to be uneven. Unlike my neighbors, who were intent upon the spectacle within the rope circle, I watched the competitors outside the circle, curious if they would observe and take note of the techniques on display or ignore the opportunity to get to know their opponents.

Rhys was sitting half in shadow on a bench at the edge of the waiting group with his sword resting on his lap. From here, his eyes appeared closed, though I suspected they were open. I felt the slightest twinge of a headache, followed by my stomach clenching, and I closed my eyes, willing it to go away. Even with my eyes shut, I could still imagine how Rhys looked on the bench. His black hair pulled back at the nape of his neck, full beard almost long enough to touch his chest, and the brilliant blue eyes, like sapphires, their depths endless.

My heartbeat sped up. The longer my thoughts lingered on Rhys, the more I craved his touch again. *I cannot afford to get attached to him. The odds are high that he will fail.* Opening my eyes, I returned my attention to the sparring match only to find it had ended. Guards were carrying away three unconscious men. My eyes widened in concern, and I shot my grandfather a glance. He gave me a pointed look, as though saying "So what?" before resuming his conversation with a noblewoman I did not recognize.

Rhys walked into the rope circle, and my eyes met his. Daggers pierced through my skull, my vision went black, and I fainted.

Eighteen

TRISTAN

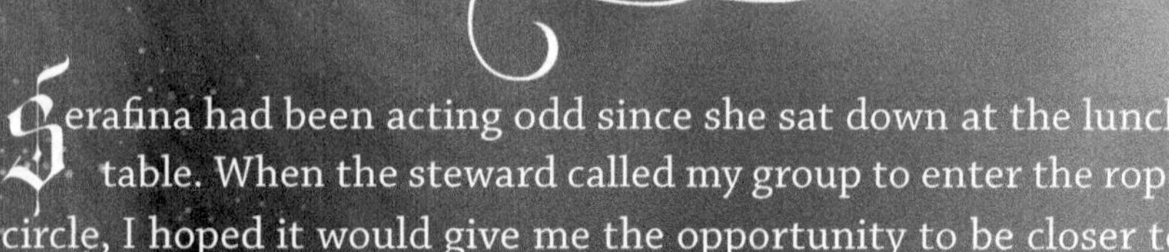

Serafina had been acting odd since she sat down at the lunch table. When the steward called my group to enter the rope circle, I hoped it would give me the opportunity to be closer to her and ensure she was fine.

I gave my sword an experimental swing, and as her blue-green eyes met mine, intense pain flashed across her face, and she toppled sideways in a dead faint. I jumped over the rope and was about the leap onto the table when firm hands gripped me.

"It's not your concern," Thomas warned. I shook my arm as though to dislodge his grip, like the guard was nothing more than a nuisance.

"She needs me," I replied under my breath, swallowing hard when I realized I should not have let the words escape my mouth.

Thomas's face reddened. "The only person she needs right now is the doctor. If you speak like that again, you will be thrown out of the competition and into the dungeon. The princess would be out of your reach forever."

I clenched my jaw, the muscles in my neck bulging as hot anger coursed through me. Loathe to admit the guard had a valid point, I stood in silence, not making a move to retreat or to be perceived as a threat to the princess.

Metal pounded on stone. I craned my neck so I could see the source of the sound. Lord John was attempting to capture the room's attention by thumping his metal-tipped staff on the stone floor.

"Quiet!" I shouted, and the silence was immediate. The steward cast me a grateful look.

"We have concluded the demonstration. His Royal Majesty and Her Highness look forward to seeing everyone first thing tomorrow for phase one," Lord John announced, then thumped his staff again. The effect was instantaneous: The guests stood, and though quiet conversations sprung up among them, the mass drifted toward the exit.

My fellow competitors were slower to leave. Our belongings were in small piles along the back wall. I believed most of us were staying at various inns throughout the city, but since I was keeping to myself, not wanting to befriend anyone, I had not discovered where.

Callyn stepped out of a shadowy corner of the luncheon room and joined me on my way out.

"I didn't realize you were here today," I said with barely masked surprise.

"Did you think I wouldn't observe? I want you to have the best advantage possible. Which means studying your opponents. Serafina is a distraction. I was not certain you would be capable of obtaining the information we need if she was here too," Callyn said tartly.

I bit the inside of my cheek. Callyn was right. Serafina was a distraction. *I need to focus tomorrow, or I am going to lose my only chance to get her back.*

"Would having sex help?" Callyn asked as we passed the blacksmith shop where I had first seen Serafina.

Peering at her out of the corner of my eye, I couldn't decide if she was serious or not. "I don't think being intimate with anyone other than Serafina is going to help me."

"I expected you to feel that way. I just wanted to be sure instead of assuming incorrectly. Are you hungry?" Callyn asked, but before I could respond, she took off at a sprint.

"Callyn, wait!" I shouted, sprinting after her. "Fuck," I growled under my breath as I quickly lost track of where she went among the milling humans. Sniffing the air, I caught a faint trace of Callyn and—*another Fae!* I gasped. *I guess Callyn was right. I* trusted that Callyn would be able to pursue this unknown Fae without my help.

I returned to Wayside Inn. Weary from worry for Serafina and the day's exertions, I lay on the bed and fell asleep.

Pushing the bookcase open, my breath caught in my throat as I saw Serafina. Her russet hair had been braided into a crown with small pearls threaded on a nearly invisible wire through her locks. Her shoulders were bare, with the dress's heart-shaped neckline drawing the eye toward her luscious breasts and down lower toward her sweeping ivory skirt and the body it hid.

Serafina closed the gap between us and kissed me, her lips velvet on mine. A moan escaped my lips, as desire erupted through my entire body. Craving her touch, I pulled her close, our bodies fitting together perfectly.

"I love you," I spoke into her mind as we kissed, tongues dancing.

"Claim me," she demanded in my thoughts.

My cock strained against my pants. She ground her hips against me, and I almost lost control. With a wicked smile on her lips, she slid her hand down my pants and cupped my cock.

"Claim me," she repeated.

A shiver ran down my spine. I didn't need any more encouragement. Her wants and mine were the same. She undid the laces on my pants, and they slid down around my boots. She gave my cock a long, appreciative look, then gathered the folds of her dress in her hands and pulled it up.

"Are you sure?" I murmured, hand raised but unwilling to make another move until I was one hundred percent certain she wanted me.

Serafina nodded. I pulled her to me, my cock bumping the apex of her thighs. I kissed her deeply and with one thought made her dress disappear. One hand I kept on her waist, and the other I ran up her thigh, delighting in her reaction as I lightly ran my thumb over her clit. I plunged two fingers into her, swirling and teasing, and she moaned against my lips. Gently lifting at her waist, I raised her up, and she encircled her legs around my hips loosely. Slowly, to be sure I was positioned correctly, I slid inside of her. A shudder rippled through her.

I nipped her lip. "Not yet, my love."

I took my time pulling out. Savoring how tight she clenched against me, her soft whimpers of pleasure. Without giving her warning, I thrust my cock hard and fast into her. I went deeper than I had ever gone before, and she took my entire length. I gasped as my muscles clenched, but I was determined to draw it out as long as possible. Who knew when we'd be together again? I refused to not savor every second our bodies were one. Sliding my fingers between us, I plunged them into her folds alongside my cock, brushing against her clit, then reached up and pinched her nipple between my fingers.

"Tristan!" she screamed as spasms rolled through her body. With one more thrust, I pulled her tight as our bodies convulsed together, wave after wave of pleasure.

"I love you," I whispered against her lips.

I woke up drenched in sweat. A quick assessment and I realized it wasn't just sweat. *The dream was so vivid.* My pants were damp with fluids. I was shocked to realize that my pent-up longing for Serafina had finally gotten its release. *I guess I didn't need to have sex with anyone but Serafina after all.*

Nineteen

SERAFINA

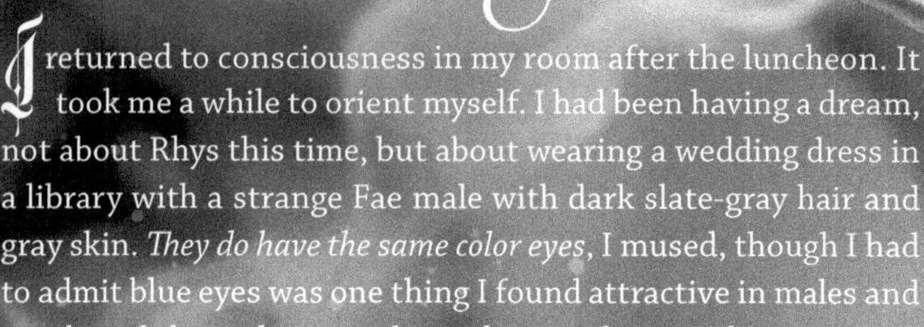

I returned to consciousness in my room after the luncheon. It took me a while to orient myself. I had been having a dream, not about Rhys this time, but about wearing a wedding dress in a library with a strange Fae male with dark slate-gray hair and gray skin. *They do have the same color eyes*, I mused, though I had to admit blue eyes was one thing I found attractive in males and attributed the male in my dream having them to that.

A fire roared in the hearth, and I could hear Violet and Mary quietly chattering at the dining table. My stomach gurgled, and I realized I hadn't eaten any lunch and had no idea what time it was.

"Mary?" I called.

"Yes, Your Highness?" Mary's voice became louder as she approached.

"Would it be possible to get some food?" I asked.

Mary gave me a thoughtful look. "Of course. Are you feeling better? You gave the king a scare when you collapsed again."

I'm sure I did. "Yes, the rest has helped. After I eat, I would like to go into the city."

"As you wish. I will inform Thomas of your intentions," Mary said.

Trays of food were laid out before me on the low table in front of the hearth: a selection of bite-sized sandwiches, fresh fruit, and vegetables. I ate three sandwiches and a bowl of fruit before I decided I was full enough and ready to go out.

While I ate, Mary had set out a plain burgundy dress and petticoat.

"Thank you," I said and proceeded to get dressed. Though I did not feel entirely myself, I was determined to go into the city and find Ghilanna. *I need answers.*

I suggested that my guards and I take horses into the city and was surprised when neither of them disagreed. *How bad do I look?* I mused. The black mare was tacked up in a sidesaddle, and I opened my mouth to protest when I glanced down and realized it was my mistake, not the groom's—I was wearing a dress. Sighing in frustration at myself for not putting on pants before we departed, I resolved to ride sidesaddle, something I hadn't done since I was six. I mounted, and we rode slowly through the city. Our pace was slow, sometimes barely moving due to the number of people on the street and the guards' desire to stick to the well-used roads.

"Your Highness, if we're looking for your Fae friend..." Thomas began.

"Her name is Ghilanna," I offered.

"Ghilanna," Thomas said. "I have heard that there are a couple of Fae staying at Wayside Inn. Perhaps she is one of them."

Thirty minutes on a horse and I was regretting my decision to come into the city at all. Lower back pain from the miscarriage combined with the ghost of a headache, and the horse's movement was not helping matters. Thomas's idea was well-timed. I nodded, and he took the lead, though he constantly threw worried glances over his shoulder at me.

Sooner than I expected, we reached a large building that took up the better part of a block. At the corner, a sign saying Wayside Inn swayed slightly in the wind.

Thomas dismounted and tied his horse to the post, then held my horse while I dismounted. The other guard would stay with the horses while Thomas escorted me inside.

The inn was noisy and full of customers. Tables overflowed with people, and even more patrons leaned against the walls, clutching mugs of ale to their chests. I exchanged a glance with Thomas. *How am I supposed to identify anyone here?*

We made our way around the room, peering at the inhabitants of each table.

"Serafina?"

I recognized the voice immediately and spun around. Rhys was just coming off the staircase. Our eyes locked; I took a step toward him, and my vision wobbled. He must have seen something in my expression, because suddenly he was there, holding my hand. Everything straightened out.

"Thank you," I mumbled, not sure how anyone could hear with so much noise.

Someone bumped into me hard from behind, and I stumbled into Rhys's arms. His arms wrapped around me. *Safe.* I tipped my head back, searching his face. I knew I shouldn't be here, in a public place, embracing a man. Especially one who was competing for the privilege of marrying me. But right now, what I really wanted was to know what it felt like to kiss him. *Are his lips like velvet as they were in my dream, or do they feel entirely different?* My lips parted, and I rose onto my tiptoes. His lips brushed my forehead, and he stepped back, keeping his hands on my arms but distancing himself from me.

Confusion filled me. *Am I misjudging his feelings?* Thomas tugged on my arm from behind.

"Princess, we need to go," Thomas said. When Rhys didn't respond, either to encourage me to stay or to agree I should go, I made my own choice. I twisted out of his embrace and followed Thomas out of the inn. I swallowed hard, my throat dry. Frustration blended with weariness threatened to overwhelm me.

I must be misreading Rhys, or my dream has interfered with my memory of what happened in real life. He is merely another suitor who has entered the competition, nothing more and nothing less. In silence, we mounted the horses and took the shortest route back to the palace.

Twenty

TRISTAN

I should have kissed her on the lips. The words kept repeating over and over. When Serafina had tipped her head toward me with parted lips, I knew immediately that was what she wanted. But Callyn's words of caution had won, and I placed a chaste kiss on her forehead.

Deep inside, fear coiled that if I kissed Serafina on the lips I wouldn't be able to stop there. Wayside Inn was very public; even just the random chance meeting was likely to get back to the king. *I made a smart choice.* Confident in my decision, I returned to my room. Sleep would likely bring dreams, but it would be better than sitting at a table worrying over the kiss. Besides, tomorrow was the first phase of the competition, and I needed to rest as much as possible.

Travaran's hands held my arms in a vise grip as he shook me like a rag doll. "You'll never betray anyone again." His cold voice wrapped around me.

I woke up to my arm being shaken. Callyn's white hair fell over her shoulder and tickled my arm as I woke up. Blinking at her, I massaged my arm when she let go of it. Her grip had been light and friendly; Travaran's grip in my dream had hurt. It was a relief to see there were no marks on my arm. *Just a dream.*

"Sleep well?" Callyn teased.

I grunted. "Better than I expected until Travaran showed up," I replied, standing up and stretching.

Callyn shot me an inquiring glance, but I wasn't sure now was the best time to explain the dreams I was having to her. We were to assemble at the palace gates at sunrise. I had an hour before I was expected to be there, and I intended to make the best use of my time.

I ran through a series of stretches, letting my muscles loosen up before easing into strengthening exercises. I finished the routine with a few sets of kicks and punches. When I was done, all traces of sleep were gone, and I was ready to face whatever awaited me in the obstacle course.

Callyn had used her magic to create a light breakfast for us. Eggs, sausage, and fruit juice. The pack I was permitted to take into the obstacle course contained an assortment of dried meat, fruit, and nuts as well as a canteen of fresh water.

"Delicious," I murmured as I polished off my plate.

"I figured if I treated the competition as though you were going to fight in the arena, that would be close enough to how you need to prepare," Callyn explained.

She was right as always. Though the human-designed competition was not likely to have the magical creatures—dragon, griffin, and leon—I was certain it would not be a short race over a few natural obstacles. Tanyth's hatred for humans meant I had had little time to study them and learn information that could aid me. *I have over fifty years of training and combat experience. Far more than any of my human opponents. That will be enough.*

My hair was pulled back tightly at the nape of my neck. I wanted to make sure it would stay out of my eyes. I had a black tunic underneath a thick hardened-leather breastplate. Lord

John had said we would be permitted to wear arm and leg guards as well, but I wanted to preserve my agility. The human-made leather armor was functional, but too stiff for my liking. My dark-brown pants were wool-padded cotton. After inspecting my sword and dagger carefully and deeming them sharp and without flaws, I strapped the scabbards onto my waist with the dagger on my right hip and the sword on my left.

"Ready?" Callyn asked, examining me.

"As I'll ever be," I said with a half-smile.

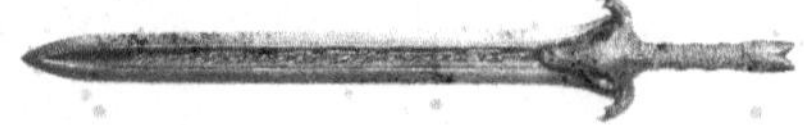

I was one of the last to arrive at the palace gates. It seemed my opponents felt being early would give them bonus points. *I know better.* The only thing that mattered in an event such as this was how we performed once it started. What happened before or after meant nothing.

The nobles were scattered around the courtyard, some astride horses, others in open carriages, leading me to believe phase one was not being held within the palace grounds. I wasn't surprised. The palace, at least to the extent that I had explored, was quite efficient in its use of space.

When the last competitor arrived, Lord John rode over to us atop a small brown pony. "You will get into the wagon." He waved his hand at a covered wagon that was just pulling through the gates. "When we get to the starting point for phase one, I will explain the rules."

When no one made a move to approach the wagon, I rolled my eyes and walked over to it, pushing the flaps on the back open and climbing the two steps. *It's going to be tight.* It wouldn't matter, though. If this was how the king wanted us to travel, then we would.

The trip was surprisingly short. I believe we spent more time not moving than we did moving.

Lord John shoved the flap open. "We're here."

As the first to enter the wagon, I was the last to leave. The other competitors huddled together, chattering nervously. I ignored them and gazed at our surroundings.

There was a medium-sized lake several hundred feet down the hill from us. Beyond the lake was a small mountain with a deep hole at its base. It took me a few moments to realize that the small flecks moving were humans and that the mountain and deep hole were Gaskal's gold mine. I focused my attention on the lake and identified the telltale signs of the sides having been carved out. *It's an old mine.* At the end closest to us was a narrow wooden dock with small boats tied at even intervals. *Twenty boats.*

Pulling my attention from the lake, I forced myself to scan the surroundings, hunting for more clues of what we would be facing. But aside from the dock with twenty boats, nothing was obvious.

"Competitors!" shouted Lord John. Silence fell as we turned to face the steward.

"Your phase one task shall be to make your way through the ruins of the old watchtower, hike down to the lake, select and row a boat to the other side of the lake, then remove the boat from the water entirely. You will then enter the canyon between the old and new mines. The finish line is at the top of the water-fall. Not completing any of the four elements will result in elimination. The order you finish in will determine the starting order for phase two. You have until sundown. Failure to reach the top of the waterfall before dark will result in disqualification," Lord John explained, his hands clasped in front of him.

The steward was skilled at keeping his expression neutral. Many of the competitors were not. *Idiots.* They were whining about what the steward had told us; I was more concerned about what had been omitted and why we had almost twelve hours to complete the phase.

The old watchtower was a crumbling ruin about halfway between where we were standing and the edge of the lake. Initially, I had overlooked it because it was unremarkable. Clearly, King Leonard felt it was important. *Or some feature of it is.* Judging the overall distance we had to travel, if I was running it would take maybe two hours. *As a Fae, which I am not,* I sharply reminded myself. For a human, that would likely be four. I had found that with the pendant around my neck, I had lost some of my strength and energy levels. However, that still did not explain why we would need so much extra time. I shrugged. I would find out soon enough.

"Stand in line," Lord John ordered.

We assembled into a loose formation just behind a red line painted on the grass.

King Leonard approached us, mounted on a snow-white stallion. "Good luck in phase one," the king said solemnly, raising his hand high in the air. When he dropped it, a loud crack reverberated across the grounds. Half of the competitors shot off as though from a cannon. I jogged down the hill about one hundred yards before slowing to a walk. Ahead of me, Pierre lost his footing and slid haphazardly down the hill, hitting rocks along the way. *Ouch.* I winced in sympathy.

I wanted to win, but that did not mean I should be reckless or stupid. Sprinting when I had many hours till the deadline would only result in me draining my energy too fast, when I might need it later. My preference was to let the humans stumble into whatever challenges awaited us.

Twenty-One

SERAFINA

As I listened to Lord John announce the obstacle course, concern welled up within me. *The old watchtower—with its rotting floor and the mineshaft beneath it. The lake.* I shuddered at the memory of the year it had been drained and the thousands of human skeletons that had been found at the bottom.

No wonder they had called phase one an obstacle course. It was sure to put all twenty men to the test. Could they adapt to changing situations, or would they perish?

I turned away as Pierre rolled and slid down the hill. This whole competition was ridiculous.

"Serafina," Ghilanna whispered in my ear. I knew she was using magic. It would be dangerous for her to approach me here, especially with my grandfather so close. Thankfully, I had talked my grandfather into having a tent set up for me in case I began to feel unwell.

"Thomas, I need to lie down," I informed him, clutching my forehead and swaying in the saddle. His response was immediate. A twinge of guilt went through me for faking it, but it was the only way I'd be able to talk to Ghilanna.

Thomas helped me off the horse and guided me to the tent, then watched as I carefully lay down on the sofa and closed my eyes. I waited until I heard his footsteps retreat, then opened my eyes and sat up. The back canvas of the tent shimmered, and Ghilanna appeared. She placed a finger to her lips, then raised her hands, and white magic flowed out of them until we were surrounded by a faint bubble.

"They won't be able to hear us," Ghilanna said.

"Thank you," I replied, then rushed into what I wanted to say before Ghilanna could distract me with her news. "The headaches get really bad when I'm looking at Rhys, but go away when he touches me."

Ghilanna's eyebrows rose. "Rhys?"

"Yes, the human with shoulder-length black hair and a thick beard," I replied.

"Do you by chance recall his last name from the formal introductions?" Ghilanna asked.

I closed my eyes, trying to recall his introduction before I had fainted. "Rhys Mongan of Eagle Rock."

"Eagle Rock is part of the Lord of the West's kingdom," Ghilanna said.

I raised my eyebrows that she knew this when I did not. "Does it matter that he's from a different kingdom?"

Ghilanna shook her head. "Probably not. Other than not very many people here will know anything about him."

"I was under the impression that since the competition is a last resort to find a husband, there would be fewer well-known men entering. Otherwise, my grandfather would have invited them to meet me instead of having to rely on the competition to find them," I replied.

"Eagle Rock is not too far from the border shared with the Court of Dusk," Ghilanna muttered, though I was certain the words were thoughts spoken aloud and not directed at me. I failed to see why Eagle Rock being close to the Court of Dusk territory was an issue. All the human kingdoms shared borders with a Fae court.

"Sorry," Ghilanna said, meeting my gaze. "I'm still trying to figure out the connection between magic and your illness. Clearly, there is a Fae who harbors ill will toward you. I'm still leaning toward the possibility that it's Prince Tanyth, given he is rumored to use dark magic."

"No, he wouldn't do that," I said harshly. "We were engaged. He loved me."

Ghilanna stood up and paced. "While he might have loved you, you are no longer engaged. I was able to confirm that he did receive your letter and King Leonard's. He does not forgive easily. I would not put it past him to have a fail-safe that allows him to activate a spell should an unforeseen event occur, such as you breaking off the engagement."

I struggled to believe that Tanyth would stoop so low. *He loved me.*

"For as long as I can remember, I have known two things about Prince Tanyth. The first is that he *hates* humans. The second is that he wants King Pharaan's position as king of the Fae and has been searching for three magic objects that, if the prophecy is true, would grant him the power he needs to overthrow King Pharaan," Ghilanna explained patiently.

My fingers tightened in the folds of my skirt. "If Prince Tanyth hates humans as you say, then why the hell would he have agreed to marry me?" I stood up and paced. "Not only am I a half-human, I also *look* like a human." *How could I convince myself to love someone who hates what I am?* Fear worked its way through me as I comprehended how close I had been to marrying a lie.

"Precisely my point. Something is not right. Either he lied to you, or ..." Ghilanna said.

"Or he's the one who did the dark magic on me to influence my feelings for him," I finished. Silence filled the tent as we let the words settle over us and what it meant if Prince Tanyth had worked dark magic on me. *Could Tanyth also be tampering with the competition?*

I stood to pour myself a glass of water. As I sipped, tendrils of fear wove through me. *How much of what I remember of my engagement to Tanyth is real and how much is what he wants me to remember? Did he only alter my memories, or did he do other things as well, like get me pregnant? Can I even trust myself?*

Ghilanna spoke again, breaking through my thoughts as they spiraled darker. "There is another matter I wanted to discuss."

What now? I wasn't sure if I could handle another matter, especially not if it was on the scale of the previous one.

Ghilanna patted my hand and then spoke. "Your mother was able to establish camaraderie with hundreds of human families over the twenty years she lived in the city. They have been waiting for you to return, Serafina, and fulfill the promise she made to them. That one day you would be Lady of the South and would put an end to the hatred for non-humans and those who fraternize with them."

"How is that supposed to help me now? My grandfather will never cede his power to me until he takes his last breath. Perhaps if I were a man, he would consider it. But to a woman? And a half-blood at that? *Never.* While it is a relief to know I have supporters in the South, as long as King Leonard is alive, they are in danger of discovery. I would hate to see them make mistakes now that I am here, before it would be wise." My voice wavered.

"There are secrets known only to the Lord of the South and his direct heir. Secrets you will soon be privy to. Know this: Even if your grandfather hates Fae, his family has been entwined with them for centuries. He cannot change that," Ghilanna said.

"The South's secrets are tied to Fae." I gave a strangled laugh, though it sounded more like a choking sound. "There's no way."

Ghilanna shrugged. "You'll find out soon enough."

I heard a crunch of footsteps on gravel and shot Ghilanna a worried glance. "You need to go."

Ghilanna stood and kissed my cheek. "We will figure this all out. Remember, you're not alone."

I squeezed her hand and settled myself back on the couch, feet propped on the armrest. My stomach churned, and I sipped at the water, praying I could fight off very real nausea. *A dark spell has been cast on me, and there is a group of Fae-loving humans in the city.*

I had expected Thomas to enter the tent; instead, it was Violet. She curtsied to me. "Your Highness."

"Violet, it's good to see you. Are you enjoying watching phase one?" I asked politely.

Violet fiddled with the folds of her dress. "If I may be honest?"

I nodded. "Of course, and please sit."

Violet sat, then replied, "Now that the competitors have all made their way down the hill, it is quite difficult to see them. We can hear the rocks sliding and the occasional clang of a sword near the watchtower, and the screams of a large bird, but they're out of view."

I chuckled. *So much for entertaining our guests.* "I see. Have they tried moving to a different location for a better view?"

"That's the problem, there isn't really a better place. Or at least not one that has been deemed safe enough for the entire group," Violet admitted.

"Once they reach the lake, we should be able to see something," I replied.

"Are you feeling any better?" Violet asked.

I took a sip of my water, buying some time to decide my response. "A little. I'm still getting cramps, and that's making it uncomfortable to sit on a horse."

Violet gave me a sympathetic smile. "My mother had terrible cycles. I've been blessed with easy ones, but I'm familiar with the struggles. But ... can't you just use magic and make them go away?"

I sucked in a breath sharply, trying to keep my voice even. "I can't do magic."

Violet's eyes widened and her face paled. "I'm so sorry, Your Highness! I thought …"

"Yes, I know what you thought. But I can't do magic." I took another sip of my water, not sure what else to say.

The tension between us grew. I was relieved when Thomas stuck his head in the tent to announce most of the competitors were approaching the lake and it was time for us to move to the next viewing location.

Twenty-Two

TRISTAN

I drew my sword as I approached the edge of the watchtower ruins. Two of my opponents had entered the area and had yet to reappear farther down the hill. I was uncertain if that meant they had perished inside or were still working their way through. *It doesn't matter.*

Taking a deep breath, nostrils flaring, I recognized the metallic scent of a griffin den and the sharp tang of griffin blood. *Is this where Marek is hiding?* Callyn had never told me where she'd found the griffin rider. I crept through the crumbling archway, senses on alert. Prince Tanyth had had a bonded pair in his collection—a griffin and its rider. There were so few still alive. *Does King Leonard know what a treasure he has in his kingdom?* Sorrow filled me. Griffins, whether bonded with a Fae or a mated pair of their own species, were incredible to behold.

A skittering of rocks, followed by a high-pitched click. I whirled, sword raised. A large griffin with deep bronze-colored feathers and light-brown fur spattered in blood faced me, its molten gold eyes boring into mine. Its razor-sharp beak snapped in anger. Droplets of blood splattered my face.

"I don't want to harm you," I said calmly, sheathing my sword and raising my hands.

The griffin tilted its head to look at me but did not make a move to attack. I noticed a severed arm behind the griffin in a puddle of blood and briefly wondered where the rest of the man was, for I was certain the arm belonged to one of my opponents. My heart rate returned to its usual steady rhythm. A sharp needle poke, directly into the old wound from Dragonfang, sent me to my knees.

"What do you want, *traitor*?" the voice demanded.

I closed my eyes, old memories flooding me, and a tear trickled down my cheek. "Marek." Marek had made the pendant; it was no surprise he could see through the enchantment and recognized my Fae form.

"Give me one reason why I should allow you to live," Marek demanded, his blade pressing into my back deep enough to pierce the skin. I could feel the blood trickling into the waistband of my pants.

"I'm sorry," I whispered.

"You murdered her!" Marek snarled, shifting position so his blade was at my throat and I could at last see his face.

"I had no choice." I choked out the words, my throat dry.

"There is always a choice, Tristan. You could have refused. Instead, you murdered Iylane and collared Beck," Marek said in a cold voice.

I knew he was right. I could have refused, but at the time I had valued my life—and keeping my own secrets—more than Iylane's. I had no way of knowing what impact my refusal would have had on the situation. Marek had every right to be angry, and I would not fault him if he chose to take my life.

"Then kill me," I rasped.

Marek lowered his sword and moved around so he was standing in front of me. "You're bonded."

"How do you know that?" I asked incredulously. I couldn't feel Serafina. The king of Fae couldn't find evidence of the bond either. Yet a griffin rider could? Even through the magic of the pendant that was supposed to turn me into a human? *A pendant Marek helped cast the spell on.*

The griffin rubbed its head along Marek's shoulder. "Asteria can feel it. Just as she can feel your mate is among the spectators."

I rubbed a hand across the wound in my back, processing the new information. *Griffins can sense soulmate bonds. I wonder if Asteria can do magic too.* "You're right. My mate is up there. Her name is Serafina. But Prince Tanyth did something to her, to our bond, and it is not working as it was."

Marek gave me a thoughtful look. *I guess Callyn didn't give Marek much information.* "Your mate is the prize in this competition? How does it feel to know that she is within your grasp yet could be lost to you forever if you fail this human test?"

"It's almost unbearable. To make matters worse, she doesn't remember anything. It's as though we met for the first time when I made my intent to compete known," I replied, deciding I had nothing to lose by being honest.

"I cannot solve your problem. Or not the one you're about to ask me about … the issue of removing Prince Tanyth's magic and restoring your bond," Marek said. "However, I do have a suggestion. Treat it as though you do not have a history. Win her love again. Sometimes the way to break dark magic is a matter of the heart instead of finding the correct spell."

Marek's words were similar to what Callyn had already suggested.

I bowed my head. "Thank you." I stood up and gazed upon Marek and Asteria, wanting to offer them something in return. "Beck is alive. Or he was a few weeks ago when I was last at Dorcha Palace. I am no longer bound by my blood contract to do Prince Tanyth's bidding."

Marek gave me an unreadable look. "Yes, your blood contract is gone. Instead, you have something even worse. You've been marked by Dragonfang."

Not sure how to take Marek's opinion that being marked was a terrible thing, I responded with information I doubted Marek had, whispering, "Rethys is alive."

Marek's eyes burned even brighter. "The prophecy is true."

My breathing hitched, and I crossed my arms. "What prophecy?"

A spray of pebbles showered us. Marek ignored my question, concern flickering across his face as he shot a glance toward where the pebbles had come from. Then, he put his hand in the small of my back and propelled me forward. "Go. Around the bend. If you look behind the rock, there is a tunnel. It leads to our nest, but if you keep going it'll take you through the hillside and down close to the dock."

I followed Marek's directions, wondering what prophecy he was talking about. *We talked of being marked by Dragonfang and Rethys being alive.* It must have to do with those two things. I shook my head, promising myself to ask Callyn if she had her copy of *Bedtime Tails* when I returned to the inn tonight. Perhaps I would get lucky and it would contain the prophecy Marek was referring to.

Ducking to avoid hitting my head on the ceiling of the tunnel, I wound my way through the hillside, passing by the body the arm belonged to just past the nest. Unable to hear anything beyond the occasional cascade of pebbles and dripping water, I had no way to track the time. I wasn't sure how long I spoke to Marek, or how long I trekked through his tunnel down to the lake. I swallowed hard, thinking of Iylane. Like many of my shapeshifter kills I had done on Prince Tanyth's orders, she was one I still deeply regretted. There was nothing I could do to reverse their deaths, only strive to be a better Fae now that I was free of Prince Tanyth's influence. *Yet here*

I am, disguised as a human, behaving no better than I did under Tanyth's control.

My stomach knotted, and each step I took felt like weights were in my boots. *I can't do this. I need to tell Serafina the truth.* I stopped walking and turned, my hand on the pendant, ready to take it off and return to the king and Serafina, apologize for lying, and accept whatever punishment King Leonard saw fit.

I made it back to the nest just as Asteria was settling on top of it. The griffin stood up and hissed at me, snapping her beak, wings flaring. A high-pitched voice entered my thoughts. *"Stupid Fae."* It took me a moment to realize it was Asteria talking to me.

Blinking, I stared at her, unsure how to respond. *Do I ignore her and keep going back up to the king to announce my withdrawal from the competition?*

Asteria cocked her head and raised a paw, flashing her sharp black claws at me. *"Turn around and finish the competition. Stop trying to sabotage yourself."*

Cheeks burning, I averted my eyes from Asteria. "It's not that simple," I whispered.

Asteria charged me, snapping her razor-sharp beak dangerously close to my fingertips. *"This isn't just about you."*

My eyes snapped up. "What?"

Asteria fluttered her wings. *"We are mere pawns. Now go, before you ruin your chances because you run out of daylight."*

This time when she dove for my finger, she clamped down on it with her beak. Hissing in pain, I opened my mouth to say something, but she twisted and slammed into my back with her hip, shoving me down the tunnel. The uneven ground combined with the momentum of being pushed gave me no choice but to go forward. The tunnel became steep, almost too steep to walk down. I slowed my steps and used the narrow walls to brace to prevent my feet from sliding. Sniffing the air, I could smell the brackish lake water.

My calf muscles were tight with the strain of the steep slope, and relief coursed through me as the ground leveled out. One moment I was in shadows; the next, the lake water was lapping at my boots, the sunlight directly overhead making it difficult for my eyes to adjust. Asteria had been right about one thing. If I wanted to complete today's phase, I had no more time to waste, which meant I would have to ponder her words about us being pawns later.

A ripple in the water caught my attention. I stood immobile, watching as a shadow rose to the surface and large scales broke the water, followed by the tip of a broad snout and large reptilian eyes. The creature must have caught my scent, for it sped toward me.

I ran, not caring if I drew more attention to myself and my precise location. My feet skidded across mossy rocks that were just below the lake's surface and made it challenging to keep my footing. I knew with every fiber of my being that if I fell, this creature, whatever it was, would attack.

Just as I set my feet on dry ground, there was a loud roar. The animal launched itself into the air, snapping. It was huge, more than twenty feet long, with short legs, long claws, and a broad mouth filled with hundreds of tiny teeth. I could see bits of flesh caught in them. *Perhaps this beast is why the lake is one of the obstacles.*

Digging my heels into the ground, I sprinted for the dock, angling away from the edge of the lake, hoping that even though it had legs, it would not come after me on land. When I reached the dock, I halted and bent over, panting. Taking stock of myself, I noted that I still had all the belongings I had begun with—pack, sword, and dagger. Out in the water, I saw the beast swimming toward the two boats in the middle of the lake, their passengers oblivious to the danger.

While it's distracted, I should get my boat and rush to the other side. Moving quickly, I chose a boat from the five remaining and climbed aboard, then untied the rope and cast off. There were two oars fitted into loops of metal on either side of the boat, in line with the single bench.

The boat was small, just large enough for one adult human or Fae. It would not stand a chance against the lake beast. Wrapping my hands around the oars, I began rowing. Sticking to the edge of the lake would take longer, but I hoped it would not draw attention to me.

Thump.

A plank landed a few inches from my foot at the bottom of my boat.

"Help! Help! He—" The last scream was cut off. Closing my eyes briefly, I sent a prayer to the gods that the poor soul had a swift death. I had seen the beast's teeth and knew it was not a painless one.

I found my rhythm and sped up as fast as I dared go. The small boat did not seem to be very well made. Water began seeping into the bottom after about ten minutes, and the whole boat shuddered under the strain as I increased my speed, my human muscles protesting at how hard I was pushing.

I heard a huge splash to my left. Droplets of water landed on my arms and the back of my neck. Rowing momentarily forgotten, I turned my gaze to the churning, bloody water. A thud against the bottom of my boat drew me back to myself. *Hurry.* The water was the beast's domain. A sword might not be enough. The best chance of survival was to get to the end of the lake as fast as possible.

Exhaling slowly, I gripped the oars and dug in. *The boat will hold together*, I informed myself, *if I believe it will happen.* The alternative was unacceptable.

The thumping against the bottom of my boat stopped and was replaced by light scraping. I could barely believe my luck that I was at the end of the lake. Releasing my hold on the oars, I grabbed the rope and leaped out of the front of the boat and into the edge of the water. With one deft yank, I dragged the boat behind me and up the embankment. When I was certain it would not slip back into the lake, I dropped the rope and sprinted away. I could see the canyon ahead between the mountain and the lip of the tiered mine. The sun was well past its zenith, which meant if I wasn't careful, I ran the risk of losing simply because of the sunset deadline.

The canyon sloped downward before curving to the right. I had to weave around boulders and scraggly trees, but it was easy to keep the steady, ground-covering run I was accustomed to until I reached a pile of boulders three times my height that spanned the entire width of the canyon. I walked its span twice, hunting for a way through the boulders, before concluding the only option was up.

Spying handholds a foot out of my reach, I bunched my muscles and jumped straight up. My fingers scraped the stone, finding purchase in the small cracks I'd earmarked. I was careful to choose handholds that were accessible by my human body and not the longer distances I could normally manage. I quickly swung left to right until I gauged I had enough power to sail the distance to my next mark, and so it went until I was able to pull myself up to the top. Unlike the side I had just scaled, the other side was smooth, as though polished. The easiest way to get down was to jump.

One, two ... Before I could get to three, someone yanked my foot hard, and I tumbled forward off the boulders, catching a flash green as I saw my opponent balanced precariously on an almost invisible ledge about four feet below the top of the wall. At the last moment, I tucked into a roll, protecting my neck with my arms as I crashed into the hard granite. My breath left me in a whoosh. Gasping, I tried to orient myself and draw my dagger, but it wasn't at my waist. In fact, my scabbard was several feet away and out of my reach.

Slowly, I sat up. Whoever had attacked me was nowhere to be seen, except for a puff of dust up ahead. I grabbed my scabbard tightly and stood. There was a sticky feeling on my cheek. I buckled the scabbard around my waist before touching my fingers gingerly to my face. I was not surprised when they came back with blood. I eyed the top of the boulders; the drop was higher on this side than it had been on the other.

Urging myself to continue, I started my trek down the canyon at a walk. But time was of the essence. Sore from the fall, I made myself speed up until I was running again, albeit half my usual speed. Callyn had been right about the competition; it was not going to be easy.

I could hear the roar of the waterfall long before I was able to see it. I had not come across any of the humans since being yanked from the boulder and was unsure if that was a good or bad thing. *It doesn't matter. I only have an hour before I have exceeded the allotted time.*

As I rounded the corner, the pounding of water was deafening. The waterfall was unexpectedly massive. The pool it fed into was lined with large rocks like the ones I had seen throughout the canyon. *Maybe this is not usually a canyon, but a river from here to the lake*, I mused. There was no obvious path from the canyon floor to the top of the waterfall. The canyon walls were smooth and far too high for me to scale without magic. Which left climbing the rocks on the face of the waterfall. They were slick with water, and I could see hints of moss.

This is the task. If I want to be with Serafina again, there is only one way out of here, and that is up. Determined to finish within the allotted time, I skirted the pool of water until I reached the shortest distance I would have to swim.

Plunging into the pool, I was surprised that the water was warm. I had expected it to be icy. *Focus.* I swam to the rocks and scanned the lowest one for the start of my route. There were several options. I chose the one that had several flat rock platforms, deciding that being able to pause the climb would be better than going straight up.

When I reached the second platform, I tugged my canteen out of the pack and took a swig, then nibbled on some dried venison. There was a whizzing sound, I twisted slightly, and an arrow clattered onto the platform. More arrows came rapidly. Cursing under my breath, I slung my pack over my shoulder and climbed as fast as I could, dodging arrows to the best of my ability.

My arm and cheek stung from grazes when I hadn't been fast enough to get out of the way. I passed the next platform without stopping and the arrows ceased. Panting, I clung to my perch with my fingers and the edge of my boots. *Something on the platform must be the trigger.*

Gritting my teeth, I continued my upward climb. *Don't stop on the platform*, I reminded myself as I passed yet another one. Not that I had time to rest. The sun was setting.

Soaked from head to toe, wet clothes clinging uncomfortably to me, I dragged myself over the edge at the top of the waterfall.

"Congratulations! You have completed phase one," King Leonard said from a few feet away.

I peered up at him, surprised he was personally telling me that. His attention on me didn't last long before he turned to the guests and my opponents. He spoke in a voice that carried. "This marks the conclusion of phase one. There are now fourteen of you going into phase two tomorrow."

I took my time to move over to the rest of the group. The trial was at an end, and I was not inclined to rush, nor did my exact location seem to affect the king's choice to speak.

King Leonard continued, "Phase two is a foot race. You are not permitted to bring weapons, though you can have a pack with a canteen and food should you choose to bring one. There will be a day of rest between phases two and three."

The king walked away, his guards closing in and blocking him from view.

Lord John stood in front of us, his gaze moving down the line. "Those of you who remain are dismissed. We will once again meet at the palace entrance at sunrise."

I was tired, scanning the faces of the other competitors. Some looked far worse than I felt, and two appeared unscathed, as though they had not exerted themselves at all today. *Or they just changed clothes.* Either way, it was no concern of mine. I had completed phase one and needed to focus on phase two. I noted neither Lord John nor King Leonard had mentioned how the foot race would be judged—if it was based on meeting a certain time, surviving, or some other specific criteria. *I will have to find out tomorrow.*

When it was clear that the steward had no other information for us, I made my way back up the hill. I could see the palace in the distance, and it was not too difficult to pick out the road, even in the dwindling light.

Twenty-Three

SERAFINA

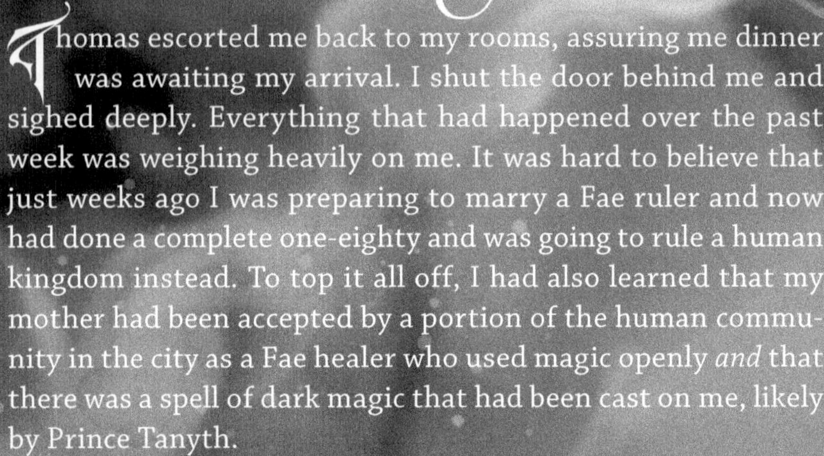

Thomas escorted me back to my rooms, assuring me dinner was awaiting my arrival. I shut the door behind me and sighed deeply. Everything that had happened over the past week was weighing heavily on me. It was hard to believe that just weeks ago I was preparing to marry a Fae ruler and now had done a complete one-eighty and was going to rule a human kingdom instead. To top it all off, I had also learned that my mother had been accepted by a portion of the human community in the city as a Fae healer who used magic openly *and* that there was a spell of dark magic that had been cast on me, likely by Prince Tanyth.

I sat down at the table, with tears trickling down my face. *I wish you were here, Mother.* For the first time in many years, I felt lost. Everyone wanted something from me, but I hadn't given myself a chance to figure out what it was that *I* wanted. As I wiped my eyes, I noticed a piece of paper tucked under the silver tray of food.

Swiping at the tears, I snagged the paper off the table. My name was written in a familiar hand. With shaky fingers, I unfolded the letter.

To my beloved daughter, Serafina,

In the thirty years your mother and I were together, there was always one thing she was certain about. That no matter how much neither one of us wanted the responsibility of heir to fall on your shoulders, one day it would. We vowed that you would grow up among friends and family who loved you dearly so that you would learn to value others not because of a title they might hold or a particular way they looked, but because of the individual they are.

Being a lord or lady does not make you a good person. In fact, many let the power created by their position go to their heads. Though you likely did not know, your mother was a seer. As I'm sure you have discovered, the Fae have many prophecies. Most never come to pass, but some do. You, my dearest, happen to be the subject of several. I imagine it is due to your mixed heritage and the potential you possess that would allow you to unite Fae and humans in a way that has never been accomplished before. Take courage that you are equipped with the skills needed to succeed and will have friends to help you along the way. The years you spent with us and then the years you will spend with the Fae are equally important. As is the time you will be lost.

The pages fluttered to the floor. "He knew this outcome was

likely … yet they led me to believe that we would always be together as a family, *forever*."

Curiosity finally got the better of me, and I scooped up the pages to continue reading.

As you take your place as the heir of the South, you will learn the family secrets that my father desperately wants to bury. There is a book. You are the key. Be brave and know that you are never alone. Your mother and I are always in your heart. Just close your eyes.

Love always,
Your father, Gareth Helias

Tears streamed down my face. *Who brought this letter?* The timing was impeccable. Though given the words my father had written, I knew it had to have been planned. *Perhaps another one of Mother's visions.*

It was unnerving to think that there was not only one Fae prophecy about me, but multiple. I thought I had packed my book of *Bedtime Tails* when I left Jade Wilds. Now would be a good time to review it. I wasn't sure if I would be able to identify which stories might be about me, but it was a place to start.

Will the knowledge I gain add to my confusion or help solve it? My father also stated I would be lost. I was unsure if he was referring to the dark magic plaguing me at this precise moment or when I had been betrothed to Prince Tanyth.

I dug through the trunk of belongings and found the book at the bottom. Tucking it under my arm, I decided to peruse it while eating my dinner.

Heaping plate in front of me, I studied the cover of the book. The S was a gray tail with black spots on it. *Like the snow leopard in my dream*. Intrigued, I opened the book to the first story and sighed at the sight of the familiar title: "The Lost Fae Queen."

The title page featured an illustration of the Fae Queen in full plate armor and a helmet adorned with a crown set with emeralds. In her left hand was an old book with metal corners and in her right hand a gigantic sword. A cloud of darkness rose behind her.

When tension rises and war with the humans has come, the
Lost Fae Queen will return.
First, she will prove her battle prowess.
Look closely or you might be blinded, for when the Fae Queen
returns, not all will know her, yet everyone will follow her.

The illustration on the second page was of a snow leopard prowling.

Be warned, the Fae Queen must stay pure until the Great Cat
finds her and their souls unite.
With their souls bound, the heir will be found.

The story concluded on the final page.

The Fae Queen's magic will return and together they will
defend the Fae from the end of time.
Time is of the essence, or the Fae will fall to the darkness.

The final illustration was of the Fae Queen side by side with a snarling snow leopard with piercing blue eyes and swirls of vibrant green and gray magic surrounding both.

My hand froze as I peered at the image. The snow leopard felt familiar, as though I might know it. *Ridiculous. I have never seen a snow leopard in person.* I took a bite of stew and flipped to the next page.

An illustration of a dark green dragon named Rethys was there. Eyes wide, I realized I had heard the name Rethys somewhere. As I focused on when that would have been, a piercing headache arose behind my eyes. Shutting the book, I set down the last bite of stew and took a long drink of water, hoping the headache would go away as quickly as it came.

When the glass was almost empty, the headache had faded enough that I was confident I could once again focus on the book.

The book opened without me touching it and stopped on a page at the very end. *Strange.* The first illustration showed a sword peeling the skin from a human's face, revealing the skull beneath. I shuddered in revulsion. *What a horrible drawing to include in a book for children.*

The second illustration was of a beautiful dagger with a handle in the shape of a dragon's head with green eyes. *Dragonfang.*

My eyes widened in recognition. I knew with certainty I had seen this dagger before, when King Pharaan had taken me to the emerald mine. *The dagger appeared when I touched the emerald worktable.* Making the connection between the strange event at the emerald mine and this story left me with many questions. I hoped Ghilanna would have the answers.

Returning my attention to the book, I noted that the poem was short.

> *Become one with flesh*
> *Summon the dragon with his fang*
> *Bloodsong sang with glee*
> *The one who can tame the three*
> *Can maim all foes against thee.*

The third drawing was of a worn book with heavy gold decoration on it and what looked like blood seeping from the pages. *Bloodsong Grimoire.*

My eyes flicked back to the letter sitting on the sofa. *The letter mentioned a book.* I shook my head. There was no way the book my father referred to was mentioned in this story. There were many books at my grandfather's palace. Even if the *Bloodsong Grimoire* were real, why would a Fae-hating human have a Fae book?

So far, all reading *Bedtime Tails* had accomplished was raising more questions and causing me to feel unwell. I stabbed a piece of sausage and shoved it in my mouth. The flavors were intense—garlic, pepper, and chili flakes. *I'll finish eating and then sleep. I'd rather not get sick enough to need another sleeping draught if I can avoid it.*

Twenty-Four

TRISTAN

Upon my return to Wayside Inn, I paid to use one of the private bathrooms, wanting a hot soak for my sore muscles. Instead of looking for Callyn, I went straight to the private bathroom. Steam wafted from the large metal tub. I shed my wet clothing in a heap and eagerly stepped into the bath.

The water was deliciously hot. I sank beneath it, running my hands through my hair before emerging. A contented sigh escaped my lips as I leaned back, closing my eyes. *One down, two to go.*

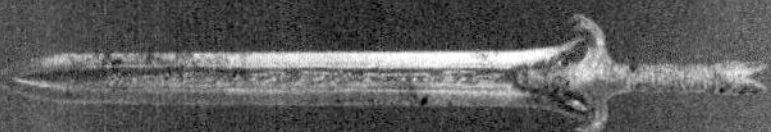

I woke up with a start and fell off the bed. "Oof."

Callyn stirred, and I felt bad when I realized it was in the wee hours of the morning, waking her earlier than necessary. Deciding to leave the room dark in the hopes my friend would go back to sleep, I quietly began my stretches, the exact same routine I had gone through yesterday morning.

I anticipated as the second phase, the number of competitors eliminated in the foot race would be higher. I doubted they wanted the final phase to have most of us still participating.

I was starting the pushups when Callyn threw off the covers and sent small balls of Fae light around the room. "I figured out who the Fae I have been sensing is," she announced.

I kept going, assuming she would tell me without needing to be prompted.

"Her name is Ghilanna Qira. She is one of Serafina's best friends. They met twelve years ago when Serafina started training at Jade Wilds," Callyn shared with me. The surname Qira felt familiar, though I couldn't quite place where I'd heard it before. It was not a name that originated in the Court of Dusk.

"Ghilanna's mother is Cithrel Qira, niece to Prince Almar Vacaryn," Callyn added.

Leave it to her to anticipate my next question. I licked my lips, trying to wrap my thoughts around a relative to the ruler of the Court of the Moon being entwined with Serafina. A line from the Lost Fae Queen prophecy came to mind: "Not all will know her, yet everyone will follow her."

"What is Ghilanna doing here?" I asked.

Callyn rolled her eyes. "I would think it's obvious. Her best friend is now heir of the South. What reason would Ghilanna have *not* to be here?"

She had a point. Ghilanna's reasons for being here were the same as Callyn's. I stood, exercises momentarily forgotten. "We know she is unwelcome in the palace, which means seeing Serafina would be complicated."

"Since you have been cavorting around as Rhys Mongan, you likely haven't noticed, but not all areas of Gaskal care about Fae. There have been a few times when I have strolled down a street with my features visible, and no one confronted me saying I didn't belong. If anything, I would've sworn some went out of their way to greet me once they knew I was Fae."

Very odd.

"Perhaps that is another reason she is here, because she has a foothold in the city already," I said. "There is no rule that states every citizen of the South shares King Leonard's feelings about Fae. Think about it. I didn't hate shapeshifters, but I was ordered to hunt and kill them by Prince Tanyth. It would be reasonable to assume the people here might be under similar pressure, where their true feelings must stay secret."

"Fine, say you are right. How does that help us?" Callyn demanded.

"In the immediate time frame, It doesn't," I replied. *The citizens of the South might be more amenable to the idea of their queen having a Fae consort than I expected.* I swallowed hard. *If Serafina will forgive me for deceiving her.*

My stomach gurgled, disrupting my thoughts.

"You're almost out of time. Do you have everything you need in your pack? No weapons today," Callyn reminded me.

"Yes, the pack is ready," I replied, tugging a fresh dark-blue tunic over my head and quickly lacing up a pair of tan pants, then settling the pack on my shoulders. There was a puff of purple magic and then Callyn offered me a wrap. By scent, I could tell it contained eggs, potatoes, and venison. I could eat while we walked.

Callyn had a wrap in her hand as well, and we briskly made our way from Wayside Inn to the palace gates. The exercises combined with our fast trek here did exactly what I had hoped: I was now warmed up for the foot race.

When we arrived, Lord John was standing next to a large canvas. The canvas appeared to have a map of the race. From the back of the group, I had to guess what the map said. It seemed like the race would start with us running up to the wall and racing its entire length before returning to ground level and continuing around the lower perimeter.

Lord John coughed to get our attention. "Welcome to phase two! Today is the foot race. The map beside me is your route. You will complete five laps. The top six fastest will advance to phase three. Any placing lower than sixth is disqualified."

Five laps, I mused. From my visits, I knew the palace wall spanned the entire perimeter of the building. Because we would be racing on both levels, we would have to go up and down the stairs each lap.

Today, the nobles were sitting on a large platform that must have been erected in the middle of the night. It provided them with a view of the wall on this side of the palace, though they would not be able to witness the entire race. I doubted it would be possible to see the entire race from one location, unless one went to the highest tower in the palace. It made sense that the king would have wanted his guests to see the beginning and end of the race. The location's platform guaranteed that much.

"Follow me," Lord John ordered. The fourteen of us followed him in a disorganized group. *I guess humans tend to not fall into a line unless explicitly told to.*

The beginning of the race was at the base of the staircase to get to the top of the wall. We halted a few feet from it. "The order you begin depends on the order you finished yesterday. Number one and two," Lord John said motioning for them to come closer. "On my count, you will start."

A light-haired human who looked barely old enough to shave spoke. "How much time between the groups?" I had to give the kid credit; it was a smart question.

"Thirty seconds. Now, ready … One! Two! Three!" Lord John's arm came down and the light-haired young man and a man with a red beard made their way up the stairs. True to his word, at thirty-second intervals, the steward sent everyone up in pairs. As the last to finish phase one, I was starting a full three minutes behind the first pair.

Lord John dropped his arm, and I ran up the stairs, taking them two at a time. I reached the top and took off as fast as I could. I passed three more competitors, which put me in eleventh place. Raising my speed just a hair, I settled into a steady pace.

A quick glance over my shoulder and I realized we were now out of view of the platform. Guards were posted every fifty feet or so, otherwise the top of the wall was void of traffic.

By the time I reached the stairs going down, I had passed one other competitor and was now sitting in tenth place, halfway through the first lap. At this point in the race, anything could happen. I slowed my pace going down the stairs after almost slipping on the first step. I hadn't realized it was wet and set my foot on it.

As I reached the bottom, I saw Pierre sitting to the side, clutching his head. Blood trickled from a gash in his forehead. Grimacing in sympathy, I made myself keep going. If the wound was serious, he would be tended to. *And eliminated.*

There were either posts and ropes or colorful flags marking the course. The route was not straight as I had assumed. We wove around barracks, the palace blacksmith, stables, and other buildings that were critical to the palace. My pace slowed more as the path narrowed and I had to squeeze between two buildings. Then, the path widened again.

Ahead, I could hear the cheers of the nobles. *The leaders must have just started their second lap.*

Twenty-Five

SERAFINA

I was being followed in the forest. I thought it was the snow leopard, but every time I tried to catch a glimpse of it, it was gone. My destination was just ahead. From here, I could make out the shape of the stone pedestal and the shaft of light that streamed down on it.

An abundance of caution kept me from rushing to the pedestal to inspect the object sitting on it. Instead, I hovered at the edge of the small clearing. To my surprise, the snow leopard sat down on the opposite side. I could see its fur rippling in the slight breeze and was certain it was real, not just a shadow.

When the snow leopard did not make a move toward me, I gathered my courage and closed the distance between myself and the stone pedestal. The shaft of light had made it difficult to make out what was on the pedestal from a distance, but now, with my hands resting lightly on the edge of the stone, it was quite clear it was an old book. The cover looked like some sort of leather, and there were brown stains on it and on the edge of the pages.

Just as I set my hand on the book, the forest became unbearably bright.

"Serafina! The race has already begun. We must hurry." Violet's worried voice came from the other side of the bed.

Reluctantly, I extracted myself from the cocoon of covers. I wasn't particularly interested in watching the foot race today, though I knew I should. The cramps were finally starting to subside. With another day of rest, they might go away altogether. However, the king had told me my presence would keep the prize visible, encouraging the competitors to try harder.

"How are you feeling this morning, Your Highness?" Violet asked as she poured a cup of tea for me. Mary was bustling around the room.

"A little better. Having the tent to rest in yesterday helped tremendously. Will we need to make similar arrangements for today?" Just like the competitors, I had not been privy to any of the details for the competition.

Violet shook her head, her carefully curled ringlets dancing around her face. "No. The race is short. A few hours at most. Which is why we must hurry. The king will be displeased if you're not there to see who will be advancing to phase three. Besides, don't you want to see them running?" Violet asked, voice quivering with excitement.

I sighed and took a few sips of my tea, then nibbled on a biscuit. I had seen enough males running during my training at Jade Wilds to know it was not terribly impressive. I didn't want to quench Violet's excitement though. *There's no rule that says we have to like the same things.* "Honestly, I'd prefer to be racing with them," I replied.

Violet coughed on her tea. "Really?"

I nodded. "Yes. I did train for twelve years. I'm sure I'm more fit than half of them at least."

"You want to run with men?" Violet said.

For a woman who trained horses—a man's job—I was surprised that running with men was something she was hung up on. *Unless she is still too caught up in the need for women to do certain things separately.* "When I train, I don't pay much attention to gender. We're all the same, trainees or warriors. We want to be the best."

"Even when you're having your monthly cycle?" Violet asked hesitantly, as though she expected a reprimand for the question.

I wondered if Mary had been doing exactly that when they were together—reprimanding Violet for asking questions that a palace maid would consider inappropriate conversation to have with a princess.

I took a deep breath, then replied, "Enemies do not wait to attack on your terms. Monthly cycles, broken limbs, it doesn't make a difference. If you're not ready to defend in any situation, then you're at a disadvantage. To answer your question, yes, if I were given orders to run with the men today, I would do it."

"Your clothes are ready," Mary called, a welcome interruption. I could tell I wasn't going to make any progress in the conversation with Violet other than increasing my annoyance. *Maybe if she would finally agree to let me train her a little bit, she would warm up more to the idea of women having the same roles as men.*

I stood up and gazed at where she had laid the dress on the bed. A bright-purple gown, with frothy lace at the sleeves and collar. I wrinkled my nose in distaste. "There isn't anything else I can wear?"

Mary tutted. "No. If you had woken up early, then perhaps I could have found another suitable dress. But we're running late. This is what you are wearing."

Cramming the biscuit into my mouth, I moved into the open area of the room where they liked to dress me and pulled my nightshirt off. Mary handed me the paper-thin undergarments. I slipped them on and stood in a wide stance, waiting for the petticoat, the middle layer, and then the corset.

Mary's haste was impressive. Apparently, my maid was concerned about angering the king. A small part of me felt bad about sleeping in, while the other part pointed out that it was the maid's duty to ensure I was ready on time, and she had failed to wake me up sooner.

I heard a quick series of knocks on the door, then it opened.

"Are you ready?" demanded Thomas.

"Yes!" I replied.

"Hurry, the race is almost over. The top three have just reached the bottom of the stairs," Thomas replied.

Linking my arm through his, we ran down the hallway, dodging servants who were carrying trays laden with food to an unknown destination. We finally emerged through one of the side doors; ahead, I saw the raised platform adorned with ribbons and large swathes of fabric. Our steps slowed as we went up the stairs, not wanting to appear in a rush to the courtiers. Thomas shoved me into my seat next to my grandfather just as the competitors came into view.

Three of them were running almost stride-for-stride as they barreled toward the finish line. My grandfather murmured to me, "The top six will move on."

Dipping my head to indicate I had heard, I gazed beyond the three. Frederick Hunter was next. He was also sprinting for all he was worth, though there was no one immediately behind him.

A tall, broad figure—I knew immediately it was Rhys—was in fifth. His stride was effortless compared to the others. If Rhys had gone through knight training at Eagle Rock, this race should have been easy for him. *Then why is he not first?* Nibbling on my lip, the answer came to me. This was still only the second phase. Why expend the energy to win the race when the third phase was the only phase where coming in first place meant winning the competition? The strategy was smart. Rhys must have felt my gaze on him, for his eyes met mine. I half rose in my seat, intending to wave my scarf at him, when the platform tilted sideways and I fell to my knees, clutching my head. Intense pain rolled through me.

Cool hands touched my forehead. "Serafina." My grandfather crouched next to me. I sucked in a short breath through my teeth, willing my body to cooperate and the pain to subside enough to open my eyes.

"Grandfather," I whispered, slowly opening my eyes. Our gazes met.

"Since you have arrived, you have been unwell. It pains me to see you this way. What can I do?" my grandfather asked. Once again, the words were kind, but the tone was harsh, as though he blamed me for the illness.

The timing of the conversation was awkward, and I wasn't entirely sure if my grandfather wanted the truth. "Dark magic is making me sick," I whispered.

The king's face turned mottled red, and his eyes darkened in anger. "I see. Well for now, if you think you are able, we must greet the top six who will be advancing to the final phase." He stared at me, daring me not to get up.

Unwelcome tears trickled down my face. I wasn't sure I could stand. Thomas pushed his way through the guests until he was in front of me. He crouched down and offered me his hand. I took it and slowly managed to stand. I wobbled as I adjusted to being upright, taking shallow breaths and praying the headache would ebb away.

Upon the conclusion of the royal congratulations to the winners advancing to phase three, the skies opened, and huge drops of rain fell. Shrieks of noblewomen, concerned about ruining their dresses, grated my ears. The king's guards swept around him and whisked him out of the bad weather and back into the palace. Thomas and a few other guards surrounded me, and we made our way into the hallway where my rooms were. Before we reached the door, I halted and turned to Thomas. The king's anger when I revealed dark magic could be making me sick had gotten under my skin. Now that the headache was gone, I needed an outlet for my own pent-up frustration.

"Find me a room I can practice in. Better yet, find me a willing partner. *And* I'll need to borrow a sword." My tone was firm. I did not want to debate my request. I wanted him to make it happen. If everything my grandfather said was true, then Thomas and the other guards should have instructions to follow my orders as well as my grandfather's. My title of heir made me the second-highest-ranking individual in the kingdom. My patience for being ordered to stay in my room or only practice weapons in certain areas was gone.

Thomas gave me a concerned look, then sent two of the guards on the errand to find a suitable room. "We will let you know when they return and the room is ready. For the time being," he said with a pointed look at my dress, "I'm assuming you want to change?"

"Is that a challenge? Do you not think I am capable of fighting in a dress?" I demanded testily.

Thomas raised his hands defensively. "I am not doubting your skill with a sword, Your Highness. Merely assuming you would be more comfortable in your usual practice attire of tunic and pants, and noting that there is sufficient time for you to change if you would like."

"Thank you for the consideration," I said softly, then entered my room.

Twenty-Six

TRISTAN

Large raindrops pelted my shoulders and head, obscuring the visibility. Everyone else had bolted for shelter. My tunic was plastered to my back, and my hair that had escaped its tie was now stuck on my jaw. Had I also bolted, there was a small chance I'd have stayed drier, but at this point, seeking shelter was pointless until I knew what I was doing. It was tempting to return to Wayside Inn to find a dry set of clothes, since the pendant prevented my magic from working.

Clearly, no other activities are scheduled for today, which means I can do as I please. Though most of us were staying in the city, other than not being assigned a room for an overnight stay in the palace, there had been no indication that we were unwelcome to linger there.

Shoulders back, chin up, I walked confidently past the guards. They made no move to prevent my entrance, cementing my assumption that I was welcome to loiter if I wanted to. I could hear the king's voice and laughter coming from a room down the hallway to the left. I veered to the right, in the direction I knew Serafina's rooms to be. I was not naïve enough to believe I could just waltz up to her rooms.

From the time we had spent together in Dorcha Palace, I knew that Serafina enjoyed training as much as I did. I did not believe for one second that King Leonard would be able to prevent her from practicing. It would be like denying her food or water. Wishing I had magic to dry myself, I wandered down the hallway, opening doors until I came across a small closet with a stack of towels. I took two, and between the towels and wringing out the fabric, I dried my clothes as best I could manage. *It'll have to do.*

As I dried myself, I could hear the faint sound of metal striking metal. *Likely swords.* I knew it could be anyone practicing. The guards had to hone their abilities to be able to adequately protect the royal family and the residents of the palace.

I'll see who it is. Maybe I'll find Serafina on the way. Decision made, I strolled through hallway after hallway, past centuries-old suits of armor, paintings of every Lord of the South for the last five hundred years, statues, and the occasional vase. I was surprised how few people were roaming the hallways here, allowing me to penetrate deep into the heart of the palace without anyone questioning me. A stark contrast to Dorcha Palace, where the guards were on a frequent patrol schedule.

The sound of swords clashing was just behind the next set of doors. Gently, so as not to alarm whoever was inside, I opened the door. To my delight, I found Serafina. I stepped inside and let the door close silently behind me, content to observe.

The first thing I noted was that Serafina had changed out of the gaudy purple dress from spectating the race into appropriate training clothes. Black leather pants that were thin enough to see the subtle definition of her leg muscles, short black boots, and a black tunic with the sleeves cut off, leaving her tanned arms bare. Sweat glistened on her forehead and biceps. Tendrils of her russet hair had escaped the braid and stuck to her face and cheeks.

The guard she faced had black hair with threads of gray. His wore a white tunic that clung damply to his chest, pants with heavy leather leg guards, and metal-toed boots. I grimaced in sympathy, knowing quite well how hot the leg guards could get. The guard had wisely discarded the leather breastplate and chain mail tunic near the table, where two other guards were playing a card hand. I briefly wondered how long they had been sparring.

Serafina noticed me first. She lowered her sword and skipped to the side as the guard thrust his. If she hadn't moved out of the way, she would have been stabbed in the stomach.

"Your Highness. Please forgive me." The guard's voice shook, though I couldn't tell if it was from fear that he had almost killed his princess or from the physical exertion of sparring with her.

I stepped out of the shadows of the door, bowing deeply. "Your Highness, I did not mean to intrude."

She glanced at me, then away quickly. In our previous meetings, she had met my gaze. *What changed?* Then I remembered her illness. She couldn't look at me because we weren't touching, and with the guard watching my every move, it would likely be taken as a threat if I were to reach out to touch her now, especially without an invitation.

Keeping her eyes averted from mine, she spoke. It took me a moment before I realized her words were directed at me, not the guard. "How is your skill with a sword? I didn't have a chance to see you spar at the luncheon." She spun her sword in her hand. "Do you have the guts to spar with me?" Her eyes met mine for the briefest moment in challenge before they slid away again.

The lack of eye contact was unnerving. I swallowed. She had offered me a chance to spar with her. It was the exact opportunity I had been hoping for, so why was I hesitating? "It would be my pleasure to spar with you, Your Highness," I replied with another bow.

The guard gestured for me to take the floor; his relief was palpable. I set my pack down and unsheathed my sword. Holding it loosely in my left hand, I used my right to unbuckle the scabbard and laid it on top of my pack.

Approaching the center of the room, I raised my sword, feet spread to give me the most maneuverability. Serafina's sword lightly brushed mine. "One, two … three."

Instead of striking first, she twirled to the left. I followed with a high strike. Serafina parried, sending bright orange sparks into the air as our blades slid together.

Ignoring the tingling as a few landed on my skin, I stepped to the left, then initiated a middle-low combination. Serafina pressed close, feinting a parry, before swiping her sword to her left and jabbing in the middle through my guard. I felt the tip of the sword scratch my abdomen before she yanked it back, eyeing me.

Rolling my shoulders, I darted toward her with a low feint followed by a high strike. She barely got her sword up in time and gave up several steps as I pressed down on her sword. Just as I was about to let up, she slipped away, freeing her sword and coming up behind me.

"I thought knights were supposed to be fast," she taunted.

"We are," I replied.

"Not today!" She smirked and launched into a fast combination. Her footwork was nearly perfect. I was so distracted by how her body was moving that I almost didn't get my sword up in time to block her thrust to my groin.

There were moments when Serafina's stride would waver. No matter how long we sparred, I could not figure out what was causing it. She still would not meet my gaze, and I found myself wishing she would.

She darted to the side in a low feint followed by a high strike. I blocked and twisted to the left, chopping down toward Serafina's shoulder. Realizing my mistake, I pulled back on the sword but was unable to halt my momentum. Serafina ducked under my arm and sliced across the leather covering my hamstring. I bit my lip, fighting the reflex to snap my foot back into a kick.

The guards might tolerate a sparring match, but if I were to hurt her, that would be an entirely different story.

Strength sapped from the morning race, I had to concede we were very closely matched. *Would that be any different if we both were at full strength?* I didn't know the answer since at Dorcha Palace, she had been constantly training or forced to fight in the arena with minimal opportunities to rest. I had no idea how her days were scheduled during her time among the humans. I doubted it involved days full of training.

Sweat trickled down my back. I lost track of how much time was passing. The guards did not seem inclined to make us stop. *However long she wants to spar for,* I told myself.

Watching Serafina's movements, I thought she was getting tired, or at least getting close to the end of her pent-up energy. Her tunic adhered to her breasts, leaving very little to the imagination. My fingers twitched as I remembered how it felt to have them under my hands. Smooth like silk.

Our swords clashed together, and I almost dropped mine. Blowing out a breath, I reminded myself to focus, forcing my eyes to Serafina's face, not her chest. Her sword whistled through the air, and I reacted in time. At the last moment, she dipped her wrist, and my sword popped out of my hand and sailed through the air.

I couldn't help it. I burst out laughing. I was the exact same move I had used on Serafina when she had been distracted. *Serves me right.*

Giving me a quizzical look, she leveled both weapons at me, our eyes finally meeting.

Her lips parted, I took a half step forward, and her face crumpled in pain. She dropped the swords and fell to her knees.

"Serafina!" I gasped, dropping to my knees and gathering her in my arms. The guards shouted, but I didn't care. *"My love, what is wrong?"* I said softly into her mind along the bond. Silence met my words; the threads of our bond were still dull.

She stirred in my hold and cautiously peered up at me. I kept my hands on her, unwilling to let go. "What happened? Is it … ?" I didn't want to ask about her illness with her guards so close. Thomas seemed trustworthy, but I wasn't sure about the others.

The guards hovered nervously in a tight circle around us. Serafina's blue-green eyes searched mine. I could only hope she found the answers she sought. "Your touch helps," she whispered.

My eyes widened at her admission, but the guards didn't react. She had seemed so much like her old self when we sparred that I had almost forgotten her condition. *Hadn't Marek said something … I reviewed my memory of that conversation but was drawing a blank.* Lips by her ear for fear the guards would overhear me, I said, "I'm sorry my presence causes you pain."

"Not your fault," Serafina mumbled against my chest. Worry flooded my thoughts. She was confirming what I had already known, which posed a significant challenge for me. *This is bad.* I could not maintain physical contact with her. Or at least not forever. I might be able to manage it for the remainder of the day, depending on what her guards had to say about it.

"We could try hand-to-hand combat," I suggested.

Though I wouldn't be holding her hand, without the swords between us we'd be in almost constant contact throughout the entire bout.

"Sure," she replied. "But first, let's get some water."

Twenty-Seven

SERAFINA

Knowing it would be taken the wrong way if I continued to hold Rhys's hand on the way to the refreshment table. I walked beside him but was careful not to look at him too long for fear of the headache returning.

I was tired, but in a refreshing way—from pushing my body to the limits of its training. I am not sure why I had accepted Rhys's offer of switching to hand-to-hand combat when I should have declined. *I'll just have to see how it goes and try my best to not make a fool of myself.*

Thankfully, neither Thomas nor the other two guards had protested at the prolonged sparring session Rhys and I had engaged in. When my heart rate had returned to normal, I moved back toward the center of the room. I could hear Rhys's steps confirming he was just an arm's length behind me.

With my eyes trained on his shoulder, I set up—fists raised, balancing lightly on the balls of my feet. Controlling my breathing until it was steady, I reviewed hand-to-hand combat maneuvers in my mind. There were a few new ones that Commander Meriel had taught me when Ghilanna and I worked on my stealth skills before I arrived in Gaskal.

"One, two, three!" I did a right, then left jab at Rhys's middle and ducked to the side as he returned the favor, except his punches were aimed at my upper torso. Bobbing and weaving, we used almost the entire room.

I yawned. Rhys took the opening to execute a series of six right-left jabs at my stomach. Not to be taken advantage of so easily, I ducked and rolled, popping up behind him, leading with a left hook, then a right jab aimed at his kidneys. Rhys spun and covered my fist with his hand, preventing me from completing the move. I pulled away, expecting him to let go, but he wouldn't. His expression was intense, but I could not sense any malice in him. I jerked my arm backward, and he released my fist. I stumbled a few steps, then regained my balance.

We circled, appraising each other.

I lunged low with a right-left, then an uppercut, then pivoted and thrust back with my elbow.

"Oof." Rhys grunted as my elbow jabbed him in the gut.

Not wanting to lose my momentum by gloating over the small victory, I skipped to the side as Rhys's fist sailed past my jaw.

On and on it went. Our pace slowed as our breathing became more ragged. Debating if I should call it quits, I decided to do a few more punches and kicks, just for fun.

I backed up a few steps, then sprinted toward him. Right hook, left hook, jab, jab, right hook, and I sank to the floor, rolling behind him. Surprised feinting worked a second time, I leaped up. Confirming I had enough space, I pulled my left leg in toward me and spun with a kick, aiming for his kidneys. Moments before my kick connected, he caught my foot in one hand. His grip was firm but light as he twisted his hand, pulling me off balance.

"You've tried this before," he whispered before releasing my foot.

Eyes wide, I retreated. *This is the first time we've sparred together, ever. Why would he say I've done the kick from behind before?* I let my eyes drop, and when I raised them again, realized my mistake. He charged and scooped me up over his shoulder and spun, before depositing me on the floor.

Not to be outwitted, I scissor-kicked and swept his feet out from under him. Tristan landed with a thud on his back beside me. Before he could beat me to it, I twisted and rolled on top of him. Pinning his arms to his sides with my hands, clenching his hips tight with my thighs. I peered down at him, breathing heavily.

His bright blue eyes locked with mine. Slowly, I became aware of how I was positioned, and the slight pressure that was increasing between my thighs. I glanced down at his groin and saw the unmistakable bulge of his cock.

Shaking, I stood up and walked away, unable to decide if I was angry at Rhys for desiring me or at my stupidity for straddling him. The last thing I needed was for word of this to get to my grandfather—or anyone outside of this room, for that matter.

"We're done here," I announced, pouring myself a glass of water and hoping no one would notice the tremors. My back was to Rhys; the last thing I wanted was to see his face and what he thought of my reaction. I had no inkling of what time it was. What I did know was I was sweaty, tired, and quite hungry.

Keeping my attention on the water, I almost dropped it when Rhys's hand brushed lightly on my waist. The water sloshed dangerously close to the rim. He moved next to me, so our shoulders were touching. "Would you like to practice with me tomorrow?"

"Phase three is tomorrow," I replied hurriedly, wanting to shout *yes*.

Rhys cast a glance at me. "No. Tomorrow is our rest day. I train every day. I figured you'd understand given the years you spent at Jade Wilds."

Relief and uncertainty filled me. *Would word get out I am favoring Rhys over the others, or are my activities not newsworthy?* I had no idea what the answer to my question was. My eyes sparked with an idea, a way around whether it was proper for me to invite him to practice. *Hopefully, he will catch my meaning.*

"I will be practicing in this room tomorrow after breakfast," I said.

Rhys replied, "After breakfast, I usually go for a run."

"I'll see you around," I said, then turned away before Rhys could respond. "I'm ready to return to my rooms," I informed Thomas and the other guards. Without comment, they followed me out of the practice area and down the hallway.

My belly was full of hot food and my body clean after a soothing bath. Thankfully, the bleeding seemed to be almost completely gone. Exhaustion wrapping around me; it was no surprise when sleep came almost instantly when I laid my head on the pillow.

Fists curled with my thumbs in the correct position, I threw punch after punch at Rhys. Using my smaller size and speed to my advantage, I was able to pummel him with quick, sharp right and left jabs, followed occasionally by a hook. Rhys had little time to do more than block. I grinned wolfishly at him. He might be better with the sword, but I was not going to let him win this match.

Determined to prove my point, I backed up a few steps, then sprinted toward him, tucking into a dive at the last moment and snapping my foot out to catch him in the ankle. Rhys hopped one-footed away from me. Not wanting to give him a chance to recover, I pulled my right leg in toward me, then spun, landing the kick—not in his kidney, as I had intended, but in his right forearm as he pivoted, trying to snatch my foot with his hand.

Every time he touched me my body felt like sparks were blazing trails all over it. Not wanting to become distracted by these unnamed feelings, I twirled out of the way as Rhys spun in a left crescent kick. My eyes twinkled in excitement at the opening Rhys had left, and I quickly schooled my face back into a mask, lunging forward.

188

Before I could land my punches, Rhys's arms wrapped around me. I expected him to throw me back and was caught off guard when he pulled me tight to his body and dipped his face down for a kiss. His mouth was gentle and tasted like honey. My lips parted, wanting to taste more of him. Tendrils of desire wound through me. The longer we kissed, the more I wanted his hands everywhere.

Rhys ran his hands down my back and cupped my buttocks, pulling me closer. He made a small thrust with his hips, and I was surprised when his cock bumped against me. We were entering new territory, and I was at a loss for how to respond. Though my body certainly seemed to know what it wanted.

Seeming to sense my uncertainty, Rhys cupped my cheek with his hand. "I can slow down if you need me to," he murmured. But I found myself not wanting to slow down.

"I need you in me," I replied, nipping his lips.

Rhys chuckled. "In time, Sera. I don't want to do anything you're not ready for."

"For some reason, it feels like I have always been ready for you. Even though we just met," I replied. I had no idea where the words came from, since we'd only known each other for a few days.

He ran his hands down my sides, then his thumb brushed against my nipple. I moaned, arching against him as my core began to throb.

"Please," I whispered.

"Well, if you're going to say please, then of course my answer is yes," Rhys responded, capturing my lips with his.

I woke up with a start, feeling around the bed for Rhys, my concern with how much trouble we would be in if someone found out we had had sex and told my grandfather a crushing weight.

The other side of the bed is cold. Then, it hit me. I had dreamed about our training session turning into far more than what it had yesterday. Sitting up in bed, the blankets pooling around me, I realized how ridiculous it was that now of all times I was having dreams of kissing males. Especially when the one in the dream might not be the one I married. *I cannot let myself get attached to the idea of Rhys,* I warned myself. *Or any male. If the king or anyone else finds out I'm not a virgin, then heads will surely roll.* I took a shaky breath. I couldn't remember anything surrounding my pregnancy, which kept gnawing at me. I knew I could get pregnant with only one sexual act, but I couldn't remember being intimate with anyone at all.

A tantalizing memory nagged me, just out of reach. *Maybe if I ignore it, I'll remember.* Deciding to try that, I swept the covers onto the other side of the bed and slid out, cringing as my toes missed the rug and hit the icy stone. I slid a pair of fur slippers on and padded over to the table, where someone had had the wherewithal to place a steaming pot of hot water and a fresh pouch of tea leaves.

Scooping the tea into a cup and adding the hot water, I settled onto the sofa to wait for it to brew. When it was the perfect rich amber color, I removed the bag of tea and took a sip. "Ah," I said with a smile as the tea trickled down my throat, just enough to warm me without burning my mouth.

Gazing into the lightening shadows around the window, a memory came back to me.

I was standing in the library in Dorcha Palace waiting for Prince Tanyth to take me to our wedding. My whole body was drawn tight, fear and apprehension about the fate awaiting me if I went through with it. There was a noise, and I spun, ready to fight, when I recognized the snow leopard.

"I love you," *the snow leopard said in my mind. I could feel the words wrapping around my whole body. The soulmate bond between us so bright I could almost see it.*

"I love you with all my heart," *I replied.*

I lost my grip on my teacup as I clutched my head, screaming as the pain threatened to rip me into pieces. Falling to the floor, I hit my head on the edge of the table. I could feel the blood flowing freely, but that was just a small pain compared to what was happening to my eyes.

Hands gripped me, but I couldn't stop screaming. Nothing in my life had ever prepared me for experiencing pain on this level. Eventually someone shoved a cup of liquid in front of me and tipped my head back, pouring the thick, syrupy substance down my throat. I gagged and spit half of it back up, but the pain started to ebb away, and I drifted into unconsciousness.

Twenty-Eight

TRISTAN

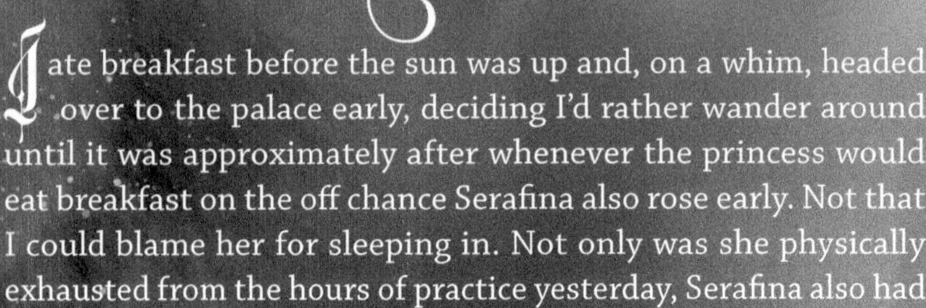

I ate breakfast before the sun was up and, on a whim, headed over to the palace early, deciding I'd rather wander around until it was approximately after whenever the princess would eat breakfast on the off chance Serafina also rose early. Not that I could blame her for sleeping in. Not only was she physically exhausted from the hours of practice yesterday, Serafina also had to be mentally exhausted from her duties as a princess.

Mindlessly weaving down the hallway, examining statues on one side and then drifting to the other, I froze when I heard screams. *"Serafina!"* I shouted down the bond. Sprinting, I followed the screams until I reached her rooms. They cut off as abruptly as they had begun.

I pounded on the door. "Let me in!"

Eventually, someone decided to investigate who was making such a ruckus. The guard Serafina had been sparring with yesterday opened the door. "I'm sorry, but she is unwell. You cannot be here."

I growled. Thomas, Serafina's primary guard, nudged the older one out of the way and gave me a wary look. I swallowed hard, realizing to the humans the sound I had emitted sounded far more like a snow leopard than I had intended. Thomas yanked the door sharply shut and brushed past me, giving my sleeve a light tug. I followed him in silence, knowing he likely wanted privacy from the other guards to either throw me out or give me useful information.

"If I hadn't seen the two of you interacting yesterday, I would not be telling you this," Thomas said quietly. "The princess has had these episodes where she is fine and then not. Plagued by excruciating pain. She claims to have no idea why it's happening, and we are at a loss for how to help her. The king's doctor has been able to give her sleeping draughts, which seem to help. But if I'm being honest, that is not a long-term solution."

"The king allows his granddaughter to be drugged instead of trying to find a *real* solution to her illness." I practically spat the words out. "I appreciate your willingness to share with me. If you will not allow me in there, then I am not sure how I can aid you." It was a risk to push Thomas into allowing me to see her.

I was not a healer, though, and even if I was, with the pendant on, my magic was unreachable. Callyn wasn't a healer either, which meant if Serafina truly needed a Fae healer, then there was not much either one of us could do for her. Watching Thomas's face, I could see his struggle plainly: concern for the princess versus letting a virtual stranger into her room.

Finally, it appeared Thomas came to a decision. "I will allow you to see her. But you're going to have to be patient. I would rather do this without witnesses. Why don't you go find some-where to wait, and I'll get you when the coast is clear."

"As you wish," I murmured and headed down the hallway looking for somewhere to wait that wasn't glaringly obvious.

I found a bench next to a window overlooking a garden. Stretching out my legs in front of me, I gazed out at the garden while keeping my ears peeled for any footsteps that would indicate Thomas was heading my way.

The hours ticked by. Finally, when the sun had long since passed its zenith, Thomas found me.

Leaping to my feet, I demanded, "Has she improved?"

Thomas shook his head. "Not really. We had to give her more of the draught. Now, if you would come with me. We have some time before the king plans to check on her again himself. I would recommend being long gone before he arrives."

Anxiously, I followed Thomas to Serafina's rooms. He led me inside and showed me where she lay on the bed, wrapped in blankets. A fire burning in the hearth provided extra heat as well. Other than the three of us, the room was—remarkably—empty.

When I reached her bedside, I hesitated, unsure what Thomas expected of me.

"I am going to go sit over there," Thomas said, then abruptly pivoted and sat on the sofa by the fire. With the distance the guard was allowing, we were as close to alone as I imagined we would get.

"Serafina," I said softly, trailing my fingertips lightly along her face, brushing stray strands of hair away. Her blue-green eyes opened the barest of slits, as though even that much was painful. I lightly began massaging her scalp. Under my ministrations I could feel her relaxing as she uttered tiny whimpers of pleasure.

My body was responding, and I knew I would have to tread carefully or risk whatever trust Thomas had placed in me. *A few more days*, I promised myself.

"Rhys?" Serafina whispered.

I stopped massaging her scalp and knelt next to the bed so my face was next to hers, though I kept my hand touching her skin. "I'm here for anything you need."

A smile curved her lips, and a little bit of color was returning to her cheeks. "You might change your mind if I told you about my dream."

My curiosity piqued. *What kind of dream was she having about me? Perhaps the bonding process is starting again of its own accord with dreams, like it did in Dorcha Palace.*

"I had some tea and then ... pain, so much pain," Serafina said. Tears glistened in her eyes.

Steeling myself, I kissed her eyelids. "Please don't cry. Has the pain lessened now?"

"With you here, yes. Whatever the doctor gives me has only been putting me to sleep. It does nothing for the pain. Not this time," she admitted.

The condition is getting worse. Having had my share of lengthy recoveries from battles, I had an idea of how exhausting high levels of pain were, coupled with the grueling schedule her grandfather had set. *Callyn and I must find a way to break through the magic.*

"Has Ghilanna Qira come to see you today?" I asked, considering that the other Fae might have the answers we sought.

"How do you know about Ghilanna?" Serafina asked, her voice getting stronger the longer we touched.

I realized my mistake. My planned answer—that Fae can sense one another—was not going to work, not when to everyone here I was a human. "Thomas told me about her. Does she have any answers about your sickness?"

"Nothing that you would believe," she replied.

"Try me. I've heard lots of things before," I said softly.

"Ghilanna thinks it's dark magic caused by a Fae," she replied.

I gasped, feigning surprise like a human would. "How would you be mixed up in dark Fae magic?"

Serafina pressed her lips together and shook her head, not willing to share. I couldn't blame her. She had barely spent any time getting to know Rhys. Why would she trust me with details of her past?

I tried another tactic. "Do you remember what you were thinking about when you got sick?"

She shook her head. "No. I was drinking tea, and that's all I remember." Though her face had been cleaned, I could see the cut along her hairline where she'd hit her head. I couldn't imagine the headache that typically accompanied a cut like that that would help matters.

There was a commotion at the door. "I must go, or the king might decide to throw me out of the competition altogether."

"Kiss me," Serafina said suddenly.

"What?" I asked, certain I had misheard her.

"Kiss me," she repeated, her hands sliding out from under the covers to wind themselves in the fabric of my tunic. She tugged, and my chest bumped into the edge of the mattress. Our faces were less than a hairsbreadth apart.

Mustering all the strength I had, I replied, "I can't. Not yet."

She rolled over in bed, clearly unhappy, but with Thomas on the sofa and the king's entrance imminent, the last thing I could afford to do was kiss the princess. If we were already betrothed, I might be able to get away with it, but not today.

Reluctantly, I stood. Thomas appeared at my elbow, and he led me deeper into Serafina's suite of rooms and out a door into a silent hallway. "The king won't know you were here. Now go."

Twenty-Nine

SERAFINA

The morning of the final phase of the competition, I was feeling marginally better, at least physically. Mentally, I was still worrying over my missing memories and what could be hidden within them. Every time I tried to remember, the headaches returned at full strength. Taking a deep breath, I decided to focus on something that would not make me sick.

I knew preparations for the wedding were underway somewhere in the palace. It felt strange to be left out of such a momentous life event, but I was not sure I could handle more conflict with my grandfather over the details. I had given Lord John my meager guest list—Ghilanna, Fiera, Commander Meriel, and King Pharaan. As long as the invitations could be delivered, I doubted King Leonard would object. The guests on *his* list encompassed many of the ones already here for the competition. It was one of the reasons for the tight schedule.

Will more guests arrive in the three days before the wedding? I wondered. It had not escaped my thoughts that as granddaughter of not one but two kings, there was a distinct possibility there would be a large group of guests. I secretly expected there was a possibility no one would come too.

Heirs come and go. Look at how many King Leonard had to begin with. Is the wedding of an heir really going to draw that many people? I doubted the king's illness was widely known, which created even less of a reason for people to make the trip to attend. *Unlike a coronation, where the outcome is certain.*

I reached for the door, intending to head to phase three, when Thomas stepped in front of me. "We need to go through the garden."

"Why?" I demanded. Normally, I would take his recommendation for where to go, but I could tell he was tense. His hand was resting on top of his sword, eyes examining the room.

"It's not your concern," he said.

I gave his shoulder a shove, and he wisely moved out of the way. "I will decide what is my concern."

I opened the door and froze. "Leave or you'll end up like Gareth" was painted across the wall in bold red brushstrokes.

"Why did you want to hide this from me?" I demanded, stepping back into my room and facing Thomas.

"Because whoever did it has never taken the time to get to know you like I have. I wanted to spare you from reading such a terrible thing," Thomas said. His voice sounded normal, but his gaze was wary.

It did not escape me that he said he had gotten to know me. Which he had, or at least as much as a guard could get to know a princess. *He cares.* My anger faded. "Thank you, Thomas. I appreciate you." I patted his arm, swallowing hard. I was going to have to have a discussion with my grandfather about palace security. First a note and now paint on the wall—clearly the palace guards were not doing their jobs adequately. My request to increase security had met deaf ears. Would the transgressor hold a dagger to my throat next time? *Is that what it'll take to get a response from King Leonard, a death threat?*

"Let's go," Thomas said and led me through the garden and out the gate. There was a cold breeze, and I shivered. The dress

I was wearing today had cap sleeves. Neither Violet nor Mary had mentioned anything about today's weather. *Now I'm going to freeze.* With the number of guests sure to attend the last phase, I briefly contemplated trying to find Ghilanna and asking her to place a warming spell on me. I had no illusions that the joust would take hours. *I suppose I could ask someone to retrieve a cloak for me once we get there.*

The pace Thomas set led me to believe that we did not have time to run back to get more clothes to keep me warm. I quickly recognized our destination: the meadow where Grandfather and I had shared our gallop just a few days ago. A logical place for a phase involving horses, since there was plenty of room for six horse and rider pairs to maneuver. A large grandstand had been erected, and the benches were already filled with spectators. In front of the stand was a large riding arena; the ground had been tilled to provide soft footing for the horses, and in the center, a long pole ran the length of the arena, about waist high, dividing it in two.

"This is what a joust looks like?" I asked as we made our way to the elevated seats in the front corner, positioned no doubt for the best view.

"Yes. Though it's been over one hundred years since a kingdom hosted a joust," Thomas said, his excitement evident.

I rolled my eyes. "Wasn't that because it was outlawed?" I replied, unable to suppress my surprise.

Thomas shrugged. "Your grandfather decided the third phase would be jousting. I am but a guard in his palace. It is not my place to disagree with the king's choice."

Thomas was right, and with the competition starting in less than an hour, nothing I could say would prevent the joust from happening. He indicated which chair was mine. Before I could sit, he held open a bulky fur-lined robe. Grateful, I slipped my arms inside and pulled it tight around me, then sat. Warmth spread through me that Thomas cared enough to know I would be cold.

Shortly after I settled in my chair, a short, clean-shaven man with cropped, straw-colored hair, wearing polished plate mail and a bright red cape fluttering around his shoulders, strode confidently into the arena. He bowed deeply to King Leonard and me before facing the stands full of our guests.

"Welcome, guests from far and wide and residents of the South! I am Declan Green, master of the guard, and for the joust I will be your master of ceremonies. Today, you will witness the third and final phase of the competition to decide who Princess Serafina will marry," he bellowed. A spattering of claps could be heard throughout the crowd. *Apparently, no one is excited about this.* Or perhaps they just wanted to be entertained and didn't care about the purpose of the event.

Unperturbed, Declan continued his monologue. "Today you will watch our competitors compete in a maximum of four jousting rounds. The first two rounds will eliminate two competitors; the rest will compete in the elimination round for Princess Serafina's hand in marriage. Each round consists of multiple matches, and each match includes three passes. Two points are awarded for unseating and one for shattering a lance. Now! Please welcome Frederick Hunter of Hunter's Hollow!"

There was a flurry of movement at the far side of the arena, and then a man encased head to toe in full plate armor on a white horse charged toward Declan. Clumps of arena dirt flew high into the air. Seconds before Frederick would have trampled Declan, he reined his horse into a sliding stop. A spray of dirt fell on Declan, but he continued smiling as though nothing had happened.

"Frederick will be wearing brown!" Declan shouted and handed Frederick a brown piece of fabric. Frederick took it in his hand and pumped the air with his fist. The guests shrieked and clapped. I rolled my eyes.

Declan waved Frederick away, and Frederick moved over to stand near Grandfather and me. He was too far below us to strike up a conversation, and for that I was grateful.

A hush fell across the crowd as we waited for Declan to announce who the next competitor would be. "Sorrel Ward of Glass River!"

If I recalled correctly, the Glass River went from the west border of Gaskal and wound through the edge of the lands belonging to the Court of the Sun.

Lost in my thoughts, I missed Sorrel's entrance. His armor was almost identical to Frederick's, but his horse was quite different. It was a heavier draft breed, built for carrying cavalry. It was a light tan color with white feathers around each of its saucer-sized hooves.

"Sorrel will be wearing yellow!" Declan announced and handed Sorrel a yellow strip of fabric.

Determined to pay more attention, I kept my eyes riveted at the end of the list where the competitors were entering.

"Rhys Mongan of Eagle Rock!" Declan announced.

I tensed in my seat as Rhys, astride a brown horse, shot sideways across the arena. It took me a moment to realize Rhys wasn't causing the horse to go sideways. Muscles bunched, the brown horse was bucking and twisting, doing its best to dislodge Rhys. The crowd was eerily silent as we watched them weave their way toward Declan.

Rhys pulled the horse to a halt in front of the master of the guard. The horse's sides were heaving and I could see the whites of its eye, but, momentarily at least, Rhys had gained control.

Declan offered him a bright-blue piece of fabric. "Rhys will be blue!"

The crowd remained silent as Rhys convinced his horse to walk, albeit slowly, over to where Sorrel and Frederick were waiting.

Thirty

TRISTAN

I had a tight grip on the reins. My horse had made it clear as soon as I was on his back that he didn't want anything to do with me. It was impossible to know if the horse was reacting to the pendant's magic or if it could still sense the snow leopard shifter part of me. *Just my luck to get the one with a strong opinion.*

At least I know how to ride, I reminded myself. My father had made sure of it. A matter simplified by Elre Gilvrye being a horse shifter. Not only had my father taught me how to ride, he had also made sure I knew how to stay on, regardless of what tricks a horse would pull. I had mostly hated those lessons, but looking back, I understood now why he had taken the time.

Declan, master of the guard, worked his way through introducing the other three competitors: Wictor, Peter, and Jack. I resorted to allowing my horse to walk in small circles to keep him from bucking again.

Finally, Declan approached us. "The order of the first round is Rhys versus Peter, Frederick versus Sorrel, Wictor versus Jack. If your name was listed first, then you start at this side. The rest of you need to go around the back of the stands to the other side."

Declan met each of our gazes with his own and held it for a moment. "Remember, it's the best two of three. To get one point, you must hit the lance on the shield. You will be awarded two points if you hit the shield and unseat the rider. All six of you are guaranteed two rounds. Then, the two lowest scores will be eliminated."

I had jousted twice. Both times were at Embergate and were not my finest moments in training, mostly due to the horse not liking me. It's hard to aim a lance when the horse is trying to throw you off. Grinding my teeth together, I moved myself into position, then slid down my visor. A guard handed me a lance. I rested it against my boot, waiting for Declan to drop the flag signaling the charge.

The horse shifted underneath me, and the flag dropped. Digging my heels into his sides, I rose in my stirrups and held the lance level at an angle. My horse shot forward a few strides and then began crow-hopping. Peter blew past me, his lance missing by several feet due to my inability to control my horse, not his technique.

Taking a deep breath, I relaxed my hand on the reins, and we bounced our way to the end. A guard took my lance and gave me a moment to breathe before handing me a fresh one.

"I'd recommend controlling your horse or you risk disqualification," the guard said with a smirk.

Breathe, I reminded myself. Declan was standing in the middle of the arena again. He glanced at me and I bobbed my lance, indicating I was ready. Peter did the same.

"GO!" shouted Declan.

This time, I dug my heels in and loosened my reins, praying the horse would not use the room to take off bucking. To my surprise, he dug in deep with his hind end and charged forward. I rose in my stirrups to position my lance. My focus narrowed in on the center of Peter's shield.

There was a metallic crunch and a spray of wood as both lances shattered on impact. My horse slowed of his own accord as we reached the end of the list and quietly turned around. I took the fresh lance the guard offered, noting that the lances were painted in the colors we had been assigned. A quick glance at my shield told me it was still in one piece.

"GO!" This time I loosened my reins even more, and we barreled down the line. As the lance hit Peter's shield, I twisted my wrist, taking advantage of how far forward Peter tipped. With the added motion, I popped Peter out of his saddle. Freed of its rider, the horse took off bucking in a wild circle, precariously close to Peter.

The crowd shrieked, "Save him!"

I trotted back to the end of the line, relieved that I could dismount and take a water break while the others completed their first round. A groom showed up to take my horse. I set the shield and helmet on a stand marked with my name.

A heavily cloaked Callyn met me on my way to the tent set up with snacks and water. "You scared me that first round. I thought the king was going to eliminate you."

I shrugged. "I figured I could sort something out with the horse. I doubt he'll ever be my fan, but hopefully we can get through this tournament in one piece."

"Are you going to watch the rest of the rounds?" Callyn asked.

I shook my head, sending strands of damp hair swirling around my face. "No. I'd rather wait back here, out of sight."

Thirty-One

SERAFINA

The excitement I had felt watching the first round quickly faded as the second was drawn out. However, Grandfather and our guests were still enthralled by the jousting. *I suppose this is for them more than me.* I realized that I would have to get used to being bored by events like this. *Another royal duty.* At Jade Wilds, I never had to worry about organizing entertainment. Life at a Fae training camp was simple: eat, sleep, train, and repeat. Once or twice a year there would be parties, but attendance wasn't required. As a princess and eventually a queen, I would not have the luxury of attendance being optional.

Perhaps I can also organize events that I want to participate in as a way to get to know my subjects. Not just parties for nobles, creating an even more obvious divide between us. I lifted my head as a hush fell over the crowd as a healer and several guards carried Jack out of the arena.

Declan strode toward the stands. "Guests! It is my honor to announce the competitors who will move on to round three!" Whistles and cheers rose in the stands. Declan had to wave his arms to get them to settle down again. "Round three is an elimination round. Best two of three and the loser doesn't get a second chance. Rhys and Wictor will start, followed by Frederick and Peter."

After Rhys's challenges with his horse, I had not expected him to advance to round three. Of the four competitors, there was only one I did *not* want to marry—Frederick. Both of our meetings left no doubt in my mind that he was in the competition for one reason—to get the throne of Gaskal. What worried me the most was my grandfather seemed to favor Frederick. If he were to win, I knew that it was possible that he would take the throne and I would turn into little more than a broodmare, suited for producing heirs and not much else. I gripped the arms of my chair, knuckles turning white. *I won't let any male treat me that way.*

The crash of metal yanked me firmly out of my thoughts. Rhys swayed precariously in the saddle, his lance in pieces on the ground. Wictor was on the ground holding the handle of his lance with the other half at the end of the list. It had snapped in two instead of shattering as a lance was supposed to.

Declan and several other guards helped Wictor to his feet and back into the saddle. Without having watched, I assumed Wictor had one point and Rhys two since both lances had broken. Determined to watch the next round of the match and not get distracted, I stared at the middle of the arena, where they should strike each other.

"Wictor! Wictor!" chanted the crowd. Wictor and Rhys thundered toward each other. Clumps of dirt sailed through the air; some I was certain landed in the stands. Moments before the impact, I noticed Wictor subtly shift his position, tilting away from Rhys. Wictor's lance slid off Rhys's shield, and Rhys's hit the bottom of Wictor's. With Wictor's tilted, off-balanced position, it was no surprise when he toppled sideways off his horse.

I shook my head. *Wictor had been centered. Why'd he shift?* That made me wonder if the man was aware he had altered his position. It was possible he had no idea. Woe to him, because he had just lost. With two unseatings, it was impossible for Wictor to earn enough points to beat Rhys.

I took a deep breath as it sank in that there was now a fifty percent chance that Rhys could end up winning. I shot a glance at my grandfather, but his face was a careful mask. A cramp was forming in my calf. I stood, hoping moving around some would help, when the urge to pee hit me. Blushing at the thought of telling anyone as though I were a child, I caught Thomas's eye and headed down the stairs. I knew there had to be a latrine set up somewhere around here.

Walking felt better than I expected it to, and the cramp worked its way out of my calf. After using the latrine, I opted to wander around the bottom of the stands. Thomas dutifully followed me without commenting. From the roar above, I knew the winner of the match after Rhys's was about to be announced. I held my breath, hands shaking slightly.

"Frederick!" Declan shouted.

Even though his voice was muffled with the stands between us, I could still easily make out the name. A shiver ran through me. *Fifty percent chance a man who treats me like an equal wins. Fifty percent chance the man who wants to steal the throne wins.* I hadn't paid enough attention to Frederick's rounds to know if he had also had difficulty with his opponents like Rhys had or if he'd breezed through as though he jousted regularly. *Would it matter?*

Swallowing hard, I couldn't help but wonder how I had ended up here, with my husband and likely the future of the South being settled by a joust. *Maybe I was wrong and I should have tried to smooth things over with the suitors; at least that way I would have had a better idea of who I was going to marry.* I realized now that being able to complete an obstacle course, run a foot race, and win a joust has very little in common with ruling a kingdom. *I hope King Leonard doesn't regret his decision to choose my husband by competition when he finds out the real nature of the winner.*

I heard a cough behind me. I turned and saw Thomas was trying to get my attention. "Princess Serafina, shouldn't we return to watch the final round?"

I fidgeted with the folds of my dress. He had a point. *It would look bad if I wasn't there to witness who would win my hand.* "Very well. Let's return."

Thirty-Two

TRISTAN

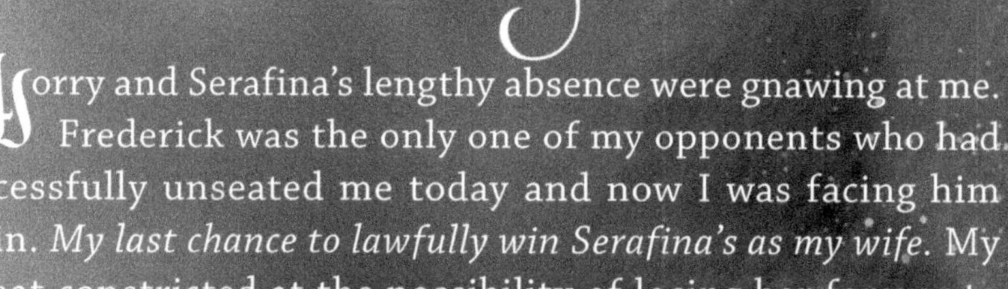

Worry and Serafina's lengthy absence were gnawing at me. Frederick was the only one of my opponents who had successfully unseated me today and now I was facing him again. *My last chance to lawfully win Serafina's as my wife.* My throat constricted at the possibility of losing her forever to Frederick.

A flicker of movement that caught my eye, and I blew out my breath in relief when I saw it was Serafina returning to her seat. The other competitors had been whispering about her disappearance with a candid debate about why she had left. I was worried she had been overcome by one of her bouts of sickness.

To give Frederick a short break, Declan rode out into the arena and did some tricks on his horse. The crowd found his antics amusing. I did not. *What is the purpose of doing a handstand on a horse?* Demonstrating archery from horseback, or something along those lines at least, would be a useful skill. I also found it strange that the master of guard, who should be in charge of the king's safety and overall security of the palace, would have time to practice stunts. *Maybe that is why security is lacking at the palace.*

I could see from where I patiently waited precisely when Frederick gave the signal he was ready. Moments later, Declan returned to sitting astride his horse. "Ladies and gentlemen! The final round!"

"One, two, three!" Declan dropped his hand and backed his horse out of the arena.

A light bump in the sides was all it took, and my horse shot down the arena. I rose in the stirrups, and my grip on the lance slipped just a hair in my sweat-slicked palm. The impact of Frederick's lance hitting the center of my shield sent a jolt through my shield arm, followed by the sharp tug as my lance skipped off the side of Frederick's shield.

Growling in frustration, I stopped at the end of the list and traded out my lance for a new one. As the fresh lance hit my hand, my horse let out a sharp kick, just a hairsbreadth from hitting the poor guard in the arm. Clenching my jaw, I shifted in the saddle. *Don't fall apart on me now.* I was close to my goal, winning Serafina's hand—far closer than I had expected to get.

Taking a deep breath, I exhaled, relaxing my jaw and settling deep into the saddle. The signal came, and we charged down the list again. I waited longer to rise into the stirrups and set my lance, tipping my shield arm slightly. The move was either brave or stupid. If it worked, Frederick's lance would slide off the shield. If it didn't, then I could end up with a lance in my arm or side. Luck was with me this time; Frederick's lance slid off and mine shattered as it slammed hard into the center of his shield. *Tied.*

As I trotted to the awaiting guard, I contemplated my options. My best bet would be to try to unseat Frederick. Both of us falling out of the saddle was far less likely to happen than one. The guard handed me the lance. My horse started pawing the ground, then let out a few small bucks. I loosened my grip on the reins even more, considering doing away with them altogether, but that could be dangerous too if they went over the horse's head and got tangled in his legs.

After wiping my hands on the saddle blanket, I took the lance and adjusted my shield. *This is it.* It was hard to believe everything had come down to this. If I won, Serafina and I would marry. Together, we could try to solve the mystery of the bond and get her memories back.

If I lose … I chomped hard on my tongue and a rush of coppery blood flooded my mouth. There was no option to lose.

"Your Majesty, the time has arrived for the last run of this three-day competition. Frederick Hunter the bold, hailing from the eastern side of Gaskal, vies for Princess Serafina's hand against Rhys Mongan, from Eagle Rock, training grounds for the knights of the West," Declan announced. His voice projected to reach everyone's ears. The crowd stirred, some clapped, then the stomping began. Soon, I could almost feel the vibrations of the stands moving from the sheer number of feet stomping on the wood.

My horse gave a half rear. "Hush," I murmured, hoping my voice was soothing to the animal.

Declan waved his flag in the air. It was half blue, half brown, representing both of our assigned colors. I briefly wondered who had been assigned the task of sewing it on such short notice.

"One … two …"

I couldn't hear the three because of how loud the crowd roared as the flag dropped. My horse tucked his chin in to his chest and rounded his back. *Shit.* I could feel the muscles bunching when to my surprise, he shook himself and took off at top speed. My balance was off, and I had mere moments to recover before it would be over one way or another. I rose shakily in my stirrups, the tip of the lance wavering.

I let go of my lance on impact, swaying dangerously in the saddle. A shard of Frederick's lance had pierced my side, finding the only gap in my armor. Bouncing uncomfortably as my horse trotted in a tight circle, jarring the wound even more, it took me a few moments to pull my attention from myself to my opponent. To my shock, Frederick was on the ground while I had stayed in the saddle. The outcome was quite clear.

Yet the grandstand was utterly silent. Pain and exhaustion wove through me as the adrenaline seeped away. Reminding myself that I had just won and should at the very least thank the king for hosting the competition, I lightly nudged my horse and rode over to the part of the grandstand where Serafina and King Leonard sat. I removed my helmet and tucked it under my arm, bowing awkwardly in the saddle.

Moments ticked by. King Leonard finally stood and stepped to the edge of his box. "May I present the winner of the competition, Rhys Mongan!"

A spattering of claps could be heard, but nothing like the cheers that had erupted when Frederick had managed to unseat me in the second round earlier in the day. It was blatantly obvious that the guests in the grandstands preferred a local as the husband for their princess.

Bitterness flooded my mouth. *Too bad their king chose to let the competition decide. Once invoked, he could not back out.* My gaze flicked to Serafina, but she was so wrapped in her fur robe that all I could see were her glittering eyes.

Lord John approached me and held my horse while I dismounted. "Congratulations," he said, offering me his hand to shake. I took it, noting his firm grip.

"You seem to be the only one who doesn't mind the outcome," I said.

Lord John chuckled. "You caught them by surprise is all. As the outsider no one has heard of, they expected you to lose by a lot. Many of the lords bet large sums of money on it. Can you imagine how you'd feel if you had just lost millions?"

I had to confess that he did have a point. I just prayed it wasn't an indication of what Serafina and I would be facing for our entire future together. Never having the acceptance of our people and being barely more than figureheads. Biting the inside of my cheek, I realized I should know better. Serafina would not let her people treat us that way. *And how will she treat me, when she finds out I am not the human Rhys Mongan, but a Fae?*

Part Two

Thirty-Three

SERAFINA

Rhys, a man from the West, just won my hand in marriage. The information slammed into me and sent me reeling. An outcome that had felt unlikely, since lately it seemed as though nothing I wanted happened. I buried my face in the soft fur lining of the robe. *Is this what my mother foresaw? That if I were to marry an outsider, we could lead the kingdom and its people in a journey of acceptance?*

Digging my fingernails into my palm, I inhaled slowly, trying to halt my whirling thoughts warring within. Relief that the wait was over—the competition had determined Rhys would be my husband. But my relief was not enough to wash away the fear that Rhys or someone else would learn my secret and call off the wedding. The last thing I needed was to be accused of dishonoring my family and the king for an act I had no recollection of.

Maybe Rhys won't care, even if he does know. I barely knew the man. It was impossible to predict how he'd react to the information. *Won't he find out when we consummate the marriage?* I thought someone had told me once it was possible to tell if a female was a virgin by a physical examination.

"Serafina," King Leonard's voice broke through my thoughts.

"I would like to meet my betrothed," I said before I lost my nerve.

"No. There is a set time for you to see each other tomorrow. Now, it is time for you to go see the seamstress. There is much work to be done for your wedding in three days," the king replied.

"No," I said, anger flaring.

"You will obey my orders," growled my grandfather.

"The competition is over. My soon-to-be husband has been identified. There is no reason why I cannot meet with him. A chance to get to know one another before the wedding," I replied, gritting my teeth. I had followed his orders for the most part the past few days, but now that the competition was over, nothing I did would change the fact that Rhys and I were to be married.

"You can get to know each other after the wedding. When you're making an heir," King Leonard snapped.

Preparing for my next move, I dropped the robe in my vacant chair, not wanting to be hindered by its thick folds, and backed up a few steps. "I have put up with your rules. But this is my life, my husband. Why do you care if I want to speak with him, other than proving you have control over me?"

He stepped close to me, cheeks mottled red in anger. "You've already done more than just speak to him. Given the chance, I wouldn't be surprised if he'd fuck you in public."

My neck snapped back as though he had slapped me. *Does he know?* He continued speaking. "It is against our laws for a female heir of the South to bed her betrothed before the wedding. The other lords can demand your execution for fear of you conceiving an heir that is not pureblooded."

I laughed harshly. "A pureblood heir? How can you even say that to my face? I'm half-Fae, half-human. There is no part of me that can ever be 'pure.' If that was a legitimate criterion for your heir, then you should never have demanded that I come here." Pulse pounding, I took another step back, toward the narrow staircase behind me. "Now. I am leaving. Goodbye." I spun on my heel and ran down the stairs. When my feet hit the soft grass, I kept running, weaving around people. When I looked up, I found I was out by the temporary pen the horses were being kept in.

A large black stallion noticed me and eagerly approached the edge of the fence. He had a thick black mane that fell well past his shoulder. His hooves were larger than my hands and his legs were adorned with feathers. I climbed the fence. The stallion sidled closer. Wrapping my fingers tightly in his mane, I swung my leg over his back and sat up. He took a few steps, then curled his neck around and nudged my foot. I stroked his neck.

"Dubhar," I said. It was the Fae word for shadows and fitting for a horse of his color. I had the strangest feeling I'd called another horse that before, though I couldn't remember the precise circumstances.

Dubhar nickered softly. I nudged his sides with my heels. There was a commotion from the direction I had come. I could see the bright blue of my grandfather's cloak and knew I was running out of time for whatever it was I was doing. Dubhar was smart. Without any instructions from me, he trotted around the pen, and the other horses clustered in a corner, wisely staying out of our way. He then shifted into a canter and aimed for the fence. As his muscles bunched, I anticipated his intention and adjusted my position. *One, two, three.* Dubhar launched us into the air. We sailed over the fence with ease and thundered down the meadow. With the wind in my face, Dubhar's effortless stride carried me farther away from my grandfather and our confrontation.

My hair streamed out behind me, the pins holding it up no match for the swift wind in the meadow. Dubhar galloped to the edge of the meadow and then followed the perimeter, careful to stay away from where the jousting had been. The stallion's stride changed, and I knew someone was approaching. I was surprised when we circled around to face the intruder to see Rhys, alone and on foot. *Perhaps my outburst worked.*

Dubhar spiraled in toward Rhys and halted, far enough away that he would not be able to pull me from his back. I studied Rhys, ignoring the headache that was starting to form in my temples. His hair was a mess from wearing the helmet to joust and then running his fingers through it. His white shirt was tight enough I could make out his muscles through the fabric There was a small but noticeable bright-red bloodstain near his abdomen. I hadn't realized he'd been wounded during the competition.

"You have caused quite a ruckus with your departure," Rhys informed me. I could hear the amusement in his voice, which was a relief.

"It's good that you are not expecting me to be a well-behaved, order-obeying wife," I replied, tone sharper than I intended.

Rhys grimaced. "That was never my expectation, Your Highness," he said with a bow. Dubhar snorted and pawed the ground impatiently.

"Pray tell me, what is your expectation, *betrothed*?" I demanded. *Will he be honest?* It was just the two of us here in the meadow. No one else could hear what we said.

"To serve the Lady of the South in whatever capacity she deems me worthy of." His blue eyes sparkled as the sun emerged from behind the clouds. I adjusted my gaze to his shoulder, so as not to bring on the sickness. "Whether that is leading your army by your side or as your bedroom slave. The choice is yours."

My face paled as he implied he'd be willing to marry me for the sole purpose of fucking me. *Wouldn't that make my grandfather happy if we provided him not one but a horde of heirs?*

"Or you can send me away, and I'll leave you alone forever," Rhys said softly.

He must have seen my reaction to his mention of the bedroom. Given he was currently the only solution to my mysterious illness, the last thing I wanted was to send him away, at least not until it was resolved.

Licking my lips, I glanced at him, then back toward the grand-stand. "I heard you were quite the fast runner in the foot race. Care to demonstrate?" I shouldn't ask him to race me. He was wounded, but I wasn't sure how much time we'd have together, and I was curious to see what he'd do.

"Race you on foot?" Rhys asked.

I smothered a laugh with my hand. "No, I want to race you on Dubhar."

"Interesting name," he said, though I thought I heard approval.

"The stallion's name is not relevant. Will you race me?" I asked again.

"Yes, I accept your offer," Rhys replied.

Smiling at him, I leaned forward over Dubhar's withers and tapped him lightly with my heels. We shot forward, clumps of grass spraying in our wake. Shooting a glance behind me, I saw Rhys a few lengths back and returned my attention forward. Belatedly, I realized I hadn't designated where we were racing to. *The tree line.*

Less than ten lengths into the race, Dubhar's strides faltered. *He's exhausted.* I ran my hand along his damp neck in a silent apology. I had not considered my mount's needs, only my own. Sitting up straight, I asked Dubhar to walk. "Thank you," I said softly. His ears flicked back in acknowledgment.

Rhys shot past us, then skidded to a halt when he realized I was no longer racing. "Is everything okay?" he called.

"Dubhar is tired," I replied as the horse halted. I could feel it now, the way his legs were shaking from the exertion. I dis-mounted; strong arms wrapped around me. I closed my eyes, and a flicker of a memory reached me of another male holding me the same way. I took a shaky breath, praying with Rhys touching me the illness would stay away. Over the past week in Gaskal, the only person who honestly did not seem to want anything from me was Rhys. I couldn't decide if it was because he did want something and was just better at hiding it or that he was content to just be in my company.

Rotating in Rhys's arms so I could see his expression, I said, "My grandfather is of the opinion that we should not spend time together, unless it's at a formal function, until after the wedding."

"What is your opinion on the matter?" Rhys asked curiously.

"That as the second-highest-ranked individual in the South, I should be allowed to get to know my betrothed better *before* the wedding. Though honestly, there are many things about being heir my grandfather will not tell me yet." My mouth twisted. "If I were a man, I would have known long ago what he is keeping from me."

"Then I promise you that I will do everything in my power to ensure that we have as much time as you desire to get to know one another before the wedding. By law, we are required to marry, but that does not mean we have to go into it blind," Rhys replied.

I could hear the sincerity in his tone, making me want to believe that to him I was not just a prize that would give him the keys to a human kingdom, but a person who perhaps one day he might fall in love with, even just a little. What I wanted the most was for him to respect me and my people.

I could see movement over Rhys's shoulder. "It seems like someone is going to come retrieve me if we don't head back. It was nice to feel free though, if only for a little while."

Rhys stayed silent. His jaw tightened slightly, making me wonder if my words had hit a nerve. I shrugged, brushing past him, and began the trek back toward the jousting arena. Dubhar followed me closely, which was a relief. I wasn't sure how I would have explained that the stallion got away because I was riding without tack and had to get off to preserve his health.

Thirty-Four

TRISTAN

Serafina's comment about being free had really gotten under my skin. It was extremely clear that she did not remember any of her time as a prisoner of Dorcha Palace. In her mind, she was akin to a prisoner at her grandfather's palace, being forced into a marriage she didn't want but had to accept for the good of her people. While he was restricting some of what she could do, he was not preventing her on pain of death from doing anything. *Or not that I know of.* I couldn't help but worry about how she was going to react when she got her memories back and learned exactly what kind of prisoner she had been at Dorcha Palace.

I was already devising ways we could meet to get the face-to-face time Serafina was craving before the wedding. *Just like I did at Dorcha Palace.* Keeping secrets from a ruler was a task I had many years of experience doing. *And am doing right now*, I reminded myself sharply. I could not afford to forget that I needed to reveal my true identity to Serafina sooner than later.

We got about halfway back when the guards and Lord John reached us. One dismounted and quickly put a halter on Dubhar, who until that very moment had been following Serafina as though he were a puppy. As soon as the halter went on, the stallion reared, striking with his front hooves and narrowly missing the guard's face. The guard tugged hard on the rope.

What does he think that is going to accomplish? I wondered.

The stallion dropped back to all four feet. Another guard approached from the side. Lightning fast, a hoof flashed out sideways, and the guard fell to the ground, clutching his stomach. Dubhar snorted and snapped his teeth at the guard holding his lead.

I kept my hand in Serafina's, praying she would not interfere. To my surprise, the guard took Dubhar's momentary stillness as a sign of submission and reached out a hand to pat the stallion. Dubhar lunged and bit him in the shoulder, then shoved the guard to the ground. Rocking back on his haunches, he wheeled around until he found Serafina and shot toward us. He stopped directly in front of Serafina, sides trembling. His muzzle twitched, and he stretched out his neck until he was able to touch her face with his nose. Then, he started licking her face.

I swallowed hard at the abrupt behavior change. Serafina giggled. The stallion proceeded to wash her face with his long tongue. Confident Dubhar had claimed Serafina as his person, I peered over at the guards. One was approaching again.

"I'll be right back," I said to Serafina and Dubhar. "Just stay here." My words were directed at the stallion, who had already injured two guards. I did not believe it was necessary to make the list grow.

As I walked toward the guards, I felt a tingling sensation between my shoulder blades, but then it was gone. I glanced back over my shoulder, but Dubhar was still contentedly washing Serafina's face. *How odd.*

I blocked the guards before they could approach Serafina and Dubhar. "Do you really think you're going to lead him anywhere?" I demanded.

Lord John frowned from atop his horse. "What do you mean?"

I rolled my eyes. "You ride a horse, yet you seem to know nothing about them. The stallion injured and could have killed all your guards and now is licking Serafina. What does that tell you?"

"That he is a dangerous, unpredictable animal that should be put down," Lord John replied coldly.

"If that is really what you believe, then you do not deserve to ride a horse at all," I growled. Licking my lips, I willed myself to calm down and offer a better explanation. "Horses can bond to people. This stallion has chosen Serafina. Would you take your princess's horse from her?"

The guards started muttering. Lord John repeated his previous sentiment. "He is dangerous."

"To you perhaps. Clearly, you are unaware of anything that has happened between Serafina and Dubhar. She took him for a ride, no saddle, no bridle. He galloped faster for her than he did for his rider during the joust. You can see her over there right now. She is in one piece. I ask you again, are you going to take Dubhar from your princess and future queen?" I demanded.

Lord John shifted in his saddle. "You have a point. However, King Leonard does not want her anywhere near this stallion. He is my king. I will allow you to escort them back to the stable with the guards following respectfully behind. I cannot predict what King Leonard will do once they are both safely separated."

"Understood," I replied. *I pray King Leonard makes the right choice.* I returned to Serafina. Dubhar had ceased washing her face and had his head on her shoulder. Once again, I felt a brief tingle. I would have sworn it was magic, but it came from nearby and I couldn't sense any other Fae. *Maybe Marek is checking in on me.*

"Lord John has promised no one will try to take Dubhar away right now, but we need to return to the stable," I announced. Dubhar stamped his foot and stared at me for a moment before returning his attention to Serafina.

"Then let's go," Serafina said, and together the three of us headed back toward the stable.

Thirty-Five

SERAFINA

Once Dubhar was settled in the stable, Rhys and I entered the palace. Lord John was there waiting for us. "Rhys, it is time for you to retire for the night."

It was an order; one I had expected that either I or someone else in the palace would have to give to Rhys. Honestly, I was exhausted, and my bed was calling my name. Though we might be officially betrothed, Rhys had no business in my rooms. After the momentous events of today, I didn't want company right now, even if it had been an option.

Turning to face Rhys, I gave him a tired smile. "Thank you for standing up for me today."

Rhys bowed, then brought my hand to his lips. "I am yours to command. Good night, Princess."

Lord John's face was blank, making it impossible for me to decipher what his thoughts were on my exchange with Rhys. I followed the steward down the hall, leaving Rhys to go wherever he was staying. I briefly wondered if now that we were betrothed he would be given his own rooms here to ensure his safety, or if that would only happen after the wedding.

As we reached my rooms, Lord John paused in front of the doors. "You have a visitor."

I raised my eyebrows in surprise. "Who?"

"Ghilanna," Lord John said. "I know you're tired, but she was hoping to talk to you immediately after the joust, and well, you know how that went."

"Does the king know?" I asked tiredly. I did not want to stir up any more trouble for myself tonight.

"No, I did not feel this was important enough to bother him," Lord John said and patted me on the arm. "Now. Go, visit with your friend, and then rest."

I nodded and slipped through the door, locking it behind me. The room was bathed in warm lamplight. Ghilanna was sitting on the couch near a low table filled with bite-sized snacks, a pitcher of water, and tea.

"Quite a day, eh?" said Ghilanna with a wry smile.

I sighed and sat on the edge of the couch. "You could say that. After the joust, I just needed to be away for a moment."

"Well, you caused quite a stir among your guests and the king. He was furious, you know," Ghilanna said.

I shrugged. "To be expected. When I inquired about taking the stallion out for a ride a few days ago, the guards told me the king forbade it." I ran my fingers over my dress, noting how filthy it was from riding bareback and slogging through wet grass. "Lord John said you wanted to talk. I'm tired and I love you, but can we just get to the point?"

Ghilanna sighed. "Yes. Do you remember how I told you that Solana built rapport with the locals and that many of them have been seeking close ties to the Fae since then?" I nodded, wondering why this couldn't have waited until the morning. Ghilanna continued, "Well, they want to meet you tomorrow."

"Tomorrow?" I replied, then snagged a biscuit off the table and nibbled on it.

"Yes. They feel it is important to get to know you before the wedding," Ghilanna explained.

"They have agreed to come to the palace?" I asked.

Ghilanna shook her head. "No. You must go to them. They want to meet you at your old house."

My lips trembled as sadness swept through me. My father had been murdered in our garden, and then my mother and I found horses and ran. Meeting at the house meant I would have to face the memories. "Anywhere but there," I whispered.

"I'm sorry. They were quite firm on the location and unwilling to explain why. Though Commander Meriel gave me some information about Solana before I left Jade Wilds, she did not tell me everything. Perhaps there is something special about the house?" Ghilanna suggested.

I bit my lip, trying to steady my breathing. "Not that I know of."

Ghilanna gave me an apologetic look. "Okay. I will make sure we have time before they are supposed to arrive so that you can settle yourself. I know this is going to be hard, but I will be there if you need me."

Ghilanna poured cups of tea for us and offered me one. I took a sip: chamomile, and it was the perfect temperature. I let the tea soothe me as we sat in companionable silence. I didn't have the energy to carry on much of a conversation. Not wanting to be rude and throw my friend out, I couldn't muster any words to fill the silence.

"How do you feel about Rhys Mongan winning the competition?" Ghilanna asked.

I had just taken a sip of my tea and gasped, sending me into a coughing fit as it tried to go into my lungs. Eyes watering, I finally got myself under control and took a tiny sip of tea to soothe my raw throat.

"Of the six competitors who competed in the joust, he was the only one remaining who seemed to have a genuine interest in me as an individual and not just as a prize. I can't imagine my grandfather is pleased that an outsider won. However, he was the one who approved the competitors," I replied.

Ghilanna studied me as though debating her next words. "I swear there are times when Rhys behaves as though he knows you. Did you meet growing up?"

"No, I've never met him before," I replied and nibbled on my lip in thought. "Though I think I told you the headaches seem to go away when he touches me."

"Maybe he knew your mother and has a family connection somehow?" Ghilanna replied thoughtfully.

"Perhaps. I don't know much about him yet. We have sparred a few times," I said and blushed as I recalled almost kissing him.

"Is that all you did?" Ghilanna teased.

I rolled my eyes. She must have noticed my blush. "Yes."

"Do you want to do more?" she pressed.

I took a long sip of my tea, not sure how to answer. I had not even confided in Ghilanna about the miscarriage, and now, when I was so tired I could barely think straight, was not the right time.

When the cup was empty, I set it down and looked at her. "Now that we are betrothed—soon to be wed—I won't have a choice in the matter. It is our duty to provide the South with an heir."

Ghilanna scooted closer to me on the couch, so we were touching. "You always have a choice. No one can force you to have sex if you don't want to, Serafina."

I frowned. That was not how my grandfather had phrased things. And I had no idea if I had had a choice the time that resulted in becoming pregnant. But she was right, I always had a choice to stand up for myself. It was possible Rhys would even be willing to help me lie to the king about having sex.

"What do *you* think of Rhys?" I asked, turning the question back on her.

Ghilanna chuckled at my tactic, then grew serious. "I did some digging. Rhys Mongan served as a sergeant for the knight training facility at Eagle Rock for ten years before he was discharged for disobeying a direct order during a skirmish with the Fae."

"What did he do?" I asked.

"I have no idea. I couldn't find any details of what the order was. Only that he was discharged. He must have *some* leadership skills; otherwise, he would never have earned the title of sergeant," Ghilanna said.

"What about ..." *Commander Meriel* was on the tip of my tongue when pain lanced through my eyes. I lost my grip on the teacup and it fell to the ground, shattering. I clutched my face with my hands.

Ghilanna wrapped her arms around me and rubbed my back. "What happened?" she said keeping her tone soft.

"Daggers in my eyes," I mumbled. Closing my eyes did not help. My breathing became shallow as I struggled with the pain.

Ghilanna's fingers spread out on my back, and I felt them warm up. I cracked my eyes open a slit and the space around me was glowing in the soft white of Ghilanna's magic. The pain decreased by a hair. "Better?" she asked.

"Not really," I whispered, squeezing my eyes shut again.

"Let's get you in bed," Ghilanna replied.

I wanted to protest that I was dirty and needed a bath, but the words would not come.

I don't know if I blacked out or not, but one moment I was on the couch and the next I was tucked into my bed, eyelids heavy. Ghilanna was lying on top of the covers next to me, her hand still on my back. I let my eyes shut and slid into a deep sleep.

I was riding Dubhar in the field. There were several fallen trees. Nudging him into a canter, I used my seat to direct him toward the nearest one. Wrapping my fingers in his mane, I raised my butt off his back into a jumping position. Dubhar's muscles rippled beneath me as he gathered himself.

"One, two, three," *I said softly, more for myself than for the stallion. Dubhar launched us into the air, and we sailed over the tree with ease. I focused on the next tree, the wind tugging my hair out of its braid, sending loose strands into my eyes.*

As we approached the tree, I became aware of a presence nearby. I glanced over my shoulder and was surprised to see a snow leopard following us, though by its demeanor, we were not being hunted, just followed. Dubhar snorted, as if to say, "What took you so long to notice?" Otherwise, the horse clearly had no concerns about our predatory shadow.

Thirty-Six

TRISTAN

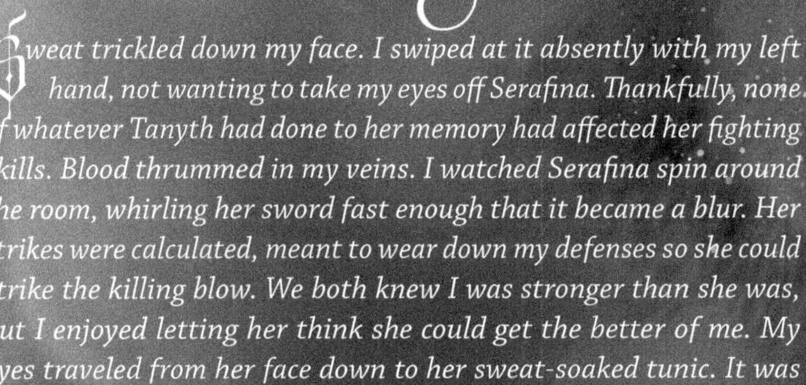

Sweat trickled down my face. I swiped at it absently with my left hand, not wanting to take my eyes off Serafina. Thankfully, none of whatever Tanyth had done to her memory had affected her fighting skills. Blood thrummed in my veins. I watched Serafina spin around the room, whirling her sword fast enough that it became a blur. Her strikes were calculated, meant to wear down my defenses so she could strike the killing blow. We both knew I was stronger than she was, but I enjoyed letting her think she could get the better of me. My eyes traveled from her face down to her sweat-soaked tunic. It was a light enough color that I could see the outline of her nipples as the fabric clung to her.

Desire wove through me. Serafina clucked her tongue when she realized I was staring at her breasts and darted in, jabbing me lightly with her blade. I smirked, letting go of my sword. It clattered to the floor, and her eyes followed it. I took her sword blade between my two hands and tugged. The metal sliced into my palms.

"Tristan!" she gasped as the blood dripped down the sword. She let go of the hilt, and I released the blade before it could do any more damage. Pulling my hands toward her, she inspected the cuts, but even as we watched, I could see the wounds healing.

"I'm fine, see?" I replied.

Serafina's eyes were wide. She let go of my hands and wrapped her arms around me. She tipped her face up, and her lips met mine. Eagerly, I deepened the kiss, pulling her tight against me. "I love you," I whispered against her lips.

"Did you grab my sword to just to tell me that?" she demanded.

I kissed her again. "Yes. Do you mind?"

Instead of answering the question, she reached between us and ran her hand along the length of my cock. I hissed in pleasure. Serafina nipped my lips and then unlaced my pants and fell to her knees in front of me.

Freeing my cock with her hands, she guided it into her mouth. I gasped as she sucked on the tip, then wrapped her hands around my hips and tugged. As she consumed me, her nails dug into my buttocks. Taking the hint, I thrust with my hips and bumped the back of her throat but let her have full control.

My whole body was wound tight. Serafina drew me into her mouth, her teeth grazing my tender flesh. Pleasure rolled through me as I spasmed with my release. Serafina's mouth released me and she stood, then deliberately swallowed my cum while watching my expression. I pulled her toward me and kissed her, thrusting my tongue deep into her mouth, relishing the taste of my seed.

"My turn," I said, smiling and trailing kisses from her breasts to her navel on my way down to my knees. I was reaching for the tie on her pants when I noticed someone was watching from the shadows. I shot to my feet, gray magic swirling around my hands.

"Betrayer," snarled Travaran.

My eyes widened in shock as my best friend stalked toward me as though I was his prey. Travaran, Prince Tanyth's heir, had died at Serafina's hand before she was captured and taken to Dorcha Palace.

"I would never betray you, Travaran," I replied calmly.

Travaran spit at my feet. "Yet you're the one fucking the half-blood. Hell, you're even marrying her. How is that not betrayal? Does everything you've ever stood for mean nothing now?"

My hands curled into fists. "We might have been friends, but you only knew the part of me you wanted to know. The part that your father approved of. You, Travaran, never took the time to ask how I really felt about humans. But you wouldn't have accepted my answer anyhow, not if it wasn't the same as yours."

"Well, the good news is you no longer have to pretend, because your life has been forfeit," Travaran announced. There was a swirl of teal magic, and Fleshrender appeared in Travaran's hand. I could not hide my grimace.

Travaran ran toward me, sword raised. I tried to move but found I was rooted in place.

"Stop!" I shouted.

My shoulder hit the wood floor first. I thrashed against the blankets that were wrapped tightly around me, trying to make sense of where I was.

"Tristan?" came Callyn's voice from a few feet away.

I took a deep breath. *I'm at Wayside Inn. In the room I share with Callyn. Travaran is dead.* "It was just a dream."

"You were shouting," Callyn said tiredly.

I shoved the sheets away from me and stood up. "I'm sorry."

"Do you want to tell me about it?" Callyn asked.

"No," I replied. "It was just a dream. It's not important." I put my sheets back on the bed and slid under them, hoping I could go to sleep. Images of Travaran calling me a betrayer kept flashing through my mind.

I must have fallen asleep again, because when I woke up the small curtain was open and daylight streamed onto my face. Callyn's bed was made, as though no one had even slept in it.

Sniffing the air, I cringed. I smelled like sweat, sex, and *horse*. I realized I had climbed into bed without bathing. I quickly made my bed, noting I would have to change the sheets before sleeping in it again.

"Going to take a shower?" Callyn teased.

"Yes. I can't believe you didn't force me to take one last night," I muttered.

Callyn chuckled. "You were tired, and rightfully so. I figured you needed the rest and that I could survive one night of you smelling terrible." She gave me a sly glance. "Who did you find to sleep with you in this city? Most of the humans hate Fae."

"I didn't. I had a dream," I said flatly. Callyn didn't respond. I assumed she knew who the dream was about.

"Soon you will have her back," Callyn said softly.

"And if the bond can't be fixed?" I asked.

"You can love her without needing the bond. I can see that with my own eyes. It will simply take longer for her to be as comfortable with you," Callyn said.

I blew out my breath. I knew she was right, but part of me craved the feel of the bond that we had shared. Knowing what it meant to have found a soulmate only to have it ripped from us was unbearable at times. "I'm going to shower."

"Don't take too long. I heard some rumors about a gathering on the northwest side of Gaskal, and I want you to come with me," Callyn said.

"A human gathering?" I asked incredulously. *Why do we suddenly care about human gatherings?*

"It has to do with Solana," Callyn said.

Serafina's mother, my mind supplied. "I'll be fast." *What a strange new development.*

Thirty-Seven

SERAFINA

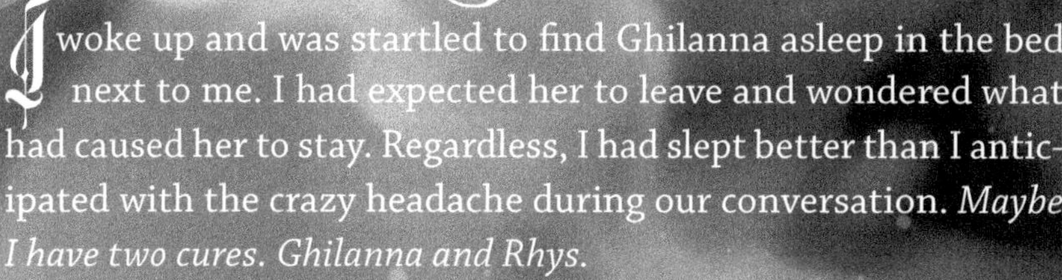

I woke up and was startled to find Ghilanna asleep in the bed next to me. I had expected her to leave and wondered what had caused her to stay. Regardless, I had slept better than I anticipated with the crazy headache during our conversation. *Maybe I have two cures. Ghilanna and Rhys.*

Shifting the blankets, I slipped out from underneath them and padded into the bathroom, throwing a few looks over my shoulder to reassure myself that Ghilanna was still sleeping on the bed. Running the bath, I let my thoughts drift to the dream I'd had of riding Dubhar. *I have a connection to him. I will have to put in a request to the stable that Dubhar become my personal horse.*

When the height of the water in the tub was to my liking, I stripped out of the nightgown and climbed in, relieved that I had no traces of illness of any sort. *Hopefully it stays that way.* The water was the perfect temperature. I found myself wondering if Rhys liked his baths as hot as I did or if he preferred the water cooler. That, among other personal preferences, would soon be known to me.

Not wanting to worry about what might face me at my parents' old house, I instead focused on getting clean and deciding what I would wear for this meeting.

Clean, dressed, and fed, I only had one last task to do: inform Thomas of the plans. "Ghilanna is taking me to my parents' house," I explained.

"I'm going with you," Thomas declared. I had expected him to not want to allow me out of his sight. Especially not going into the city.

Ghilanna frowned. "The humans we're meeting will be suspicious of a guard. I doubt they would even show their faces if you're there."

Thomas stood his ground. "Except you're wrong. I sat in Solana and Gareth's kitchen drinking tea and listening to Solana's stories of Fae when I was a young boy. The only reason they have insisted on a meeting *now* is because I have kept them apprised of the situation here. Just as by their orders I delivered Gareth's letter to Serafina."

I sucked in a breath. Thomas just admitted to essentially spying on me. Though I didn't feel like it was malicious, it made me uneasy nonetheless.

Ghilanna examined Thomas from head to toe. She didn't seem surprised by his revelation. "They said they had a man on the inside. I didn't realize it was Serafina's personal guard. Fine, you can come. Now please, let's go before we're late," Ghilanna said.

She led us through the small courtyard where I practiced weapons and out the nearly invisible door in the wall. On the other side, we found ourselves in the labyrinth that was part of the palace's largest garden. Though I had been this way before, Ghilanna was far more confident than I was as we wound our way through the garden, squeezing through a hedge here and a statue there until we reached the outer palace wall. We followed the gravel path until we reached the small gate the servants and guards used.

My apprehension grew the closer we got to the house. My feet felt heavier and heavier, as though someone was adding weights to the bottom of my boots. We rounded the corner, and I stumbled to a halt.

The three-rail wood fence, with stone columns to support the rails, was surprisingly in good shape. The rosebushes were neatly trimmed. The wood gate was shut, and it looked like someone had repaired the hinge that caused its tilt. Tears welled and dripped down my cheeks as memories flooded me.

From inside the house I heard a thud. Thud. *Mother shot out the back door. I dropped my messy embroidery and followed on her heels. My father was face-down in the grass, two arrows protruding from his back and others scattered around the lawn and in the fence. Blood, too much blood, seeped from the wounds onto his shirt.*

My mother whispered something I couldn't hear and then turned to me. "Quick, Sera. We must go."

"But Papa!" I protested, digging in my heels as her fingers wrapped around my arm and pulled me toward the door.

"Sera, Papa is dead. The only thing we can do now is run," Mother informed me. Her voice was harsh.

Does she not even care that Papa is dead? I wondered.

Reluctantly, I turned away and followed her into the house. Shouting began in the street, and I heard more thumps of arrows hitting the house. The threat is real. Knowing this, I stopped fighting with my mother and rushed into my bedroom for my bag. The one Papa asked me every night if it was ready.

"Just in case we want to sneak away to go camping without telling Mother," he'd tell me in a whisper.

Now I knew it had been a go bag in case we were no longer safe here. A neighbor who had horses was waiting for us at the front of the house. He helped me mount as my mother swung into the saddle.

As soon as we were on, mother kissed to the horses, and we took off at a gallop, weaving through people milling around the city street.

I shuddered. Ghilanna placed a hand on my arm. "We need to go inside."

I nodded mutely and led the way through the gate and into the house. Just as the exterior remained the same, so had the interior. A neat stack of logs by the fireplace. Pots on their hooks over the sink. The pink quilt laid along the back of the couch. I walked around the room, trailing my fingers over the surfaces. Even though my last memory was of running away, I had lived in the house for ten years that were filled with good memories. It was just difficult to recall them through the veil of emotions surrounding my father's murder.

I sat on the couch, pulling the pink quilt over my lap. "Are you going to tell me what they want to talk to me about before they get here, or is that going to be a surprise?" The words came out sharper than I intended.

"You are the heir of the South but also granddaughter to the King of Fae," Ghilanna explained.

I shrugged. "King Pharaan has many daughters and granddaughters. I am no different than the others and certainly don't have any claim to his throne. You and I both know Fae titles only pass to a male."

"Yes. I know that. But these people seem to think that it's not that simple. Nothing I have said will sway them. They want to see you," Ghilanna replied. "I suspect that this has to do with information Solana gave them that Commander Meriel doesn't know."

I opened my mouth to respond when there was a knock on the door, then an audible creak from the hinges as it swung open. "Good morning!" called a cheery voice.

"Josiah?" I said in surprise.

"You remember!" he exclaimed.

I stood up and walked over to him. Josiah Blackthorn was a burly man with a thick gray beard, bald head, and twinkling brown eyes. His hair had been solid black the last time I saw him, but otherwise he seemed unchanged.

"Of course." I hugged him. "How are the horses?"

Josiah shrugged. "Good. I heard about what you did with the king's black stallion. Riding *without tack*!" He tsked.

I shrugged. "It was safe."

"I taught you better than that, missy," he said, wagging his finger at me.

"Yes, and when I rode your horses bareback, you always mysteriously disappeared," I commented.

Josiah grinned. "You remember that?"

"Yes! And how angry Mother was," I said, then sucked in a breath.

Josiah stumbled forward as someone shoved him out of the way. I hopped to the side to avoid getting knocked over.

"Why are you blocking the door, Josiah?" demanded a strong woman's voice.

"Valerie," I said. She was Josiah's youngest sister, and, if I remembered correctly, had married a blacksmith on the other side of the city. Valerie had curly coal-black hair that framed her face and green eyes.

Valerie didn't hug me, not that I had expected her to. We only crossed paths when she was visiting Josiah, so we had never gotten close. Neither of my parents wanted me anywhere near the forge.

Valerie gave me a curt nod and then stepped out of the way. People continued to file into the room. *Where did they all come from?* A few other faces were vaguely familiar, though most I didn't think I'd ever met before. They certainly seemed comfortable in my parents' house.

"If everyone will find a seat, we can begin," announced Ghilanna.

I returned to my spot on the couch with the pink quilt draped over my legs. It made me feel like a child again, but I didn't care. It was challenging enough to not let my grief and old memories overwhelm me.

To my surprise, Josiah stood up and moved in front of the fireplace so he could address the whole room. "Thank you, Serafina, for coming here to meet with us. When you were born, your mother, Solana, made us swear to protect you as if you were our own. She also made us promise to allow you to grow up as a normal human child would, free of the responsibilities of a princess. Though we were reluctant, when she told us of her vision, we immediately agreed. I am sorry that you are learning this from us and not from Solana herself.

"As you have recently learned, your mother was a Fae seer. The majority of her visions revolved around the same thing: uniting humans and Fae to face an unimaginable enemy. One who, without both species united, would destroy everyone and everything in its wake. Originally, she came to Gaskal to spy for King Pharaan and to use Gareth to get close to King Leonard. However, she fell in love with Gareth, and soon after they married, she started having visions urging her to find common ground between humans and Fae, to prove that we can live together in harmony."

Valerie stepped forward and took his place. "Solana worked with our healers, taught them herb lore. She strengthened the potency of our herbal medications. An alternative to using magic, but better than traditional human medicine.

"Solana freely shared her knowledge with any who were willing to learn. Twice a week, she would train the youngsters in weapon skills and self-defense. We developed strategies for different types of attacks that could occur here in the city," Valerie explained.

Surprise and awe wound through me. My mother had truly dedicated herself to encouraging Fae and humans to accept each other as allies.

"You are the heir of the South and are marrying an outsider. Together you will lead the South and use our kingdom to set an example for the other human kingdoms to strengthen our relationship with the four Fae courts," Valerie asserted.

I moistened my dry lips with my tongue, then I spoke. "You make it sound easy. As though I can just demand the lords of the East, North, and West accept Fae as allies and all will be well. *And* you assume that the four Fae courts will willingly work with me." *I have faced animosity for being half-Fae before. I have no doubt I will do so again.*

Valerie chuckled darkly. "No one said anything about it being easy. Only that Solana had foreseen that the task would rest on your shoulders. Should you fail, then we will meet the end of time."

End of time? The words were familiar, but I was trying to place why. My gaze flicked to Ghilanna. To my surprise, she handed me a book. I ran my hand over the familiar cover. *Bedtime Tails.*

I flipped through the pages, skimming the various stories and hunting for the one that mentioned the end of time. I noted that most of the illustrations that had been in mine were missing from this copy.

Finally, I came across it.

When tension rises and war with the humans has come, the Lost Fae Queen will return.
First, she will prove her battle prowess.
Look closely or you might be blinded, for when the Fae Queen returns, not all will know her, yet everyone will follow her.
Be warned, the Fae Queen must stay pure until the Great Cat finds her and their souls unite.
With their souls bound, the heir will be found.
The Fae Queen's magic will return, and together they will defend the Fae from the end of time.
Time is of the essence, or the Fae will fall to the darkness.

"You think I am the Lost Fae Queen?" I demanded incredulously.

Valerie shrugged. "Solana never referred to you as such. But it's a rather large coincidence that it's mentioned in the Lost Fae Queen prophecy, don't you think?"

I couldn't decide what was stranger, the fact that Valerie knew so much more about my mother than I did, or that the humans in this room were clearly very comfortable with the idea that Fae prophecies could come true.

"I won't be queen of the South until my grandfather dies. I don't know if you spend much time around him, but he is quite healthy and has a very strong dislike for Fae. I doubt any maneuvers I would make within the South to encourage alliances with the Fae, even with our neighbor the Court of the Sun, would go over well. Then, you have the matter of the other things the prophecy addresses. I've never come across anyone called or resembling a Great Cat, and the possibility of being able to have a soulmate bond is low given I'm only half-Fae. Besides, Rhys is human. Humans can't have soulmate bonds," I said.

"We are confident that you will find a way to bring humans and Fae together. Prejudices can be softened. Perhaps the king has never had the opportunity to get to know a Fae himself. We know of the tension between you and King Leonard. Take the time now, while you can, to show him that you are more than just an heir in name alone. That you, mixed bloodline and all, are worthy of his title," Valerie replied. Murmurs of agreement spread throughout the room.

I sighed, feeling as though their confidence in me was strongly misplaced. I didn't know anything about diplomacy. Give me a sword and an opponent over the delicacies of politics any day. "I cannot promise you that I will be successful, but I will do my best." I had already tried to soften my relationship with my grandfather, but with every attempt, it felt like we ended up clashing even more.

Josiah nodded. "That's all we ask. We understand that the changes we want to see are not going to happen overnight. But unless you try to implement them, humans and Fae will continue to regard each other as potential enemies."

Tracing the floral pattern on the quilt, I considered my next words carefully, not sure I wanted the answer. "Do you have any idea how much time I have?"

Josiah shook his head. "Unfortunately, no. That was one thing that Solana was never able to tell us. Her visions did not give her a precise *when*, only that certain events would happen if specific conditions were met."

"I see," I responded. As good as it felt to see Josiah again, at this precise moment, I really wanted a chance to be alone. To process what they had just told me, preferably away from my parents' house. Josiah, Valerie, and the others expected me to encourage not just the South but the other three human kingdoms to form alliances with the Fae kingdoms. I was going to have to tread carefully and gather as much information as I could about the kings before I approached them.

Even if I fully trusted Rhys, I knew he couldn't help me. At least not with the first task. King Leonard disliked Fae as a rule, and the other kings were not likely to be any better. The only thing in my favor was that because I did not look Fae, they were more likely to at least listen to what I had to say instead of immediately dismissing me.

Whispers filled the room as small conversations broke out among everyone. I stood, the quilt sliding to the floor. "I must return to the palace. I promise to do what I can to help." I started to curtsey, then stopped myself, realizing that if anyone were to bow or curtsey, protocol stated it should be them to me, not the other way around. *Something else to get used to.*

I set the book on the couch, and before Ghilanna could block me, I strode out the front door and through the gate and began winding my way back to the palace. The crunch of gravel behind me indicated Thomas had caught up. I didn't slow my steps. Right now, I needed a chance to process on my own. *A ride on Dubhar?* The idea was incredibly appealing.

Head spinning with information from the meeting with Valerie and Josiah, I walked briskly toward the stable. Ghilanna had stayed, presumably to talk more to Valerie and Josiah, which suited me just fine. I wasn't sure I wanted her to add to the pressure I already felt from that meeting.

Valerie's words repeated over and over in my head. *"You are the heir of the South and are marrying an outsider. Together, you will lead the South and use our kingdom to set an example for the other human kingdoms to strengthen our relationship with the four Fae courts."* It was a lofty expectation for me to lead a human kingdom *and* strengthen relationships between humans and Fae. *Are they blind to the fact that not everyone wants me here?*

I slid into the stable through the barely open doors and rushed to Dubhar's stall. The striking black stallion immediately came to the front of his stall, smacking his lips together in greeting. I threw my arms around his neck and hugged him, grateful for one constant in my life who wouldn't judge me or give me nearly impossible tasks.

I heard the scuff of boots and half turned, keeping one hand on Dubhar's neck. Thomas had his arms full with the saddle, bridle, and brush box. I took the brush box, and he set down the saddle and hung the bridle on a hook.

"Thank you," I said warmly.

Thomas shrugged. "It's nothing."

It wasn't nothing, but I wasn't sure what else to say. It felt good to have someone in my corner who was willing to accept me without judgment. Knowing that he was part of the group my parents started was comforting because the last thing I needed was a guard who was going to stab me in the back—or watch someone else do it—for being a half-blood.

While I groomed and tacked up Dubhar, Thomas did the same for his own horse. I was half expecting him to insist on another guard coming with us, but to my surprise he didn't. About half the stalls were empty, but I wasn't in the stable enough to know if that was because many people were out riding right now or if they were usually vacant.

"Ready?" he asked as he led his horse, a bright red gelding with two white front socks, out of its stall.

"Yes," I said, smiling, and followed him out of the stable.

We mounted outside. Once on Dubhar's back, I could feel his muscles bunch like a spring waiting to be released. I patted his neck. "Easy, Dubhar." The last thing I needed was to take off at a gallop while still within the palace grounds.

Thomas took the lead, and we headed out the side gate and toward the big field. I loosened my reins as we got farther from the palace. When the gravel path disappeared into the field, I lightly tapped Dubhar's sides with my heels, and we shot forward like a cannonball.

As I found my rhythm with his stride, it felt like we were flying over the ground, he was moving so fast. I could hear the hoofbeats, but his gait was so smooth it was difficult to perceive each footfall. A quick glance behind me showed Thomas was following, but his horse was not nearly as fast as Dubhar.

The edge of the field approached and Dubhar's stride slowed until we were walking. I halted and waited for Thomas to catch up, feeling significantly better after the run. When he caught up to me, I noticed a chatter of voices coming from the trees.

"Who is that?" I asked.

Thomas's hand rested on his sword hilt, and we both stared at the trees as the voices came closer. "I don't know. The groom mentioned there were other riders out, but he didn't elaborate."

I blew out my breath. "Oh." *Hopefully they'll leave us alone.* The last thing I wanted right now was to be criticized by courtiers for one of many "transgressions" I was taking part in. Riding astride, riding a stallion, and wearing pants were the three most likely to get mentioned.

The group of riders became visible. I noticed Violet first since she was also riding astride, though unlike me, she was wearing a riding suit, not dressed like a man. I also recognized Duchess Oriana; Oriana's husband, Duke Herman; and their granddaughter, Lady Geneva. There was another lord with spiky red hair and a tiny mustache who looked familiar, but I couldn't remember his name.

Lady Geneva was the same age as Violet and myself. Her grandparents had been quite vocal about their concern for my half-human bloodline in conversations I'd overheard during the welcome banquet for the competitors. I was not looking forward to talking to them now.

Violet raised her hand and waved to us. I looked over at Thomas. "Can we leave?"

He gave me an amused smile. "No, because they have seen us. It would look bad for you as heir to not at least be polite and greet them."

I grimaced. "I was afraid you'd say that."

The group of nobles quickly closed the gap between us. Duchess Oriana eyed me with a slight curl in her lip before she noticed I was watching and her face became a careful mask. "Your Highness, it is wonderful to see you!" the duchess gushed.

I shifted in my saddle and reminded myself to be polite. "It's good to see you too, Your Grace." Sifting through what I knew about them, I came up with a suitable topic. "Were you able to settle the deal on your last wagonload of wool?"

Duke Herman gave me an appreciative smile. "Yes. The terms were quite favorable indeed. Thank you for remembering, Your Highness."

I opened my mouth to say something else polite and mundane when I heard hoofbeats behind us. Twisting in the saddle, I peered behind me and saw a pair of guards riding our way.

They halted an arm's length away, and I immediately recognized George. "Your Highness, my apologies for the interruption, but the seamstress was looking for you."

I sighed in relief. "I will come at once," I informed George, then returned my attention to the duke and duchess. "Please excuse me, I have wedding preparations to handle."

Without waiting for them to respond, I whirled Dubhar around and nudged him into a canter. The last thing I wanted was the duchess to mistakenly think I was inviting her to come with me.

Thirty-Eight

TRISTAN

When I returned to the palace after observing Serafina's meeting at her parents' house with Callyn, I couldn't help but think it had largely been a waste of time. The only piece of information we had gathered was she was meeting with humans at her parents' house, but since we hadn't been able to overhear anything, we had no idea what they had discussed. Bored and wanting to do something physical, one thought was foremost in my mind: sword work. Returning to the practice room Serafina and I had been in the other day, I opted to leave the door open just in case anyone was looking for me. I was working my way through a combination of high and low sword strikes followed by a crescent kick when I became aware of someone in the hallway. A telltale clink of metal told me it was likely a guard wearing chain mail. He paused in the doorway as I swapped my sword into my left hand, repeating the same combination.

"Pardon the intrusion, Master Mongan. I was informed you needed a sparring partner," the man said.

Who informed him? I lowered my sword and turned around. He was a short, stocky guard wearing a chain mail shirt, with an axe strapped on his back and a sword in a scabbard on his waist.

He had short, curly brown hair threaded with gray, a crooked nose, and warm brown eyes. His cheeks were dusted with brown stubble.

"And you are … ?" I asked, keeping my voice even. It wasn't his fault that someone had mistakenly assumed I wanted a sparring partner.

"Guard Nolan Westson, at your service," he said with a slight bow.

"Did you receive orders to come here, or do you honestly want to spar with me?" I asked, wanting the truth.

Nolan shrugged. "A bit of both, I suppose. Master Guard Declan has assigned me to you. I've heard rumors you have been sparring with the princess, and since she is busy, I thought you might want a partner."

I adjusted my grip on the sword to hide my dismay. I had known I would get assigned guards eventually, but I didn't expect them this soon. "I'm fully capable of defending myself from anything that comes my way."

To my surprise, Nolan nodded in agreement. "I am aware. However, orders are orders."

"Fine. Then yes, you can spar with me. Axe or sword, your choice," I replied. It wasn't worth the effort to pressure Nolan into ignoring his orders. *This is the price of marrying an heir of a human kingdom. Even if she were heir of a Fae court, the need for guards would be the same.* Until now, that hadn't sunk in all the way. All the years at Dorcha Palace, I had been the one doing the guarding, whether it was Travaran, Tanyth, or other protection details. This was the first time I had to consider the ramifications of having someone who was not directly under my command with me, our roles essentially reversed from my norm. *He'll be under my command when Serafina is queen.* But I had no idea how many years that would take. Until then, I was certain Nolan and whoever else ended up assigned to me would be reporting to Declan, who in turn would report directly to the king.

Maybe it's best to be upfront with Nolan now. I took a deep breath. "I want to get it out in the open that I have friends who are Fae, and I do not intend to alienate them now that I am betrothed to Princess Serafina."

Nolan gulped as though he had something stuck in his throat and then spoke. "As long as your friends do not pose a threat, whether they are human or Fae is of no consequence."

"What do you consider a threat?" I asked, genuinely curious. *Some might consider sparring a threat.*

"Attacking you unprovoked," Nolan said.

I raised my eyebrows. "What do you consider sparring, then?"

Nolan turned bright red. "You can spar with approved guests," he grudgingly conceded.

Not wanting to get into an argument, I did not ask what it would take to get a guest of mine approved to spar with me. I highly doubted that King Leonard, who had made his dislike of Fae very clear, would allow me to spar with one. Not at the risk of me accidentally dying or being rendered incapable of fathering a child.

I had no illusions that King Leonard's primary intention was anything other than to ensure the Helias bloodline continued as soon as possible. *What about when he finds out I'm not human? Is King Leonard going to want me to sire a child to continue the Helias line then?* Though I knew that Serafina would have to still want me first before King Leonard's opinion would come into play.

Which brought me back to my concern over the pressure on Serafina to have a child and how she would take it. I understood all too well what it meant to fulfill one's duty, but I held out hope that we would be able to warm up to each other and decide on our own terms when we attempted to create an heir.

Nolan unbuckled his scabbard and set it on the table, then tugged his axe out of its sheath. "I'll use my axe," he announced.

I nodded, wondering if he was going to remove the chain mail or keep it on.

The guard made no move to remove the armor, so I stepped into the center of the ring and gave my sword an experimental swing. Nolan set himself up an arm's length from me, legs wide, axe balanced evenly in his hand. I noted how comfortable he appeared with the axe. In making me human, the pendant's magic had also slightly diminished my energy levels, which meant I tired easier than before. *Like a human.* I was curious to see how well my guard handled himself.

"One, two, three!" I called.

On three, Nolan swept his axe to the right, arcing into a high strike and then bringing it down hard. I blocked, my sword vibrating from the impact. Sliding my blade along his, I thrust, disengaging the two weapons. Spinning to my left, I entered a low-mid combination, forcing Nolan to react fast.

The guard met each strike with an appropriate block. I had a feeling that if I wanted, I could outmaneuver Nolan, but there was no reason for me to do so. Not all sparring practice had to be about proving one or the other was the best; it could simply be about getting time with the weapon in your hand against someone else. *Maybe if I don't pound him into the ground, I'll earn his respect.*

Nolan swung the axe up in an underhand mid-strike, and his grip loosened, making the axe slide closer to his hand. I knew the strike would fall short and didn't bother blocking it.

"Let's take a water break," I suggested.

Nolan gave me a relieved smile. "Good idea." The guard's face was red from exertion, and sweat beaded on his brow and cheeks. Even his hair was damp. I was tempted to suggest he remove the chain mail, knowing it would reduce the load, but Nolan had made his decision to wear it when we started, and I wasn't sure my suggestion would be appreciated now.

We were facing off again in the center of the room when I heard booted feet, at least two sets, heading our way. I lowered my sword and turned toward the door. Master Guard Declan entered first, guards fanning out around him, and then King Leonard entered.

I bowed deeply, and Nolan did the same. He seemed as surprised as I was by our royal visitor.

"It is time you and I have a chat, Rhys," announced King Leonard.

I glanced around the room, wondering if this was where we were going to conduct our chat. Other than the table and one chair, there wasn't much in here; just open space to practice.

"Yes, Your Majesty," I replied.

Declan beckoned to someone in the hallway I couldn't see. Several palace servants walked in carrying a heavy chair that was well padded and covered in gold jacquard fabric. They set the chair down and stepped out of the way to make room for a round table and a second chair. Next came a tray of tiny sandwiches. When everything was arranged, the servants filed out.

King Leonard sat down in the chair facing me and motioned for me to sit in the other one. I did so, and Nolan took up a position on the wall with the other guards. I tucked a strand of hair behind my ear and waited for the king to tell me what he wanted.

King Leonard took a sip of water and then spoke. "From your wedding night until my death, your only role is to ensure the Helias bloodline continues."

I swallowed hard, the topic and the king's bluntness catching me off guard.

"Of course, I do not want you to force Serafina to have sex against her will," the king continued.

I coughed. *He thought I would follow his order if he said to rape her?* My dislike for King Leonard was growing by the moment. I clenched my jaw, not wanting to anger the king by speaking.

"You will have most of my resources at your disposal to woo her and produce the heir. However, you will not be permitted to take her outside of the city walls or palace grounds without my express permission. A trip out of the kingdom is forbidden as well," King Leonard said. I could hear the edge in his tone.

Freedom to do as I please if my objective is getting Serafina into bed? I couldn't decide if I was happy at the chokehold being loosened or angry that it was only for one purpose—and not because he wanted Serafina to have freedom to be herself.

"I understand." I ground the words out, then took a sandwich and shoved it in my mouth to keep from spewing my real thoughts.

King Leonard's mouth twitched as though he was amused by my reaction. "I want to make sure you understand that you do not have an official position within my court until Serafina becomes queen. If you had arrived in possession of a noble title, then the situation would be different. However, if you prove yourself, I might be able to give you responsibilities."

Prove myself how? By getting Serafina pregnant quickly? I wasn't sure I wanted to know what responsibilities King Leonard thought I would be worthy of. The background Callyn and I had devised for Rhys was that he had grown up at the knight training facility in Eagle Rock and had been involved in training knights. If I was in King Leonard's shoes, I would take advantage of having another individual who could help with training the guards and keeping them brushed up on their skills. I doubted King Leonard had any intention of doing that.

Declan approached the king and bent over, whispering in his ear. A smile flickered across the king's face, then was gone. "I am needed elsewhere. Remember what I said, Rhys."

I stood hastily and bowed as King Leonard stood up and departed. The room emptied out till it was only Nolan and me left with the additional furniture and the tray of food.

"Did you want to practice more, or would you like me to show you to your assigned suite?" Nolan asked. He strapped his scabbard on and put the axe on his back.

"The suite is fine. Thank you," I said.

The first thing I did when I got into my new suite of rooms was go into the bathroom and firmly shut the door. Taking a deep breath, I tugged on my beard, mulling over the king's words. *Is Nolan only for my protection, or has he been instructed to report to the king the details of my wooing efforts?* Given I had just met Nolan, I did not feel comfortable asking him. I knew Serafina had established a good rapport with her guard, Thomas, and hoped in time I would have a similar one with Nolan.

I walked over to the sink and washed my face. When I was done, I braced my hands on the edge of the sink and stared into the mirror. A shadow filled the space behind me before materializing into Travaran.

"Betrayer!" he whisper-shouted.

I spun, fists raised, to face Travaran, but there was no one with me. Hands trembling, I combed my fingers through my hair. *Travaran is dead.* Yet I could not shake the feeling that he was right. I did betray people. Hell, I was in the process of doing so now as I masqueraded as Rhys Mongan. At Dorcha Palace, I had done terrible things under the command of Prince Tanyth. Now the only one I could blame was myself. *Maybe I should never have left. Things were simpler at Dorcha Palace.*

Closing my eyes, I took a shallow breath, trying to shake the thought that I did not deserve the freedom I had worked so hard for. It was late; too late, I assumed, for Nolan to easily agree to an excursion to down to Wayside Inn to talk to Callyn, and without my magic, I had no way of sending her a message.

I heard a soft knock on the door. "Are you okay?" Nolan called.

I opened the door. "I want to go for a run," I declared.

To my surprise, Nolan merely said, "I know the perfect place."

Thirty-Nine

SERAFINA

Sparring with a sword was akin to an intricate dance, except there was no predetermined choreography. I focused on maintaining a high level of speed with precise strikes and parries. My opponent was a Fae with slate-gray hair and gray skin. His hair was loose and cascaded around his shoulders. One pointy ear was visible.

The Fae stranger met my strikes effortlessly, driving me to increase my speed yet again. He must make a mistake at some point. I could feel his intense blue eyes as I pivoted on my left foot and then swept the sword up in an arc, aiming for his collarbone.

The Fae brought his sword up a hair too slowly. I twisted my wrist so the flat of my sword—not the edge of my blade—hit his collarbone. I gasped and took a step back, my wrist vibrating with the impact. Our eyes met, and I could feel the blood starting to thrum in my veins.

I moved away from him. *Why am I attracted to a Fae?* He took advantage of my distraction, and I gasped when his sword lightly nicked my throat. Not wanting him to think I was weak, I backed up and launched into a middle-high combination with a middle strike finish. As I thrust my sword at his stomach for the finishing move, he *grabbed the sword blade between his two hands and yanked. Blood flowed from his hands to the floor.*

I let go of the sword in shock. As soon as the Fae dropped the sword, I grabbed his wrists, staring at his palms. Yet, he was healing. With my hands on his wrists, I became aware of desire snaking through me.

As though he sensed my intention before I took action, the Fae wrapped his arms around me and placed his velvety lips on mine. I parted my lips and let his tongue explore my mouth. The longer we kissed, the more my core throbbed, driving me to want to do far more than kiss.

I reached between us and ran my hand along the length of his cock through his pants. I smirked at his hiss of pleasure. A wicked idea came to me as we kissed. I unlaced his pants and then dropped to my knees. Wrapping my hand around his cock, I stroked, then wrapped my tongue around his tip and gently sucked. His moan was all the encouragement I needed. I drew him into my mouth until his cock bumped the back of my throat. Hands around his hips, I found my rhythm, occasionally scraping my teeth along his shaft to enhance his pleasure. His whole body was taut. With one more tug, his cock spasmed, and his seed flooded my mouth.

My body was strung tight as I wrung the last bit out of the Fae, then stood, gazing at him. He kissed me deeply and slid his hand eagerly down my pants, plunging his fingers into my drenched folds. Small tremors went through me as the Fae used his fingers expertly, then, with one small flick to my clitoris, I got my release and sagged into his arms.

I woke up with a start. My hand was between my legs and covered in fluids. I wrinkled my nose at the idea that a *dream* had made me do that. Not only any dream, but a dream about a *Fae.* I sat up, confusion filling me. *Why am I dreaming about being intimate with a Fae?* I understood a dream like that about Rhys, especially given it was inevitable we would have sex at the very least on our wedding night. Even a dream about Prince Tanyth would have made sense given we were engaged mere weeks ago. I had no idea where this gray-haired, gray-skinned Fae had come from. I blushed in embarrassment, praying this was not how it would be for me, married to one man and mooning over someone entirely different.

I heard Violet's footsteps before she appeared at the edge of the bed and threw back the bedcurtains. "Good morning, Serafina," she said cheerfully.

I hastily wiped my hand on the sheets before shoving the covers away and swinging my legs over the side of the bed. "What's on today's agenda?"

"Breakfast with Duchess Oriana and Lady Francesca," Violet replied.

I bit back a groan, wondering who had scheduled a meeting with Duchess Oriana. That marked two interactions in two days. *Too many, in my book.* It dawned on me that the ride had not been scheduled and if anyone was to blame it was me, but the idea of seeing her again so soon was less than appealing. Raising my arms above my head, I stretched, working the kinks out of my lower back.

Breakfast was in one of the rooms designated as "the queen's parlors." The walls were decorated with rose wallpaper. The flowers were so detailed that I was tempted to touch them to make sure they weren't real. The servants had set up a buffet-style breakfast with an assortment of meats, eggs, and fresh fruit for us to select from.

My mouth was full of eggs and sausage when Duchess Oriana spoke. "I saw one of the Fae filth in the city today. Shopping among the humans as though they have a right to be here."

The food turned to lead in my mouth, but I forced myself to swallow. "There is no law saying Fae cannot walk freely in the city." My words were harsh.

Duchess Oriana looked at me like she had just noticed I was present. "Why would you want them to walk freely? They're terrible creatures."

Lady Francesca echoed her agreement and kept from meeting my gaze. Offering Duchess Oriana my opinion was useless. Her mind was set, and nothing I said would sway her.

To my dismay, Duchess Oriana patted my hand as though we were friends. "When you become queen, you can do what King Leonard has not: make it illegal for Fae to set foot in the South."

I snatched my hand away from her and shoved my chair back, fuming. I shot a glance at Thomas and his look was full of warning. I swallowed hard and looked at Duchess Oriana, then Lady Francesca. "I will keep your request in mind if I become queen. I am unwell, and we will have to resume our conversation later." I clutched my stomach to sell the lie, and Thomas rushed over to usher me out.

"Are you really sick?" he asked.

I dropped my arms and straightened once we were away from the rose parlor. "No, I'm fine. I just can't stand women like that. Obviously she thinks that I have no loyalty to Fae whatsoever; otherwise, she would realize that as a half-Fae, I'm the last person she should be talking to about making any anti-Fae laws."

"She'll get what's coming to her," Thomas murmured.

Casting him a sharp glance, I said, "What do you mean?"

"How do you expect people to accept your plan of bringing Fae and humans closer together unless you eliminate the ones like Duchess Oriana who are extreme in their views about human superiority?" Thomas demanded.

"I will not condone violence simply because she has a different view than I do," I said firmly.

I wandered blindly through the halls of the palace, not paying attention to where my feet were carrying me. *Anywhere but that room.* I shuddered. Duchess Oriana was not shy about disliking Fae—and almost certainly didn't like me either—but this was the first time she had spoken openly about wanting to ban Fae from the South entirely. Even if there were times I was frustrated by my dual heritage, I did not want to see Fae forcefully driven out of human territories. As it stood, very few Fae were willing to interact with humans for precisely this reason.

Eyes focused on the pathway, I walked straight into someone. Strong hands gripped my arms to steady me. Startled, I lifted my head fast and clunked it on the chin of the person gripping me.

"Ouch," grunted Rhys.

"Sorry," I mumbled, rubbing the top of my head. "I should watch where I'm going."

Rhys gave me a lopsided grin. "You can run into me any time."

I rolled my eyes. I didn't make it a habit of smashing into people in hallways. "Care to walk with me?"

"Sure. Is everything okay?" Rhys asked.

I sighed and slid my arm through his, and we turned down the hallway that neither one of us had been coming from, continuing my random wandering. "It's nothing. Just a lady with a strong opinion."

To my dismay, Rhys asked the question I had been hoping to avoid. "Opinion about what?"

"That Fae deserve to die," I finally said. I was curious to hear Rhys's response and get a better gauge of his feelings about Fae.

"Harsh," Rhys murmured.

"Yes. I think that because I look human, they feel more comfortable telling me their true feelings, assuming I share the same opinion."

"It's not a bad thing for a noblewoman to believe that she can relate to you. It could help you win her support if you need it in the future," Rhys said wisely.

I grimaced, thinking about how I had left the breakfast. "I ruined that chance."

Behind us, Thomas chuckled and then coughed, presumably to hide it. I wasn't convinced that befriending Duchess Oriana was worth my time. There were others in this court who were not as extreme.

Rhys patted my hand. "What is your favorite weapon?"

I bit back a laugh, grateful that he could read me at least that well. "I prefer a longsword."

"I prefer the broadsword," Rhys said.

I stopped walking, eyeing Rhys. *A broadsword?*

"Doesn't that tire you quickly?" I asked.

Rhys's eyes got wide for a moment, as though he just realized what weapon he had said. "It does. What I should have said is I like to train with the broadsword so that when I use a longsword in actual battle, it's easy in comparison. The extra weight helps build muscles and stamina."

His explanation was sound, though I still thought it was odd he said he preferred a broadsword. I shrugged and let it drop. "What about archery?"

"Bow or crossbow, I can use both," he replied.

"Me too," I said. *What else can we discuss besides weapons?* I'd never spent much time hanging out with males. I had no idea what we should talk about.

I peered around us and was surprised to see we were approaching one of the gardens. Walking outside in the sunshine was appealing. I adjusted our course, and we walked through the doors leading us into the garden.

Rhys cleared his throat, then spoke. "We are soon to be wed, and one day you will be queen. What role do you want me to have?"

I considered the question, knowing my answer could have a significant impact on the future we had together. "It is my hope that you will serve as an advisor to me." I wasn't sure if I wanted to offer a virtual stranger the possibility of also being co-ruler. I knew once it was on the table it would be harder to retract. Whereas as an advisor, there was room for me to place different values on his advice depending on the situation or even how our relationship was faring.

I blushed, thinking of the most urgent responsibility that my grandfather had put on my shoulders: making an heir. *No time like the present to discuss it.* "How do you feel about children?" I asked, blush deepening as Rhys paused our walk so he could face me.

Rhys replied in a calm voice, "I am open to however many children you want, whenever you are ready."

I sighed in relief at his response. "Thank you. I've always wanted at least one." I swallowed hard as I realized that I had almost had one, but that had been ripped from me, like my memories. Shoving those feelings away, I continued, hoping Rhys wouldn't notice I wasn't quite myself. "Honestly, children have been far from my mind. At the battle of Emerald Valley, I was made a full warrior. Ready to take more responsibilities at Jade Wilds or potentially a Fae court."

Rhys took my hand and kissed my knuckles, sending shivers down my spine. "Like I said, whenever you are ready. Now or in ten years or longer. It is of no consequence to me."

What would King Leonard say if he thought we might wait ten years! I admired Rhys's openness and commitment to allowing *me* to decide when I would be ready. It was a far cry from my grandfather's pushiness.

Lips parted slightly, I tipped forward, my eyes lingering on Rhys's mouth. Rhys dipped his head down, but before our lips could touch, there was a commotion. I sprang away from Rhys as though his touch scalded me. Face heating, I refused to look at him and instead waited for whoever was coming to appear.

Violet darted around the corner and almost ran into Thomas. I choked back a laugh at her surprise. *She knows Thomas is everywhere I am.* "The seamstress is waiting, Princess Serafina."

I frowned, then I remembered the seamstress was coming for us to figure out the wedding dress. I half turned to Rhys. "Sorry, but I need to go. We can finish later."

Rhys nodded, though his expression was unreadable. I departed with Violet and Thomas bringing up the rear. *Finish what later?* My cheeks heated again as I realized had left it open to interpretation.

Following the lengthy appointment with the seamstress, I was desperate to get out of the palace. Thankfully, Violet was up for a late afternoon ride. Once in the stable, Violet and I took our time grooming the horses. Dubhar was thoroughly enjoying his lengthy brushing session. Peering across the aisle, I could tell Violet's horse, whose eyes were closed and lip was drooping, was also enjoying the attention. My wrist was starting to cramp from the continuous brushing. I decided Dubhar was clean enough and stepped half out of the stall to grab the saddle blanket and saddle. I snagged the bridle off the hook, slipped the bit into his mouth and the leather over his ears, then fastened the buckles. Dubhar rubbed his face on my tunic. I chuckled. "We're almost ready, promise."

Shooting a glance over my shoulder, I saw Violet leading her horse out of the stall. *We're ready.*

After exiting the stable, we mounted up and then took off at a brisk trot heading toward the meadow. Thomas was close behind us with the other guards fanning out a bit farther away. A reminder that I was never really going to be alone again. "For my safety," I muttered.

"Did you say something?" asked Violet. I shook my head, surprised she'd heard me.

Dubhar's gait was smooth as we crossed the palace courtyard and slipped through the gate out to the field. Thankfully, no one else had decided to come out for a ride—likely because it was colder in the mornings and less favorable conditions for riding. Neither of us minded though.

"Let's go!" I shouted and nudged Dubhar with my heels. He burst into a ground-covering gallop, but Violet was neck and neck with us. Dubhar slowly lengthened his stride, keeping us just a hair past Violet. I was certain if I had wanted we could have galloped far faster than Violet, but we were out to have fun, not for me to win a nonexistent race. The tree line was approaching; Dubhar slowed into a smooth canter, and we turned to go around the perimeter. At this pace, Violet and I could have a discussion and hear each other.

"Are you excited about the wedding?" Violet asked, eyes sparkling with her own eagerness.

"Honestly, I'm not sure. Part of me wants to get it over with as quickly as possible. The other part I don't think has had a chance to digest that I am getting married tomorrow. The pace that we're going through everything is so quick. It's a lot to wrap my mind around. I wish sometimes that I could just freeze time," I explained.

Violet's eyes widened. "Is that something Fae can do? Freeze time?"

I laughed. "No. That's not a real magic ability. Fae seers can foretell events that might come to pass in the future, but they can't manipulate time itself."

Disappointment filled Violet's face. "Oh. I thought that was possible."

I shook my head. "Unfortunately, no. Most Fae magic is tied to elements. There's also shadow magic and shapeshifting."

"I think I've heard of some of those before. Aren't shapeshifters animals who can become Fae?" Violet asked.

Dubhar slowed down to a bouncy trot. I took a moment to consider my response as I used my legs and seat to encourage Dubhar to smooth out his gait. "As far as I know, shapeshifters are Fae who can take on an animal form."

"Have you seen one before? A shapeshifter, I mean?" Violet asked.

I could feel the beginning of a headache coming on. "No. I haven't seen a shapeshifter." Instead of elaborating on my answer, I dug my heels into Dubhar harder than I intended and he half-reared before shooting forward. The conversation made me realize how much I missed Jade Wilds and being able to ask Commander Meriel questions instead of having to guess. *How am I supposed to teach humans about Fae and encourage tolerance when I don't have any way of answering questions that might come up?* I doubted King Leonard's library had books with information on Fae, especially not with his obvious dislike of them.

Forty

TRISTAN

After Serafina left to see the seamstress, I wandered the garden for over an hour before selecting a black granite bench in front of a bird fountain to sit on. Moments later, the crunch of footsteps on gravel alerted me to a visitor. I looked up quickly, hoping perhaps Serafina had returned. Instead, I was met with the steely gaze of a noblewoman. Her brown hair, heavily threaded with gray, was in a severe bun. She was wearing a dark-red gown with gold beading at the cuffs and collar.

I stood and bowed. I had a fleeting memory of seeing her at one of the events but couldn't recall her name.

"Master Mongan, I have been hoping we would have the chance to talk," she said. Her voice was cold, calculating.

Keeping my tone neutral, I replied, "Forgive me, Your Grace, I do not believe we have been formally introduced."

The noblewoman laughed, but it sounded forced. "My apologies, Master Mongan. I am Duchess Oriana."

"Nice to meet you," I murmured politely.

"There are some matters I would like to discuss with you. I know you have Princess Serafina's ear, and there are those of us who feel that as a newcomer to the South, the princess doesn't quite understand the situation," Duchess Oriana explained.

She was close to me now, directly in front of where I was backed up to the bench. There was no room for me to maneuver. I could not make the space between us larger. *Has she forgotten I'm new to the South as well?* Not wanting to draw attention to my made-up backstory, I asked, "What situation?"

"The presence of Fae in Gaskal. Prior to the princess's arrival, there hadn't been one in the city in a decade or more. Now, there are several, behaving as though they own the place," she said with a disdainful sniff.

This must be the noblewoman Serafina told me about earlier. Given Serafina's comments about Duchess Oriana, I knew I was going to have to tread carefully. I wasn't sure I wanted to make the duchess an enemy. As long as I was disguised as a human, I wanted to be as neutral as possible, allowing Serafina to decide her stance on certain topics, including how to handle the relationship between humans and Fae. Even so, I was confident I knew her well enough to predict her feelings on that matter.

"What about the Fae currently in Gaskal?" I asked when it became clear the duchess was not going to elaborate.

"It is critical that they depart," Duchess Oriana said vehemently.

"How do you propose I accomplish that? You know better than I that I do not have power within this court," I replied.

The duchess laughed. "That's where you're wrong. You have the princess's ear, which gives you immense power, because she can make decisions like barring Fae from entering the city—and even the kingdom. You just need to convince her."

I found it intriguing that the duchess was not taking her case to King Leonard. *If his people feel this strongly about Fae, why isn't the kingdom already closed?* Or perhaps King Leonard was wise in this matter, understanding the implications of closing a border versus open dislike. *Closing borders is likely to provoke a war.*

I didn't know King Pharaan well enough to have any idea if a move on King Leonard's part would cause him to go to war against the South. The Fae relied on iron for weapons, but I wasn't entirely sure the gold mines controlled by the Lord of the South were of critical importance. *It might give Prince Tanyth the fuel he needs though.* Technically, the Court of Dusk did not share a direct border with the South, but I knew Prince Rhangil of the Court of the Sun would often side with Prince Tanyth, and he most definitely shared a border with the South.

I shuddered, remembering vividly the last time Prince Tanyth had battled against a Lord of the South. Though the battle had been more even than expected, Prince Tanyth had won. *Because of me.* My stomach roiled. I swallowed hard, praying I wasn't going to throw up in front of Duchess Oriana.

"I will consider your request," I told her hastily. I made a motion to Nolan, and he came forward. Giving the duchess a short bow, I departed without allowing her time to object.

Memories of violent battles against humans flooded my thoughts. *Can I do that to Fae I have served side by side with within the Court of Dusk?* Tremors ran through me as I considered what it meant to stand beside Serafina as an imposter. *No better now than I was under Prince Tanyth's iron fist.*

"Are you okay?" Nolan's voice broke through my thoughts. His hand hovered just above my shoulder, as though he was afraid to touch me.

Sucking in a sharp breath through my teeth, I exhaled slowly and then nodded. "I'm fine. Old memories resurfacing, that's all."

"I'll have food sent to your room," Nolan declared.

I am hungry, I admitted to myself, though I had no idea how the guard knew. Food and a chance to be left alone would likely make a significant positive impact on my mood.

I rounded the corner, focused on food and the possibility of taking a bath, when I stopped mere moments before plowing into someone. Nolan bumped into me, but my feet were far enough apart that I prevented us from bowling into the person. *Fae.*

After Duchess Oriana's comments today to Serafina and me, I was surprised to see a Fae within the palace at all.

Her skin was dark brown, almost black, and her hair was black with tight ringlets. I couldn't see her ears because of how her hair was styled, but there was no mistaking that she was Fae. The air shimmered with her magic, and then it vanished.

Nolan came to my rescue. "State your business," he demanded, stepping between us.

The Fae sighed as though she was frequently asked to explain herself. "I'm Ghilanna Qira, Princess Serafina's friend."

The look Ghilanna was giving me had me wondering how well the magic in the pendant would hold up.

Then, she blinked. "Sorry for staring," she apologized.

I shrugged. "I'm used to it." As Serafina's betrothed, and before that, as the lord commander of the Court of Dusk, people openly stared at me. Over the years, I had learned to ignore the extra attention.

"Is there anything I can do for you?" I asked.

"No, I was heading back into the city. Serafina is still with the seamstress," she replied.

"I see," I replied automatically, though I suspected Ghilanna had gotten bored or at least had things she wanted to talk about with Serafina that were not appropriate for prying ears. "Will you be at the wedding?"

Ghilanna frowned. "I'm not sure."

Her words surprised me. I knew King Leonard did not like Fae, but to deny Serafina the ability to have one of her friends at such a momentous event was cruel. *Something Tanyth would have done.* Until now, I had not thought of King Leonard as a cruel human. *Maybe I've misjudged him.*

"I will make sure that you can be a guest," I said. "From the way she talks about you, I can tell you're important to Serafina."

Ghilanna's lips twitched, but no smile came. "Thank you," she replied, though I wondered if she believed I would fail.

"My pleasure," I replied and gave her a slight bow. Ghilanna stepped around Nolan and departed.

We continued our trek to my suite. My stomach gurgled loudly, echoing down the hall.

Nolan chuckled. "See, you *are* hungry."

"I didn't deny it," I muttered as we reached my door and went inside. A servant was placing a tray on the small dining table. *He must have sent word for food while I was chatting with Ghilanna, I mused.*

Helping myself to a full bowl of venison stew and two rolls, I dug into the meal. It tasted far better than I expected. Humans tended to cook with a very different selection of herbs and spices, and I was acclimating. Belly full, I moved from the dining table to a more comfortable position on the couch to meditate. Taking a deep breath, I leaned back into the firm cushions and let my eyes shut.

Travaran stood behind a kneeling Serafina, his hand wrapped around her throat. Blood trickled down her split lip.

"Betrayer!" Travaran shouted. "You chose her over me, and now she'll pay the ultimate price."

I lurched forward to stop Travaran but found I was chained to a wall and could only get a foot closer. Serafina's blue-green eyes, rimmed with red, met mine. "I'd rather die by his hand than marry you. Betrayer!"

Legs thrashing, I lost my balance on the couch and rolled off, catching myself just in time to not hit my head on the table. My heart thundered in my chest. *So much for meditation helping me relax.*

Frustration welled within me. *If I can't meditate without Travaran creeping into my thoughts, I doubt a nap will be any better.*

Even though I had already spent time practicing with my sword today, I knew it was the best bet. The windows rattled from the harsh wind outside; I didn't think Nolan would appreciate it if I decided to go for a run. Mind made up, I buckled the scabbard around my waist and departed, intent on my destination.

Leaning against the wall, I sipped water from a canteen during my second break from practicing sword work. My breathing was returning to its resting rate, and I was considering switching to hand-to-hand combat when Serafina strolled into the practice room.

I smiled. "Good evening, Your Highness."

"Good evening, Rhys," Serafina replied cheerily. She unbuckled her scabbard and placed it on the bench. Then, she started stretching. I observed her, making note of the differences in our routines. Sticking to her prescribed plan of avoiding my eyes to prevent herself from getting sick, Serafina's gaze remained focused on the floor or the wall for the duration of the warmup.

"How was your appointment with the seamstress?" I asked.

Serafina shrugged. "It was uneventful. What about your afternoon?"

Grimacing and earning a giggle from Serafina, I replied, "I encountered Duchess Oriana."

Serafina rolled her eyes. "Let me guess, she is trying to get on your good side to get to me?"

"Yes," I confirmed. "She is quite pushy."

Serafina nodded in agreement. "She is. But I am not going to let her dictate how I should feel about Fae."

"What would you say to a sparring match? To clear our minds," I suggested.

Serafina gave me a smile. "Precisely what I was thinking."

Close proximity and my frequent dreams of Serafina were making this practice session a struggle. If I'd had my way, I would have sent everyone away and had sex with her right there in the practice room. *Maybe when we're married.* Though I had discovered that humans felt strongly about keeping sex and intimacy a private matter that was not to be shared outside one's relationship. I had no idea what repercussions there might be if the king caught wind of us making an heir outside of our designated suites.

"I was planning on switching to hand-to-hand combat. Does that work for you?" I asked.

"Hand combat is fine," Serafina said with a smile.

She has no idea what she does to me. I smiled back, unable to do anything else. The wedding was tomorrow. Then, I'd have more freedom.

I walked to the center and positioned my feet, then raised my fists. Serafina mirrored my movements, then counted, "Three, two, one! Begin!"

I ducked her one-two jabs and went for her unprotected stomach. Serafina twisted at the last moment, and I connected with air. She hooked her foot around my calf to sweep my legs from under me. I tsked and did a right hook. She blocked and spun with a roundhouse kick aiming for my ribs.

Dodging and weaving, we landed few punches and even fewer kicks. I spun out of the way to avoid a kick to the groin, and Serafina came up behind me, wrapping her arms around my shoulders. Surprised that she tried the maneuver, I tucked my chin to my chest and flipped her over my head and onto her back. She let go with a gasp as the wind got knocked out of her.

I waited for her to recover a few moments before offering her my hand. She took it, and I leaned forward, putting all my weight on my right foot. She gave my arm a deft pull, and, unbalanced, I fell forward onto my stomach.

Chuckling, Serafina climbed onto my back, straddling my hips. I lay there, panting, debating what to do. Decision made, I rolled, jostling Serafina, but she stayed rooted in place. I peered up at her and licked my lips. I wanted to thrust my hips up and brush her thighs with my cock, but I was afraid to scare her away. Or to anger the guards.

Her blue-green eyes locked with mine, and she dipped her head down and kissed me. Hesitantly at first. I ran the tip of my tongue over her lips, and she parted them. The kiss slowly deepened, and Serafina melted into my arms.

A loud cough and I remembered where we were. Reluctantly, I put light pressure on Serafina's shoulders to encourage her to sit all the way up.

"Perhaps we should continue practicing," Serafina whispered.

"I will do as you command," I replied loud enough for the guard to hear. Curiosity gripped me. *How bold is my princess?*

When I fell into bed the night before the wedding, I had been certain I would sleep. My arms and legs felt like noodles from how thoroughly I had worked them. Yet sleep eluded me, and the few times I had fallen asleep, dreams of King Leonard calling everything off had plagued me. I knew I needed to be at the top of my game today for Serafina. I just hoped what little rest I had gotten would be enough to keep me energized for the whole day.

As a foreigner marrying the princess and heir, I was not permitted to wear gold to my wedding. In fact, Lord John had informed me it was expressly forbidden. Through hasty research about the marriage traditions of Eagle Rock, I knew that I would not be breaking any of "my" own traditions.

Regret filled me as I considered that by continuing the charade of being Rhys, I was also denying myself the opportunity to perform the tradition held by shapeshifters to shift during the wedding ceremony. I had not yet decided when the right moment was to reveal my true identity to Serafina, but it was too risky to do before the wedding.

274

I scanned the room full of guests, trying to see how many I could identify. The ceremony was being held in the large gallery adjacent to King Leonard's throne room. The reception afterward would move into the grand ballroom: the Golden Rose, built for Queen Rosalie by the Lord of the South who had ruled Gaskal four hundred years ago.

The human kings were easy to identify based on their individual crowns—each of the metal that was mined in the kingdom. Guests from each kingdom seemed to be dressed in colors similar to those of their metal. Whether I liked it or not, I would shortly be bound not only to Serafina as her husband, but also to the humans of Gaskal. *How many of them have realized what that will mean when King Leonard dies? That they will have to bow before a half-Fae?*

My attention was drawn back to the arriving guests when a mass of bright pink feathers entered the room. I examined her from top to bottom. Her outfit had a tall top hat with a matching shawl. Underneath the shawl was a skintight dress, the bottom of which was also covered in feathers, though these were vibrant pink at the top and faded out to white at the bottom of the dress.

Smoothing my hands over my pants, I watched the next group enter. They were a small contingent of Fae. I noticed Commander Meriel near the front, King Pharaan, and Lord Commander Onvyr. Serafina's friend Ghilanna brought up the rear. Unlike the peacocking human, the Fae wore natural colors. Robes in tans, browns, and shades of gray. I silently prayed to the Fae gods that tempers would stay checked and all guests would be content to witness our celebration, no matter their feelings for one another. *Is this how Solana and Gareth felt when they were married? Like the whole world hung in balance and even a pin drop could throw it into chaos?*

There was another woman who was not quite as flamboyant as the pink one. She wore a frilly silver dress covered in swaths of sheer fabric. A flash of Serafina in a sheer gold dress at Dorcha

Palace hit me, and I winced. The dress had been spectacular; the circumstances had not. *Today is my wedding. I should not dwell on the terrible things that happened in our past.*

Guests mingled among themselves until the music changed, and Lord John made his rounds asking guests to please take their seats. The ceremony was about to start.

Forty-One

SERAFINA

Only through grit and determination had I been able to accomplish my goal of getting to know Rhys better before the wedding. Though the past two days had been a whirlwind, I at least felt confident that we were a good match for each other, and I could feel the foundation of trust falling into place.

I suspected the wedding would be easy compared to what awaited me in the bedchamber tonight. *Will he know I'm not a virgin? How does it feel to have sex?* Heat flooded my face at the thought of asking a stranger the latter. In the past two days, I hadn't had an opportunity to ask Ghilanna for any advice. Now, with my wedding night looming before me, I regretted not carving out the time to talk to her. I gasped as deep sadness seeped through me that my mother would not be present on my wedding day, a day no daughter should have to go through without her mother.

Though there was no shortage of women at my grandfather's palace, I had yet to feel any kind of connection with them. I doubted Violet knew any more than I did about sex since she was not married either. It was one thing to discuss the weather or the latest fashion and entirely different to talk of intimate things. Or at least that was how I felt. The culture within the South strongly emphasized that intimacy between husband and wife was meant to *stay* between them.

I ran my hands across the surface of the steaming bathwater, reluctant to get out of the bath because that would mean it was time to go. Instead, my thoughts drifted to Rhys's touch being the key to minimizing my illness. Deep down, I knew this was not going to work long term. I couldn't keep him at my side forever. The vision I had was for us to work together to solidify my position as heir among the people of the South. Just as my mother had foreseen.

Closing my eyes, I sank under the water. *Today I must focus on getting through the wedding without messing up my vows too much.* My grandfather had been close-lipped about who exactly he had invited to the wedding. *Not that he has felt like sharing much about anything else either.*

"Your Highness," called Mary's voice. I realized I had drifted off and the water was now lukewarm.

"You can come in!" I replied, standing. Goosebumps rose on my arms as the chilly air caressed my skin. Mary hastily approached with a towel. I stepped out and wrapped it around me, relishing its heat. *She must have warmed it by the fire.*

Back at Jade Wilds, I wouldn't have had a thoughtful maid. If I had let the water cool off, then I would have had to use a cold towel in my cold tent. *I guess there are perks to being a princess.*

I stood in the center of three mirrored panels, affording me a view of almost the entire dress without having to twist and turn. I was required to have a dress of gold. Thankfully, I had been permitted to have a say in its design. The result achieved the desired effect and comfort while also meeting the royal requirements. The bottom layer was metallic gold silk that whispered when I moved. Over the silk was ivory satin, paneled in such a way that the golden silk was visible as I moved. If I were to twirl, it would flare out around me. The ivory satin had an intricate design of pearls and gold beads. The long sleeves were made of gold silk with solid gold cuffs to hold them in place. As with my other dresses, the neckline was high, though I had convinced the seamstress it was okay to have my upper shoulders and collarbone visible by using a scoop neck.

My hair cascaded to my waist. Unlike the ornate dress, my hair was left plain. The tradition was strange, but I was not going to argue. Avoiding having pins digging into my skull was fine by me. The last piece of my ensemble was the crown. Thin strands of gold had been woven together as though they were a rope, not metal. Each strand had a different texture: one was polished, one was hammered, another brushed. The crown, just like the gold dress, was simply following tradition. In fact, Mary had informed me that this crown was exclusively reserved for a princess's marriage ceremony.

Violet did a final inspection and deemed everything to be in place. Hoping no one would notice the slight tremor in my hand as I opened the door, I put my shoulders back and headed into the hallway to meet my grandfather.

The hallway was empty save for us and our escort of guards. As we trekked toward the hall where the wedding would take place, an iron grip on my nerves was all that kept me from bolting screaming back to my room. The closer we got, the more nervous I got. Not about Rhys, but about the circumstances of the marriage, forced into it because of a stupid law in a kingdom that had discarded me years ago.

I could run away. The thought drifted by, but I rejected it. If I had truly wanted to run, I should have done so days ago. Not now, after I agreed to go through with this. *For the good of the South. Eyes forward, right foot, left foot,* I ordered myself as we got closer and closer to the doors.

These are my people. No matter what my grandfather believes, I at least owe it to them to try. My mother had foreseen that I would become queen. Even if the circumstances were not quite ideal, or not how I had dreamed my wedding would happen, I believed in my mother. Decision made, I stiffened my spine and stood taller.

"Here we are," Grandfather said.

I gave a slight nod, and the guards threw open the doors. Silence fell upon the hall. A piano melody my mother used to play drifted toward us, calling me. I easily spotted the contingent of Fae in the sea of humans with Ghilanna closest to the aisle. I was pleased that she had been allowed to attend.

Halfway down the aisle, Grandfather stopped and took his place among the guests. I proceeded the rest of the way without him. My gaze was focused on the vase of white roses behind Rhys. I was afraid if I looked at him, fear of the unknown and giving up control would send me careening out of the room.

I could feel Rhys's gaze on me. Imagining his intense blue eyes, a shiver went down my spine that was decidedly not caused by fear, but something else I was afraid to name. When I reached Rhys, I pivoted ninety degrees and held my hands out. Rhys took them. My gaze flickered to his for a moment before focusing on the priest. The single song might be of Fae origin, but the way the ceremony would run was human.

"Starting with the princess, each of you will repeat after me," the priest announced.

I nodded, and Rhys gave my hands a squeeze of encouragement.

"I, Serafina Wyantha Helias, give you my body, that we two might be one," I said, keeping each word clear and precise. "I promise loyalty and friendship to Rhys Mongan with all that I am and all that I have to give. And I accept him as my lawful wedded husband for life. I freely make these promises to you, for today and all our tomorrows, for all our lives together."

Then it was Rhys's turn. "I, Rhys Mongan, give you my body, that we two might be one. I promise loyalty and friendship to

Serafina Wyantha Helias with all that I am and all that I have to give. And I accept her as my lawful wedded wife for life. I freely make these promises to you, for today and all our tomorrows, for all our lives together." Rhys paused and then added, "From the depths of my heart and soul."

Tittering arose in the hall among the guests, and I became aware that the vows we had been told to repeat said nothing about love or hearts. The wedding wasn't happening out of love. It was happening because Rhys won the competition and, therefore, my hand in marriage. Thankfully, the priest did not make a fuss about Rhys's additional words.

At the priest's signal, Violet walked over and handed him the rings. The priest nodded in thanks, and she returned to her position.

The priest handed me a ring first. Rhys offered his left hand, so I could place it on his finger. Repeating after the priest again, I said, "With this ring, I thee wed." Then, I slid the ring on Rhys's finger. I was surprised when I realized it wasn't just a plain band. The ring on Rhys's finger was very similar to the crown sitting on my head: intertwined strands of gold, hammered and brightly polished.

The priest coughed, and I blinked, remembering that there was still more to the ceremony. I held out my left hand and Rhys put the ring on my finger. "With this ring, I thee wed," he said softly.

This time I did meet his gaze, confident that with his hands on mine, the illness would stay away.

"You may kiss the princess," the priest said.

Face heating with the eyes of so many guests on us, I tipped my chin up toward Rhys, and he kissed me. His lips were soft against mine, but unlike our kiss from the other day, this one was quick.

The crowd clapped, and the priest cleared his throat again. "I now introduce Princess Serafina Wyantha Helias and her husband Rhys Mongan."

I sighed in relief. *It's over. For better or worse, I am now married to Rhys.* Rhys lightly held my hand, and we walked down the aisle. A smile played across my lips. The past two weeks had all been leading to this moment, and now it was over. The reception would be an opportunity for guests who had recently arrived for the wedding to offer their congratulations.

There will be food, I reminded myself, though I wasn't sure if I was hungry or not. Now that the ceremony was over, I could at least say I had fulfilled my primary duty as heir. Hopefully for a few hours at least, I would be able to forget about the second duty that was looming over me.

Ghilanna caught my eye as we passed and waved. I waved back. A few guests murmured words of congratulations, and then we were out the doors and into the hallway.

Forty-Two

TRISTAN

A swell of happiness coursed through me. *I am married to my soulmate, Serafina.* After being discovered by Prince Tanyth and everything I had gone through the last few weeks to win back Serafina's hand, it was hard to believe that all that was left was the reception and consummating our marriage.

As soon as we emerged from the wedding hall, Thomas appeared and escorted us to the Golden Rose ballroom. Serafina was silent. Not wanting to intrude on her few moments of peace before the onslaught of guests, I instead examined our surroundings. I became aware of the increasing number of roses in the palace decor. There were rose patterns inlaid in the wood flooring, stenciled onto the columns, and even engraved into edge of the ballroom's heavy wooden doors, with a rose in full bloom in gold inlaid in their centers.

Serafina's fingers wound through mine as we made our way to the middle of the ballroom where we would greet guests. The center of the floor featured a mosaic masterpiece: an inlaid circle with a massive bouquet of roses, all made of colored stone.

Thomas stopped when we were standing over the top of the rose. "This is where you will greet the guests."

"What happens after we greet the guests?" I asked.

Thomas pointed at tables along one wall. "There is a buffet of food over there, and servants will walk around with drinks. There will be dancing, of course, and mingling with guests." Thomas bowed and then walked over to a position by the doors the guests would come through.

I took a deep breath and faced Serafina, thrilled to see the relaxed set of her jaw and the brightness of her eyes, telling me, at least for now, she was happy. When she had first walked down the aisle, I had half expected her to turn tail and run. Not that I could blame her. There was an immense amount of pressure on her to prove that she was worthy of being the future Lady of the South.

Her blue-green eyes met mine, and her lips curved into a smile. I leaned down and kissed her. "*Wife.*" I sent the word along the bond, which was still dull. "Wife," I whispered against her lips. She started to wrap her arms around my waist, pulling me closer, when someone coughed from close by. I reluctantly stepped back from Serafina and turned toward our first guest.

Serafina smiled at the couple as they approached us. From the silver crown on the man's head, it was not difficult to guess who it was. "Rhys, may I introduce you to the Lord of the East and his wife, Queen Chantilly."

"Nice to meet you," I said, and we shook hands with both and then moved onto the next guests.

After greeting more than half the guests, I felt Serafina stiffen when Duchess Oriana and Duke Herman approached us with their granddaughter trailing behind them. The duchess was wearing a teal dress with a gem-encrusted belt and a thick gold choker, and the duke wore a matching teal jacket with black pants and a white shirt.

"Duchess Oriana and Duke Herman, have you met Rhys?" Serafina said. I could hear the tightness in her voice.

"Thank you for coming," I said. Not wanting to encourage the couple to stay longer, I opted for a polite greeting instead of explaining we had already met.

Sensing that Serafina was a bit frustrated after seeing Duchess Oriana, I turned to face her. "Would you like to get some food?"

Serafina flashed me a brilliant smile. "Yes, thank you."

Once we had finished our food, I was debating what to do when I spied King Leonard heading our way. Shoulder to shoulder with Serafina, I could feel the quiver in her arm as she plastered a smile on her face and greeted the king. "Grandfather."

"Serafina, will you do me the honor of a dance?" King Leonard asked.

She nodded. "Of course."

I watched as they settled into a waltz among the other guests on the dance floor and then let my attention be pulled elsewhere in the room.

Pleased that Serafina was enjoying dancing with various guests, I was surprised when Ghilanna sat next to me. "Be kind to her tonight," she said firmly.

"I would never to anything to hurt her," I replied sincerely. *Except betray her trust,* my mind reminded me darkly. I clenched my fist and then slowly released my fingers, trying to relax.

Ghilanna looked as though she wanted to say something else when Serafina suddenly appeared and crooked her finger at me.

"I'm being summoned," I said apologetically.

Ghilanna smiled. "Go. Enjoy yourself."

I hurried to do as she asked, setting my hand in Serafina's and allowing her to escort me onto the dance floor.

I lost track of time as we twirled our way around the dance floor. I caught a glimpse of King Pharaan, his black hair pulled back in a ponytail at the nape of his neck and a thin gold crown with tiny emeralds on his head. He wore a dark-green jacket with black piping, a white tunic, and black pants. When Serafina noticed him, she tugged me to a halt and led me off the dance floor.

"Grandfather," Serafina cried with a smile and ran the last few steps. His arms wrapped around her. "It's so good to see you again." I could barely make out the muffled words she said into his shoulder.

He released her from the hug and stepped back, peering at her from head to toe. "You look well, Serafina."

"I'm glad you're here," she replied. "Rhys, this is my grandfather, King Pharaan." She grabbed my hand and tugged me forward.

I bowed deeply. "It is good to meet you, King Pharaan."

"We're going to go sit down for a bit. My feet are tired," Serafina said apologetically. I kept the smile off my face that she was openly admitting her feet hurt.

King Pharaan smiled. "It's your day, Serafina. I would like a dance later."

She kissed him lightly on the cheek. "I will find you."

We walked over to the chairs that had been set aside for us. They were on a small platform, so we could see better.

Serafina sighed and leaned back into the plush cushion. "This is better."

I nodded in agreement. The chair was comfortable, but my feet, unlike Serafina's, had not gotten too tired. I'd spent too many years spent building my stamina to allow an event like this to cause much of a problem for me. But I was happy to ensure Serafina was comfortable.

A few minutes after Serafina and I were settled, I could hear King Pharaan's voice in my mind. *"I don't know what game you're playing disguised as a human, Tristan Gilvrye, but if you mean ill toward Serafina, then this is the only warning you'll get."*

I sucked in a shaky breath. *He could expose me.* If he could tell, it was only a matter of time before others figured it out too. *I need to tell her soon.* Reluctance filled me. As much as I hated lying about who I was, now that I was here, married to Serafina, telling her the truth could end things permanently between us. *Can I give up everything I've worked so hard to earn in the name of truth?*

My emotions churned as I considered what the consequences of telling her versus not telling her would mean. By not telling her, I was breaking my promise to myself to be a better Fae for her.

A tingling sensation broke through my thoughts as King Pharaan's voice entered my mind again. *"You were right. The soulmate bond is there, but it's faint."* The connection disappeared as abruptly as it had come.

The bond cannot be broken except by death. Hope spread through me that if magic was binding us together, then perhaps somehow, someday, Serafina would find it in herself to forgive me. *If I tell her soon.* I gave Serafina's hand a gentle squeeze. *Tomorrow. I will tell her tomorrow,* I vowed.

I glanced at my wife, and she seemed at ease among our guests, more so than I had expected. It was tempting to ask her if she wanted to leave, to perform the last duty expected of us on our wedding day. *Consummating the marriage.* I dared not hope that we could also break whatever was hindering our soulmate bond, but it was a place to start. However, I didn't merely want to drag her to bed. I wanted to seduce her and have her begging me to leave the reception. Which meant there was only one way to accomplish that in a room full of people.

"Would you like to dance again, my love?" I said, facing Serafina.

Forty-Three

SERAFINA

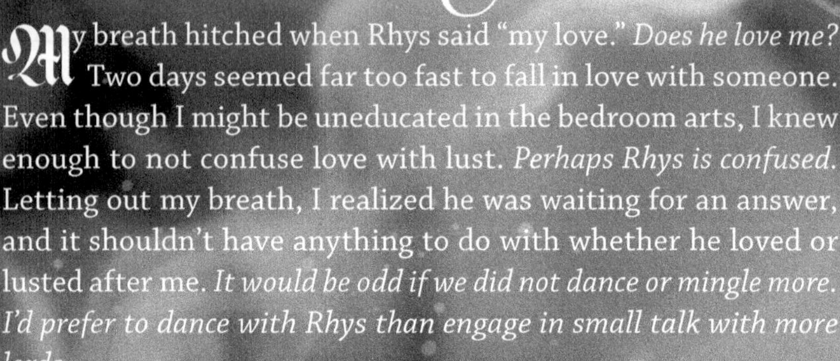

My breath hitched when Rhys said "my love." *Does he love me?* Two days seemed far too fast to fall in love with someone. Even though I might be uneducated in the bedroom arts, I knew enough to not confuse love with lust. *Perhaps Rhys is confused.* Letting out my breath, I realized he was waiting for an answer, and it shouldn't have anything to do with whether he loved or lusted after me. *It would be odd if we did not dance or mingle more. I'd prefer to dance with Rhys than engage in small talk with more lords.*

I smiled at him and stood up. "Dancing would be wonderful."

"Very well. I will be right back," Rhys said with a sly smile. Not sure what that was about. I watched him walk over to where the orchestra was taking a water break and consult them briefly before returning to our table.

Rhys bowed and brought my hand to his lips.

"You're being silly," I muttered as people watched us. "Please, let's dance."

I tugged my hand out of his and brushed past him onto the dance floor. Rhys stalked after me, wrapping a hand around my waist, twirling me so I was facing him. His eyes were bright with amusement and something else I couldn't place. The orchestra began playing a waltz. I set my right hand in his left and my left on his shoulder. We danced around the room. At the end of the second song, I was reminded of exactly why we had taken a break in the first place. My shoes were pinching the sides of my feet.

"What's wrong?" Rhys asked as I stumbled a few steps.

"The shoes hurt," I said into his ear.

"I can fix that," Rhys replied, his lips just a hairsbreadth from my neck.

"You want me to toss my shoes somewhere?" I asked.

Rhys shook his head and chuckled. "No." He fell to his knees in front of me and lifted the edge of my dress. Wrapping his hand around my foot, he tugged one shoe off, then the other. He stood, holding them.

Thomas walked over. "May I?" he asked with an amused smile.

Rhys smiled. "Yes, thanks."

I watched as Thomas departed with my shoes. "That was cheating."

Rhys shrugged. "How else did you expect me to solve your problem? I don't have magic."

I shook my head. Honestly, I had no idea what I had expected him to do.

"My feet feel much better without the shoes, thank you." I was also grateful my dress was long enough that no one would notice my bare feet.

Music filled the room, and the quiet chatter of guests rose again. I allowed Rhys to lead me to the other side of the dance floor. When the musicians finished their piece, Rhys raised his hand, and the music changed.

I could immediately tell it was of Fae origin, even though the musicians were human. *Did he give them sheet music he had hidden in a pocket, or are they just well-traveled?* The tempo was stronger, aggressive even. Earlier we had glided across the dance floor; now each step he took was filled with purpose. His gaze met mine, and his expression was intense. He pulled me sharply toward him. Our bodies collided, and sparks erupted across my skin. I closed my eyes momentarily at my body's reaction. I opened them just in time for him to twirl me away from him. The gold silk of my skirt flared around me, just as I envisioned.

When I spun into Rhys, he pulled me to him, his movements possessive. Anyone watching would know that I belonged to him. *But would they question that we haven't tasted each other?* My steps hesitated as that thought hit me before I realized it didn't matter. We were married. If we had sex tonight, no one would be able to challenge the legitimacy of our wedding.

Rhys gave my hand a gentle squeeze, tugging me back into myself and sending more sparks along my arms. The next time he spun me, he kept me close, never releasing my hand. When I was facing him again, he dipped me down over his knee and kissed me. His lips were soft and tasted like chocolate from the dessert earlier.

I returned the kiss, and the sparks traveled from my lips all the way down to my core. I gasped, and Rhys swept me upright. As he readied himself to spin me away again, I wrapped my arms around him, pulling him to me and kissing him. I parted my lips, and without any more encouragement, he deepened our kiss. Intense desire wound around me, and a moan escaped my lips.

Rhys chuckled. "We can take our leave."

I nodded, peering up at him under my lashes, grateful he knew what I wanted without having to vocalize it here in front of the guests. For me, this was uncharted territory.

Rhys brought my hand to his lips, and then we walked over to the orchestra. He murmured thanks, and we made our way to the door at the back of the room.

Lord John was waiting for us in the hallway. "Your room has been prepared."

"We're going to my bedroom," I replied with a glance at Rhys.

Lord John shook his head. "Unfortunately, no. There must be witnesses."

Shock ran through me. *I have to have sex for the first time with people watching?* Instead of replying, I merely nodded and tightened my grip on Rhys's hand.

I was shaking as we walked down the hallway. Rhys tugged me to a halt and took my hands in his, holding them between us. "You will be fine. I promise. You won't even know the witnesses are there."

He handed me a note, in Ghilanna's handwriting. I gave him a quizzical look and pulled it open.

Your grandfather told me about the witness requirement in an off-hand remark. I have put a shield in the room that will block you from seeing or hearing the witnesses. Enjoy your husband. Yours, Ghilanna

I crumpled the note in my hand, wondering what Lord John would think if he knew I wouldn't have to see or hear the witnesses. It was a horrendous tradition, and I felt sorry for any woman who had had to go through it.

Firmly gripping Rhys's hand, I followed him into the room. There was a large four-poster bed against the far wall, and above it was a narrow walkway with a railing and an assortment of empty chairs. *For our witnesses.* I felt almost afraid to let go of Rhys, but I realized that we both needed two hands to get undressed. Pressing my lips together, I moved over to the bed, unable to still the nervous tremor in my hands. *What if the witnesses think I'm incompetent?* I bit my lip and watched as Rhys undressed himself. I was wearing a sheer sleeveless tunic, and that was it. Everything else was in a heap by my feet.

"Are they up there?" I asked Rhys, so quiet only he could hear. He nodded.

I glanced up and was relieved to see Ghilanna's shield was holding; the chairs had moved, but they still appeared empty. *Let's see if I can forget about people being up there.*

"Look at me, Serafina," Rhys ordered softly.

My gaze dropped till I was looking into his blue eyes, darker now in the dim light within the small room. As his hands went to the laces on his pants, I couldn't help but watch. When his pants slid down, they revealed Rhys's cock, longer than I had imagined and already ready, the tip glistening with fluids. I gulped and took a step back. *I can't do this.*

Rhys stepped forward and wrapped his arms around me. He pulled me close, and my nipples, already sensitive, brushed against his chest. I sucked in a breath at their tenderness and the fluttering in my core. Rhys's cock bumped against the apex of my thighs, and I gasped as need wound through me. A smug smile on his face, he dipped his head down and kissed me, hands holding me in place. I lost track of how long we stood there, kissing. I kept expecting him to lead me to bed, but he didn't. I lost myself in his mouth and was surprised when I felt dampness between my legs.

"Serafina," he whispered, giving a small thrust of his hips to bump his cock harder into me. I kissed him back and moaned as his cock brushed my entrance. I ran my hands down his back, unsure what else to do. Rhys tipped his head back, meeting my eyes.

"You should lie down on the bed," he suggested, softly nipping my lips.

Deciding his advice was the most comfortable option, I scooted onto the bed, lying against the pillows, watching him. Rhys followed me and nudged my legs open, kneeling between my thighs. His cock brushed against my folds, and my back arched as my core began pulsing. I whimpered, and Rhys leaned down and kissed me. "I'm going to enter you slowly."

I blinked, confused, then I realized he was talking about putting his cock *in* me. I bit my lip and nodded. "Okay." He kissed me again, and then I felt slight pressure as his cock slowly slid into my canal.

A hiss escaped my lips at the pressure, but it eased as quickly as it began.

"Are you okay?" Rhys whispered in my ear, before taking it between his lips and sucking on my tender lobe. I grabbed his hips and pulled on them, wanting him deeper inside of me.

"Yes," I said desperately. My whole body was throbbing with unanswered need. *How could I forget something that feels like this?*

Clearly satisfied by my answer, Rhys surprised me and ran his thumbs over my nipples, sending shivers down my spine. My breasts tightened, and I clenched around him. Rhys dipped his head down and took one of my breasts in his mouth and sucked on it. As he did, his thrusts became faster and deeper. He dragged his teeth on my nipple, and I screamed, "Rhys!" Waves of pleasure rolled through me. Rhys didn't stop. He kept thrusting until I felt his cock spasm inside of me. He kissed my lips, his gaze sleepy. I felt his body relax as the waves of the orgasm sizzled out.

As Rhys arranged himself beside me and pulled the sheet over us, I realized the magic shield was gone and the witnesses were departing. *It's over. They saw what they needed to see.* Part of me wanted to leave this room now that we had performed our deed. The fact that anyone could enter whenever they chose and observe us was unnerving. I turned toward Rhys to ask if he'd mind returning to my rooms when I realized he was asleep.

Yawning, I decided it didn't matter where we were if we were just going to sleep. I closed my eyes and drifted off.

I was sitting on the blue velvet couch in front of the fireplace in my suite at Dorcha Palace. Feeling slightly nauseous, I was pleased when there was a light tap on the door and the healer came into the room, smiling and with a fresh cup of tea. Prince Tanyth emerged from the shadows and brought it over to me. The teacup looked tiny in his large hands.

He gently offered me the cup. "There's a good girl."

I took a sip and smiled; the tea was delicious. "How good of you to remember my favorite tea blend."

"Of course, my love," he replied.

The following morning, Rhys and I were eating breakfast in the small sitting room across from where we'd spent our wedding night. "Remind me later to tell you about my mother," I said, earning me a curious look from Rhys.

Before he could ask me what it was about my grandfather walked in. I hastily wiped the crumbs off my face. We both rose. I curtsied, and Rhys bowed.

To my surprise, my grandfather waved us off. "If it is just the three of us in a private room like this, you can drop the formalities."

We stayed standing. I assumed whatever task I had with my grandfather this morning was not going to take place in this room.

"If you're ready, Serafina, we should go," King Leonard announced.

I squeezed Rhys's hand in farewell and followed my grandfather out of the room. We strolled down the hallway in silence for a while.

The king coughed a few times, then spoke. "Now that you are married and have consummated the marriage with witnesses, we can address the matters of critical importance to your position as my heir."

I licked my lips, hoping he wasn't going to tell me I needed to prioritize making an heir again.

Grandfather continued. "As you are aware, the gold mine transfers from king to heir. There is a rite we must go through to do that. And ..." The king paused. "There's the matter of the book."

The gold mine made perfect sense, but before I could stop myself, I blurted out, "Book?"

The king spent a few moments surveying the dimly lit stone hallway we were walking down, making me realize that the guards were no longer following us. *How odd.*

He returned his gaze to me. "Yes ... the *Bloodsong Grimoire*."

My jaw fell open. I stopped walking, shock and disbelief coursing through me. *The* Bloodsong Grimoire *was in the* Bedtime Tails *book. A Fae magic object.* My grandfather turned to face me.

"You know of the book?"

Lips pressed tightly together, I nodded. "Not much," I whispered.

He motioned for me to walk toward him. "Come, we must reach our destination at a certain time."

I hurried toward him and he grabbed my hand, then continued to walk down the hallway. I was certain he was holding my hand to ensure I kept walking, not out of companionship.

"The book," he said, lip curling. "You must go into its chamber and touch it, then repeat a phrase so it will acknowledge you as the heir."

"What do you do with it?" I asked.

"Nothing. Its pages are blank," he replied, voice tight.

What a strange tradition. "Why do all heirs have to do this if it's just a blank book?"

My grandfather shrugged. "Just like the ritual with the gold mine, this is one I was told *must* happen. The gold mine of course is far more obvious. It is our blood that allows it to continue to operate and gold to be found."

"What do you mean, our blood?" I asked, praying he didn't mean what I thought he did, that we had to give the mine our actual blood.

He shook his head. "We shall not discuss that now. The first task is the book. The mine we will do tomorrow."

I bowed my head in acceptance. The hallway ended at a large wooden door with a plain bronze plate in the middle of it. The door had no handle, though it was the only way we could continue down this hallway.

"Watch and remember. This is how you will get down here when you have your own heir," my grandfather said.

He must not have been down here since his father showed him the door. I watched as he set his hand on the bronze plate. The plate flashed briefly with red-tinged-brown magic. *Almost like old blood.* Then, the door swung outward.

The hallway narrowed ahead, forcing us to walk single file. The walls shimmered with Fae light, the only source of light in the hallway—an odd light choice for a kingdom that dislikes Fae. The door shut behind us with a soft thud. I shivered. *Hopefully it will open the same way from this side.*

I lost track of how long we walked when the narrow hallway opened into an egg-shaped chamber. In the center was a stone pedestal with the *Bloodsong Grimoire*. The walls of the chamber were smooth obsidian, and high above was an opening with a single shaft of light creating a column that centered on the book.

"What am I supposed to do?" I asked. The room was oddly familiar, yet I was certain I'd never been down here before.

"Put your left hand on it," he said, his voice paper-thin.

I shot him a worried glance, but in the dimness of the chamber, I had no way of reading his expression. I closed the gap between me and the pedestal. As I got closer, my skin started to crawl. I stopped in front of the book, keeping my hands at my sides. It was larger than I expected, several inches thick, with dark stains on the leather cover and tarnished gold corners.

I reached out my shaky left hand and placed it on the book. A blast of the same reddish-brown magic rolled out of the book, through me, and around the room. Then, it disappeared. I tried snatching my hand away but it was stuck. The book pulsed under my hand. I shuddered at the slimy feeling in my mind, as though something was trying to get in.

Another pulse of magic rolled through the room, and the book freed my hand. The cover whipped open, and the supposedly empty pages were covered in a scrolling text accompanied by images.

Fourty-Four

TRISTAN

Left to my own devices, I decided to go back to my room and get in some sword practice. I walked as quickly as I could toward my room. I had no idea how long Serafina was going to be busy with the king this morning, but I needed to share my new knowledge with someone I trusted, which left Callyn.

Debating if I should return to Wayside Inn and leave her a message or wait until the luncheon to talk to her, I thrust open the door to my room. Callyn was standing by the bed, rotating a dagger in her palm.

"What are you doing here?" I demanded, shutting the door and facing her.

Callyn smiled. "When I learned that Serafina had some tasks to do this morning, I figured you would likely need a distraction. Would you like to spar?"

"Maybe," I replied. "I wasn't expecting King Leonard to take Serafina away this morning. I was planning on telling her."

Callyn's eyes widened. "Telling her you're Fae?"

Running my hand over my face, I sighed. "Yes. We're married now and have consummated the marriage. I think it would be in my best interest to come clean today." I hesitated.

"What?" asked Callyn.

"King Pharaan was able to see through the pendant's magic," I admitted.

"I see," murmured Callyn. "If you are going to tell her today, I would recommend doing so when you she is not able to readily reach a weapon, just in case she takes it the wrong way and wants to kill you."

I growled low in my throat. "That's not funny."

"I wasn't trying to be funny. I only want to make sure you are prepared for her to react violently and to take into consideration the location of the discussion as well as who might overhear you. Confiding in Serafina is one thing. Having someone report the information to King Leonard is quite another," Callyn said seriously.

She had a valid point. Serafina was likely to be very angry. If I told her when there were witnesses, there was a high chance it would be reported back to King Leonard, which would put me in a precarious position that Serafina would not be able to get me out of—if she wanted to.

"I'll take her for a ride. Her guard Thomas is part of the human contingent that was working with Solana and Gareth. I doubt he will report anything I tell Serafina to the king."

"Aside from your decision to tell Serafina, how did last night go?" Callyn asked.

I shrugged. "Fine. Ghilanna was able to shield the witnesses from Serafina's view. I got the job done, if that's what you're worried about."

Callyn swatted me. "I'm glad it went well. Now ... how about that sparring match?"

"Well ... what would you think about going for a run in the forest?" I countered as a desperate need to shift hit me.

Callyn headed for the door, then stopped mid-stride, her mouth slightly open. She was gazing at the floor. I opened my mouth to ask her what she was doing, but as I did so, I felt magic awakening deep within the palace and wondered what on earth King Leonard had taken Serafina to do. For a human who hated magic, it seemed quite odd that he would be in possession of a magic object somehow tied to his family. *Do humans ever make sense?* They didn't, or at least not most of the ones I had spent time around the past week while in Gaskal.

"Did the king elaborate at all on what their task is this morning?" Callyn asked.

I shook my head. "No. He mentioned a book and that they would be back in time for the luncheon."

"You can feel the magic object now, right? I wonder if it's the book that they were going to see. It would make sense ..." Callyn looked troubled as she trailed off. "The only magic book I know of that has that much power is the *Bloodsong Grimoire*. I don't know why Serafina's family would be in possession of that book, but if we can feel it and it *is* the *Bloodsong Grimoire*, now any Fae in the palace will know exactly where it is too," Callyn pointed out.

It was strange that two of the three objects in a *Fae* prophecy were found in direct connection to humans. Perhaps in the long-forgotten past, the two species had not been as distant with one another as they currently were.

Serafina had mentioned this morning needing to tell me something about her mother but said that it could wait. *Does Serafina's information have to do with Fae and humans interacting?*

Forty-Five

SERAFINA

With Grandfather leading the way, we departed the chamber with the *Bloodsong Grimoire*. The whole interaction with it had unsettled me, and I craved Rhys's reassuring touch to wash away any residual sliminess from the book. Unfortunately, we were headed straight to the luncheon, where Rhys would meet us.

The Golden Rose ballroom was the location for the luncheon. It felt strange to be back there during the daytime. Sunlight streamed through the glass ceiling, making it difficult to appreciate the gold roses woven together to create the braces holding the glass panes in place.

The roses on the white marble columns were easily visible, though. I marveled at how detailed they were, realizing that perhaps I should spend more time exploring the palace and getting to know my new home.

One long table was set up in the middle of the room. A set of two gold-encrusted chairs with dark-red velvet cushions were arranged at the head of the table. A single, slightly elevated chair was at the other end. *Two for us and the one for Grandfather*, I assumed. Guests were already filtering in and taking seats at the table. I noticed that each plate had a small card with a name on it. As Rhys escorted me to my chair, I saw our names.

As I settled into my chair, I became aware of someone gazing intently at me from the seat to my right. I glanced up and was surprised to see my other Fae best friend, the red-haired Fiera, glaring at me. *When did she arrive?* The last time I saw Fiera was after the battle at Emerald Valley, before my stay at the Court of Dusk. Then, during the two weeks I was at Jade Wilds after the postponement of my wedding to Tanyth, she'd been out on a long hunting trip.

"Hello, Fiera," I said with a smile, trying to hide my confusion at her hostile expression.

"Princess Serafina," Fiera replied tersely.

Unable to understand her tone, I asked, "Did I do something wrong?"

"You abandoned me," Fiera hissed.

I licked my lips, trying to hide my confusion. I had no idea what she was talking about. We had fought side by side at Emerald Valley. Never once, either there or at Jade Wilds, had I been in a position to abandon her.

A teal hand settled on top of Fiera's fist. "There now, my love. Her Highness is not to blame," said a smooth voice I recognized immediately.

I stiffened, tightening my grip on Rhys's hand. *Prince Tanyth, ruler of the Court of Dusk.* He was the last Fae I expected to see here given I had broken off our engagement in a letter. Not to mention my suspicion that he could be the one causing my illness.

I forgot to breathe as I studied him. The prince's blue-black hair had two braids falling in front of his shoulders with the rest of it loose down his back. His crown was made of antlers but was a simple circlet. He wore a black jacket with teeth and claws sewn into the cuffs and collar. Trying to tear away my gaze, I coughed, realizing I'd been holding my breath and was out of air.

I thought I saw a faint teal glow of magic around his hand, but I blinked, and it vanished. I took a sip of water, trying to make sense of everything, including why the prince was here at all and how odd it was that Fiera was accompanying him.

"Serafina, did Fiera tell you our news yet?" Prince Tanyth asked.

I shook my head, wondering when Fiera would have had time given I hadn't seen her in weeks. "No. What news?"

Rhys entwined his fingers with mine and gave me a reassuring squeeze.

"Fiera and I are soulmates. I was quite surprised when it happened. There are rumors, of course, that Fae can be blessed with two soulmates in a lifetime. Given how long I was bonded to Travaran's mother, I never expected it to be possible. But here we are!" Prince Tanyth said cheerily.

I watched as Fiera turned toward Prince Tanyth and kissed him deeply. I even saw a flash of tongue. Cringing, I met Rhys's gaze, afraid to say what was on my mind aloud. But the whole thing was quite strange. *Fiera accusing me of abandoning her and then Prince Tanyth declaring they are bonded soulmates. We were still engaged less than three weeks ago. Were they going behind my back?*

Prince Tanyth was handsome and his teal skin unusual for Fae. I could understand why Fiera would find him appealing. *She must have run into him on her hunting trip.* It proved a solid explanation for why I hadn't heard from her, and since she hadn't returned prior to my departure from Jade Wilds, supported the idea that they had met after my engagement ended. I couldn't imagine what it would feel like to have a bond with another Fae. Though the formation of a soulmate bond was common, sometimes it could take a lifetime before a Fae found the individual destined to be their mate.

I could feel twinges of a headache coming whenever I looked at Fiera. Thankfully, Rhys was content to keep his hand in mine.

Though it was difficult to eat with one hand, it was better than having to leave feeling unwell.

As I ate, I wondered where Ghilanna was and if she had had a chance to talk to Fiera. Given how close the three of us had been, I assumed Fiera would have at least opened up to Ghilanna. *Unless bonding changed her an extreme amount.* I fleetingly wondered if Ghilanna knew anything about Fae soulmate bonds and if they could cause personality changes in a Fae.

Trying to wrap my mind around Fiera and Tanyth as a couple, I realized I needed to pay attention to the guest on the other side of us as well. Politely, I made eye contact with the man sitting next to Rhys. I was surprised to see it was King Hanover Atwood, the Lord of the West. *Ruler of the kingdom Eagle Rock is in.*

My grandfather had a strong relationship with King Hanover. The iron produced in his mines was the only source of metal to produce weapons. Whether they were the traditional iron or the lighter weight silver-iron version, both required the raw ore. Though gold was beautiful and highly desirable, iron was a necessity. King Leonard's first wife, Glenora, was King Hanover's oldest daughter. The alliance the marriage created had further strengthened their standing with each other. I realized then that perhaps part of my grandfather's opinion toward my father was not exclusively tied to him marrying a Fae, but also the circumstances of his birth—which killed Glenora.

"Princess Serafina, I am looking forward to getting to know you better. King Leonard has told me many wonderful things," King Hanover said. He smiled, though it did not reach his eyes.

"Thank you, King Hanover. I heard your lower mine experienced some flooding a few months ago. Did you get that resolved?" I asked, choosing what I hoped was a safe topic.

King Hanover's eyes widened in surprise. "Yes. We were able to siphon most of the water into the river and the rest evaporated on its own. In some ways the flooding was helpful."

"How so?" I asked. I thought my grandfather had said over one hundred lives had been lost in the flood.

"The water removed many layers of debris and uncovered several large iron deposits. It would have taken the crews months to get through that much material, likely longer, since we were focusing on a different area this year," King Hanover explained.

"How fortunate," I murmured, trying to hide my dismay at how dismissive he was being about losing lives in the flood.

"I have heard that Fae have trouble conceiving. I've wondered if that is true for a half-blood such as yourself," King Hanover said.

I gripped Rhys's hand tightly at the abrupt change to the immensely personal topic. It struck a nerve since I had miscarried, which could be construed as struggling to conceive.

"Should you fail to conceive, given that you are of my blood, the South would then pass on to my heirs." Though his voice was low, I was certain that Rhys and I were not the only ones at the table who had heard King Hanover openly admit he has an eye on the Southern throne for himself or his heir.

If the magic of the mines is tied to heirs of blood, could I also gain access to the iron mines? The idea was intriguing and led to more questions. How many other marriages between the human kingdoms have created heirs like me with the potential to operate more than one mine? My fingers twitched. I knew somewhere there was a book with the genealogy of the royal family of the South. The only recent kingdom bloodline mix that I was aware of within me was my ties to the Lord of the West.

I wished I could tell Rhys what I was thinking. It would be extremely convenient at that moment. Schooling my face into a bland expression, I tried not to let King Hanover's words get to me. I knew it was a tactic to attempt to get under my skin to see how I would react.

A flurry of movement caught my attention. The servants made their entrance with steaming platters of food. Conversations around the table quieted as everyone focused on the meal.

I was grateful for the distraction. With Fiera unwilling to have a civil conversation with me, I was hard-pressed to figure out what a suitable topic would be to discuss with Prince Tanyth or King Hanover. Rhys hadn't tried to help either.

When the meal concluded, we milled around the room talking to the guests. Grandfather came up to me as King Hanover departed. He kissed me lightly on the cheek.

"Enjoying yourself?" he asked. I could tell he was.

"It's a good opportunity to get better acquainted with my future subjects," I replied.

King Leonard nodded. "Precisely. That was why the tradition was started. The wedding plus the events of the two following days are dedicated to the new couple and provide the opportunity for guests who traveled far and wide to get here to know you better. Historically, trade agreements and alliances have been made at events such as this."

He paused and surveyed the room before returning his gaze to me. "Which brings us to the matter of the agenda for tomorrow. First thing in the morning, you and I will go to the mine. There is a farewell ball in the evening. However, the afternoon event is traditionally decided upon by the heir. What activity would you like to host?"

I peered at him, wondering if this was a trick.

Grandfather smiled. "This is your chance to show the guests a piece of you."

My lips twitched. "Do you really mean that, or do you just want them to see the parts of me you fully approve of?"

His smile faltered slightly. "Pick something, Granddaughter. They want to know what kind of a person you are, and the ruler you will one day be. I'm sure it won't be an embroidery party."

I swallowed; my throat felt dry. *He's serious.* What I wanted the most was the opportunity to demonstrate my skills as a warrior. That they would believe I was worthy of ruling Gaskal because I had valuable experience. "A skirmish."

Rhys coughed and covered his mouth. I shot a glance his way and saw his eyes sparkling with amusement.

My grandfather did not look amused. "A skirmish? Like a training exercise?"

"Yes. Except I want to participate," I explained. Crossing my fingers and praying Rhys would forgive me, I added, "I will lead one team and Rhys the other."

"I can't allow you to get hurt," King Leonard said.

But I was expecting his response and had prepared mine. "There's an easy solution. Practice swords and arrows that have chalk on them. That way, the weapons are not real so no one will get injured, but it's still possible to determine if someone should be dead."

"You *really* want to skirmish with your guests?" King Leonard finally responded.

I nodded. "Yes. You just told me to pick something that would allow them to get to know me better. This is how."

"Very well. I will ensure that they are informed and can prepare," King Leonard said and then stalked away.

"Skirmishing with the guests," Rhys said. "Frankly, I'm surprised he agreed."

"Me too," I murmured. I surveyed the room, noting that many of the guests were starting to leave. While my grandfather was right that the two days after the wedding were to allow us to get to know the visiting nobles of the four human—and Fae—kingdoms, they were not fully packed with activities. There was time for them to have their own meetings among themselves, explore the city, or merely relax.

As we made our way through the palace, Rhys's words broke through my thoughts. "Care to share the secret?" he teased.

"Secret?" I asked. It took a few moments before it dawned on me that I hadn't explained what our task was. "Oh, we're going to the library, or my grandfather's version of it, anyhow. When I was talking to King Hanover, he made a point about my grandmother being his daughter. Which means, if I understand the way the magic with the metal mines works, that I could in theory be able to link or control both the gold and iron mines. The primary requirement is to be an heir of blood. So, of the royal bloodline, which I am, since King Hanover is my great-grandfather."

When we reached the library, I peered around the room. There had to be thousands of books filling the rows of bookcases. A spiral staircase on one side led up to the next level, a narrow walkway allowing access to even more books. Sliding ladders made the hard-to-reach volumes on the highest shelves accessible. Rhys agreed to help me, and we began our search.

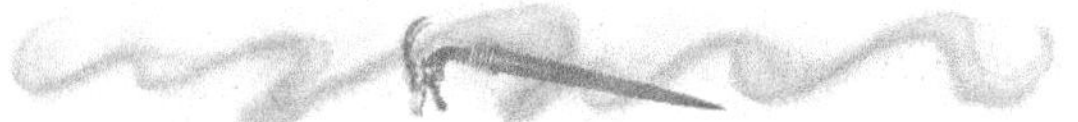

Hours later, I was hungry and tired, wanting nothing more than to retire to the solitude of our chambers for the night. Unfortunately, Lord John caught us just as we entered the corridor to our new rooms with the announcement that we would be having dinner with King Leonard.

Lord John escorted us to the dining room where the king was waiting for us. The seats we were offered were positioned side by side. I couldn't decide if that was a good or bad thing, because every time Rhys set his hand on my leg it sent sparks running through my body. I don't think he had any idea what his hand was doing to me, but I was starting to get desperate for him to remove his hand entirely—or do something else. Unfortunately, my grandfather was still enthusiastically devouring his venison.

Keeping my eyes fixed on my plate, I wrapped my fingers around Rhys's and tried to remove his hand from my leg. I couldn't get him to budge. I shot him a sideways glance, hoping he'd get the hint. Instead, he gave me a wicked smirk. I blushed, and he slid his hand up my thigh.

I bit my cheek hard enough to draw blood and turned my head away from him. He might find what he was doing amusing, but I did not. *At least not with present company.* I took a small sip of my wine. I felt eyes on me, and I turned to face my grandfather. He was openly staring at me, his fork hanging in the air.

"What?" I demanded.

"It seems as though I am keeping you from what the two of you would prefer to being doing at this moment—making an heir. By all means, you may take your leave," my grandfather said.

My cheeks heated in embarrassment that he had noticed what Rhys was doing, and was *pleased* by it. I rose from my seat. "Thank you, Grandfather." I curtsied and then rushed out the door Thomas was holding open for me, not waiting to see if Rhys was coming. My grandfather's words had acted like a bucket of ice water on my desire. But I was not going to tell him that, nor did I want to spend more time being scrutinized. *If he wants an heir that badly, maybe instead of ordering us to eat with him, he should let us have alone time.*

My shoes clicked on the polished marble. About halfway to the rooms I stopped abruptly, remembering we had been given new ones.

Rhys bumped into me. "You forgot about the new rooms."

"Why didn't you tell me when we left dinner?" I demanded, tone sharp, still annoyed at him for being so obvious at dinner.

"You're angry with me. I figured letting you cool down would help," Rhys said, taking my hand in his and running his thumb over my knuckles. I wanted to hold on to my anger—though it was difficult to decide if I was really angry at Rhys or at my grandfather—but even the slightest brush of his finger was enough to send sparks of desire rushing through me.

Not trusting my voice, I adjusted my route through the palace, heading to our new set of rooms. This would be our first night staying in them. Rhys pushed open the door, and we stood in the entryway, gazing inside.

"It's the size of a house!" I gasped. There was a foyer designated by four white columns, beyond which the room split into different areas. A large dining room table with seats for twelve was on one wall. Couches surrounded a massive fireplace in a semicircle. There was a mahogany desk with bookcases lining the walls near it. Each wall had several doors leading from it.

I glanced at Rhys, and he also seemed taken aback by the size of our new home. "Should we explore?"

"If that is what you desire, then of course," Rhys said.

I shivered, and a few sparks skittered across my skin. I tugged my hand out of his and strode toward the first door. It was another room, decorated in cream and gold, with a white painted crib and matching wardrobe. My stomach plummeted to my feet at the harsh reminder of what I had already lost. Choking back a sob, I tugged the door shut, keeping my back to Rhys and attempting to regain my composure. *The last thing I want is a constant reminder that we are supposed to produce an heir and the secret I'm keeping from Rhys.* I was certain if I got rid of the crib the maids would inform Grandfather, but I could at least keep the door shut.

The next room was the same as the first with another crib. "Apparently, he expects us to have twins," Rhys muttered.

"Uh, I don't think he expects twins. He just expects more than one child as quickly as possible," I replied in a strained voice.

"Twins would be faster," Rhys said.

I shuddered at the thought of giving birth to two babies at one time. *What if I have another miscarriage?* The only thing I knew for certain was I *could* get pregnant, but I didn't know if I'd carry to full term. *Whose child did I lose?* Squeezing my eyes shut, I took a shaky breath, trying to let go of the pain of loss and focus on Rhys and our new home.

I opened my eyes and continued our exploration, walking past the columns to the other side of the main room. There were two more doors. I had to assume one was the bathroom and the other our bedroom. I debated between the two, then decided the one closest to the wall with windows overlooking the garden was most likely to be the bedroom. *Because what use would a bathroom have for garden windows?*

I pushed the door open and stepped inside. This bedroom was at least double the size of the other two. A large bed was centered on the back wall. The wood was honey colored, a stark contrast to the dark tones of the other wood furniture, though the cream and gold theme continued. Currently, the room had a bed and two wardrobes, but there was space for more furnishings. *Maybe we can select our own together.* It would be nice to put a personal touch on this room and this suite that was now ours. From the scale of everything, I expected this was intended as the queen's suite, and my grandfather had opted to give it to me now.

"What do you think?" asked Rhys, tentatively wrapping his arms around me from behind.

"There's a lot of space. We could do training without ever having to leave," I replied. Even though I was angry, Rhys's arms were reassuring, and I felt the anger ebbing away. He nuzzled my neck with his lips and butterflies fluttered in my stomach. I tried to stamp them out as Rhys trailed tiny kisses from my ear and neck to my shoulder.

I closed my eyes. My body reacted to his touch and sparks ignited along my skin. I pressed tighter against him, and his right hand slid down my waist to my thigh. Blood throbbing in my veins, I thought, *Clothing is so annoying.* Rhys took my earlobe into his mouth and gently sucked. I gasped when I felt dampness between my thighs.

"I need you, Serafina. Do you want me?" Rhys asked softly against my ear.

"Yes," I murmured as he kissed my neck, unable to resist the demands of my throbbing core. Distracted by his kisses, I was surprised when my dress pooled around my feet. Unhindered by my clothing, Rhys ran his fingers along my thigh, before plunging them into my folds. I hissed in surprise and pleasure as he flicked my clitoris with his thumb.

I tipped my head back on his shoulder, back arching as his fingers thrust deeper and deeper. With his other hand, Rhys ran my nipple through the tips of his fingers. I bit my tongue hard as waves of pleasure rolled through me, then I sagged against him, barely able to stand.

"I'm not done," he whispered against my ear, then withdrew his hand from between my legs and swept me into his arms.

Intrigued by his comment, I kept myself limp, wondering what his next move would be. Thankfully, Rhys laid me on the bed, face up. Then, he straddled me but stayed kneeling. Locking his gaze with mine, I watched as he took the hand that was still glistening with my fluids and sucked on it.

A tendril of need wound through me. I glanced down between us and was met with the breathtaking view of Rhys's cock. *He's huge! But*, I reminded myself, *he fit once, he'll fit again.* Pulse pounding, I realized how ready he was for me. Pre-cum glistened at the tip of his cock. Tentatively, I reached out my hand and brushed it with my finger.

Meeting Rhys's gaze with my own, I raised my finger, now covered in pre-cum, to my lips, slowly slid my finger into my mouth, and sucked on it. Rhys growled. I smirked. "You did it first."

He nudged my legs open with his knee and then lowered himself over me, sliding his cock slowly into me. My muscles tightened in response.

"You okay?" he asked.

"Yes," I replied, grateful he cared enough to ask.

Bending over me, Rhys captured my lips with his as he thrust deeply into me. In and out. As I got a sense for the rhythm, I moved my hips in time with Rhys's, discovering that it was driving him even deeper. The sparks I had felt earlier intensified. Every movement of his cock inside me sent them skittering throughout my body. For the briefest of moments, it felt as though I was thrusting my cock into my own body beneath me. I let my eyes flutter shut, and the feeling went away, leaving only building pressure.

"Good girl," he murmured into my ear. Then he grabbed my calves and lifted them so they were on his shoulders. I bit my lip at the intensity of the new position. Rhys's strokes became faster, filled with need.

I was wound impossibly tight, and my foot was cramping when Rhys reached between us and slid his finger inside of me too. A moment later an orgasm far more intense than the first one exploded through me. "Rhys!" I screamed.

Seconds later, Rhys gasped, "Serafina!" as pleasure crested through him.

Rhys rolled onto his side, and we lay there for a long time gazing at each other. I still had trouble believing that I was married and was also the heir of the South. It felt surreal. Yet here we were in an opulent room within the palace in Gaskal.

"Is this how it will always be?" I asked.

Rhys gave me a quizzical look. "If you're asking if having sex will always be that pleasurable … I promise to do my best."

I giggled and blushed. "I meant being married."

Rhys shrugged. "I have no idea. I've never been married, nor spent much time around married couples. As a child, I can assure you that I did not pay much attention to how my parents interacted with each other. My concern was what they thought of me."

Unable to stop myself, I spoke the words on the tip of my tongue. "Do you *want* to have children?" Holding my breath, I awaited the answer.

Rhys was quiet for a moment. "I want *you* to bear my yo... children."

I nipped his lips and asked, "Is that a promise of fidelity?"

"It was in our wedding vows," Rhys said softly. He took my hand in his and squeezed it. "Are you worried I am going to break my vow?"

I pressed my lips together and looked away. Rhys's fingers cupped my chin. I let him turn my face back to his. "It's the nature of men to do so."

Rhys's eyebrows rose in surprise. "How do you have experience with this?"

I realized I had no idea. I could not remember ever witnessing a married man breaking his vows.

Rhys gave me a light kiss on the lips. "I don't intend to break my vow to you, Serafina. I will do everything in my power *not* to break it. Just as if we are blessed with children, I will protect them with my life."

"Okay," I replied. I had been wanting to tell Rhys about the book all day. My grandfather had not forbidden me to tell him.

"There's something else I need to tell you," I started.

Rhys gave me an encouraging smile. "You can tell me anything."

"This morning my grandfather wanted to take me to do something with a book. Well, the whole thing was very strange. The book was in a special obsidian chamber. It has a name. *Bloodsong Grimoire*."

Rhys's breathing hitched. I couldn't tell if it was from recognition or disbelief that a Fae object could have a name.

I shuddered, remembering the slimy feeling in my mind when I touched it. "Grandfather said it's just a blank book, and I was supposed to put my left hand on it and then we'd leave. Well, I followed his instructions, and ..." I shivered, and goosebumps rippled on my arms. "The pages have words on them now," I said.

"Did you get a chance to read it?" Rhys asked.

I shook my head. "No. He wanted to leave, so we left. Honestly, I am not sure I want to read what's on the pages. I don't know if it's possible for a magic object to be evil, but it did not feel like ordinary Fae magic. It felt *wrong*."

"Do you think you could take me down there, so I can look at it?" Rhys asked.

I tugged on my lip, trying to remember exactly what my grandfather had said. "I believe the book is intended only for the current Lord of the South and his heir. Given you hold neither position, I don't think I should take you down there. Not unless an emergency arises and the book could prove useful."

"Except you have no idea what information the book contains. How will you know when it might be useful?" Rhys observed.

I stuck out my tongue at him. "Good point. Maybe when the dust has settled from the wedding, we can go down there and learn more. For now, though, I would prefer to leave the book alone."

"As you wish," Rhys replied. He kissed my forehead and then tugged the covers up over both of us. I rolled over and scooted backward so I snuggled against him as I fell asleep.

Fourty-Six

TRISTAN

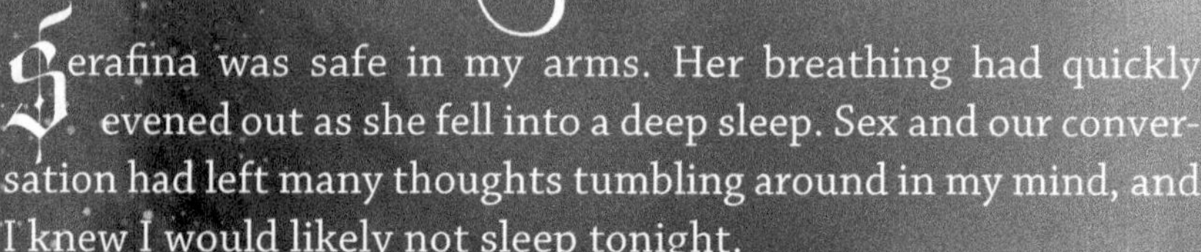

Serafina was safe in my arms. Her breathing had quickly evened out as she fell into a deep sleep. Sex and our conversation had left many thoughts tumbling around in my mind, and I knew I would likely not sleep tonight.

In my mind's eye, I could sense our bond. Before the wedding, it had been dull; now it was muted green entwined with dark gray. There had been a few moments when we'd had sex where it felt like we swapped positions, and I thought as I thrust into her that the bond would reawaken, but the feeling disappeared as quickly as it had come.

Hope coursed through me that we could repair whatever Prince Tanyth had done. We just needed more time. *And more sex?* I fully intended to put that theory to the test. I suspected Serafina's interaction with the *Bloodsong Grimoire* had cracked Prince Tanyth's magic, given the ripple that had gone through the whole palace.

Which meant Callyn's theory about the three magic objects of the prophecy Prince Tanyth was obsessed with was true. He had used either Dragonfang or Fleshrender to bind Serafina's soulmate bond, and only by using one of the objects would we be able to reverse it. The other concern hovering at the surface of my thoughts was that Prince Tanyth and the *Bloodsong Grimoire* were both here in the palace. The prince would do *anything* in his power to get his hands on the book.

With my magic blocked by the pendant, my greatest weapon against Prince Tanyth was out of my reach. *Except it's not. Remove the pendant, and I will have my magic back.* I had promised myself I was going to have revealed my identity by now, but with the soulmate bond stirring between us, I hesitated. If the bond were to restore fully, it would give us a deeper connection, making it easier for Serafina to understand my reasoning because she could feel me through the bond rather than only hearing the words. Deep down, I knew we were close to unlocking it. While it was a risk to put off telling Serafina my identity, I felt, given the evolving situation, this new plan was in both of our best interests.

I must have drifted off to sleep. I woke up to Serafina's hand lightly brushing against my cock. It took me a moment to realize she was still asleep. The sparks that I knew were tied to our bond spread throughout my body, and need throbbed in my core.

My eyes adjusted to the not-quite-dark room. Serafina lay on her back, the sheet rumpled around her waist. Her chest rose and fell with each breath. Unable to resist, I scooted closer and ran my tongue around her nipple, before taking it into my mouth and gently sucking.

Serafina twitched but continued to sleep. I switched to her other breast and gave it the same treatment. Her back arched, and a whimper escaped her lips, but her eyes didn't open. Determination filled me, and I let my hand slide under the sheet onto her thigh, slowly working my way into her folds. It didn't take much before she was drenched and ready.

"Mmmm," Serafina murmured, and I knew I had her full attention.

"Roll onto your stomach," I said softly and withdrew my fingers.

Serafina rolled onto her stomach and cast me a sleepy smile over her shoulders.

I moved so I was kneeling behind her and tugged her hips up so her butt was in the air. Positioning myself correctly, I guided my cock inside of her channel, gasping as I almost came. Biting my tongue, I tried to rein in my body's response. I wanted to take my time so she would be satisfied too.

"Is this okay?" I asked. I could feel her relaxing against me, but I still wanted to be sure.

"Yes," Serafina replied. Bending over her back, I held her hip steady with one hand and massaged her breasts with the other. Then, I found my rhythm. Each stroke sent me deeper than the last. The sparks that had woken me were almost painful. I could feel the bond thickening. The colors were getting brighter. *Serafina,* I called on the bond, but she didn't respond. I let go of her breast and set my hand on her other hip. Each thrust into her, I also pulled back on her. Serafina's breathing was heavy, and I knew we were both close. With one more thrust, I sent us both careening over the edge.

"Rhys!" she shouted.

"Serafina?" I gasped. But the connection that had been there moments before was gone. Sadness filled me, swiftly followed by determination. I thrust again. Serafina whimpered against me, and I withdrew.

"I'm sorry," I said, crouched on the edge of the bed.

Serafina rolled over and looked at me. "For what?"

"I hurt you," I replied.

Serafina shook her head. "No, you didn't. I just wasn't expecting you to try again so soon. Or for my body to respond at all."

"You want to try again?" I asked, surprised. *I'm going to have to learn her tells.*

"Honestly, I'm not sure I can be very helpful. You seem very skilled at wringing everything out of me," Serafina admitted.

I chuckled. "For you, my love, I can go all day if you want."

Serafina gave me a wry smile. "I'm not sure my grandfather would be happy about that. I do have duties to attend to."

"He did say that creating an heir was of utmost importance," I replied.

Serafina swatted at me. I caught her wrist and kissed it. "I just need to know what you want me to do, wife. I'm yours to command."

Serafina gave me an appraising look. "I suppose a bath is in order. I can't exactly attend a meeting smelling like ... well, however I smell to someone else."

"A bath for two?" I asked.

"Absolutely," Serafina replied.

Thankfully, Serafina had been satisfied with simply taking a bath. We shared a few kisses, but that was it. *I think she's worried about someone walking in on us.* When we were clean and dry, I helped her get into her clothes. She denied my suggestion to call for help, claiming between the two of us, surely we could manage.

I admired our work. Serafina was wearing a deep green satin gown and corset, complimented by a simple gold circlet on her dry hair. I didn't know enough about female hairstyles to feel comfortable doing more than towel-drying her hair though.

I then turned my attention to my own attire. Thankfully, the wardrobes had clothing in them. I selected a simple black jacket and pants with a white silk shirt. Without knowing what was on today's agenda, I wanted to make sure I appeared like the princess's husband. *Consort? Prince?* I wasn't entirely sure if I even had an official title at this point. *I should ask.*

We entered the main gathering rooms together. There was a selection of breakfast foods awaiting us, though Mary had forgotten to include food for Lord John, who was present too.

It seems privacy is hard to come by in this palace. I swallowed hard. *Just as it was in Dorcha Palace.*

I knew Serafina and King Leonard were going to the gold mine today. Unlike the book, it was common knowledge that there was magic of sorts that tied each human kingdom to its metal ore mines and only an heir related by blood to the original kings could keep them in operation. I pinched my lips together and pulled out a chair for Serafina, then sat in my own.

"What's bothering you?" she whispered before loading her plate with food.

I followed suit, considering my words. "Do you not find it odd that a human kingdom has two things that are significant—and magic—and require not just an heir, but an heir of blood to keep the kingdom running smoothly?"

"If you're referring to the mines, the library that held the information about how they were created and the magic involved was lost in a devastating fire two hundred years ago. None of the books were recovered, nor were there spare copies anywhere," Serafina replied, her fork hovering in the air by her mouth.

I raised my eyebrows, and she hastily shoved the food in her mouth. "Lord John, what is on today's agenda?" I asked, remembering my manners.

"Rhys, thank you for the question. Serafina and King Leonard will be going out to the mine. Ghilanna has requested a meeting with you while Serafina is out," Lord John explained.

Intriguing. Though Serafina had told me of Ghilanna, beyond bumping into each other in the hallway and our brief interaction at the wedding, she had made no attempts to meet with me. I assumed it was due to my current appearance as a human who was not her top priority. "Has the location of my meeting been determined?"

Lord John nodded. "Yes." He slid a piece of paper across the table toward me.

I scooped it up and studied the address, then offered it to Serafina. Her eyes widened immediately in recognition. "Is this a joke?" she demanded, staring at the steward.

"No, Princess. Is there something wrong with that location?" Lord John asked.

Serafina's gaze dropped to her plate. Her lips pressed into a thin white line. I reached over and caressed her cheek. "What's is it?"

"It was my parents' house." Her words were so faint I almost thought I had misheard her.

Why are we meeting there of all places? I recognized the address, having been there spying on Serafina's meeting, but I hadn't realized it was the house she grew up in. Knowing the house's history and Serafina's relationship to it didn't give me confidence that this wasn't a trap.

"Ghilanna knows things … about my mother. I was going to tell you myself, but the timing was never right. Now it seems she has decided to take matters into her own hands," Serafina said.

I could see her hands shaking slightly as she picked up the teacup and took a sip. Returning my attention to the steward, I asked, "Is there any chance we can change the location to here in the palace?"

The steward shook his head. "I'm sorry, but she was adamant that you meet her there. It is within your rights to refuse. She is merely a guest."

"No, I'll go. I don't want an escort either. The location is upsetting to Serafina, so I would prefer to investigate on my own," I replied, my tone firm, borderline an order.

To my surprise, Lord John acquiesced. "I will allow it this time. But I must warn you that the king intends to set strict limitations on both of your movements until an heir has been produced."

I rolled my eyes. "We're fully capable of protecting ourselves. Besides, hasn't he been around Serafina long enough to know that she does what she wants?" An image flashed into my mind of her galloping away from the jousting tournament on Dubhar, bareback, without so much as a halter.

The steward cringed. "I know. However, I am simply relaying the king's words."

Serafina jumped into the discussion. "I plan on discussing it with the king today. As well as establishing what other duties I will be handling."

"Good. Now, I will let you two finish eating and return when it is time for you both to go your separate ways," Lord John announced, then departed.

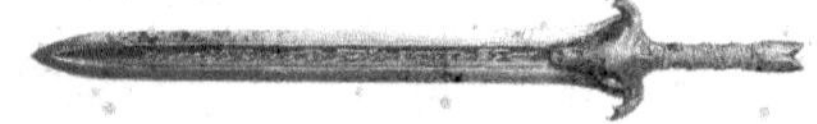

Lord John was not gone for long before he returned to take Serafina to wherever she was meeting King Leonard. There was no reason for me to delay meeting with Ghilanna. I left a few minutes after Serafina did and made my way out of the palace, opting for the less-busy servants' passageways.

I was curious to learn what it was Ghilanna felt was important to share with me. A shiver of apprehension when through me. *Does she know I'm not Rhys, but Tristan?* King Pharaan and Marek could feel me through the pendant's magic; it was not too far-fetched to think Ghilanna might have figured out what was going on too. Biting my cheek hard enough to draw blood, I forced myself to think about something else.

Serafina mentioned needing to tell me something about her mother ... and I knew the house I was going to had belonged to her parents. Quicker than I expected, I halted in front of Serafina's parents' house. The gate was held open with a small rock; as soon as I set foot through it, the front door opened.

"Hello," I greeted Ghilanna.

She beckoned me into the house and then shut the door firmly. "Hello. I didn't meet to be rude, but it is important we do not flaunt your presence here too much. Not everyone is thrilled that you are Serafina's husband."

"Yes, I am aware," I replied conversationally. "What is it you wanted to discuss?" I peered around the inside of the house, making note of the worn pink quilt draped over the back of the couch and the bookshelf above the hearth.

"Serafina's mother was a seer," Ghilanna said jumping straight to the point.

My jaw dropped open in surprise; that was the last thing I expected Ghilanna to tell me.

"Yes, shocking, isn't it? I don't know how much you know about Fae seers, given you're a human and from Eagle Rock. But essentially what it means is Solana could sometimes see the future. Or a *possibility* of a future. Many of her visions have been of Serafina," Ghilanna revealed.

Remember you are a human who knows nothing of Fae prophecies, I reminded myself sharply. I could not afford to make Ghilanna question who I was, not now. "Why is it important if Solana had visions of Serafina?"

Ghilanna blew out her breath sharply. "She foresaw Serafina would marry an outsider, which you are."

Fascinating. It was strange to think that there was more than one prophecy circulating about Serafina and I being together. However, it also cemented my belief that everything I had done through this moment to ensure I could be with Serafina was for a just cause.

"The other thing that Solana's visions foretell is that Serafina will play a critical role in reshaping the relationship between Fae and humans. As her husband, your duty is to support her in these efforts. From what I have seen of your actions so far, you do not seem to harbor ill will toward Fae. It is critical that both of you lead by example and show Serafina's subjects exactly how you want them to behave. To treat Fae with grace and fairness," Ghilanna said.

There were four strong taps on the back door. My hand instinctively went for my sword.

"I'll be right back," Ghilanna said and retreated to the back door, tugging it open just enough to speak to the person. The conversation ended quickly, and she rushed back to me. "There is a mob of armed individuals heading this way. You must leave quickly. Go straight back to the palace. Josiah has a horse for you in the back."

I frowned, but did as she ordered. Sure enough, there was a heavyset bearded man in the back holding a bony gray horse that wore a halter and nothing else. "I didn't have time to saddle him up. Rocky may not look like much, but he's surefooted and fast even in the city."

I had no choice but to swing my leg onto Rocky's back. I grimaced as his spine poked into my groin in the most uncomfortable way. *It's only a quick ride to the palace, then I'll never ride Rocky again.* "Thank you," I said. The man slapped Rocky's butt and the horse shot forward. We burst through the open gate and galloped up the road.

Forty-Seven

SERAFINA

The horses were waiting for us when we reached the stable. I smiled when I saw that Dubhar was saddled next to the king's chestnut stallion. *A small win*. But a win nonetheless—one I hadn't expected. For the king to have ordered Dubhar to be tacked up for us to ride together meant something.

"I have seen how well the two of you get along and wanted to give you Dubhar as your wedding present," the king said. His tone was flat, as though he wasn't thrilled with his own decision.

I rushed over and gave him a hug. "Thank you." He took the hug but made no move to return the affection. I released him and stepped back. No matter how he was behaving, I knew with this gift that he did care about me, at least a little.

"We will get there faster on horses, with fewer bumps," King Leonard explained.

Our entourage made its way down to the gold mine. We had two squads of knights, which I thought was overkill, though I refrained from saying so. The matter of the *Bloodsong Grimoire* had been simple. I was certain whatever we were doing at the gold mine was not a simple matter of touching an object.

The journey was silent save for the sound of the horses' hooves. We exited the palace grounds and rode down a gently sloping grassy hill at the back until grass gave way to rocks and the path became small pea gravel. The path wound down the hill until it leveled out a few hundred feet from the mine. From here, I couldn't even see the lake, though I knew the general direction it was in. I hadn't realized before how large the mine truly was.

Our group halted and the guards fanned out around us. King Leonard motioned for me to dismount. I did and waited while he was helped from his horse. His back was to me, but I could see from the movement of his shoulders that he was shaking. *Is he having another seizure?*

Declan noticed my gaze and held his finger to his lips. I sighed. I would have to talk to him later to find out more. *Or confront Grandfather directly?* Our relationship was still strained, though at times I thought maybe he was willing to accept me for who I was. I couldn't imagine he would welcome questions about his health from anyone, let alone me.

"What are you waiting for, Serafina? Come here," King Leonard barked.

I snapped my head up, realizing the king and Declan had moved ahead, toward what I thought was a large rock. The shadows from the mountain made it difficult to fully discern the shape.

Walking quickly toward them, I realized it was a rectangular block made from gold. The top reached my hip, and if I had lain on it, my feet would have barely reached the edge. My eyes widened as I took it in, wondering if it was pure gold or if it was covering a stronger material, given how soft gold was. The sun was behind the mountain, but if it emerged, I could imagine the block would be blinding to look at directly. I ran my fingers lightly over the edge.

Inside a tall room carved within the mine were two giant natural emeralds framing an intricately carved emerald table.

"This is where the Court of Dawn creates magical objects," King Pharaan said.

I blinked rapidly; Declan gave me a concerned look but didn't comment. "What are we supposed to do here?" *Why does a human kingdom have a table like one in a Fae mine? Maybe it's just a mine thing.* It was a logical explanation, but I didn't feel convinced. However, my grandfather had told me there was a task we must perform to link me to the gold mine as his heir. Perhaps I would soon learn if there was a connection.

"It is time," King Leonard announced. He stepped up next to me at the gold table. Thomas and Declan moved out of earshot.

"What do I need to do?" I asked.

King Leonard pulled a dagger out of the folds of his robe and set it on the table. I studied the dagger. It was a simple, utilitarian design, without any wrapping around the hilt for a more comfortable grip. The only part that wasn't simple was that it was gold. *Can gold even hold an edge?* I wondered, though it was possible the dagger was just for show.

"Hold out your hand over the table," he ordered.

I stretched my hand out, palm up. He picked up the dagger and sliced the full width of my hand, then did the same to his. "Put your hand in mine," he explained.

I set my hand in his, and he squeezed it, then turned them, so the mingled blood would drip onto the table. The drops bubbled as though boiling hot as they connected with the gold.

"Repeat after me," King Leonard ordered. "'With this blood, I bind myself to the gold mines as the future Lady of the South.'"

I dutifully repeated the words. When I finished, a bright golden glow emitted from the table, encasing our hands. The glow continued to expand beyond our hands.

The king sent me a wary look. "Are you doing this?"

I shook my head. "I don't have magic." Worry coursed through me. *What is happening?* I tried to remove my hand from his, but they were stuck together. I swallowed and knew that we would have to wait out whatever was happening.

The king pressed his lips together into a thin line, and we both watched in apprehension. The entire table was glowing. I could feel the blood continuing to drip off the bottom of our hands. *Maybe if we stop feeding the table blood, the magic will stop?* Except our hands were locked in place too.

The table was almost completely hidden by the brightness of the magic. Suddenly, it felt like all the air was being sucked out of me. I gasped and tipped forward. There was a loud pop, and the glow disappeared. Our hands released.

Below where our hands had been was a gold crown, unlike any I had seen before. It had four points, one on each corner, like a compass. A unicorn, a griffin, a dragon, and an emerald. I sucked in a sharp breath. *Why is there a crown with Fae court symbols at a human mine?*

I opened my mouth to ask my grandfather when he collapsed, convulsing. Declan ran over, holding the king and giving orders.

Please be okay, I prayed. The little I knew about the seizures was that they could happen at any time, but high stress could make them occur more frequently. *As if ruling a kingdom is never stressful.*

I waited to the side, giving my grandfather space to recover when the seizure ended.

"I need to go back to my parents' house," I told Thomas. I knew with certainty that there had to be more answers there. Ghilanna and the others had said my mother was a seer. She must have kept a journal or something to track her prophecies.

"Are you sure? I know it was not easy for you to be there," Thomas said softly.

I nodded. "Yes. I need answers. That is my best option for getting them. I just need to confirm that whatever we just did was all that needed to occur. Then we can leave."

Thomas nodded. "Very well. I will bring Dubhar over."

My grandfather was sitting up, though still on the ground. I crouched next to him. "Is there anything else we need to do?"

He shook his head slowly, as though in pain. "No. The task was to slice open our hands and recite the words."

"Can I take the crown with me?" I asked.

He shrugged. "I have no idea where it came from. My only assumption is it is *for* you. The ritual establishes your tie to the gold mine. Otherwise, it would have shown up many years ago when I did the ritual as heir."

"Thank you. I am going to do some research and see if I can find any answers about the crown," I explained.

"As you wish," King Leonard said tiredly.

Taking that as my dismissal, I snagged the crown off the gold table and tucked it into the bag on my saddle.

Unhindered by the two squads, Thomas, George, and I made good time from the gold mine to my parents' house. I wondered if Rhys would still be there for his meeting with Ghilanna and couldn't decide if I hoped he was there, or if I wanted to investigate the crown on my own.

When we reached the house, there was no sign of Ghilanna or Rhys. After doing a quick sweep, Thomas motioned for me to enter the house. George kept watch outside. It was eerily quiet after the meeting with Josiah and Valerie on my last visit. A quick scan around the kitchen and family room confirmed that the book likely wasn't there. I moved into the small healing room that had served as my mother's office and a place to treat patients.

The shelves were filled with a hodgepodge of jars and books. None of the books had titles on the spines, so I had to pull them out one at a time and scan their contents. The third book I pulled out was my mother's copy of *Bedtime Tails*. I looked at the cover, then at the spine. The cover had the same cover design with the snow leopard tail as the S, but I could have sworn it was way thicker than the ones I'd seen in the past.

I sat down in the chair at the desk and began flipping through it. The first story was "The Lost Fae Queen," which I was well acquainted with. The second story was about a dark green dragon named Rethys. The illustration depicted a dark-green dragon with black belly scales standing over a treasure hoard of gold and jewels.

> *The treasure of Rethys is hunted far and wide by seekers of fame and fortune. Hundreds have perished in their quest, intent only on their personal gain.*
>
> *One day, a Fae accidentally stumbled upon Rethys's cave, seeking shelter from the storm. He saw the sleeping dragon and could feel the warmth radiating off the creature. The Fae curled up in a ball against Rethys's side and fell asleep.*
>
> *When he awoke, the first thing he noticed was a mark on his arm. The light in the cave was dim, so he stepped outside to inspect it. In the sunlight, the mark became clear: It was a tattoo of a dragon.*
>
> *"You are the first to come here not to steal, but because you needed shelter. If you are ever in need, you can summon me through the mark. If your heirs are worthy, they too will be able to summon me through the mark, if they can earn it," Rethys spoke into the Fae's mind.*
>
> *"Thank you," the Fae said.*

I raised my head from the book. The story was much longer than I remembered, though it seemed to be in the same vein as the one in my copy of *Bedtime Tails*. The idea that Rethys was able to mark a Fae with a tattoo that would allow him to be summoned was strange. Fae creatures had been only briefly glossed over in my history lessons while at Jade Wilds. I knew a short list of species and which courts they were most commonly found in, but that was the extent of my knowledge. *Maybe it's normal for them to mark Fae.*

I turned to the next story and was surprised to see it was in my mother's handwriting. I traced the words with a shaking finger as emotions welled within me. I was confident this was a sign I was on the right track. *I wish you were here, Mother.*

TRUTH IS IN THE BLOOD
BEFORE THE WINTER FLOOD
TWO SPELLS WILL BIND
FIGHT THE END OF TIME

There was no drawing on this page, which made me felt like it wasn't as much a story as it was a real prophecy. *Whose blood? What spells?* I sighed. It was vague and could reference almost anything.

The next pages had the story about the three magic objects, Fleshrender, *Bloodsong Grimoire*, and Dragonfang. I shuddered and hastily turned past them. The images alone creeped me out. I didn't want to consider if it was true that someone was hunting for my family heirloom, the *Bloodsong Grimoire*.

The following spread had a lovely drawing of flowery vines. *I guess I'm not the only one who isn't a fan of the skull image.* I kept going. Next was my mother's writing again.

TABLE AWASH IN GOLD
THE BLOOD RISES WITHIN
BUILDING THE BRIDGE
FOLLOWING THE COMPASS
THE BLESSING WILL COME
THWARTING THE MESS
THE COURTS WILL BE RENEWED

There was a rough sketch in colored pencil of a yellow rectangle

331

and a circle on top. *The gold mine ritual and the crown.* I reread the words three times, trying to decipher them. My best guess was that the crown appearing was simply an indication that I was supposed to be a bridge between the Fae courts and the human kingdoms—at least *my* human kingdom. This prophecy spoke of gold, which most certainly was a representation of the South, but it said nothing of the other metal ores.

Thomas walked in to check on me. "Find anything?"

I gave him a strained smile and patted the book. "Yes. This book seems to be where my mother was writing her prophecies. Or at least I've found two so far. Would you mind looking at them?" Thomas may not be Fae, but he seemed to know quite a bit about my mother and her prophecies. *He might understand this better than me.*

"I would love to look at the book, but let's return to the palace. We've been here quite a while, and we should make sure your grandfather is still okay," Thomas said.

He had a point, and I realized I was hungry. "Sure, as long as we can eat before I go check on the king?"

Thomas chuckled. "Of course. I can send George ahead to alert the kitchen."

"Are you sure?" I asked.

"Yes. I'm confident the two of us can defend you from anything."

An idea came to me. I shut the book and handed it to Thomas, then went to the closet in the office. Rummaging through the stack of boxes and hanging clothes, my hand finally felt what I was looking for: my father's sword. It took some strong tugs to remove it from the boxes it was wedged between. I shut the closet door, then ran my hands over the scabbard. The leather was starting to crack.

"With this, I *will* be able to defend myself," I said.

"Good idea," Thomas replied. Apparently, he had forgotten I hadn't brought a sword with me to the gold mine this morning.

"Let's go," I said and settled the scabbard around my waist.

Forty-Eight

TRISTAN

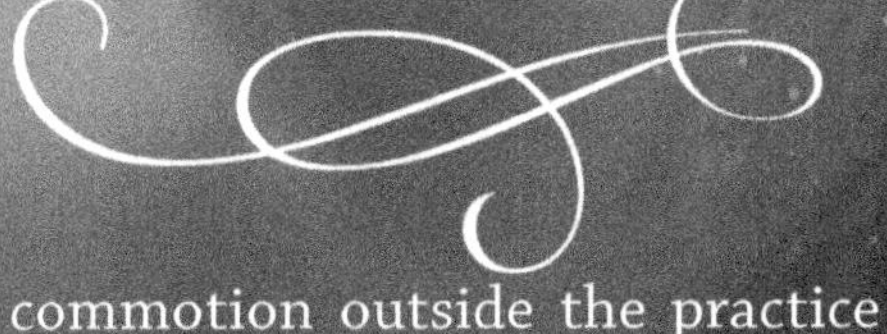

There was a commotion outside the practice room where Nolan and I were sparring. I took several steps back and lowered my sword, wondering what was going on. Serafina and King Leonard had gone down to the gold mine along with a large contingent of guards. I assumed the noise signaled their return.

Nolan took it upon himself to step into the hallway. He came back a few minutes later. "From what I gather, there was strange magic during the ritual, which has the guards spooked. In addition to that, the king had a seizure. Sounds like everyone is in a tizzy about both things. It'll take a while for them to settle down."

My interest was piqued by the "strange magic" comment. I had gathered from Serafina that the gold mine was bound to the Helias bloodline through a spell of some sort. I assumed that like with the book, the ritual was typically uneventful. The heir and current king would go through the motions of the ritual and then it was over.

Two human kingdom traditions involving magic have behaved differently now that Serafina is heir. That's one too many to be a coincidence. Given my recent entanglement in not one but two Fae prophecies, it was difficult to keep my thoughts from heading in that direction. I recalled Ghilanna telling me this morning that Serafina's mother was a seer and Solana had her own prophecy about her daughter.

Running my hand over my face, I considered the available options. Talking to King Leonard about Fae prophecies would be useless. I doubted he'd believe a word I uttered on the subject, especially since as Rhys Mongan, I shouldn't know much about Fae prophecies anyhow. However, Callyn would be worth talking to.

"I am going to go into the city to meet a friend at Wayside Inn," I announced.

Nolan grunted in agreement. "Walk or ride?"

"I'd prefer to walk," I replied.

"Suit yourself," Nolan responded. I assumed he would have preferred to ride, but I wanted time to think.

About ten minutes into our walk, I realized we going the wrong direction. I rolled my eyes. *This is what I get for not paying attention.* Halting, I eyed the street signs, recalling the map of the city and trying to chart a path.

Nolan watched me with amusement. "I wondered when you'd notice we're walking in the opposite direction of Wayside Inn."

"Why didn't you say anything?" I demanded.

Nolan shrugged. "You wanted to walk, and we don't have a pressing agenda. I knew you'd eventually realize we were going the wrong way."

I bit back a sharp reply. He was right. We had nowhere to be, and odds were Callyn wasn't even at Wayside Inn right now. "Which way do we go to get to Wayside Inn?" I asked.

"If we go down Green Street, it'll get us almost all the way there," Nolan replied, pointing at a narrow alley between the two buildings.

"That's a street?" I asked in surprise.

"Yep," Nolan said with a smile. I shook my head and walked between the two buildings onto Green Street. It was narrow, barely large enough for me to pass through.

A loud clang that sounded like swords hitting each other resounded from behind us. I froze, ears straining. It came again, followed by the distinct whinny of Dubhar.

"Serafina!" I shouted and spun, plowing right into Nolan.

Nolan squeezed to the side to let me pass by and then followed closely on my heels. I sprinted out of the alley, toward the swordfight.

A thread of fear worked through me, and I quickly squashed it. *Serafina can handle herself.* We arrived in the middle of chaos. Dubhar was rearing and striking while Serafina tried to slice the hooded and masked attackers with her sword, but they were just out of reach. Thomas was fighting two against one. His arm was bleeding heavily, though it wasn't slowing him down yet. There were two dead on the ground, but still seven or eight doing their best to injure Serafina.

I launched myself into the fray. Sweeping my sword left and right, there was no finesse in my movements, just speed. I knew if I could catch them by surprise, it was my best shot at ending this mess before Serafina *or* Thomas got killed.

The first two attackers were focused on dodging Dubhar's hooves. I drove my sword through the back of one and across the neck of the other, splattering myself and the stallion in droplets of blood. Nolan shouted on the other side of Serafina, and I could hear the clank of his axe against a sword.

From the corner of my eye, I saw Thomas sweep his sword in a high strike—too high. Leaping forward, I closed the gap between us and spun in a high crescent kick. My boot connected with the back of the attacker's head. His neck snapped to the side, and he crumpled. I twisted, narrowly missing getting skewered by a blade that looked more ornamental than utilitarian. *Who are these people?* I wondered.

Serafina shrieked and I pulled my attention away from Thomas, who had things under control. Dubhar was bleeding from wounds on his chest and neck and two of the attackers were trying to pull Serafina off.

Dubhar cast me a look as though to ask if I was going to solve the problem or just gape. I shook myself, and swinging my sword with both hands, sliced across the hamstring of one attacker and the lower back of the other. They released their grip on Serafina, and she kicked one in the face. I grabbed the other by the arms and shoved him to his knees.

"Who sent you?" I demanded, yanking off his hood and mask.

The man spit on my feet, and I backhanded him with my fist, letting my emotions get the better of me.

I felt a light hand on my shoulder. "I'm fine, Rhys. We can take him back to the palace to be interrogated."

Thomas took hold of my captive, and I met Serafina's gaze. Her face had a smear of blood on it, and her sword was still dripping.

"You scared me," I admitted.

Her gaze softened. "I told you before, I can handle myself."

Thomas coughed. *I guess her guard disagrees this time.* "There were a lot of them. I don't think one guard is enough from now on if you're going to come into the city."

Serafina didn't reply, so I inspected Dubhar's wounds, then decided they were not severe enough for her to get off. *It's safer this way.*

"Let's go back," I said. It was more of an order than a suggestion. Thankfully, no one protested.

Forty-Nine

SERAFINA

Trudging back to our rooms with assurances that Dubhar would be fine, I realized how worn out I was. Rhys walked with me in silence. I hated to admit it, but he was right: If they hadn't shown up, the fight likely would have had a different outcome. The assailants had obviously been out for blood. A few had even muttered "half-blood filth" as we fought, confirming at least that they were part of the faction who had been quite vocal about disliking me. I had yet to determine if it was tied to the group of nobles who hated Fae, like Duchess Oriana, or if they were two separate organizations.

To escalate from notes and graffiti to violence was worrisome. Especially since we knew they had accessed the palace at least twice. *Or they have someone on the inside,* I mused. Not that I was any closer to identifying that individual either.

"You're a mess," I said to Rhys. He had blood splatters across his face and shoulder.

"I'm not the only one," he replied.

I winced as I caught sight of myself in the hallway mirror.

"I'd love a nap, but I might have to settle for a bath and food. We still have the skirmish later," I replied.

Thomas had reminded me when we left Dubhar at the stable. I almost asked him to cancel it. The only thing preventing me from doing so was that my grandfather had not wanted us to do the skirmish, and I felt if I canceled it, I would be giving in to his opinion that it was unladylike.

We stepped inside our home, and Thomas hovered by the door. "George is here, and I have sent for backup as well. I need to clean up. I will see you at the skirmish, okay?"

I nodded. "See you then, and thank you, Thomas." Thomas blushed and ducked his head in embarrassment.

Rhys shut the door. I was about to scold him for being rude when his lips captured mine. He pulled back to take a breath, his gaze was serious. "I thought I was going to lose you."

"But you didn't," I replied, nipping his lower lip.

"I love you, Serafina. I know it seems like things are moving fast, and maybe to you it is crazy that I can have feelings like this for you already, but I do. I want you to know that I love you. Whether you say the same words now or never. This is how I feel," Rhys said. His voice never wavered.

Warmth spread through me. *He loves me.* I wasn't ready to say the words back, but it felt wonderful to hear them.

"Bath," I squeaked as Rhys tried to kiss me again.

Rhys chuckled. "Right ... bath." Taking my hand in his, he led me to the bathroom.

Before the attack outside of my parents' house, my plan had been to discuss Solana's prophecies with Thomas. Now, that discussion was going to have to wait. I blushed, thinking about how it had felt to have Rhys's cock thrusting into me while submerged in the tub. Blinking, I forced myself to focus. Violet was helping me dress for our skirmish with the guests. The last thing I needed was to be daydreaming about what position I wanted to try next time Rhys and I were alone together.

I smoothed my hand over my pant leg. It was stiff leather, far stiffer than anything I had worn at Jade Wilds, but it was all they had been able to find in my size on such short notice. Violet had had to help me shimmy into them. The waist was snug and the laces more for looks than necessity. They flared out at the bottom, as though intended for fashion rather than utility.

I had a long-sleeve royal-blue tunic on with a leather vest that was styled more like a corset than a traditional armored vest. Inspecting it by touch alone, I determined it likely was leather strips sewn onto a corset, with straps added at the top to give it a more vest-like appearance. I sighed.

"Is something wrong, Serafina?" Violet asked. She tied the lace to the vest and moved on to brushing my hair.

"I wish they had accommodated my request for a leather armored breastplate or vest, not whatever this is," I said.

I could see Violet pursing her lips from the reflection in the mirror. "What you're wearing looks very nice. It's important everyone knows you're a princess."

I bit the inside of my cheek. I doubted anyone here was going to forget I was a princess regardless of whether I was wearing a corset or armor. "Rhys is wearing exactly what I wanted to wear," I protested.

Rhys crossed the room and posed for me, his hands on his hips. I rolled my eyes. "I'll trade you."

"Not a chance!" he said with a grin.

I stuck my tongue out at him. If we had time, I would fight him for his vest, but we didn't. As it was, I thought we might even be late, even though Violet hadn't said anything.

I had requested she put my hair into two braids, and she was finishing tying off the second one. Rhys had his pulled back with a leather tie.

Violet let my hair slide out of her fingers. "Does that look okay?" she asked.

I peered into the mirror and nodded. "Better than I could do myself." The last thing I needed was to crush Violet's confidence. Our friendship was growing, but it was still new.

I heard a knock on the door, then it cracked open. "Hurry up!" called Thomas.

"Thank you!" I told Violet, then took Rhys's offered hand and departed.

Thomas led the way and Nolan brought up the rear, with the rest of the guards trailing behind. Deciding not to mention that if the extra guards were that far behind, they would likely not do much to prevent an attack, I paid attention to our surroundings. Each statue and suit of armor was in the same place they had been the last time I passed through.

I was jumpy as we walked out of the palace and over to the courtyard, where things had been set up for the skirmish. The attack earlier unsettled me far more than I had admitted to Thomas. Guests were on a patio that was raised by two steps from the skirmish area. There were two racks of wooden swords, one with blue chalk and the other green. It took me a moment before I realized that Rhys was wearing a green tunic. *Blue and green teams.* A smart idea, though I couldn't take the credit. When I explained the use of chalk or paint on the weapons, I wasn't thinking about team colors. The colors would not only identify the teams, but the guests could also track the progress of the fight.

A group of noblemen was loosely gathered near the sword racks. Though I had made certain it was clear in the invitation that men and women could compete, only men were present. I wasn't surprised. Most of the human women I had encountered at the palace would comment on how adept a husband or brother was but seemed convinced it was a man's job to wield a weapon.

The skirmish was meant to demonstrate my abilities, not pressure my future subjects into a situation they wanted nothing to do with. I only hoped the men on my team would respect my leadership skills. When Rhys and I approached, the group split in half. Not wanting to dwell on who had decided how the group would be divided, I strode confidently toward them. Shoulders back, spine straight, chin up, I met each of their gazes straight on.

"Thank you for being on my team," I said loud enough for the six men to hear me. Just then, Ghilanna appeared and joined the line of nobles in front of me.

"We are at your service, Princess Serafina," said a young man with a mop of blond curls. "I'm Brogan Green."

"Are you related to Declan Green?" I asked, and he smiled.

"Yes, Your Highness. He is my father," Brogan replied.

Studying Brogan, I could see the family resemblance: a similar nose and face shape, though the son still had some growing to do. I anticipated with a father such as Declan, Brogan should be skilled with a sword.

I smiled warmly at Lord McCormack. "Good to see you again, my lord."

"Likewise, Your Highness. Let's show your husband what we're made of, eh?" he said with a cheeky grin.

"Absolutely," I replied.

I turned my attention to a man with mouse-brown hair, beady green eyes, and a tiny mouth, who stood with his hands stiffly at his side. "I don't believe we've met, Lord …?"

The man's lip curled as he replied, "We have not, Your Highness. I am Count Xavier, cousin to Frederick Hunter."

I fought the desire to react. Of course this man who clearly didn't like me was related to Frederick Hunter. *Why is he on my team?* I wasn't going to ask. It would only alert the count to the effect he had on me. *I will have to watch my back.*

I moved down the line, though the names went in one ear and out the other. When I finished greeting everyone, they formed a semicircle around me, though there was more space between Ghilanna and Count Xavier than the others.

"Do any of you have formal training?" I asked.

Other than Brogan, the answer was "not much." They all knew how to use a sword, but none had received formal training or had actual combat experience. I expected Rhys had a similar problem. I understood my mistake—when I had said I wanted to do a skirmish, if I had been more specific, it would have shown my skills better. Instead, my grandfather had filled in the blanks, and now I was skirmishing with mostly useless nobles. It was too late now to change anything. *I will just have to make do.*

Nobles had guards and knights to protect them. In their minds, there was no reason to waste energy learning how to properly defend themselves.

"Remember, the chalk will mark you if you're hit. Waist to neck is a death blow. Arms or legs mean you are injured but not dead yet. Three hits to arms or legs means you are dead. No hits to the head or you will be out, and that is a mark against our own team, not the opposing team. Any questions?"

They all murmured no. I led them over to the sword rack, and we each selected an identical wooden sword. There were a few spares in case of technical difficulties, though I didn't anticipate any. No one should be striking hard enough to break a wooden practice sword.

Declan Green clapped his hands together. "Princess Serafina, are you ready?" I nodded in assent. "Rhys, are you ready?" Rhys nodded too. "Very well. You will have till the count of three, and then the skirmish will begin. Remember, the team with the most members still alive by the end of the hour will win, or if one of the leaders 'dies,' it will end the skirmish and the opposing team wins. Now take your positions!"

I was confident in Ghilanna and myself, perhaps Brogan, but that was it. Eying Rhys's team, I recognized Duke Herman, Duchess Oriana's husband. I wasn't surprised he was on Rhys's team. The duke and duchess seemed quite intent on winning my favor and likely thought they would earn it by participating.

"Three!" Declan shouted.

I jumped, startled. *Idiot!* I berated myself for not paying attention as one of the green team sprinted straight for me, sword forward, as though he was going to impale me. I scooted to the right and slashed his back as he shot past me. The sword connected and left a huge streak of blue chalk across his leather breastplate.

"Dead!" Lord McCormack shouted in glee. I had no idea if he was talking about the man I had just hit or if he had made a "kill" of his own.

Focus. I did not expect to win; I only hoped to prove to the participants and viewers that I was a capable leader.

Dodging another attack, I selected one of Rhys's teammates as my target and worked my way toward him. He seemed to be entranced by the courtiers on the patio and not aware of my approach. I came up behind him, adjusted my grip on my sword and started a low-low combination. To my surprise, he thrust his elbow back and nearly caught me in the stomach. I shuffled sideways and did a high strike. He met me with a high block, but I pressed down on my sword, and he gave ground.

A scuff of boots behind me had me pivoting to the left, narrowly avoiding a strike at my back. Instead of hitting me, the attacker's sword hit my current opponent in the stomach.

I jogged away, trying to come up with a plan to get to Rhys.

Fifty

TRISTAN

Try as I might, I struggled to focus on what Serafina and her team were doing. Prince Tanyth and King Leonard were having a lengthy discussion, and there had been several times where one or the other was pointing at me.

A wooden sword came down hard on my collarbone, drawing my attention back to the skirmish. Half of my team were "dead." Serafina was doing marginally better.

My palm was sweaty, causing the wooden hilt to slide in my grip. Ghilanna, who had agreed to participate on Serafina's team, swept her wooden sword toward me in a fast combination, and my sword sailed through the air. She finished her attack by stabbing me in the chest. "Dead!"

I winced, more at myself for failing to do my team justice. I should have ignored the king and Prince Tanyth, but there was nothing I could do now. *It's beneficial for Serafina to claim the win.*

I bowed to Serafina with a flourish. "The win is yours, my dear. Congratulations."

Serafina waved me off and turned her attention to her grandfather, who was beckoning us over. Prince Tanyth shot me a wicked grin, and a shiver worked its way down my spine. Even though I was no longer bound by a blood contract, I couldn't forget the feeling of being under Prince Tanyth's control.

I stood side by side with Serafina facing Prince Tanyth, who stood next to a bristling King Leonard.

"Guards!" King Leonard shouted.

I was roughly grabbed from behind. Hands yanked me; one guard held my wrists while another forced me onto my knees.

"What's the meaning of this!" Serafina shouted, her voice full of anger.

"Prince Tanyth shared with me the most appalling information that Rhys Mongan is not who he says he is at all," King Leonard replied, his voice sharp.

My heartbeat increased. Prince Tanyth's eyes bored into me, as though he could see my soul.

"Remove the pendant," Prince Tanyth said. It was a barely masked order. The guard waited for the subtle nod from King Leonard before pulling the pendant out from under my tunic and yanking. The cord snapped as though it was but a thin string.

I felt my magic return immediately. The guards almost let go of me as I regained my Fae features and size.

Serafina backed away from me. Thomas was at her side, hand on his hilt. "You're Fae?" Her voice was shaky and hardly more than a whisper, pain and anger written on her face.

I nodded, pressing my lips together. Shame washed over me. *This is not how I wanted to tell her.*

King Leonard snarled, "Tristan Gilvrye, you will be executed tomorrow for murdering King Lionel and deceiving us to participate in the competition for the princess's hand in marriage."

I lowered my gaze. The king was right. I deserved his sentence for both of my transgressions against his family. *I am not worthy of Serafina or our bond.*

The guards chained my hands behind my back and roughly shoved me to my feet. King Leonard stalked away and Serafina had vanished, which left me with Prince Tanyth.

He stepped close, lips near my ear. "Thank you, Tristan, for finding the *Bloodsong Grimoire* and laying a trap for yourself along the way."

I struggled against the chains, teeth bared. "Don't hurt her."

Tanyth chuckled darkly. "I will do anything I please. You'll be dead."

Before I could formulate a response, the guards led me away.

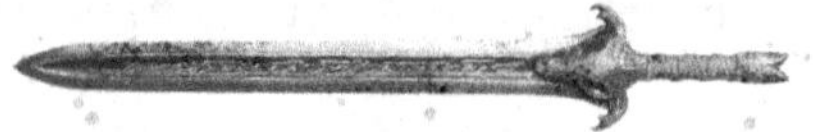

Eight guards escorted me down to the dungeon. I briefly considered fighting them and breaking free but decided against it. *Unless Serafina forgives me, there is no point. I'd rather die tomorrow than run away.*

The guards shoved me roughly into a damp cell. I stood motionless as they had a heated argument in the hallway. Eventually, one of them walked in, and I could hear the keys clanking and feel the metal loosening as the guard unlocked the shackles. I turned around, facing him.

"Remove your clothes," the guard ordered.

The clothes did not fit me well now that I was Fae and not human, but I was surprised by the order. "Why?"

"I am obeying my orders, and you will do the same. Remove your clothes, *now,*" the guard snapped.

I took my time, hesitating when I got to the pants.

"Those too," growled the guard.

I sighed and removed the pants. I could hear the other guards snickering as they watched. I ignored them, not caring what their opinions were on a Fae male body.

"Raise your arms and turn around," the guard ordered.

I wanted to roll my eyes but refrained from doing so as I raised my arms and turned. *Not that I can hide anything in my bare flesh.*

"Where'd you get the tattoo?" the guard asked when I finished turning and let my arms drop.

"It's not your concern," I replied and moved into the back corner of the cell, hoping he would get the message and leave. Thankfully, he did. The door to the cell shut with a clang that echoed throughout the hallway.

Using my magic, no longer hindered by the pendant, I called in pants and a tunic. Once dressed, I sat on the floor, leaning against the back wall, and closed my eyes. *My fate is sealed. I might as well take a nap.* Taking a deep breath, I settled into the meditation breathing with the plan of falling asleep.

I was sitting against the wall of my cell when the shadows stirred in the other corner. Slowly, the shadows moved. I rose to a half crouch, fists curled, ready for anything.

A light scraping along the stone, like a tip of a sword being dragged. Out of the shadows emerged an almost-black dragon, wings tucked tightly at its sides. We stared at each other. My breathing was rapid. I'm in a dungeon cell with a dragon and no weapons.

The dragon stepped farther forward, and the dim light showed the scales were not black, but dark green.

"*Rethys?*" *I whispered in shock.*

"It's almost time," *a voice said in my mind.*

My head thumping against the damp stone floor woke me up. Wincing, I peered around the cell, ensuring that there was no dragon sharing the space.

The air in front of me shimmered, and Tanyth emerged from a star portal. Dragonfang's glittering handle was visible from its spot on Tanyth's belt. I stood up, not wanting to give him any more advantage over me than he already had.

"I'm surprised you didn't break out already," Tanyth said with icy amusement. I stayed silent. I had nothing to say to him. "Unlike me, King Leonard doesn't have any way to prevent you from using your magic. It would be *easy*."

I clenched my jaw tight, refusing to answer his goading.

Tanyth spoke. "Without your help, I would never have found the *Bloodsong Grimoire*. You see, since Dragonfang marked you,

I can use your mark to sense if Fleshrender or the *Bloodsong Grimoire* are nearby."

I blanched. Serafina had done something to the *Bloodsong Grimoire* that must have activated its magic. *If Tanyth knows where it is, then we are all in trouble.*

"It's only a matter of time before the book is in my hands. King Leonard has been very grateful for my assistance in unmasking your deception," Tanyth said, eyes glittering with malice.

"Goodbye, Tristan," Tanyth said, and then vanished into a star portal.

I started pacing. *Maybe I should escape to warn Serafina.* I immediately rejected the idea. I doubted she would believe me after I had spent two weeks lying to her. *Hell, she likely thinks everything I ever said was a lie. All escaping will do is prove I'm just as bad as she believes I am.* I shook my head, refusing to believe that everything I had worked toward to win back Serafina was going to crumble at my feet because of Tanyth, *again*. There had to be something I could do, a way to earn her trust back. I just needed to figure out what.

Fifty-One

SERAFINA

I burst through the doors to my bedroom, barely able to see through the tears. Ghilanna pulled me into a hug. I sobbed into her shoulder. "I thought Rhys loved me. Why would he do something like this?"

Ghilanna rubbed my back, murmuring soothing sounds.

"How did we not know?" I didn't want to blame Ghilanna for not realizing Rhys ... *Tristan* was using a spell, but of all my friends, I would have expected her to know.

"It was a very powerful spell. Tristan felt human to me. I have no idea how Tanyth was aware it was Tristan in disguise," Ghilanna said.

"Who is Tristan Gilvrye?" I asked, stepping out of Ghilanna's embrace and swiping at the tears on my face.

"He's the lord commander of the Court of Dusk," Ghilanna replied.

"He works for Tanyth?" I gasped. *I slept with him!*

Ghilanna sighed. "Yes, or he did. I've heard rumors that he died. Though obviously he's alive and now in our dungeon. I don't know how much you took away from the whole exchange, given the circumstance, but I almost want to believe that Tanyth and Tristan are enemies."

My eyes widened. "That doesn't change the fact that Tristan lied to me."

"Yes, you're right. But it does make me question his motives. If he wasn't acting under Tanyth's orders, what is his interest in you?" Ghilanna asked.

I had no idea. I was still struggling to accept that the past weeks had been a lie. Rhys was Tristan. *Not a human, not a knight who trained at Eagle Rock.* "We spent hours talking. How much of what he said was even true?"

"You would have to ask him," Ghilanna said.

I laughed harshly. "You honestly expect me to believe anything he says?"

Ghilanna shrugged. "That choice is up to you. I only suggested asking him your question. I am confident in your ability to judge people."

"What a way to end a day," I muttered and began pacing. Blood throbbed in my veins as my anger simmered. Of all the unexpected events that had befallen me today, Rhys's betrayal hit me the hardest.

"How can I help?" Ghilanna asked.

I paused my pacing and peered at her. "Sparring?" I was tired and sore from the attack earlier; sparring with anyone was not the wisest choice, but it was a tactic I knew would work to let my anger cool.

With a sweep of her hand, the room filled with the soft glow of Ghilanna's magic, and the furniture rearranged itself to the edges of the room, giving us plenty of space.

"Absolutely."

My arms trembled with the effort of holding the sword. I could tell from Ghilanna's expression she was close to demanding we stop. I didn't want to. It was easier to lose myself in strikes and blocks than to contemplate Rhys's betrayal or the discovery of two new-to-me prophecies.

I pivoted, sweeping my sword in a high arc before chopping straight down.

"Excuse me," Thomas said from behind me.

I lowered my sword and Ghilanna moved over to the table for a water break. "What?" I said, sharper than I had intended.

Thomas's expression faltered. "You have a visitor."

I was in no mood for visitors. It was why I was hiding in my room instead of traipsing around the palace.

"Please, Your Highness, you should hear her out," Thomas pleaded.

Hoping the "her" wasn't Violet, I sighed. "Fine."

Thomas beckoned to someone who I couldn't see through the doorway. The visitor stepped into the room and threw back her hood. I took an involuntary step backward. *A Fae.*

"I don't want to talk to you," I said firmly. I knew she had been a member of Tanyth's court, but we had never been properly introduced.

The Fae stayed where she was. "Please, Your Highness, it's important. My name is Callyn and I am a friend of Tristan's. I know you are angry with Tristan. I also know that you are aware you're under the influence of dark magic."

"Why should I listen to you? Perhaps you should join Tristan in the dungeon as well, since you were also a member of the Court of Dusk," I snapped.

Callyn looked unphased by my comment; her voice did not waver. "Prince Tanyth put the magic on you. Why would you trust his intentions more than you would trust Tristan's?"

"I never said anything about trusting Prince Tanyth," I replied, adjusting my grip on my sword. "Prince Tanyth being the one to finally reveal Tristan's deception only proves that Tristan is not worthy of my love or my trust."

"How else was he supposed to get close to you? Your grandfather has made it clear he distrusts Fae," Callyn asked.

"Why would he need to get close to me? We don't know each other!" My voice rose as my anger flared.

Sadness filled Callyn's eyes, and she looked away. *What was that about?* I ground my teeth together.

Thomas cleared his throat and spoke. "'The outsider's veil will be broken. The souls will unite. The heir of blood will be queen of the South.'"

"Where did you hear those words?" demanded Callyn.

Ghilanna, who was now standing beside me, clenched her fists, as though familiar with Thomas's recitation.

I was frozen in place. I was certain those were my mother's words. Thomas, Josiah, and Valerie had all spoken of my mother's prophecy. How it was similar but different to the Lost Fae Queen prophecy.

Is the veil Tristan's deception? I wasn't sure I was ready to forgive him just because a prophecy told me that he did what was foretold to happen. *He'd had other options. Right?*

Thomas's response confirmed what I had guessed. "Solana spoke them."

Callyn glanced between me and Ghilanna, then back to me. "I need you to trust me."

"To do what?" Ghilanna demanded. I was grateful my friend had my well-being as her top concern.

"There's someone I want you to meet. But it will require riding there," Callyn explained.

I shot Thomas a worried glance, not sure if I wanted to ride anywhere.

"We will need a full squad," Thomas said.

"No. It can be only the three of us. A full squad will scare him away," Callyn said.

I wondered who this mysterious "him" was. Usually humans were scared of Fae, not the other way around.

Ghilanna spoke. "Who will the three be? I see four in this room."

Callyn gave her an appraising glance. "Thomas, myself, and Serafina. I do not have permission to bring anyone else."

"As long as we can be fully armed, then I will agree," I replied against my better judgment.

Callyn nodded. "That is fine. Expected even. I will meet you at the stable in thirty minutes."

Callyn joined us as we led our horses out of the stable. Once we mounted, Callyn led the way. I was surprised when she took us out toward the field and then down in the direction of the starting point of phase one of the competition.

I glanced at Thomas, and he shrugged.

We halted. I could see the ruined watchtower and the lake where the lake monster still dwelled. "We'll wait here," Callyn announced.

Callyn's attention was drawn to the sky above. I followed her gaze and was surprised to see something flying toward us. As it approached, I realized it was a bird with a rider. *What?* I racked my mind for any idea of what it could be but kept drawing a blank.

The creature glided to a landing about thirty feet away from us, giving me a clear enough view to see the eagle head with its razor-sharp beak and pale-brown-furred legs that ended in massive paws with long wicked claws. *Griffin.* The Fae rider—for I had no doubts that it was a Fae with the large pointy ears—dismounted and walked toward us.

Dubhar shifted under me, and I ran a stiff hand over his neck to reassure him, though I was also nervous.

When the Fae was a few paces away, Callyn spoke. "Princess Serafina Wyantha Helias, may I present to you Marek Fenmyar and his bonded griffin, Asteria."

Marek put his fist over his heart and bowed. "Your Highness."

I tried to place his surname. It was strangely familiar. I gasped when I realized where I'd heard it before. Prince Rhangil Fenmyar, ruler of the Court of the Sun. *What is Prince Rhangil's heir doing in Gaskal?* I inclined my head in greeting. "Nice to meet you, Marek and Asteria."

Curiosity and confusion filled me. Marek had no reason I was aware of to want to talk to me.

Callyn spoke. "Marek helped me create the pendant that allowed Tristan to become human."

I tilted back in the saddle, shocked. "Why?"

"Callyn asked for my help to aid you, and I decided that since it was in my power to assist you on your journey, I would. Callyn didn't tell me the pendant was for Tristan at first; it was only later that I learned there is a connection between you and Tristan that is critical to the survival of both Fae and humans," Marek said.

A connection between me and Tristan? His words felt like he was paraphrasing a prophecy. "Is that all you want to tell me?"

Marek frowned and Asteria came closer, staring at me with her piercing gold eyes. "No. I wanted to persuade you to give Tristan a chance to explain himself. The spell that made him human only altered him physically. It did not alter his personality. I understand what it feels like to be betrayed. But sometimes, it is worth hearing the other side of the story. Not all decisions are black and white."

I absently ran my fingers through Dubhar's mane, thinking about Marek's words. *He is not asking me to forgive Tristan, only to let him tell me his side of the story.* I realized that the request was likely the same as what Meriel would suggest if I were asking her advice.

A question nagged me. "How did you end up in the South? A human kingdom is an odd place for a Fae and griffin to spend their time."

Marek locked eyes with me, his expression serious. "I was waiting for you."

Marek's answer caught me off guard. I was expecting him to try to blame my grandfather for trapping him here or something silly like that. Not to reiterate the same words Josiah and Valerie had told me. I accidentally dug my heels into Dubhar's sides, and he reared in protest. Unprepared for the sudden movement, I slid out of the saddle and onto the ground behind him.

I sprang to my feet. "Sorry!"

Dubhar whirled, and I stumbled backward a few steps. Shimmering black magic swirled around him. His mane lightened to a striking silver against his midnight coat, and his horn was iridescent black. *He's a unicorn!*

I swallowed hard. "Emerald Valley."

Dubhar snorted and tossed his head. A deep musical voice entered my thoughts. *"I've been waiting for you too."*

My heart stuttered in my chest. *Why are they all waiting for me?* "I'm not important," I whispered.

"You have always been valued, Serafina, even if it hasn't felt that way," Marek replied. "'Not all will know her.' You are the bridge between Fae and humans. There are some who feel we would be better off without a bridge, and others, like Dubhar, Asteria, and me, who have been waiting centuries for your arrival."

I shot a glance at Thomas, feeling as though this conversation was veering toward being unbelievable.

Thomas gave me an apologetic smile. "Sorry to disappoint you, Serafina, but I too have been waiting."

I was shaking with emotions that threatened to overwhelm me. I needed time alone to think through everything I had learned and come to my own conclusions. "I will consider your request to talk to Tristan. Now, if you don't mind, I would like to return to the palace."

"You may ride me back," Dubhar offered.

"Won't the guards notice?" I asked, worried about how humans would handle the sudden appearance of a unicorn.

Dubhar stamped his foot. *"No, to them I appear as I was, a black stallion. Only you will be able to see me in my true form."*

"Then I accept your offer. Thank you," I replied. Dubhar sidled up to me and stood patiently while I mounted.

Callyn had been surprisingly quiet through the whole exchange, which left me wondering if she had arranged the meeting without having any idea what would transpire. I glanced over my shoulder at her. Callyn's expression was stoic, though she gave me a slight smile when she caught my gaze.

Nudging Dubhar lightly with my heels, we set off at a brisk trot. All too soon, we were back at the stable.

When the grooms led the horses away, Callyn motioned for me to come over. "Promise me you'll at least listen to what he has to say."

"I promise I will listen. However, I cannot commit to what my course of action will be," I replied.

Callyn nodded and then departed.

"Where to, Serafina?" asked Thomas.

"Back to my room. I'd like a snack and some quiet time," I replied.

"Very well," Thomas said agreeably.

Fifty-Two

TRISTAN

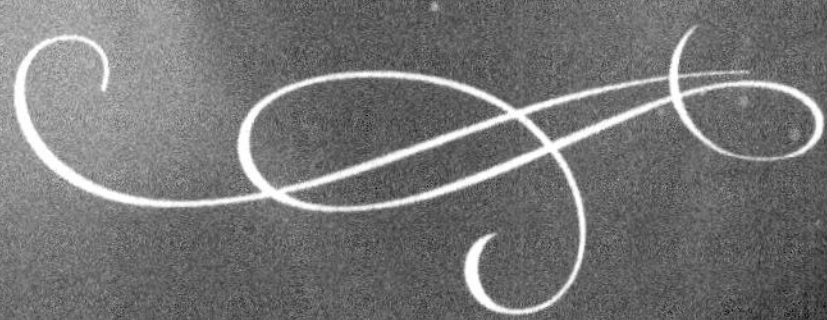

Serafina was straddling me. I watched as she wrapped her hand around my shaft. A shudder ran through me as she stroked me twice. My whole body tensed. Thankfully, before I lost control, she expertly guided my cock into her folds. I bit my lip, forcing myself to stay still, allowing Serafina to find her rhythm. Every downward stroke plunged my cock deeper inside. Unable to resist, I reached up and tugged gently on her nipple. Her response was immediate. Her legs tightened around my hips, and I felt pressure building around my cock as her breathing became rapid.

A clink of keys woke me out of my dream. A hooded figure stood at the door, unlocking it. I inhaled deeply and was certain it was Serafina—*alone.* Which led me to question who had allowed her to leave her room in the middle of the night unescorted.

I bristled but stayed in my corner. The last thing I needed when my relationship with her was already a mess was to give her more reasons to hate me. The door squeaked as she let herself in and didn't bother shutting it. *Interesting.*

"I have had several requests that I hear your side of the story," she said breathlessly, as though she'd been running. *Or having a dream?* I mused, recalling that the last time the mating bond had been solidifying between us, we discovered we had both had very vivid dreams of each otherr.

"Who made those requests?" I asked.

Serafina shook her head. "Who it was is not relevant. I am here, ready to listen. So tell me, why did you decide to lie about being a human and enter a competition to marry me?"

Direct. Though her arrival down here had been unexpected, her question was not. I debated how much to tell her. If her memories had been restored, then the conversation we'd be having would be significantly different. I was unsure how much of our past I should tell her.

"I am sorry for pretending to be human when I am not. But there was no other way to be able to win your hand in marriage," I began, deciding an apology might help.

"Why would a Fae want to marry me?" Serafina said with a harsh laugh.

"You may not believe me, but we met when you were at Dorcha Palace. I knew then that you are the one I have been waiting for. When you suddenly left, I followed, and Callyn devised this plan. If I won the competition, then my wait would be over and we'd finally be together," I explained.

Serafina took a step closer, and her hood fell back, revealing her tangled hair swirling around her shoulders. "You are not the first to claim they have been waiting for me."

A tremor ran through me. "Who else is waiting for you?"

"It's not your concern," she said.

"It *is* my concern," I growled, taking another step closer to her. "Especially with Prince Tanyth in the palace."

Serafina pinched a strand of her hair between her fingers and twisted it absently. "I haven't seen Prince Tanyth since he revealed you were not a human."

Relief coursed through me, then concern for who these others might be that were also waiting for Serafina.

"I want to know why you have been waiting for me. What is it precisely that was strong enough to risk the execution you're facing to be able to marry me?" Serafina demanded.

She was almost arm's length from me now. I could easily pull her to me and hold her, but I restrained myself, not wanting to be perceived as a threat. "I love you. I fell in love with you the first time we met."

Serafina frowned and replied in an almost inaudible whisper, "I loved Rhys."

I caught the words only because of my Fae hearing. "I *am* Rhys. Everything I said when I was Rhys was true. The conversations, the feelings—they're all real, Serafina. I *love* you."

"Then why did you lie? Why didn't you tell me immediately after the competition? Instead, you waited until after the wedding, after we consummated the marriage, and then you still didn't feel like you could tell me, that I was capable of understanding. No. Instead Prince Tanyth had to discover your secret." Serafina's voice was papery thin. I could hear her breath coming in gasps as she confronted me. "How do you expect me to trust you when you didn't trust me enough to explain?"

My cheeks heated. She was right, and what I had feared would happen had. I betrayed her trust, and now I was paying for it. "I wanted to tell you, but ..."

Serafina supplied the words. "Exactly. You were afraid I didn't love you enough to be capable of understanding." I could hear the pain in her voice. My heart ached for what I was sure I was losing.

Fifty-Three

SERAFINA

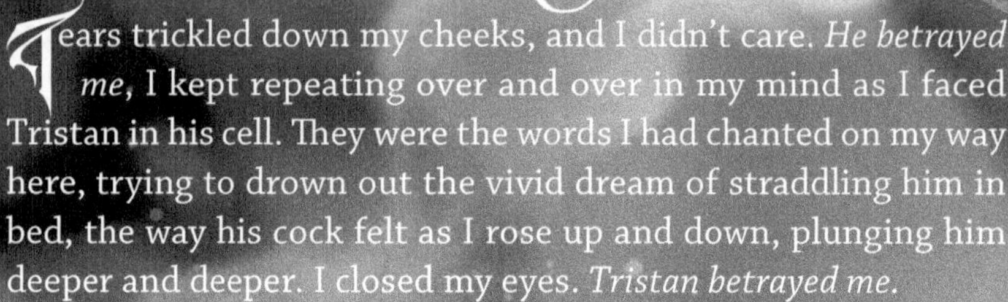

Tears trickled down my cheeks, and I didn't care. *He betrayed me,* I kept repeating over and over in my mind as I faced Tristan in his cell. They were the words I had chanted on my way here, trying to drown out the vivid dream of straddling him in bed, the way his cock felt as I rose up and down, plunging him deeper and deeper. I closed my eyes. *Tristan betrayed me.*

Every word he spoke was full of regret. I knew he was genuinely sorry. As frustrating as it was to have yet another being tell me they had been waiting for me, it also confirmed that for some reason, Tristan and I were connected.

"I forgive you," I said softly.

Tristan closed the gap between us and pulled me into his arms. I froze. Tristan's lips were velvety soft when they touched my wooden ones. My stomach fluttered, and sparks skittered across my skin. The tension drained away as he held me like I was precious.

"I can't stay here. Someone will notice I'm gone," I said, reluctantly withdrawing from his arms.

"I don't need keys. I can just use my magic to get out of here," Tristan said.

I shook my head. "The last thing I need is for you to escape. That will make matters worse. I will talk to my grandfather."

"Serafina, let me come with you, please."

It was tempting to say yes, but I was worried a guard would come down here and discover he was gone. I shook my head. "No, you need to stay."

"What if I use a star portal to take us both to your room, and then I return here? You won't risk being caught in the hallway, and we can talk," Tristan suggested.

I swallowed, my throat dry at the prospect of more alone time with Tristan. *I promised I would hear him out. This is still part of that*, I reminded myself. "Okay. I will lock the door, and then you can use the star portal."

I had never gone through a star portal that I could recall, and I wasn't sure what to expect. Tristan gathered me in his arms and opened the shimmering portal. Then, we stepped through and were in our bedroom in our suite of rooms. I blinked, trying to adjust to the change.

"Let's sit and talk," I said and took a few steps toward the door so we could go sit on the couch.

Tristan wrapped his arms around me from behind. "I don't want to sit, Serafina."

I melted against his chest. Tristan ran his hands down my sides. When he brought them back up, my clothing was gone, as were his pants. Tristan massaged my breasts, and I arched against him. I wanted to hold on to my anger, but it was impossible to deny how badly I wanted him. *Sex won't fix everything*, I reminded myself.

"How about a shower, so you won't be cold?" Tristan suggested.

"Okay," I replied, twisting in his arms and kissing him. Desire coursed through me as his cock bumped my entrance.

Tristan nipped at my lips. "We would need to get into the shower to take a shower."

"Right." I withdrew from his arms and sashayed into the bathroom. The shower was already running. *It was likely his magic.* It felt as though I could see myself walking into the shower. *This is getting weird.* I was afraid to tell Tristan about it, especially with how shaky things were between us at the moment.

The hot water cascaded over my head. I moved into the back corner, wanting to make sure Tristan had room to get into the shower. It felt far larger once I was in it than it had seemed from outside. *Not that I have been in a shower more than once or twice in my whole life, so how would I know?*

I knew Tristan was going to touch my breasts before he did. His chest touching my back, his hard cock bumped against my butt. I spread my legs a little farther, craving the feel of him inside of me again. Then came his hands. He cupped my breasts with them, thumbing my nipples.

I pivoted, my back touching the cold wall, jolting me out of the haze of desire. "You should have explained yourself before Tanyth exposed your deceit." I jutted my chin out and crossed my arms over my breasts, blocking Tristan from touching me.

Tristan's hands dropped to his side. "I already apologized. What more do you want from me?"

I shifted back and forth on my feet. "For you to understand what pain your actions have caused."

Tristan laughed sharply. "I accepted my fate to be executed. What more is there for me to do to show I understand?"

"You undermined my position at this court. My position has been shaky since my arrival. No one wants a half-Fae on the throne of the South, not even my grandfather. There have been whispers that I planned this. Disguised my Fae lover as a human to get around the laws preventing a Fae from competing," I explained harshly.

"Then let them execute me. It's an easy solution," Tristan replied vehemently.

I gulped, surprised. "Is that what you really want?"

Tristan's fists clenched at his sides, and I swore I heard him growling. "No. Of course not. I love you, Serafina, with every fiber of my being. But if you feel that the best choice for you is to execute me, then do it. I am not going to stop you. In fact …" There was a swirl of gray magic around his hands, and a dagger appeared. Tristan offered it to me hilt first. "You might as well kill me now. No reason to wait for tomorrow."

Fear gripped me. *Kill him?* My hands shook as I stared at the dagger. "No!" I shouted, shocking both of us. I knocked the dagger out of his hands and wrapped my arms around him, pressing myself as tight as possible, crushing my lips to his. Tristan's rigid posture lasted for mere seconds, then his hands were all over me, featherlight caresses that drove me wild.

"I love you," I whispered.

"I love you too, Serafina," Tristan said, then picked me up. "Wrap your legs around my hips," he instructed, and I obeyed. He took a few steps, and the cold of the wall hit my back. I winced. "Sorry," he muttered, and then the wall became warm.

I could feel his bulging cock at my entrance. Tristan kissed me and thrust into my folds. I winced at how tight it was, and he withdrew immediately. "Sorry." He kissed my lips lightly, then dipped his head down and took my nipple into his mouth, sucking.

"Oh," I whispered as my body responded, but Tristan wasn't done. While his tongue teased my breasts, his fingers swirled and tugged in my folds. My back arched as pressure built. Tristan let go of my breast and returned his lips to mine. As he thrust his tongue into my mouth, he eased his cock into my slick entrance.

"Better?" he asked as he rocked in and out.

"Yes," I hissed, cupping his face in my hands and drawing his mouth back down to mine. Reassured that I was comfortable, Tristan increased the speed of his strokes, and the throbbing in my core intensified, but there was something else too. The sparks on my skin had changed to feel like warmness enveloping me. *It's hot water,* I tried to tell myself, but deep down I knew it was not water. There was a connection forming between Tristan and me.

Tristan paused. I met his gaze with mine. "Do you feel it?"

"That depends on what 'it' is," I replied, gyrating my hips, trying to get satisfaction when Tristan stopped.

"Soulmate bond," Tristan said softly.

My eyes widened. Soulmate bonds were Fae magic, and I wasn't full-blooded Fae, so I had never thought it was possible. "Between us?" I whispered in awe. I had learned about the power of the soulmate bond and how coveted it was among Fae.

Tristan nodded. "Yes." Without saying anything else, he resumed.

Tristan kissed me, as though he had read my mind, and then dropped his hand between us and brushed his thumb against my clit. A moan escaped my lips as a small spasm went through me, causing my hands and feet to twitch. Tristan's strokes quickened, and suddenly I was looking at myself through Tristan's eyes, feeling the warmth of my walls around his cock as he—we—thrust in and out. Heart pounding, my muscles clenched. I wanted more, and before I even finished the thought, he plunged his fingers in alongside his cock, as though he could hear my desires.

"*Serafina!*" I screamed, feeling equal parts confusion and intense pleasure as my cock—*no, Tristan's cock*—jerked inside of me. I melted against his chest and knew I would have slid down the wall of the shower had he not been holding me up.

"*Serafina,*" he said. His voice wrapped around my mind.

"I can hear you in my thoughts," I whispered, confusion filling me.

"It's the bond," Tristan replied. "It's restored."

His words shocked me. I let my legs drop and pushed against Tristan. He took a step back, and I scooted away. "What do you mean it's restored?"

"We have been bonded, Serafina, but Prince Tanyth put a binding spell on the magic and was able to make it so you could not feel it and I was unable to contact you through it," Tristan explained.

"Prince Tanyth did no such thing," I retorted.

Tristan held up his hands. "You don't remember. I'm hoping that the bond reforming will help you get your memories back too. But I'm not entirely sure they are directly connected."

Hot fury rolled through me. "Why didn't you tell me earlier, when you were apologizing for the *other* time you lied?" I demanded. Once again, he had decided to withhold important information from me.

"You can feel me through the bond yourself and talk mind-to-mind. It's impossible to deny," Tristan said patiently.

"Yet you failed to inform me it had already happened. That all this time there was already a connection between us." My voice rose, tears threatening to spill over.

"Yes. I didn't want to tell you. Because I love you enough, Serafina, that I wanted you to have the opportunity to marry someone else if you chose to do so," Tristan replied. His normally bright blue eyes had darkened.

"Or let you be executed without knowing?" I snapped. "I forgave you earlier only to find out that there's more you didn't share. Is this it? The soulmate bond? Or is there even more?" I shouted. I backed up another step so he couldn't grab me if he wanted to.

Tristan's whole body tensed. I waited, wondering if he was withholding any more secrets.

"I'm a snow leopard shapeshifter," he said.

My jaw dropped. "A shapeshifter?"

"Have you never seen one before?" Tristan asked.

"No," I admitted. He closed his eyes. Moments later, Tristan was a snow leopard. His back was higher than my hip, and his whole body was covered in gray fur—lighter on his stomach, with slightly darker coloring on his back and blended throughout—and distinct black spots. His paws had to be larger than my hands.

I lifted my hand, then realized I didn't know anything about shapeshifters or rules surrounding them. "May I touch you?"

"*Of course,*" he replied into my mind.

I gently set my hand on Tristan's head, then trailed my fingers through his fur from his ears down to his tail.

"You're beautiful," I said, then dropped to a crouch, peering at his face. "I'm assuming you are the snow leopard who has been cavorting in my dreams."

Tristan shifted and our gazes met. "What kind of dreams?"

"Nothing terribly exciting. I was riding Dubhar, and a snow leopard was following me. Or I was in the forest, and the snow leopard was in the shadows, but never close," I replied.

Tristan responded, "The bond never really disappeared entirely. I could still see it. There are two Fae that I know of who have also been able to sense it."

Minutes ago, I had thought that all that stood between us was Tristan disguising himself as human. Now I knew there was more. One of his comments gnawed at me—that Tanyth had bound our soulmate bond *and* altered my memories. It fit with the theories Ghilanna and I had developed regarding my illness and dark magic blocking memories. But I was worried. *What else do I not remember?*

My thoughts drifted to my introduction to Marek and Asteria. Marek had said, "There is a connection between you and Tristan that is critical to the survival of both Fae and humans." *Is the soulmate bond the connection he spoke of?* I mused, then another thought occurred to me. *He said he was at Dorcha Palace when I was there. What if the child was his? Ours.*

Hot tears ran down my cheeks. Without my memories, I had no way of knowing. Without them, I was afraid to tell Tristan, certain I couldn't handle his reaction to the news on top of everything else. I quickly washed my hair, hoping a simple task would give me the time I needed to pack my feelings back into a tight box to deal with later.

Working the soap out of my hair, I revisited what Tristan had already told me, and I had a question. Facing him in the shower, I asked, "What are the names of the two Fae who could feel the soulmate bond?"

Tristan's lips pressed into a thin line. "King Pharaan and Marek Fenmyar."

My voice shaky, I asked, "When did King Pharaan first know?"

Tristan ran his hand through his hair, then met my gaze with his. "I followed your carriage from Jade Wilds to Gaskal. I had no idea where you were going, and when I realized your destination at the entrance to the city and our bond was not working properly, I knew I needed help. King Pharaan is the most powerful of the Fae. Since he is your grandfather, I had hoped he would help." Tristan's voice became bitter. "He didn't believe me."

"But you said he felt the bond?"

"Yes, I did say that. But when I first approached him for help—*before* you had even seen your first suitor—he did not believe me and said he was confident you were safe in Gaskal."

Safe in Gaskal. According to the very same grandfather who had promised I would have a choice where I ended up. I shivered.

"The reason Callyn and I devised the plan to enter the competition was because King Pharaan refused to help," Tristan said. He licked his lips and mine parted. I clamped them shut, not wanting to give him any ideas.

Tristan arched an eyebrow and then continued. "When King Pharaan greeted us during the wedding reception, he could see through the pendant's magic. He knew I was me, *and* he acknowledged that he could feel the soulmate bond between us."

I clenched my jaw tight enough for it to hurt. *It seems Tristan isn't the only one who has a penchant for withholding critical information from me.* I rubbed my arms. "Thank you for telling me. I understand better now why you made your choices. I thought my grandfather cared about me and would have offered you help. I see that is not the case. I am blessed with two grandfathers who value their personal agendas far more than my life."

Tristan squeezed my shoulder. "I know, and I'm sorry for that. Not all families are worth the effort. Sometimes the best 'family' is not one that is formed by blood ties, but one that bonds through friendship."

Tristan was right. When King Pharaan had introduced himself at Emerald Valley, he manipulated me into believing he had a vested interest his granddaughter. I should have known better. Only Ghilanna and Fiera had never in twelve years used our friendship for anything but what it was.

I needed to figure out what my next step was. *Tristan cannot be executed.* Of that I was certain. Except it wasn't my decision. King Leonard was very much alive. Even if Tristan hadn't hidden that he was Fae, he had murdered King Lionel and had never been punished. My grandfather was within his rights to demand Tristan's life.

There was a pounding on my bedroom door. I jumped, startled, and shot a worried glance at Tristan. "You need to hide. If they find you here, I will be punished too."

"I will stay in here and hide myself with my magic," Tristan said.

I nodded and stepped out of the shower, snagging a robe off the hook and wrapping it around myself. My hair was still dripping, but I didn't want anyone to barge in. I rushed out of the bathroom and skidded to a halt as the bedroom door opened, revealing Thomas.

"Serafina! Come quick! It's the king!" Thomas's voice was raspy, as though he had sprinted here with the news.

"I should get dressed," I protested. *A bathrobe is not proper attire to be cavorting around the palace.*

Thomas hesitated. "Fine. You have two minutes." The guard pulled the bedroom door shut behind him, giving me privacy.

Tristan came out of the bathroom dry, unlike me. I went to the wardrobe and selected the first tunic and pants I could find. I only needed to be dressed. It was impossible to not wonder what the king wanted at this unholy hour in the middle of the night.

"I will return to my cell to ensure I am there if anyone checks on me," Tristan said. He pulled me into his arms and kissed me, then stepped back and called a star portal. He stepped through before I could say goodbye.

Slipping on boots, I sighed and then headed out to where Thomas was waiting. We hurried down the corridor toward my grandfather's chambers.

"Are you going to tell me what's going on?" I asked.

"I don't know. I was only told to get you and to hurry. My assumption was he was having another seizure, but it could be almost anything," Thomas replied.

"Only Princess Serafina may enter," the guard, whom I recognized as Master Guard Declan, announced.

I exchanged a look with Thomas, then nodded. "Very well. Where is he?"

"Inside." Declan pushed open the door for me. I stepped through it, all senses on alert.

My grandfather was sitting in a chair, staring into the fire. He looked up at me. His usually vibrant eyes were dull, his face was pale, and I could see tremors in his hands.

I closed the distance between us and kneeled in front of him. "What's wrong?"

"War is coming," he said, his voice paper thin.

I inhaled sharply. "War with who? How do you know?"

"King Hanover is contesting your position as heir since your husband is not human. He is Lord Commander Tristan Gilvrye of the Court of Dusk and an obvious Fae ploy to gain control over the gold mines," King Leonard said. I had to strain to catch all his words.

I knew King Hanover had his eye on the Southern throne, but this felt wrong, especially since Tristan was scheduled to be executed in mere hours. "You are executing Tristan and thereby eliminating the problem. You should be able to reason with King Hanover. There is no reason we must go to war."

My grandfather gave me a sad smile. "King Hanover has wanted my throne since I married his daughter. I doubt anything I say will sway him."

"You could try," I said firmly.

He opened his mouth to speak and started coughing. His whole body shook. I noticed a pitcher of water on the small table beside his chair, so I filled a cup and offered it to the king. With a shaky hand he grasped it and brought it to his lips, taking a tiny sip.

"There is more," he said once the coughing was under control. "Prince Rhangil of the Court of the Sun is accusing me of holding his son and heir hostage and even now is rallying Fae on our border. I have seen it with my own eyes."

My hands balled into fists. I believed the words he said until he claimed to have seen Fae massing on the border. There was no way for him to see it, not without magical help.

"I doubt Prince Rhangil would not at the very least send someone to negotiate peacefully," I replied, keeping my tone even. In his fragile state, I was afraid to send the king into another coughing fit.

"I had several messenger reports confirming it," King Leonard revealed.

"It's fake," I responded.

King Leonard shook his head. "It's real. I trust my messengers. They were handpicked by Declan. There is no reason to doubt them."

I blew out my breath. Arguing was futile. "What is the next step?"

King Leonard took another sip of water. The liquid sloshed precariously before he got the cup to his lips. "The *Bloodsong Grimoire*."

My eyes widened. *This is what it's for? In case we go to war against Fae?* He had originally ignored my question regarding the purpose of the *Bloodsong Grimoire*. Now I knew he had been withholding information.

"I would retrieve it myself, but as you can see, I cannot make the trek," King Leonard informed me.

"You showed me how to access it. Of course I can retrieve it for you." I stood up and then felt his hand on my arm.

"I am dying, Serafina," he said softly.

"No," I replied. I refused to believe that. *How am I supposed to fight a war on two fronts alone?*

"It is true," King Leonard insisted. "Declan!" he shouted, though it was barely louder than a whisper.

The master of the guard heard him and came inside. "I am here, Your Majesty."

"We need one more witness," King Leonard said.

I glanced at him uncertainly. *A witness for what? Am I missing something?* Declan gestured toward the door and Thomas entered, then bowed to my grandfather.

"Good. With you as my witnesses, by the power vested in me, I give Princess Serafina Helias the power to act as ruler in my stead, from now until the time of my passing," King Leonard said, then started coughing. His arms flailed, sending the pitcher flying. I snatched it a hairsbreadth before it smashed into the floor.

Declain looked at me, then at the king. "You need to go. I will get the doctor."

I didn't want to leave. I wanted to make sure my grandfather was okay. *Except he gave me a task to retrieve the book.*

"I will retrieve the *Bloodsong Grimoire* and then return," I said firmly.

Declan bowed his head in acknowledgment.

My grandfather's coughing fit had temporarily subsided, and I gave him a quick kiss on the forehead. "I will be back soon. I promise."

Thomas followed me out of the king's chambers. We halted once we were far enough away that no one would overhear us. "Did he just do what I think he did?" I asked.

"If you're asking if you now have the power to reverse the execution order on Tristan, then the answer is yes," Thomas said.

Relief coursed through me. "Good, then I need to do that immediately."

"What about the book?" Thomas asked, "You promised to get that."

"Yes, I did, and fortunately the book is in the general direction of the dungeon. We can get Tristan, and then I will take him with me to get the book," I replied.

Thomas looked as though he wanted to say something. It took him a few moments, and I was getting impatient.

"Only the heir is allowed to get the book," he said finally.

"Except you just told me I was just awarded the same amount of power as the king. I can take Tristan with me. I need him to help me understand the book anyhow. It's a *Fae* object," I explained.

Thomas finally nodded. "As you wish."

Fifty-Four

TRISTAN

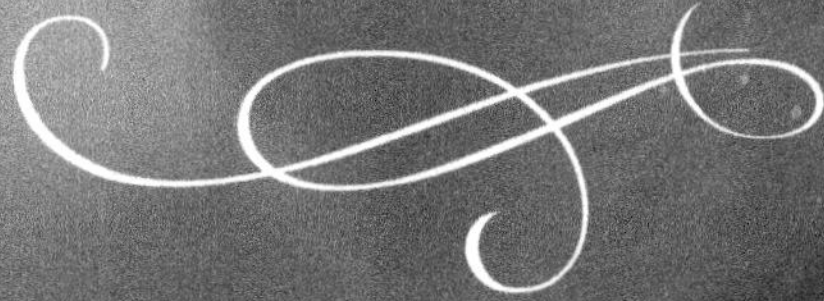

I walked through the star portal into the back of my cell seconds before the guard on patrol passed by. I held my breath, afraid the guard would notice something was off, but he didn't even look my way. *Not very vigilant.* A concern I would have to take up with Serafina if I got out of this mess alive.

I settled against the wall, arms crossed, waiting. The confrontation with Serafina had not gone how I had expected. The fact that others had told her to listen to me was a welcome surprise. I understood her anger and mistrust. I would have worried if she didn't react that way. I prayed we could put those behind us and move forward and that she would find a way to reverse King Leonard's execution order.

The dungeon was remarkably silent, unlike the dungeons at Dorcha Palace filled with various beasts and prisoners. I lightly dozed.

My eyes snapped open at the creak of the cell door. *I must have been more deeply asleep than I intended.* I recognized Serafina's guard Thomas immediately. He stepped into the cell, and Serafina scooted around him.

"I have reversed the execution order," she announced in a strained voice.

"The king is dead?" I gasped, reeling at the change in events.

Serafina shook her head. "No. But he's unwell, and he has granted me authority to use his power as I see fit. War is coming."

"War?" I asked incredulously. It was the last thing I expected her to say on the heels of announcing she had been granted everything but the official title.

"I can explain later. We don't have time. I must get the *Bloodsong Grimoire*," Serafina said, her words rushed.

"How can the book help?" I asked. A shiver of fear went down my spine. The book was safe in its chamber, a place that somehow Prince Tanyth could not gain access to. Removing the book meant we would be vulnerable to attack. *There must be a way I can dissuade her from this decision.*

Thomas inserted himself into the conversation. "Prince Rhangil of the Court of the Sun has Fae massing on our shared border. The book is supposed to help the South's defenses against the Fae."

The new information was intriguing, but it also meant that there was a need for the book; it wasn't just an order Serafina was following blindly. It was strange that Prince Rhangil would attack Gaskal unprovoked—in my experiences with him, he was not as quick to anger as Prince Tanyth.

"I can explain the details later. Right now we need to go get the book. Thomas is not permitted to come with me, but as my *husband*, I can stretch the rules for you," Serafina said.

"Here, take my sword," Thomas said shoving his sword into my hands.

I could have just called one in, but was grateful to the guard for offering his. "Thank you," I said genuinely, then followed Serafina down the sloping hallway.

Fifty-Five

SERAFINA

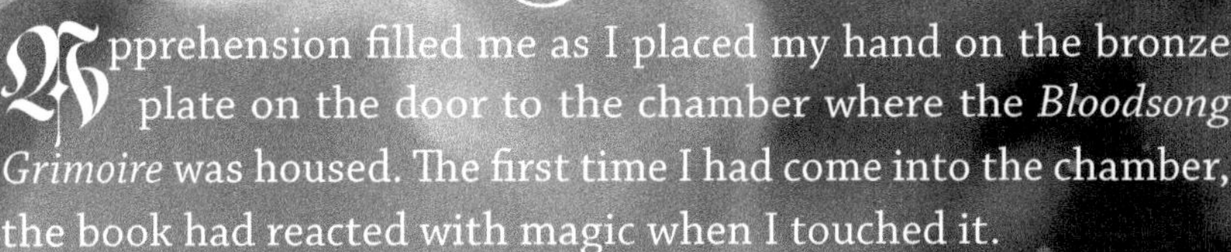

Apprehension filled me as I placed my hand on the bronze plate on the door to the chamber where the *Bloodsong Grimoire* was housed. The first time I had come into the chamber, the book had reacted with magic when I touched it.

The door swung open, and I entered the hallway beyond. Taking a deep breath, I strolled confidently toward the egg-shaped chamber. *It's just a book.* Tristan was following me in the darkness; the only way I knew he was there was through the bond. This whole plan seemed ridiculous to me, but I had decided it would at least be worth trying. *What's the harm in touching an old book*?

I refused to acknowledge that as we got closer, I could feel darkness trying to wrap around me, darkness that left a coppery tang of blood in my mouth. I paused before entering the chamber, and Tristan bumped into me. He wrapped his arms around me, and I leaned against his chest.

"We don't have to do this," he said into my ear.

"I promised I would get the book," I replied, stepping out of his embrace. I couldn't afford to get distracted.

Keeping my emotions in check, I strode to the pedestal and set my left hand on the *Bloodsong Grimoire*. Magic pulsed through the book and into me. Reddish brown like dried blood, followed by a faint green glow. A flash of deep green magic emitted from the book and then streamers of the same magic erupted from my arms, hands, and head. The room filled with deep green magic.

I gasped as memories flooded me. Killing Travaran in self-defense, being captured and brought as a prisoner to Dorcha Palace, and meeting Tristan for the first time, through being drugged by Prince Tanyth using tea, and the binding spell he had done with Fleshrender. The book released its hold on my hand, and as I fell to my knees, gasping for breath, the magic extinguished, leaving us in a pitch-black room.

Fifty-Six

TRISTAN

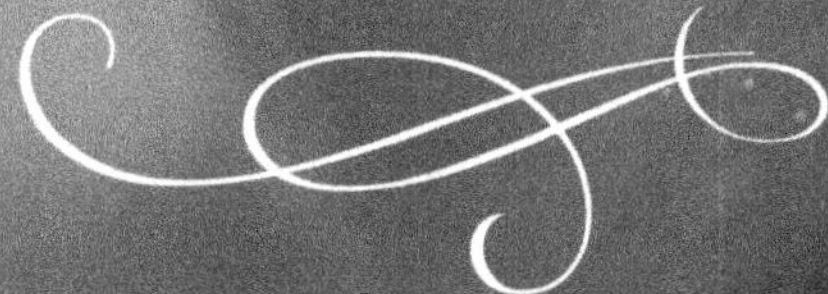

When Serafina first put her hand on the book, I felt the magic vibrate through the bond at the very first pulse. *It's working.* As much as I wanted to help her, I knew *she* had to be the one touching the book. Somehow it was tied to her family, to her human *and* Fae bloodlines. I could only pray that whatever magic the book was doing to Serafina, it would not hurt her.

My eyes widened in surprise as the magic changed from the color of dried blood to deep emerald green. *The Lost Fae Queen.* I watched in awe as the deep green magic spilled out of the book and Serafina, filling the room with light, reflected in the glossy obsidian. Love, excitement, and a tinge of fear coursed through me as I watched my wife and mate's magic unlock, proving what I had known deep down: that she was the queen in the prophecy and I was her mate, and we were destined to save all Fae from the end of time.

The instant our bond pulsed at full strength, I could feel her exhaustion. The light extinguished, and I shot forward, wrapping my arms around her as her knees hit the stone floor hard.

"I love you," I said into her mind through the bond.

"I love you," she replied.

Holding her against me, I wanted to do far more than utter words into her mind. I wanted to claim her, mind, body, and soul, to reassure both of us that this was real. But I could feel her shaking against me, just as I was aware of the memories spilling into her mind.

There was a scuff of boots from the hallway. I whirled, sword raised.

"Thank you for doing the hard work for me." Prince Tanyth's voice floated toward us, followed by small Fae lights he sent to illuminate the room.

I could feel Serafina tense and rise beside me. *I can handle him,* I told her.

"You're not welcome here, Prince Tanyth," I growled.

He released a harsh chuckle. "Princess Serafina will disagree when she hears what I have to say."

The room brightened even more, and Prince Tanyth stepped forward, shoving King Leonard in front of him. The king fell onto his knees. I could tell from his expression it was painful, but he refused to emit a sound.

Serafina stepped forward so she was even with me. "Let my grandfather go." Her voice still had a slight shake to it, betraying her feelings.

"Give me the book," ordered Prince Tanyth.

"No," Serafina replied.

Prince Tanyth raised his hand and Dragonfang appeared. He held it against the king's throat. Fur rippled along my arms. I bit my cheek, forcing the snow leopard back. Nothing I could do would be fast enough to prevent King Leonard's throat from being slit.

"Give me the *Bloodsong Grimoire*, or I will kill your grandfather," Prince Tanyth repeated, pressing Dragonfang harder into King Leonard's throat.

Fifty-Seven

SERAFINA

ear filled me. I wanted to fight Prince Tanyth. I had magic, but no training, and whatever the *Bloodsong Grimoire* had done when it had broken the dark magic the prince had placed on me, combined with the onslaught of memories, meant I didn't have the strength to even lift a sword.

I glanced back at the book. *It has been the problem all along.* Though I had no love for my grandfather, I certainly did not want him to die, especially not for a book that had no real value. Mind made up, I snatched the book off the pedestal.

Tristan opened his mouth to say something. I shook my head. "This is my choice. He's my grandfather." Thankfully, Tristan snapped his mouth shut.

I took a step toward Prince Tanyth, away from Tristan. "I will give you the book if you let him go."

My grandfather's eyes were wide, and he was shaking his head and mouthing *no*. I ignored him. If seeing him in his chamber tonight had shown me anything, it was that I was not ready to rule, not yet. I had many things I needed to learn from the king. I refused to let a book be the cause of his death.

"Deal!" cawed Prince Tanyth. Snaking his arm out, he snatched the *Bloodsong Grimoire* out of my hands. I reached out my hand to my grandfather to help pull him to his feet.

Our fingers entwined, and he was halfway up when he stumbled into my arms, blood dripping from his mouth. Prince Tanyth twisted Dragonfang as it pierced the king's back.

"No!" I screamed, clutching my grandfather in my arms.

Prince Tanyth yanked the dagger out, teal magic streaming out of his hands as he opened a star portal and walked through it.

"I'm sorry," whispered my grandfather. Tears streamed down my face. He took a gurgling breath and died.

Rocking his body against me, I cried. The past few days I had finally felt like my grandfather had at last decided to accept me as family, and now that had been taken from me. I had no idea how long I stood there holding his body when Tristan placed his hand lightly on my shoulder. "We need to go. He was the king. Preparations must be made. People must be informed."

I shook my head, barely able to get the words out. "I can't. It's too much."

Tristan kissed me lightly on my cheek. "When you became the heir of the South, you knew this would happen. It's what you signed up for."

I cringed at his words. The reality was I had been *told* that I was the heir. No one ever asked my opinion. *I could walk away. King Hanover will gladly take the throne.* I immediately rejected the idea. *I will not abandon my people*, I promised myself, straightening my spine. *War is coming.*

Tristan must have sensed my feelings through the bond, for he bowed deeply and said with reverence, "Queen Serafina, Lady of the South."

Epilogue

KING PHARAAN

I paused to admire the green glass dome high overhead in the grand entry of Uaine Palace. The sun was directly above me, and streams of flickering green sunlight bathed the room, enhancing the color of the delicate staircase made of jade that spiraled up to the dome. Rumors about Serafina's wedding had been flying since my return. I was doing my best to ignore them, knowing that no matter how much I wished she had been able to come to Uaine Palace, fate had another plan for her.

I was about to lower my gaze from the dome when there was creaking sound. My eyes widened in surprise as a crack formed in the dome, rapidly spreading from one edge to the next. Raising my hand, intending to use magic to repair it, I stumbled sideways as the ground vibrated.

The dome shattered, raining shards of sharp green glass around me. I barely got a shield up in time to prevent one from slicing into my throat.

A familiar clip-clop of hooves on marble told me Onvyr was approaching. I shouldn't be relieved he was coming to my aid. *I am not helpless.* But I was. Concern for the broken dome—and, if I admitted it, fear that I wanted desperately to bury—rose within me.

Onvyr skidded to a halt and shifted immediately. "My king!" he shouted and then inspected me.

"I'm fine," I said, my shaky voice betraying me.

"What happened?" Onvyr asked, his golden eyes full of concern.

"There's something I need to show you," I replied.

Onvyr helped me stand and then allowed me to lead the way to my chambers, palace guards forming a tight box around us. The walk took longer than I wanted, but I was trembling too much to make my feet move faster.

We entered the chamber, and Shelara, my soulmate, stood up from her chair. "What's wrong?" she demanded.

I brushed her aside. "Not now."

I went straight for the bookcase above the hearth, selecting a book with a pristine black leather cover and gold writing. *Bedtime Tails.* I flipped to the back of the book and peeled back the end page. I could feel Shelara's eyes on me. We had secrets we kept from one another, buried deep enough even the soulmate bond couldn't penetrate, and what I was doing right now was one of them.

Underneath the end page was a folded piece of parchment. I removed it and set the book down on a table. Fingers shaking, I read the paper.

*When tension rises and war with the humans has come, the
Lost Fae Queen will return.
First, she will prove her battle prowess.
Look closely or you might be blinded, for when the Fae Queen
returns, not all will know her, yet everyone will follow her.
Be warned, the Fae Queen must stay pure until the Great Cat
finds her and their souls unite.
With their souls bound, the heir will be found.*

*The Fae Queen's magic will return, and together they will
defend the Fae from the end of time.
Time is of the essence, or the Fae will fall to the darkness.
When Fleshrender, Dragonfang, and Bloodsong Grimoire are
united
The dome will shatter, and the end of time is near.
Fear not.
The wait is over, the blessing has come,
The heir of blood is found.
The compass will unite
Griffin, dragon, unicorn,
Fae and human.
Together they will battle darkness.*

Shelara's eyes met mine, and she whispered, "It is time."

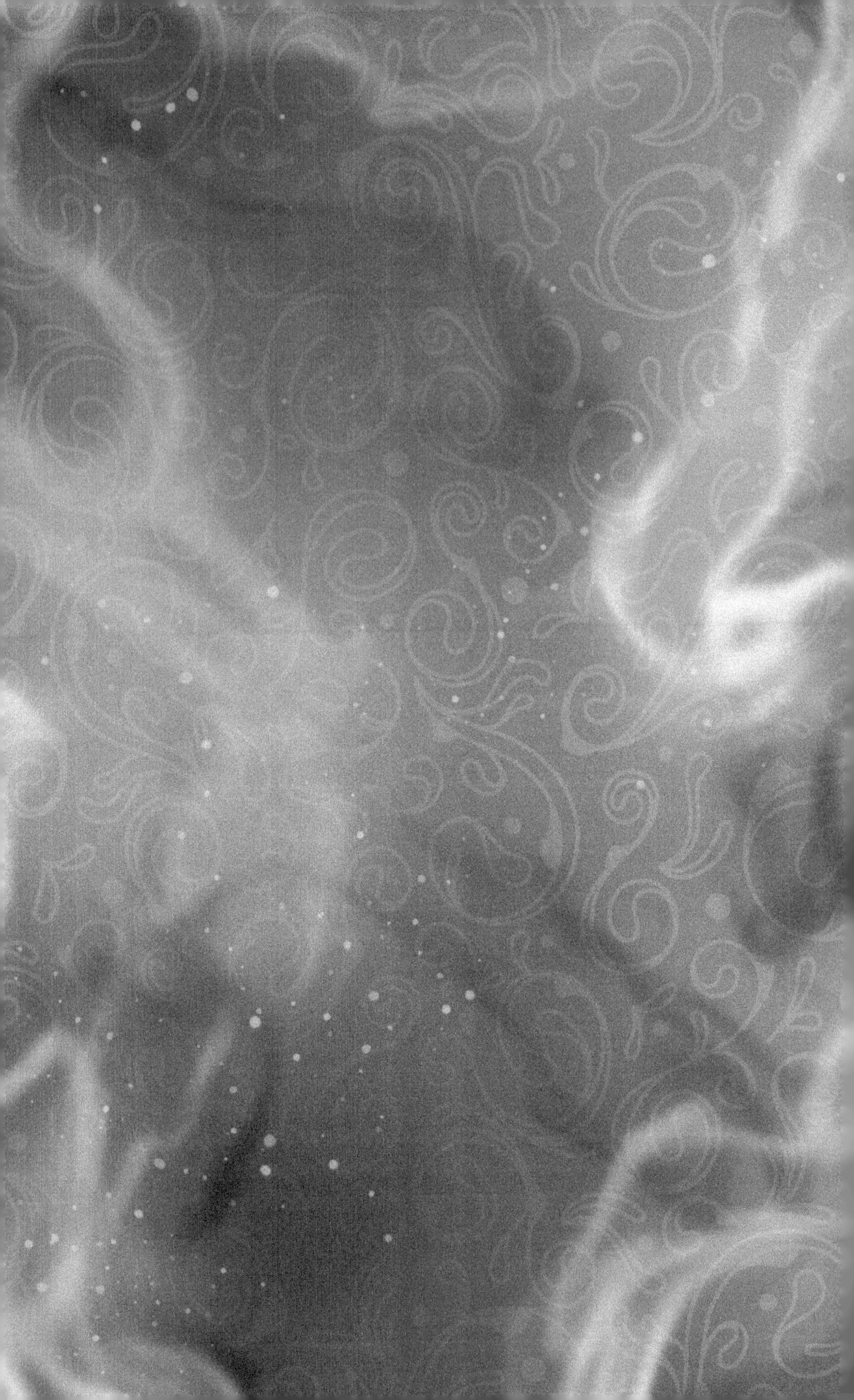

ABOUT THE AUTHOR

E.R. Jensen was born and raised in Los Angeles, California. She has lived in Oregon and Idaho, and currently resides in Atlanta, GA with her husband and three sons.

When not writing E.R. can be found enjoying her horses, traveling, and spending time with her family.

ACKNOWLEDGMENTS

Thank you to my wonderful team of artists who breathe life into the characters and scenes for my readers. Thank you to my friends and family who support this journey I'm on as an author.

COMING SOON

Crown of Emeralds
Coming Early 2026